THE
RED JEEP

DAVID ZAISS

ZAISSDA@MSN.COM

WONG PUBLISHING

© 2019 David Zaiss

All rights reserved. No part of this book may be reproduced, scanned, or distributed in any printed or electronic form without permission from the publisher. Please do not participate in or encourage piracy of copyrighted materials in violation of the author's rights. Purchase only authorized editions.

Wong Publishing
Interlochen, Michigan

ISBN: 978-0-9900062-1-3

Library of Congress Control Number: 2018958859

Printed in the United States of America

This is a work of fiction. The names, characters, places, and incidents portrayed in the story are the product of the author's imagination or have been used fictitiously. Any resemblance to actual persons, living or dead, businesses, companies, events, or locales is coincidental.

COVER & INTERIOR DESIGN BY TO THE POINT SOLUTIONS
www.tothepointsolutions.com

To the bosses I've dismissed—

Russ, Ann, Yuri, Larry, Metta, Jeff—my sincere apologies.

In memory of Matthew Hazelwood.

Strange times we live and work in. It doesn't matter how we draw a paycheck—driving a bulldozer, a string trimmer, or a laptop. Each day we get closer to conceding every last one of our precious, constitutionally-guaranteed, inalienable human rights.

Why?

I didn't know why, so I started searching. Along the way, I published *The Ping-Pong Club* and was fired.

I was writing the sequel when I received an ominous threat in the mail: "It has come to our attention that you may be planning on distributing a certain publication that could be injurious to the school. We want to warn you that if you follow through with your plans, we will pursue every legal option available to the full extent of the law."

That was why.

Suddenly, I realized there was more to why than I'd supposed. The full answer to why our rights are being threatened is waiting in the wings.

THE
RED JEEP

PART ONE
THE PING-PONG CLUB

1

"There is no statutory provision that directly
governs wrongful discharge."

THE GUIDE TO THE STATUTE OF LIMITATIONS

On a rainy Saturday afternoon, both sides of Front Street were lined with oldsters, union members, and Veterans for Peace waving handmade signs and American flags. Tourists, baby strollers, curious shoppers, and dogs wandered through and around the nearby line outside the movie theater. People were buying tickets to *How to Start a Revolution*. Pedestrian traffic ebbed and flowed as motorists paused and waited for the crosswalk to clear, many acknowledging the sign HONK IF YOU'RE PART OF THE 99%.

The early show let out and a group of students, including international teens, arrived at the crosswalk, chattering and laughing. The old slave recognized the new history teacher. Carrying his own handmade sign— OUR NEIGHBORHOODS, OUR FUTURES, OUR VOICE—he yelled, "Hey, Dustin! Join us. Give the students a civics lesson."

Puzzled looks from the international students. Why were all these old people standing in the street with signs?

"They're just kids, Tom. My sponsor group."

"C'mon, Mr. Agnew," said a long-haired chap sporting the beginnings of a beard. "Let's join them for a few minutes." His girlfriend nodded.

"We're on a tight schedule, Sven. We came to town for a movie and now we only have time for lunch."

"We don't need lunch."

The teacher was concerned about his job. "Sorry, guys. We're going to lunch." And off the little group went.

"Too bad. We need more young folks," said a woman who wasn't carrying a sign. Instead she'd embroidered her sweater with the words "We Are The 99%."

"I'm Tom. Nice combination of art and politics."

"My name is Sandra. It's starting to feel like the sixties all over again."

"Remember sit-ins?"

"I do remember. It appears you work at the art school."

"I'm the mailman."

"Those students could have been flower children."

"Remember Abbie Hoffman? *Steal this Book?*"

"Of course. MLK."

"Jerry Rubin."

"Malcolm X."

A well-dressed woman crossed the street, stuck out an elbow and jabbed Sandra hard enough to knock her off balance. "Hey, Malcolm X. Get the f**k out of the crosswalk," she laughed.

Tom reached out and asked, "Are you okay?"

"Whoa," said Sandra. "It's really starting to feel like the sixties."

"First time I've seen that. Usually we just get the finger, or somebody yelling 'Get a job!' That sort of thing."

"I know. Nobody likes protest."

"Not even protests they can believe in. Were you in her way?"

"Well, we were standing pretty close to the street."

"On the side of the crosswalk," protested Tom. "You know, the editor of the local paper is a liberal, there are liberal reporters on his staff. A few have even told me they support protests like this."

"Haven't seen a reporter here yet."

"Occupy is eight months old. I guess they're waiting for one of us to get arrested. Or killed."

"That woman assaulted me," said Sandra. "I'm writing to the editor."

On the opposite side of Front Street, the library director waved. In a minute she'd be close enough for a fist bump. Tom kept his eyes on her and put both hands firmly on his sign as she crossed the street and continued to the movies.

Sandra wondered, "Who was that?"

"The library director, my boss." Tom turned. "Why, hello, Michelle." The old slave offered his old coworker a fist to bump.

Michelle was reading Sandra's sweater. "Ninety-nine percent of what?"

"Everybody," said Sandra. "It's a protest."

"Of what?"

"Everything. The system is broken."

"No, it's not." She started to walk away.

"Wait, Michelle!" Tom called. "How long did we work together down there, in the art school basement?"

"Five years."

"All that time and not one conversation."

"You're a troublemaker." Michelle turned and walked away.

Tom was explaining this to Sandra when another acquaintance walked up.

"Hey, all the good people are here!" Sue had fled the library shortly after Melinda was fired.

Tom gave her a fist bump. "Hey, old girl, the director just walked by."

"Who? Michael Moore?"

"Different director. Your old boss, the library director."

"That sociopath?"

"Tell us how you really feel, Sue."

"She's a classic sociopath. Zero people skills, hates personal contact, sits alone in her office writing memos. Employees hate her."

"I hear," said the old slave, "the armbands may be having an effect."

"They are. Some are even appearing in employee areas. Her memo said any employee caught placing armbands in the library would be dismissed." Sue gathered an armload of armbands and said, "Good luck, Occupiers!"

Unfurling a huge banner—FORECLOSE ON BANK OF AMERICA—Occupy set off down the street—geezers, grandmas, and Vets for Peace, with the old slave tagging along, marching to the parkway and all the way to the end of the beach.

O

Tom, the mailman at Interotten Art School, loved his full-time job and especially loved meeting students from all over the world. He had, what seemed on the surface, job security.

One day, a coworker stopped by the mail room window. "My boss didn't listen to me, again."

"If you're right, Darlene, and he's wrong, tell him so."

"I can't disagree. Hamilton would fire me."

"Humpty Z. Dumpster wouldn't dare fire you. Besides, you have a First Amendment right to disagree. Go over his head."

"I can't do that."

"Your boss's bosses might be interested in hearing what you've got to say."

"Oh, well. I guess I don't mind doing what I'm told. I've been doing it for twenty-seven years."

"Darlene, you and me need a union."

"You know those old union bosses were a bunch of criminals."

The old slave resisted the urge to compare free enterprise to an eating contest where, after gorging yourself on the competition, you belch, excuse yourself, then get back to the table to throw it down again. No point in reminding the secretary that the unions had only lasted a few decades, long enough to bring about a middle class with pension and health plans and paid vacations, but not long enough to expose the greedy soul of corporations.

"Those early union organizers had a tough job," said Tom. "A few dozen slaves like you and me stood up to the most powerful economic force in the history of the planet. But, free enterprise and workers' rights are like vinegar and oil. No sooner were the unions out than paid lobbyists and corporate lackeys in state legislatures rewrote the laws to keep them out. It's been all downhill since. Today only seven percent of private workers are unionized."

Darlene admitted she was making half what she used to make when she was in a union. "It's sad," she said.

"Sad economics, certainly," said Tom. "Culture-wise, it's a seismic shift. It's clear where we're headed."

"Someday, Mr. Know-it-All, you'll have to tell me where we're headed." Darlene turned to go back to work. "Oh, I almost forgot to tell you. I'm a grandmother. Jerry and Lea had a baby boy."

2

> "Man-molders of the new age will be armed with
> the powers of an omnipotent state."
>
> C.S. LEWIS, *THE ABOLITION OF MAN*

On a picture-perfect Sunday morning, the old slave slipped his kayak into the lake and clambered in, one amiable gull floating alongside. A capricious summer wind took a break. The lake came to a standstill, reflecting the sky. The gull led the way. Tom paddled along as if on glass, in silence that was reminiscent of other Sunday mornings.

The library in the hours before opening was calm and quiet, like the lake. Tom loved shifting, re-shelving, and shelf-reading aisle after aisle in silence, sharing many of those mornings with Bob.

At eighteen, Bob was already a library veteran. He attended early church services to mentor the old slave, guiding him through reference, showing what needed little and what needed a lot of attention. Some books needed to be culled and some were checked out so often they were dog-eared. Bob frowned at the antics of the reference librarians, but reserved admiration for Melinda because "she tells you what you need to know."

The old slave stopped paddling. Wavelets slapped against the hull. The gull cocked its head, wondering what was up. Floating free as a cloud, over technical glitches and the death of unions, Tom shipped his paddle and leaned back, the morning stretching into afternoon. A job wasn't everything, doesn't guarantee a home, security, or a comfortable retirement. Get over it, move on. Slaves had to work with the temporary nature of employment. He'd forgotten more birthday candles than the director had blown out, but he could still get another job, if not here, then in another city or state. Or country. Korea would be interesting, or China's explosive free enterprise with new businesses, employment adventures, jobs for the taking ... Startling the gull, he sat up in the kayak, suddenly realizing every one of those jobs was slave labor.

He'd rounded the point of the peninsula and was halfway across the lake, the art school auditorium directly over the bow, when the sun disappeared, the wind changed, and a gust heeled the kayak over hard enough to ship water. Fighting for balance, he braced his knees and paddled hard in the opposite direction to where he wanted to go, managed to stay upright and even make a little headway. The waves doubled in size. His long, two-bladed paddle had worked some deviltry on his hands, blisters at the base of his thumbs, and those little demons were beginning to break. As the waves kept coming, he leaned into a large one, pulling as hard as he could. The bow began to turn. He pulled again, again, and then lost his point completely. At the same time, his right hand surrendered to a broken blister. The next second, he was underwater.

His life didn't pass before his eyes, but he did have a silly thought. A glitch! A change was on the way! Focusing every muscle, he kicked out and up and swam to the surface. The kayak was full of water, his paddle was gone. Inch by inch he frog-kicked the boat toward shore, but waves kept forcing him farther out. He gave up, grabbed the mooring rope, and hung on. The gull spread its wings, took off, and didn't look back.

"Help!"

Someone on shore must have heard because it wasn't long before the fireboat arrived and towed him in.

He put the kayak back in the garage, and then it came to him. He had to return to the library. Time was running out.

○

Early on a Sunday morning, the old slave punched in the security password at the staff entrance and stepped inside. How delicious. How devilish. How easy to break in. He felt like a ghoul in a mausoleum stacked floor to ceiling with dead tomes, like a thief in a graveyard searching for souls. Invading Circulation, he found no heartbeat. Neither sight nor sound in Sight and Sound. No work in the workroom, no child in Children's. The atrium was open, but the gift store was closed. Seeing nobody in the library for the blind, Tom trudged upstairs and strolled, trying doors, opening drawers, remembering six years of employment. He placed a wayward magazine back on the rack and picked up a scrap of paper from the floor. He shelf-read fiction into author order. At last, he went to work, taping black paper armbands to counters, tables, and desks, attaching them to doors and windows, slipping them into magazines. He bookmarked an Agatha Christie with an armband, imagining a little old lady's surprise, looking for a mystery and finding a mystery inside a mystery!

He stopped at the reference desk, where he'd been standing when the stranger said, "I just hate all this politics in the library."

"You mean this politics?" he asked, showing her his armband.

She turned and walked away; he continued shelf reading nonfiction. Soon she was back to look him in the eye. Silently she walked away, then walked by again. He would have enjoyed discussing politics in the library but she hadn't seemed interested.

Someone or something was moving nearby, shifting around. Watching him? Acting like a librarian, standing quietly and hardly breathing, he waited.

"Hello, Tom."

On a step-ladder changing a light bulb was an old friend and fellow slave, Jack the janitor. "Do you suppose I can have one of those armbands?"

○

"Tom? Detective Robbins, City Police. Were you inside the library this past Sunday?"

"As a matter of fact, yes."

"Figured it was you, knowing the security code. Looks like you had a few armbands to dispose of. Just a warning, Tom. Don't do it again."

3

"Working Americans without unions are deer in the company's headlights. Afraid to move, all we have is our words."

OLD-SLAVE PROVERB

The director looked great. Smiling and relaxed, she sat straight, with her head held high, while she chatted. You'd never guess she had just been released from the hospital.

"Hello, Tom," she said.

The amiable old slave almost gave her a fist bump as he took a chair. Seven library board trustees at the table in the front of the room looked up. Tom made eye contact with each, making sure none of them missed his black armband. Why wasn't the director sitting alongside the chairman? She did not belong in the last row of the meeting room ... and certainly did not belong alongside the old slave she had just fired.

The chairman rapped his gavel, everyone turned to the front, and the meeting began. "Vote on approval of the agenda. All in favor say aye."

"Aye."

"Any old business?"

What old business had the director entombed in that hormonally-challenged memory? How much dust covered that ugly business when she escorted Melinda out of the very library Melinda helped build? And why on earth had she allowed the old slave to wear the black armband with Grieving for Melinda on it every shift, three and four days a week, for five months?

She looked up, and for a second locked eyes with Tom in an old-fashioned staredown. Psychologists say eye contact is confrontational—a power struggle—the first to look down loses. In a society dominated by white, male, type-A personalities, the boss "wins" by out-staring the slave, but of course, winning and dominating are two different things. Furthermore, this boss gave every indication of being female.

"Tom?"

A single syllable. Anger? Correction? Command?

He lowered his gaze, ending the staredown, but he could feel the director's eyes boring in, trying to figure him out.

Old business continued. Tom closed his eyes to drift along an old stream of thought. Nothing seemed to change.

The chairman of the library board looked around the meeting room. "Is there any new business?"

Yes, boss, there's new business. It's good news for business too, as long as we slaves hang on to our jobs by coloring our opinions to suit your mood, as long as our visions are whitewashed by the company logo, as long as our voices only second the motions to sing the blues, as long as the soft matter between our ears is flooded with technical claptrap.

On cue, Steve stood to report on the new digital security cameras. Resolution would be out of this world, reliability state-of-the-art, technical glitches a thing of the past. The board commended the new IT director. With a grin, Steve took a seat and looked up, his eyes meeting Tom's.

Slaves love innuendo and rumor but they're a proud bunch. They reserve such gossip for themselves, and Steve belonged to another class of slaves, a category of up-and-comers and butt-kissers who smile and nod at everything the boss says, even when the boss is wrong. First to lower his gaze, Steve ended the staredown.

The chairman called for the director's report. She passed, leaving the task of reading her report to the business manager. Gwen had officiated at the old slave's termination—an assignment well above the pay scale of a bean counter. Stumbling through the list of lies trumped up to justify firing an employee for wearing an armband, Gwen had seemed apologetic, looking like she wished she were somewhere else. But the director's report was cut-and-dried finances; she finished with a smile. "It's just business as usual in the library."

In a state the governor was trying to run like a business, she meant it to be good news. Tom couldn't help imagining a governor-appointed Emergency Financial Manager swooping in and firing library director, library board, city council, county commission, teachers, firefighters, police officers, emergency responders.

The chairman asked if there was any public comment.

Tom stood. "I was a school librarian for seventeen years," he began, "and an employee here for six, but in all my years of library service, I never experienced politics like this."

The seven board members could not miss, nor could the hidden video camera fail to record, the large stenciled letters on the front of his white shirt: FIRED FOR GRIEVING. Looking around the community meeting room, Tom wondered what he could say. Etchings, paintings, and prints on the walls mixed with memories of concerts, visiting authors, book sales, in-services, and video-game contests. He thought of the special place a library has in a community, the closest thing to home for many slaves and owners alike. He remembered the hundreds of friends he'd made here. None of his coworkers, though, dared to don an armband.

"The director's stool pigeon lied. I was fired with a lie," Tom concluded his short speech and took his seat beside the director.

A few days later, his statement to the board was erased by a "technical glitch."

O

Armband Days at the library began one chilly Sunday afternoon. Three friends joined Tom at the front entrance.

"How about an armband?"

"What's it for?" The elderly gentleman seemed interested. "Why does the petition say armbands are free speech?"

"Because they are. This is a protest."

"Against what?"

"Wrongful termination. Being fired for wearing an armband in the library. Would you like to put one on?"

"Sure. Why not?"

An overweight woman stepped down from the bus. "How much are they?"

"They're free."

"Well, then," she said, holding out a flabby arm.

A bearded chap came up, took several, and said he'd wear one every time he visited the library.

In an hour, they had wrapped dozens of arms. While his three friends greeted incoming patrons, Tom went inside and made a circuit, asking every librarian if they'd wear an armband.

"My job's more important."

"I never speak up."

"Have to tell you, Tom, the armband is ancient effing history."

Upstairs at the reference desk sat Lyle. He'd supported the armband

and he'd sign the petition. "Just not here in the library, maybe later, out in the parking lot ..." Lyle stopped, tilted his head back, and studied his computer monitor.

The director was standing directly behind. "Are you asking library personnel if they'd wear an armband?"

"I suppose I am."

"You can't do this, Tom. We've had complaints."

"Can't do what?"

"Approach employees on the clock."

"How about approaching employees who aren't on the clock?"

The director shook her head and went back to her office.

Yet, only two weeks before, at this exact spot, she'd said, "I can't pay you if you're wearing that armband."

"Does that mean I'm fired?"

The director had blinked. "It means I can't pay you if you're wearing that armband."

"There's still books on my cart. How about if I finish it?"

"That's up to you."

Next day, armband in place, Tom arrived for his shift at the library.

"Oh, hey, Tom!" The director came up smiling. "You can put those hours from yesterday back on your timesheet."

And so, for five months, the old slave wore an armband whenever he went to work.

4

"Along the road of humanity the signposts are all marked progress,
except that humanity is packed like sardines into an automobile
that is traveling downhill without lights at a terrific speed
and driven by a four-year-old child."

LORD DUNSANY

Two volunteers showed up for the next Armband Day; only one
the following week. On the fourth Armband Day, the old slave found
himself standing alone in front of the library. He needed help. Then he
remembered the new violin instructor had expressed an interest. On the
tenth anniversary of 9/11, he drove to faculty lane and knocked on her
door.

No answer. He turned and was about to leave when the history teacher
opened the door. "Hello, Tom."

"Sorry, Dustin. I thought Julie lived here."

"She did, last year. She's moved to a beachfront rental on Grass."

"Any idea where?"

"Don't have a clue."

Grass was a small lake. The old slave started driving, following an
inner GPS, turning off the highway; then on impulse, into a dead-end.
At the end was a driveway. He pulled into the drive and parked behind
a red Jeep sporting a decal: WAH. What on earth did that mean? And
where was the beachfront rental?

Tom had an unimpeded view of the lake from the top of a small bluff.
There was a vine-covered split-rail fence framing a stairway beside an
outdoor dance floor. He started down the stairs and discovered that the
dance floor was actually the roof of the house. A few more steps down
revealed a series of decks under a bay of windows with views out over the

tree-lined shore. The stairs, he saw, proceeded all the way down to the lake. But where was the front door?

Lazy afternoons, calm horizons, freshwater aromas. The wash and splash of waves on the shore. Going down the stairs, Tom could hear something humming like a bass note droning. And then, an open door. He knocked softly on the door frame.

"Tom!" A flash of bare back and legs. "Just a moment! I'll be right there!"

Turning quickly, the old slave continued down. The stairs were like a concerto, introduction followed by steps of possible changes and thoughtful pauses to reconsider possibilities, but always pointing toward the finale: arrival at the lakeshore. He climbed back to the front door as the violin teacher emerged in tank top and shorts.

"So, do you like my little cottage?"

"Quite the party place."

"Have a seat." She went back inside and returned with a new paddleboard. "Isn't it something?"

"Sure is," he said, trying not to stare at trim muscular legs, testimony to hours of wake-surfing.

"When the wind is up, you can ride cute little waves."

"Sounds like fun."

"It is. What brings you to my home?"

"I'm just on my way to the library for Armband Day 5—love to have you join me."

The surfer girl hesitated. She shifted, smiled. "I'm just on my way to the UP for some backpacking. Love to have you join me."

Touché. He felt old, exposed, Cyrano rebuffed by Roxanne. "Well, I'll see you later. Just thought you might be interested."

"Maybe I could be."

Could be? Shuffling his worn deck of cards, Tom asked, "What would it take to make you interested?"

"The armband," said Julie. "Please explain."

Tom delivered a one-minute summary of six years in the library and the way it had ended. "But," he said, playing the ace, "the armbands are just the beginning."

She was still listening, so he played trump. "This isn't the first time I've taken on wrongful termination." Julie's eyebrows formed question marks. "It happened a few years ago. I went to jail. Twice, in fact, in two days."

"I knew it!"

"You know Hank's, the store down the road? ... Arrogant, short-tempered, bully to employees and sometimes customers, my boss was a jerk. For seven years I did my job, he gave me excellent evaluations, but

15

then one day he fired one of my service clerks. He told Sharon he had a videotape of her stealing beer from the back of the store. 'Show me the tape,' Sharon demanded.

"'I don't have it,' said the boss. 'It's with our security company downstate.'

"A week later, the girl walked into the store and straight up to the service counter. 'I want to see that tape, Tom.'

"'So do I.'

"'What do you mean?'

"'I'd like to see that tape too.'

"'I didn't steal anything, Tom.'

"'I know. I hate this bull.'

"'It is bull, and I need another job. Will you write me a reference?'

"You see, Julie, I knew there was no video camera. Obsessed about being ripped off, the boss suspected everyone of shoplifting or stealing. About a year before, a month before I hired Sharon, a hundred cases of beer had disappeared from the back of the store, a clean getaway. I had my suspicions about who committed that crime, and it wasn't Sharon."

Julie gazed out over the lake. A small outboard slowly powered by, trolling for bluegills. "Oh, look," she said, jumping to her feet and putting those lithe legs on display again. "They've caught one."

The fisherman killed the engine to bring in his catch.

A glitch.

While the engine is running, life sails merrily along but when the engine stops, you sit dead in the water, following the whims of the waves, turning and floating like a leaf. Progress interrupted. A bite on the line, a deer in the woods, a sudden change in weather. A kayak capsizing. A glitch causes you to wonder what you were doing before.

Not a keeper, the catch was released.

"Sharon's mother sent my reference letter to the corporate office, along with a message of her own: 'If my daughter was such a bad employee, how come her supervisor thought she was okay? We want to see that tape. If you can't provide it, we insist you give her her job back.'

"The next day the boss called me into the office. 'Apparently,' he said, 'you don't know who the boss is. Give me your keys.'

"Dazed, I walked out of the store and drove straight to Sharon's house. Her mother invited me in. 'He fired you?'

"We were on our second cup of coffee when the phone rang. 'This is Hank. We apologize for the little mix-up. There was no videotape.'

"Sharon's dad wanted to punch out the store director. I suggested a lawsuit. Her mother had the best idea: a petition."

"Which is where," presumed the violinist, "you got the idea for the armband petition?"

"Sharon took the petition to school, her parents took it to work, and I knocked on doors. One hundred and sixty signatures came from the art school. I posted the petition on storefronts, trees, and power poles. Some phoned to complain, dozens wrote the corporate office. We held protest rallies in front of the store, where I ventured inside and collected the signatures of two employees. At the last rally, the store director pulled in, strode up to me, and stabbed a finger in my chest. 'This is just to make it official,' he said. 'I'm asking you to leave.' A few days later, a sheriff's deputy handed me a restraining order barring me from my old store."

Julie winced. "Is that when you got arrested?"

"Hold on. Sharon's mother warned, 'You're not gonna do it, are you?'

"'He lied. He was wrong to fire her and wrong to fire me.'

"Sunday morning, I taped the petition to a table and set up in front of church. I met supporters, including one little, old Republican lady. 'I hate that director,' she said. 'Once I walked into the staff-only room in the store by mistake. He came up and grabbed me by the arm and none too gently escorted me out.'

"At the last rally, we heard the store director had beaten up a kid. I phoned the boy's house. His mother said Johnny and his cousin had skateboarded to the store to buy chips and pop. Johnny picked up a bottle of cough medicine. 'This is what stupid kids use to get high on,' he said to his cousin, and put the bottle back on the shelf. The boys paid and were on their way out when the manager on duty stopped them."

"'Okay, kids, where's that Nyquil?'

"Johnny led the manager to where he'd picked up the bottle and showed it to him. 'This is it.'

"'Empty your pockets, both of you.'

"They emptied their pockets, the manager said they could go, then, according to Johnny, the big boss stopped the boys before they exited the store, shouting, 'You were trying to steal that Nyquil.' He grabbed Johnny's arm hard enough to bruise him. Johnny screamed, 'Let me go!' The boss ripped Johnny's shirt, and the boy stomped on the boss's toe. He tripped Johnny and hit him in the stomach. Johnny kicked him in the leg. Finally, the boss let go. Johnny picked up his skateboard and he and his cousin went home."

"So fustimicating," said Julie. "Beating up a child is grounds for dismissal."

"It was," agreed Tom. "The actual dismissal took another two months."

"You mean, you fired the boss?"

"We righted a wrong. He'd been in charge for twenty years. The wheels of justice turn slowly and I like my politics quick and simple. Right wrong. A verb followed by a noun."

"A this followed by a that." The violinist threw her arms in the air and walked to the stairway leading down to the lake. "Morality," she said, frowning, weighing every word, "is so different from music. You're obsessed with morality. I'm not at all obsessed with music. Music is best when you don't drown yourself in it."

"Sounds like a liner note from a Miles Davis record."

"It's a liner note from my CD," she said. She took a seat on the bench. "Dear Tom, I'd like to support your sad little armbands but what do you expect to get out of them? I mean, you're saying Johnny got beat up, Sharon got lied to and fired. Two kids were screaming for justice. What did they get?"

"They learned something about right and wrong. Bosses don't give a dime about justice, they're too busy worrying about their bottom lines. Hank probably wouldn't know a wrong if it came up and hit him in the face, but he did the right thing, and two kids witnessed a lying bully get what he deserved."

Julie's bare-shouldered shrug sent jolts of dry-celled current to the old slave's loins. "You could drown yourself," she said, "in this right/wrong stuff."

He looked down, his eye landing on a Columbia alumni magazine on the table. She went to Columbia? There was a cover photo of the World Trade Center under construction, an article with dozens of pictures of the Twin Towers dominating the New York City skyline. "Yours?"

"Yes," she said. "It is."

He put a few calendar pieces together and did a little mental arithmetic. "So, you do care about justice."

"I do." She squeezed his armband. "So, Tom, tell me what is just about this?"

"I just believe it's right."

She took a deep breath and looked him in the eye. "Okay, Tom. Go on. I'm listening."

"Johnny's mom wrote the store's corporate headquarters: 'I was at work when my daughter called to tell me my son had been beaten up and accused of stealing. I apologized to my boss and drove straight home, picked Johnny up, and went to the store. I took my son's shirt off and showed the store director the marks on his body. What did he do? He smirked, said my son had intended to steal, and he was just trying to hold him until the police arrived. I've been a customer for a long time, but until you do something about your director, I promise I will not shop there ever again.' About the time the director slapped me with that restraining order, Sharon's mother and every instinct warned me."

"But you went in anyway," said Julie.

"The first time it was just to buy a pound of coffee."

"'I can't sell it to you,' the cashier said. 'There's a note on the bulletin board.' I left Hank's, went to work in the mail room and was arrested there. A few teachers and Sam, the vice president, were witnesses. I bailed myself out, went home and made two big sandwich boards—one said Hire Sharon Back and the other said Hands Off Johnny. Next morning, I wore them into Hank's. When the deputy arrived, I walked out and was waiting at his cruiser when he came out, shoved me against the car, frisked me, cuffed me behind, and muscled me into the rear seat. I bailed myself out again. 'Hope to never see you again,' said the jailer. 'You got two strikes now.'

"'The object in life,' I replied, 'is not to stay out of jail.'"

Julie leaned against the deck railing, pulled up smooth round knees and rested her chin on them, probably wishing she were wake-surfing. "I'd sure like to know the object in life."

"It's easy to say what it isn't," said the old slave. "It isn't shutting up. It isn't avoiding risk. I've been saying the object in life is not to stay out of jail since Vietnam."

"You went to jail for protesting Vietnam?"

"Only once. Come to Armband Day tomorrow."

"I'm a musician, not as bold and brave as you."

"This isn't about bold and brave, it's about right and wrong. We have a system based on power and money. Workers have given up their rights. Terminated slaves don't speak up or fight back, they just get their résumés together and move on. A few higher-up muckety-mucks like Melinda file a lawsuit now and then and end up losing not only their jobs but spending years in court and thousands of dollars in legal fees and court costs."

"Is there such a thing as rightful termination?"

"Only when it's not wrong. Six years ago, I walked out of jail totally confused. I'd worked every day for half a century and for the first time, I was terminated. The only thing that made any sense was anger. As I trundled down the road, refusing to stick out my thumb to passing cars, refusing to believe jail was the end of the story, my anger smoldered and burst into flames. By the time I reached the bus depot, I'd made up my mind. The dispatcher listened to my story and arranged a special delivery bus back to the store. But my truck was gone from the parking lot. I called around and found it in the yard of a tow operator, and drove to Johnny's. 'The jerk had my truck towed,' I said. 'I'm starting a boycott.'

"'Count me in,' said Johnny's mother."

"Wait," Julie interrupted. "A boycott? Isn't that something unions used to do to punish companies they didn't like?"

"Yeah. I should have known we were in over our heads, but over the next few days, we counted dozens in, mostly signers of the petition. Then we got the news. The store director had been fired."

"Go on."

"Like any organization, profit or nonprofit, a store needs stability and confidence. Hank's suddenly had neither. And it was suddenly management-challenged, going through store director after store director, manager after manager, only to watch killer competition build a new store across the street. Free enterprise abhors a vacuum. Herb's was making a sound business decision, positioning itself for the eventual demise of their nearest competitor."

"I wondered why there were two grocery stores right across the street from each other."

"A few weeks after I was fired, Hank's was robbed. My night cashier and I had our differences, especially after I hired her seventeen-year-old and caught him playing videogames in the stockroom. Should have fired him on the spot, instead I asked if he'd finished stocking the beer cooler. He ran straight to mama at the service counter. Marion cursed so loudly I could hear her in the stockroom. She threatened to quit—the boy beat her to it."

"You should have fired him," said Julie.

"Marion took over making the nightly deposits. One day, a deputy knocked on my door wanting to know where I'd been the night before last. 'Home, as usual, now that I'm not working anymore.' Marion had described the thief as an older man, slender, looking like a recently terminated manager who may have had a gripe against the store. Marion and I had our problems, I admitted, then mentioned the hundred cases of beer waltzing out the back door of the store. 'Has that mystery been solved?' asked the deputy. 'Marion and her son had both been on duty that night,' I said. He thanked me for my help and I never saw him again."

Slaves don't care much for politics but Julie was no ordinary slave. Searching for a natural key perhaps, an honest time signature, or a theme with logical variations, she gazed out over the lake. An afternoon of game-changing decisions had rippled the surface of the water and her paddleboard was still high and dry.

"Well," said Tom, "gotta get to work."

On cue, a twig snapped, and beside the lake, a doe and a fawn stepped out from under the trees.

"Come to my faculty recital Wednesday," said the violinist, "and I'll come to your Armband Day."

The spirits of Handel and Mozart lifted the old slave's bones through a chorus of hallelujahs and carried him all the way into town.

5

"Don't it always seem to go that you don't know what
you've got til it's gone?"
JONI MITCHELL

At the library, Tom plunged into his new project: shifting and re-shelving all of the fiction and bound periodicals. He'd reached the 1920's *National Geographic* when Karen walked over.

"Tom, would you please come with me to the office?"

Gwen did the dirty work, looking like she wished she was somewhere else. "I'm sorry to have to do this." She read aloud from an official form: "You made unfavorable comments to a patron regarding working at the library. You criticized the library, forcing the patron to excuse herself in order to get away from you. You said, 'Well, if you want to hear about working in political situations, let me tell you about this place.'"

"I said nothing of the kind," said Tom. "None of that is true."

"You've used up your credibility in this matter," Gwen replied, pushing her glasses up. "Sign here, please."

In his written response, Tom stated a patron he'd never seen before had lied and charged the library director with using a patron to achieve her goal of firing him for wearing an armband.

O

On Wednesday, he drove to the chapel. Faculty recitals normally drew as much enthusiasm as an order to report for jury duty, but Julie had filled the little theater, with standing room only and many turned away. In the

21

crowd were teachers from every discipline, including math and science. Tom found a seat next to Jake, a classical music host with the school's radio station.

The violinist strode out, smiling radiantly. "Thank you for coming!" She polished off a Mozart sonata, then a modern piece, and with everyone's attention firmly focused, she finessed phrases and spaces between notes, blending Faure into an expression of her own fiery personality. From the opening cadenza of the last piece on the program, Ravel's Tzigane, a magic spell replaced the music, setting the audience on the edge of their seats. In her musical element, Julie seemed to state, "Here! Watch, listen! Here!!" The final cadenza came fast with a flourish of bow. Or was it a wand? A dazzling smile and dainty bow drew a well-deserved standing ovation. Bravos beamed from one side of the chapel to the other.

"Tom!" Jake pounded him on the shoulder. "Was that incredible or what?!"

O

"You came!" She set her tray on the cafeteria table.

"Julie!" gushed Jake. "That's the first time I've seen standing room only for a faculty recital."

"Well, I've gotta get back to work," said Tom.

Jake went on, "I'm not kidding, Julie. Miss Virtuoso. I listen to a lot of music and spin classical every morning. Last night, you blew me and everyone else away."

"Amen to that," said Tom. "See you Saturday, Virtuoso."

O

Armband Day 6. The sun came out, turning a chilly autumn afternoon into summer. Wrapping the arm of a teenage girl, Tom cut a piece of tape and showed her where to hold it with her finger.

"What does it say?" she asked.

"'Lest we forget.' That's what the director is hoping we'll do."

"We support your armband," said her girlfriend, "but we don't understand what it is you want to see happen."

I want to fire the boss.

As the girls walked away, Tom said, "I'd like to see a change in how bosses see their responsibility."

22

Smiling, the girls kept walking.

"Managers should manage better," Tom said to their backs. "They should treat employees as resources. Treasures."

Waving, the two girls laughed and entered the library just as WAH, the red Jeep, pulled into the parking lot.

Tom beamed. "You came!"

"I promised you. How're the armbands going?"

"Let's go inside. I'll introduce you to my friends."

The atrium is an open, glass-walled, central feature with tables and couches, a gift shop, and a piano. Patrons amble through, browsing the newspapers and magazines that clutter the tables. Outside, a host of small sailboats seemed motionless on the surface of the lake, as if they were hovering in air. The old slave motioned to a bench overlooking the flower garden.

In silk top, pale-rose cutoffs, and straw sandals, Julie looked like a teenager pausing before going upstairs to check out the latest Manga. She even sported facial jewelry: a needle pierced the middle of her forehead.

"What's with the needle?"

"Allergies."

"You stick a needle in your brow for allergies?"

"My parents taught me acupuncture. It helps."

Tearing his eyes away from the needle, Tom said, "You were great Wednesday. I loved the Ravel."

"Thanks."

"I heard you're going to Panama again."

"In January. Next month, I'm playing with Mark's orchestra in Colombia."

The old slave remembered Mark. Before he felt Humpty Z. Dumpster's wrath Mark had been the orchestra conductor at the art school. "How's he doing now?"

"He's got an excellent orchestra in Bogota," said Julie, "but he's still bitter. He was fighting wrongful termination, like you."

"Naomi, Ken, Jane. Three fired in one shot. My community service kids said Mark told his orchestra to stop sitting on their duffs and speak up."

"He certainly did. Z told Jane her horns didn't sound good. That was ridiculous, one of those horns is now the principal at Juilliard!"

"I know."

Julie shook her fist. "What about Naomi, Tom?! Naomi was a diva."

"That's what we all called her."

Julie looked out the window past the sailboats to the hills beyond that were showing the first colors of the season. The old slave took a deep breath. Something about this woman connected, a musical fragrance he

23

could almost inhale. There was something else too, as disturbing as the last note of the Tzigane, terrifying and immense as the silent world just before the first pair of hands come together; in the violin's eyes burned a fire of passionate intensity.

"I didn't tell you," she said, "how much I appreciated your story about firing your boss. Forgive me, dear Tom, my mind was elsewhere."

His mind was elsewhere also.

"You knocked on my door just as I was beginning my annual rehab." She took a deep breath. "Ten years ago, I was just getting settled into my dorm when people started yelling, screaming, running. I looked outside and saw the first tower falling. Sirens, smoke, ashes in the air. I thought we'd all be killed. It was so awful I dug a grave for it, but once a year it crawls out, like a zombie."

"I was at the local public high school playing ping-pong."

"Ping-pong?"

"Not exactly playing. Coaching. Volunteering during lunch break."

"Did … did you know about it?"

"Heard the news on my radio driving in. In the recreation room it was on the TV but the kids weren't watching it, they were playing. Just another news story, something their parents might watch, not the end of the world. I didn't want to draw attention and make an issue of death and destruction."

"Not want to make an issue? That doesn't sound like you, Tom."

He could make an issue of it. "As a result of 9/11," he said, "we wasted a trillion bucks and took half a million lives."

"I understand. That's more like you."

"We got sucker-punched. For someone on the wrong side of history, Osama was right on in his reading of the American-cowboy mentality. I mean, Hitler invading Poland was wrong. Fire-bombing Dresden was wrong. Pearl Harbor, Hiroshima, wrong. But all those wrongs don't make a right. 9/11 would have been little more than a footnote in history except for our hysterical reaction to it."

"When you're afraid, you do stupid things."

"Osama wasn't stupid. Four hundred boardroom billionaire bankers, the same guys responsible for the Great Depression, the great recession, and dozens of senseless wars, got the shit scared out of them."

"Was Afghanistan senseless?"

"Idiotic. Iraq was senseless. Same with Vietnam. Korea."

"How about slavery?"

"Yeah. Slavery. Economic exploitation and politically senseless." Tom spotted Lyle coming down the stairs. "You have to meet this guy. Hey, Lyle! Over here. This is Julie."

Julie said, "Tom has briefed me about the director."

Straight to the point, Lyle said, "I hate my boss. I've hated her for two years, with good reason."

"Pretty strong words," said Julie.

"Not strong enough. She played hatchet lady at two libraries downstate and got run out of town, then they hired her to do the same thing here."

"Some librarians have quit?"

"Ten since she arrived. Seven union grievances have been filed. We're trying to form a management union. It will be tough against a boss who changes the rules to fit the situation."

"That's how she fired me," said the old slave.

Julie asked, "Are you afraid for your job, Lyle?"

"I've been here twenty years. Who's to say? Service desk hours have been cut in half. We're understaffed in almost every department. Budgets from print materials to wages have been slashed."

"The director," said the old slave, "is a liar on a mission."

"She's worse than that," said Lyle. "She's a megalomaniac, a dictator that calls all the shots and won't listen to compromise, a sociopath who sits alone all day in her office issuing memos."

"Do you support the armbands?"

"Of course. Melinda was the best boss I ever had. She was also the only staff person given an evaluation. Believe me, though, she wasn't terminated because of that evaluation."

"Terminate to intimidate?"

Ah, termination. The new workplace fact. In the last few decades, the corporate takeover of America has given rise to a new class of slaves: the wannabes, the middle managers, and the butt-kissers. For this new class, the motto is "Never say a word"; the prayer is "Yes, boss"; and becoming boss is heaven on earth. For this new class, slavery isn't the status quo, it is the sine qua non. For this new class, behaving like a slave doesn't equal being a slave; tolerating abuse doesn't equal being abused. Life after slavery is impossible to imagine; so distant, the only way out is up through the ranks, climbing over brothers and sisters, abusing as you go, trampling, backstabbing and rumor-mongering. But the road to freedom is paved with rules laid down from the top.

A subclass of these new slaves are the hatchet women and axe men who specialize in termination. Cold-blooded, these hired professionals typically arrive on the scene shortly after a new boss has taken over, when the turmoil of transition and the element of surprise can wreak the most havoc on an unsuspecting slave hold.

"Oh, yes," said Lyle. "Definitely, it was terminate to intimidate."

The director, a first-class hatchet lady, could terminate in a nanosecond. Why was it taking her so long to figure out what to do about armbands in the library?

6

"O for a muse of fire that would ascend the
brightest heaven of invention."

SHAKESPEARE, *KING HENRY V*

Julie was curious. "Can I ask where your parents are from?"

The old slave had known Lyle for ten years. Though he'd sometimes wondered about his friend's heritage, he'd never asked.

"My mother is Vietnamese," Lyle replied, darting a glance out the window. A sailboat took a buoy too close and nearly capsized, but the regatta silently sailed on and on, around and around. "My father was an American GI."

Julie had a revelation of her own. "My grandfather escaped from Korea just before the end of the war. It was horrible. Hundreds of thousands died."

"It was indeed horrible," said Lyle. "Korea and Vietnam were both destroyed, their economies wiped out, institutions wrecked, families broken. Thousands of refugees, the boat people, died on the open sea."

"Victims," said the old slave, "of undeclared wars waged for profit and power, arranged by what, in the old days we called 'The Machine.'"

It was three o'clock and time for Liz's regular Sunday gig. At eighty-six, Liz could still cover the keyboard. First on the program today was Rachmaninoff's Second Concerto.

"Did you know that our friend Tom, here, went to jail for protesting Vietnam?" asked Julie.

"I did not," said Lyle.

"A lot of others did too," said Tom. "The government wouldn't stop the war, so the people had to stop the government. Millions of slaves took the war to the streets, holding hands, singing of peace, handing flowers to cops. Occupy is doing the same thing, but its sights aren't set on the government. This time around, it's the ones who own the government— the bosses."

"I understand all that," said Julie. "But I'm still confused. Why was Melinda terminated?"

"Because she could be," said Lyle. "She was senior staff, salaried, not in the union; and so, she was vulnerable. The director and the board were gambling that there wouldn't be a lawsuit."

"Melinda called a meeting at her house," said the old slave. "There were forty of us: protesting librarians, the director's predecessor, even her previous nemesis at the director's former library."

"Ten departures have upset the entire staff," said Lyle. "Everyone's afraid. And there's Melinda's lawsuit. The board overreached."

Julie wondered out loud if Lyle was in the union.

"I am, and about ready to strike my boss."

"Doesn't the board know what's happening in their library?" asked Julie. "How can they stand by and do nothing?"

"The board is dysfunctional. They have the safest jobs in town, appointed for years, or until our dear governor fires them."

"It's so wrong."

"Vietnam was wrong," said Lyle. "Most Americans sat and watched."

"Some didn't."

"Millions didn't," Tom said. "There were protests in cities and colleges across America. Our little protest even made the news."

"When you went to jail?"

"Four of us were arrested—three students and a professor. Hundreds rallied on campus." The old slave had almost enjoyed those three silent hours of peace and quiet, reading *King Lear* while waiting to be released.

Locking eyes, Julie said, "The object in life is not to stay out of jail. What happened next?"

"I went to dinner with my future wife."

"I mean," said Julie, "with your case."

"Contempt of court charges were dismissed by a higher court."

Liz switched to Gershwin, the old slave rhapsodizing in blue.

"Well," said Lyle, "gotta get back to work. Nice meeting you."

"Wait a minute," said Julie. "Why does the board look the other way when every librarian is afraid of the boss?"

"The board is complicit," said Lyle. "They're the ones who fired Melinda."

Eyes closed, Tom said, "The board knows about Armband Days."

"Tom!" Julie took both his hands in hers. "I'm so glad you're doing

27

this. It's so right and ... so relevant." She pulled the old slave to his feet. "Let's go outside. Please? I'd like to wrap an arm in an armband."

"Not a Gershwin lover?"

"Love Gershwin, but it's warm today. We've been sitting inside in the sun for an hour, touching on some pretty heavy subjects. And ... well, I'm coming off a morning run, and ... oh, I wish I'd had time for a shower."

The old slave and the young violin stepped outside to claim possession of the bench in front of the library. Immediately, Tom wrapped the arm of a hoodied youth on his way into the computer room.

A well-dressed woman asked, "What does it mean?"

"It means opposition," replied Tom, "to wrongful termination. The armband is a protest against librarians getting the sack for no good reason."

"Was there something illegal? About, 'the sack', as you call it?"

They discussed the legality of Melinda's termination and her lawsuit. "There's right and wrong, but there's no law about wrongful discharge. May I wrap your arm?"

The woman thought for a moment. "Wouldn't wearing an armband say something about how I feel?"

"I suppose it would."

"Well, I don't feel all that strongly about it."

Thinking and feeling are such strange bedfellows. Tom picked up an armband. He folded it into quarters. "How about planting this inside a book?"

"What on earth for?"

"Well, over the last few months, we've wrapped hundreds of arms, planted dozens of armbands. Now, those little seeds are starting to grow roots."

The feeling thinker said, "Oh, I get it." She tucked a few armbands into her pocket and disappeared into the library.

A police cruiser pulled into the pick-up area and parked. A fat cop emerged and waddled inside without a glance at the two protestors. Ten minutes later, the director herself stepped outside.

"You'll have to move that sign, or whatever it is, over there." She pointed to the flagpole on the other side of the cruiser.

Julie carried the petition and taped it to the pole. "So that was the director? I don't like her." She indicated the police car. "And I don't like this."

"Next she'll tell us to move out on the lawn," grumbled the old slave. "Why, look who's here. Hello, Nancy."

"How're things, you old troublemaker?"

"Another day, another armband for your lovely arm?"

"You never give up, do you?"

"It's just the beginning."

"Let me try," said Julie. A young African-American woman walked up. "Hi, there. Can I offer you an armband?"

"Do you work here?" asked the woman.

"No, I don't. I teach at the art school."

"I'll bet you teach music."

"How'd you guess?"

"I'm a musician myself. What instrument? Violin?"

Two girls of color chatted and exchanged phone numbers. Tom wrapped the arm of a bearded chap who pedaled up on his bike, and suggested, "On your way out, leave the armband inside a book."

"I sure will."

Julie flagged down a gentleman in hospital blue. "Good afternoon, sir. Before you go inside, may I ask if you support free speech?"

"Do I? Free speech is my thing."

"Free speech is huge, that's why wearing an armband is huge." Julie wrapped his arm. "May I ask what you do for a living? Are you in health care?"

"I'm a nurse. But why is wearing an armband huge?"

"Well, look at job security. Are you secure in your job?"

"Ha. I'm new, part-time, and temporary."

"Good luck getting a job that has any job security these days. Full-time? Who wants to pay the benefits?"

"Do you have a job?"

"Yes, I do. Lucky me."

"Here at the library?"

Julie laughed. "No, this is just a part-time gig."

"They're paying you to wrap arms?"

"To tell the truth, this is a protest."

"Oh, a protest," said the nurse. "I get it. You know, I'm fed up too with the way things are going. There's only one party I support."

"What's that?" asked Julie.

"The Tea Party."

A young man in filthy jeans set his fishing rod aside and peered into the box of armbands. What's this? A tackle box? Something to eat? Julie dropped a five-dollar bill into the box. The boy grabbed it and ambled away.

She laughed. "Dear Tom, thank you for inviting me. This is so special. If only more people were awake enough and cared enough."

A woman was reading the petition. "Armbands are free speech?"

"Connie!" exclaimed Julie. "I didn't know you were in town."

"Just for a week. Then we're going back to Bogota."

"Do you know Tom? We're wrapping arms."

He'd never been introduced to Mark's wife. "I don't have too many heroes, but your husband's one of them."

"Glad to meet you too," said Connie. "But Julie, it's so good to see you. You look great."

Carrying an armload of books and CDs, Nancy emerged from the library. "Hey, kid," said the old slave, "what happened to your armband?"

"Oh, for heaven's sake, was I supposed to return it to you? I returned it to the library."

Clever Nan, leaving it where it belonged.

Connie said, "Say, would you two like to go to a concert? Cam's playing in half an hour at the Inverted Art Gallery. I have to pick up Ariel to take her to work, but I can meet you there."

The violinist's smile was dazzling. Tossing her hair back, she looked at the old slave, her eyes blazing fire. "Well?"

Was she tossing him another touché? A half-century of smoke and mirrors clouded his vision. Sorry, gotta wrap arms.

But, like the opening movement of a violin concerto, a mystery that had always seemed just out of reach, beckoned to him. How in the name of Stradivarius had this child survived the "pulverized confetti of capitalism" and become a virtuoso concert soloist sought by orchestras from New York to Bogota? What had brought her here to protest wrongful termination? Why did she call him dear? He shook his head, trying to clear it. Damn it, though, he hadn't been on a real date in years.

"I don't know," he heard someone say.

"Oh, good, I thought you were going to say no." Julie took his arm and skipped to the parking lot. "My treat," she said, jumping into the red Jeep.

Feeling younger every minute, the old slave jumped in beside. It was, after all, only a concert.

"Fifteen bucks apiece," said the attendant at the door.

The violin offered her credit card.

"Sorry. Cash only."

"My treat," said the old slave.

Julie said, "I'll buy you lunch."

A few minutes later, Connie joined them at a table in the rear. "It turned out," said Connie, "one of Mark's own orchestra kids did it. I suppose she didn't care one way or the other about politics and certainly never thought it would cost her teacher his job. Most likely she just wanted to graduate and land a principal flute job in some orchestra. It wasn't vindictive."

"She couldn't have been totally innocent," said Tom. "Nobody would do something like that without some malice."

"There were wrongful terminations all right," said Connie. "Three teachers and Mark. And how many others?"

"Seven years ago," said Tom, "Humpty Z fired fifty-three faculty at once. The Thanksgiving Massacre."

"How many teachers have quit?"

"Eight," said Tom, "in two years. Z is playing by the same new rules as corporate bosses everywhere. Bully, badger, bounce your slaves around."

"But a school," said Connie, "isn't a corporation. Good teachers are leaders. The future of the world is in their charge."

"Education was once for students, now it's for profit. Teachers like Mark are worth every penny."

"For fifteen years my husband conducted one of the best student orchestras in the country."

"It was a great orchestra," agreed Julie. "I heard them when Mark brought them to Carnegie." She turned. "Oh, there's Cam. It's about to start."

The gallery owner thanked everyone for coming and turned the stage over to an unusual ensemble of two guitars, drums, and a cello. Leaning back in his chair, the old slave closed his eyes … music hath charms … he must be dreaming.

The quartet began with a slow number, harmonically smooth, like paddling over a quiet lake in late afternoon, then changed dynamics and tempo to a primitive, rhythmic piece that featured the drummer. The old slave opened his eyes. Three musicians were making solid eye contact, playing off each other's facial expressions.

"Why is Cam the only one with a music stand?"

"He's reading the chords," a woman's voice replied. Tom closed his eyes again. The voice went on, as if from another room. "He's following the chord progression and at the same time he's improvising."

The old slave imagined the little surfer girl balanced on her paddleboard, riding waves to a distant shore.

"You said," the woman's voice becoming fainter, "armbands are just the beginning."

They are just beginning. He heard a girl's voice from long ago and far away. There was something about the tilt of her head, her smile, outstretched arms dancing in the air. Grandfather? Are you coming?

"Are you thinking of another little trip to jail?" The voice could be heard as if through trees, warm as breath on a breeze, diminishing, a child singing in a small clearing in a forest of second-growth maple and oak seeded by a copse of old growth a hundred yards upwind. Geese flocked south; a bee ruffled the petals of a thistle. It was a quiet spot to get away from things, a familiar location in the woods, close enough to visit often, still enough to hear your heart beating.

The small clearing happened to be less than a mile from the little surfer's cottage on Grass Lake.

One day, he'd stepped out of his truck into quiet so still his breath blew bees' wings and rustled the fronds of ferns. There were running steps on the road, someone training for a marathon, doing their roadwork. He peered through the trees and was so intent on who was running out in the road he almost stepped on the creature. He looked down just as his foot came down an inch from its head. Instincts screaming to remain motionless and silent, to wait for this frightening intruder to leave, it stared, large new eyes nature's miracles, wide open, two tricks of translucent and transient beauty locking him in a staredown.

"Hey, Julie! Over here. You're not gonna believe this."

The fawn jumped to its feet and ran off. Someone in the audience coughed.

The woman's voice was much closer now. "It's over, Tom. Time to go."

7

"A child will lead us."

PROVERBIAL WISDOM,
OLDER THAN AN OLD-SLAVE PROVERB

A respected twelve-year veteran on the faculty, beloved by his students, with connections in theater communities all over the country, Bernie was terminated during winter break. Humpty Z. Dumpster told the media, "Bernie didn't fit in with the school's mission or its future plans. There are a number of inaccurate allegations regarding the reasons for not renewing his contract, but for a variety of legal reasons all personnel matters are confidential. We are, of course, aware of the alumni concerns expressed on their Facebook page."

Shock and disbelief poured in; the alumni started a Facebook petition. Plans began formulating for a protest at the annual reunion, which this year coincided with the art school's fiftieth anniversary celebration. In dorm rooms and washrooms, students and faculty huddled and whispered, and began preparations for the end of May.

On Monday morning, the old slave was sorting mail when, fifteen minutes early for his community service, Morgan hurried in. "Did you hear?"

"Yesterday."

"Bernie was my favorite teacher. My parents are taking their names off the donor list."

"Good for them."

"That'll cost the school a hundred grand a year."

Tom knew parents withholding donations didn't matter. Last week, one alum had coughed up a hundred grand and the week before another had forked over a cool three quarters of a million. As long as one percenters are lined up to the last tier of Wall Street trying to invest in the art school, Bernie's termination was a donation blip. A glitch. The owners had seen this coming.

Morgan finished organizing and started on the administration run. The old slave finished sorting the dorm mail and posting the outgoing.

Right on time, Ella and Demi walked in. "Hi, Tom. What's to do?"

"Have a chair. You two hear about Bernie?"

Demi's smile would disarm a terminator, but today she was scowling. "I hate this place. I'm so angry about Bernie being fired I could quit school today."

"Me too," echoed Ella.

At the window, Sven held an envelope. "Hey, anybody selling stamps today?"

"Sure," said Demi, hopping to her feet.

Sven applied the stamps. "That was a nice comment, Tom, on the alumni Facebook page. Brave, too, considering Humpty Dumpty reads every word."

"That comment could cost me my job."

Demi danced around like a windblown snowflake. "What? Fire you? What for? Saying something about Bernie? He can't do it."

"Sure he can."

"I think," Sven commanded his little audience, "I've got it."

Ella laughed. "You think?"

"Actors think," said the actor. "Here's my idea. For a one-act or even a movie. It's even got a working title." Sven leaned over the window to whisper, "Firing the Boss."

"You're crazy," said Ella.

"Crazy like a fox," said Sven. Snapping his fingers, he chanted, "Time to go, Humpty Z, time to go," he sang, nodding his head in rhythm.

"That will never happen," said Ella.

"Why not?"

"Because nobody fires the boss." Stern-faced Ella crossed her arms.

The old slave stood silently. Such unlikely pieces of a puzzle. First Hank's, then the library. Could this be the last piece dropped into his lap like an overdue children's book?

"We could," said Tom, "wrap people's arms in black-paper bands."

"Like armbands?"

"I don't get it," said Ella.

"That's different," Sven said. "Like we're in mourning. Oh, wow! I know! We could put 'Grieving for Bernie' on it."

"We could wear armbands," said the old slave. "But maybe something else would be as good. A pin. A badge. Or a t-shirt."

"Hey, everybody!" The attractive girl opened the door and walked in. Lizbet could work like a slave but was late again. "What's this, a meeting?"

"We're talking about helping Bernie."

"I'm all for that. How?"

"We should vote on it. Armband, badge, pin, or t-shirt?

Morgan came back from the administration run and walked in. The old slave looked outside. Enormous flakes of snow were starting to fall.

"We can take a break," said the old slave. "Meeting adjourned. I want a group picture."

Shivering, snowflakes in their hair, the mail room crew stood beside the mail van. On the passenger side of the windshield, Lizbet traced WE. Sven reached over and made a heart below. Demi added TOM. They all stood back to admire their handiwork.

"Speaks to me."

"The way the words work with the love symbol."

"We heart Tom." Lizbet took the picture. "That is one cool message."

○

The newspaper article was headlined Turmoil at the Library Over. "We're just cooking with gas now," chortled the director.

Next day, another article was headlined Ex-Library Employee Sues.

"Melinda was defamed," her lawyer contended. "She was fired because of her age and gender, intentionally inflicted with emotional distress, and then victimized with a smear campaign."

"Hey, Mel," phoned the old slave, "I just read the paper. What are you doing for an encore?"

"Encore? It's not over. You know how slow the legal system works. But the director compromised your civil rights. Why don't you sue too?"

"Guess lawsuits and me don't agree. The armband's more my thing."

"What about the money you've lost?"

"Money is definitely not my thing. I might be the only slave to coerce his boss into cutting his wages."

"I don't believe you."

"Way back, when I was a carpenter's helper. One freezing winter day, while stripping concrete forms, I couldn't feel my fingers anymore and put on a pair of gloves. The boss told me I'd work faster with bare hands. Time is money."

"What did you do?"

"I left them on. Didn't need five bucks an hour. Four fifty was okay.

35

Hey, Mel, how about some armbands for the next time you visit the library?"

"Sure. Stop in next time you're in town."

O

For a few years, the old slave had supervised a ping-pong program in one of the dorm basements, donating tables and equipment and teaching basic skills. On his way to ping-pong, "Hey, Molly," he said, "filling in for a counselor?"

"Yes. And checking my email."

"Have you checked out the alum's page on Facebook?"

"Yes."

"How about it? Are you one of us?"

The tall blonde gave him a fist bump. "Of course, I am." Molly's eyes were aqua flames. "Absolutely."

He wondered how many other students were committed. Absolutely.

Three sophomores had finished a ping-pong set and were hanging out, waiting for the band concert to begin.

"You guys know about Bernie?"

"Of course," said Kylie. "I'm on Student Council. All week we've been talking about walking out of class. We will, too, the minute they fire another teacher."

The old slave was tired. "I'll believe it when I see it," he said and drove home.

His cell phone rang.

"Tom? It's Julie. Did you receive a package today for me? From a violin repair company in Ohio?"

"It's in the mail room."

"Why didn't you call me? Did you put a notice in my box?"

"I believe I did."

"I didn't see it. But … whatever. I'm getting ready to go to the airport, and I need that package. I know it's late. But if you bring it by right away, I'll show you the inside of my house."

A good delivery boy, he drove back to campus. The administration building was dark, the door locked, and there was no one in security. He called the switchboard and got the night security extension.

"Bob? This is Tom. Can I get in the mail room? Now?"

"I'm way over at maintenance. It'll be at least ten minutes."

Twenty minutes later, the old slave picked up the package and drove to the little surfer cottage. The red Jeep was gone. He called her cell phone.

"I'm at a friend's. Leave it outside the door. I'll come back and get it later."

"Off to Colombia?"

"Yes. Thanks so much, dear Tom."

Snow had covered the deck, the wind mounding it up to the door. More was coming down. Tom tried the handle, the door opened, and there was that hum again, a bass note coming from some nether region in his memory, stirring a combination of Julie's love of privacy and something else. She had trusted him. With an open, innocent heart, his femme fatale had placed herself in his hands. Shaken to the core, cursing his luck, the old slave slipped the violin's package inside her door.

The poster read A Holiday Concert—Featuring Special Guests. Julie's name in small letters staked out the center. His old chorale! It had been a year, but, throwing off the bowlines, folding up the armbands, Tom began warming up the vocal chords.

The dress rehearsal would be at the church. He pulled into the parking lot, and there it was. WAH. He parked beside the red Jeep.

In the vestibule, the violin was taping her music together.

"Tom! What are you doing here?"

"Singing, I hope."

He said hello to old chorister friends and, finding a place with the second tenors, tried to make himself inconspicuous. The conductor noted his arrival with raised eyebrows.

Though unfamiliar, the program was simple sight reading. Tom sang the high Gs down an octave and no one noticed. No one seemed to care when, during the Handel excerpt, instead of "He shall purify," he sang "He shall occupy." There was even a Christmas spiritual his basso fairly belted out falsetto.

From the top riser, he had a bird's-eye view of the four strings, and his eyes locked on the second violin. In jeans, blue pullover, and the usual smile, Julie danced her part. Lowering his music, Tom peered over her shoulder, marveling how she used her entire being to express Handel, engaging every eyelash and muscle, her legs coiled for action, balancing her driven personal center—consuming the score, seeking the meaning of harmony.

The conductor dropped his arms and stepped off the podium. Uh-oh. He's onto me. But he just wanted to work with the sopranos.

Twisting in her chair, Julie mouthed, "Can you see?" to Grace in her wheelchair. Grace nodded and smiled her thanks, shaking her head in disbelief. Supernatural! The violin's peripheral awareness bordered on the psychic! She must know every sparrow in her tree and every wave that washed up on her shore.

But can you feel my feather on your neck?

It was over. Tom congratulated himself. He'd sung the whole dress rehearsal, all the way through, without a solo.

He sang the concert without a solo also and, a few days later in the ping-pong dorm, he was working on a new under-spin serve when the violin's studio door opened. Out she came, surfing through a maze of balls.

"Why, hello, Tom. I see you're back."

"Back practicing. Um, serving, I mean."

On her way to some musical engagement, Julie brusquely hurried by and was almost out the door.

"Nice skirt." Tom's voice broke, a hoarse caw from a sick crow.

"Thanks. The chorale sounded great."

"They did? Our chorale?"

"Yes," she said, hand on the door knob, "your chorale."

"Hey, nice sweater. Looks handmade."

"It is handmade. My mother's."

"Did she knit it? It's gorgeous."

Julie closed the door and slipped off her coat. Slowly turning, she modeled a skin-tight, green-and-grey knit combination. "For her honeymoon."

"I'd love to meet her."

"Dad and Mom are visiting tomorrow."

"Bring them by. Please."

"Maybe I will."

"It's supposed to snow this weekend. I'm burning a pile of brush— maybe they'd like to watch a bonfire."

"I'll ask them." She picked up her coat.

"Wait," Tom squeaked, and held out a paddle. "Play."

"You want me to play ping-pong?"

"Just hit the ball for a minute. Please."

"Well …" She hesitated. Then, laying her coat on the table, she said, "I'm not as good as you."

"It's like riding a bike. You never forget."

She held the paddle like a bow. "Like this?"

"Sure," he laughed. "Over here, on this table. Ping-pong. It's as easy as lip-synching a Christmas carol." He served an easy one.

"You were not lip-synching, Tom." Julie changed grips and drilled the ball past him.

He served another, higher, easier. "Was too."

"Were not." Julie chopped the ball back, clearing the net and dropping short for a winner. "I could hear you."

"Sorry about that." He served a top spin to her forehand.

She looped a return into the maze of balls. "Sometimes, Tom, you don't make a lot of sense. I mean that flatteringly."

"Sometimes you remind me of a teenager." He served short, an invitation to push her return.

She killed it. "You're kidding. Are you calling me a kid again?"

"I mean it flatteringly. Yu Liu and you could be sisters."

He served an under-spin slice to her forehand, setting up her loop, but she stepped up and drove it back.

"Yu is my favorite student. You know, you looked happy up there, singing that spiritual. Like you really enjoyed singing the words."

He set down his paddle, lifted his arms. Moving his shoulders in rhythm, a slave doing an imitation of a slave, Tom sang, "The virgin Mary had a baby boy."

"That's the one."

Nodding his head, closing his eyes, he danced and sang louder, "The virgin Mary had a baby boy."

"A virgin had a baby?"

"The virgin Mary had a baby boy," Tom held the "boooy" in a long fermata.

Hands on hips, Julie asked, "How does that work?"

"It doesn't work." Tom found himself spinning in silly circles, saying, "It's not work, it's music."

"Are you finished playing around?"

Tom held his paddle like a guitar and strummed, "And they said that his name was Jesus!" He laid extra emphasis on the last syllable, like the conductor had instructed.

"Aagh! Tom, stop it!" Julie's eyes flared. "Music is work. The hardest kind of work."

"It's easy. It's Christmas."

"Do you actually believe that stuff?"

(*Fortissimo*) "Yes, believer!"

"Tom!"

(*Pianissimo*) "Yes, believer."

"Okay, that's enough."

"One more." Tom lifted a high serve, no spin. Cheesecake, a serve every beginner drools over, just before killing it.

The violinist stuck out her tongue, reached back with bow arm, let out a kamikaze shriek, and killed the ball, smashing it into ecstatic orbit inside Tom's head. He chased the ball down dizzy, giddy, reeling with happiness, and ran it back to the table.

"Saturday night!" Tom croaked. "My house. Bring your mom and dad. The flames will be eighty feet high!"

8

"Narrow your focus to the immediate present and
maintain a general disregard for the outcome."
DANNY SEEMILLER, COACH OF THE
U.S. OLYMPIC TABLE TENNIS TEAM

Darkness had fallen early; the wind had picked up. Shivering, stomping snow from his boots, the old slave peered up at the director's windows on the second floor. The library gleamed a cheerful glow, inviting everyone inside—come on in and warm up, read a good book, browse a new magazine. Throughout the summer and for several months into the winter, Armband Days continued.

"You," said the former library director, "have got to be the most persistent person I've ever known."

"Hi, Gary. Here for another volunteer shift? How about an armband?"

"No can do, Tom. These days, even a volunteer can be fired."

A young woman stopped to wrap her arm. Reading the petition, she asked, "Where can I sign? There are so many names, and every page is full."

A homeless guy and library regular came out on a smoke break, a prison release band on his wrist. "I seen you here before. What's this about?"

"It's a protest, Al."

"A protest? I'm in, bro. Been fired, too. Oh, yeah, the last time I clocked the boss and broke my hand, but he hit the ground so hard his head damn near came off." He shook his fist at the second floor. "I'll show you protest! I'll plant this little black beauty right in front of your shitty little nose."

"Before you leave," said the old slave, "plant it in a book."

◯

The next day at the mail room window, "Nice job, Molly," said Tom, "with the Martin Luther King Day yesterday. Your film brought back memories."

"It was all Mr. Agnew's doing. He's amazing."

"Yeah, great teacher. Always going the extra mile."

"He's trying to get Obama for next year's MLK day."

"By then he could be fired."

"Mr. Agnew? What's happening, Tom? Why would they fire Mr. Agnew?"

"Dustin's one of my best friends, Molly. He knows Humpty Z can fire him whenever the urge hits him."

"You're scaring me."

"These are scary times." The old slave drew the employment picture as briefly and accurately as he could.

"So, at-will means you're at the will of Z?"

"It happens wherever people work. A big boss brings in an axman to fire somebody, replacing one slave with another. It's a vicious circle. James Madison called war the nurse of executive aggrandizement. These days, it's wrongful termination. The latest victims are teachers without unions, like Bernie."

"I don't know if I can do this."

"I'm not sure I can either, but I have to try."

"Maybe ... I can give you the names of students who are in? And a few you shouldn't be talking to. Like children of trustees."

"A list would be nice."

"It can't be just the students though. We have to bring in as many teachers and alums as we possibly can."

"The alums are mostly in. Your teachers are afraid."

"But they all know Bernie shouldn't have been fired!"

"Right. I shouldn't be fired either."

Molly blinked back tears. "If you're fired, who will deliver the mail?"

"Somebody else."

◯

Rumors were flying about another faculty termination when the old slave arrived on Front Street. Still in her We Are The 99% embroidered sweater, Sandra greeted him with a hug.

"Hey, old girl. I saw your picture in the paper. I didn't know you were a teacher once upon a time."

"Once a teacher, twice a mother, three times a city councilwoman."

"You were on city council?"

"For a few years, beating my head against a wall, surveying sidewalks, parks, parking lots, and public restrooms for wheelchair accessibility. Other things became higher priority."

"Other things?"

"Oh, you know. Everything these days is so urgent. Wars, poverty. Climate change is coming on so fast. There's the environment."

"The environment is all of us."

"And the idea of leaving something for future generations."

"So, old girl, what are you leaving?"

Sandra waved at a driver with his middle finger in the air. "For thirty years I taught my students the difference between right and wrong. They got it. For fifteen years I was on city council. They didn't know the difference."

"Can I interview you? Just for fun?"

"Just don't ask me my age."

"Do you think capitalism is at a crossroads?"

"Oh, yes. Selfishness or altruism."

"Has corporate greed cost this country millions of jobs?"

"Tens of millions. We are no longer our brother's keeper. We've abandoned the Golden Rule."

"We?"

"The mega rich, those in the driver's seat. They're hanging on to their money, with our blessings, until the doomsday clock strikes midnight."

"What do you tell your children and your grandchildren?"

"I used to march for peace," Sandra said. "And I'd do it every day for the rest of my life if I felt it was doing any good. I believe Occupy Front Street is more important."

"You were a teacher, a political leader. Do you have any hope?"

"I've never stopped hoping."

The old slave asked, "Would you march against wrongful termination?"

"There's so much termination! Jobs are so scarce, finding replacements so easy."

"I mean, would you help at the library?"

"Why not? We're not getting any younger. Tell me more."

After seven months, the armband story almost told itself.

9

"The next great division of the world will be between people who wish to live as created beings and those who wish to live as machines."

JOANNE STEPANIUK, *THE VEGAN SOURCEBOOK*

Monday morning, everyone and his secretary were talking about the latest termination. Dustin's contract had not been renewed. He would finish out the school year, then be another notch on Humpty Z. Dumpster's gun.

On the spur of the moment, the old slave scribbled:

"Do you agree: 1. Bernie/Dustin deserved better? 2. I could be fired for asking? 3. Your teachers are afraid of losing their jobs? 4. Your school is being run like a corporation? 5. Firing is an administration strategy? 6. Z cares only about power? 7. Students have any power at all? 8. Protest is a way to fight back? 9. A forty-student protest would make any difference? 10. A hundred-student protest would make the news?"

He selected five seniors, one from each major department. He placed the ten questions in each of their mailboxes and included an invitation to meet with him in the dorm basement where Beethoven accompanied bouncing balls, where *West Side Story* rehearsed alongside serving practice, where art labored and ping-ponged.

Light snow was falling. The sun was setting, the road to campus a tunnel dark as the bell of a tuba. A few laggard students leaving orchestra practice hurried to a late dinner in the cafeteria. Tom walked up to the door of the dorm and drew in a deep breath. Suppose no one showed up? Crazy old coot with a cause, foisting politics off on kids. Art is supposed to live here, not rebellion. Three boys were standing at the desk, nervously looking around. The residence hall assistant had been trying to find out what they were doing in his dorm at this time of the evening. "Oh, hi, Tom," he said, relieved as he returned to his email.

"Gentlemen. Anyone for ping-pong?" The old slave led the way downstairs to a practice room.

"We didn't know what to say to him," said Ted, a motion picture arts major.

"Policing students," Tom said, "is the worst job in the world. It doesn't make any money. Slave labor."

The old slave had acted the old man in two of Ted's movies but his friends were strangers. Bruce and Jack said they wanted to learn more. Ted nodded. They were joined by Kris and Hogan, Student Council president and vice president. Molly walked in and laughed. "Hey, people. I didn't realize there were this many ping-pong geeks."

Writing majors Barb and Ravi came in and sat on the floor. By the time Demi arrived, the practice room felt like a sauna. The old slave took off his sweatshirt and wiped his brow with it.

"They're firing your teachers," he began, "as if they were ducks on a pond. Bernie wasn't the first, not by a long shot, and now Dustin."

Kris jumped in. "Student Council has been discussing this with Humpty Dumpty, how it's affecting teachers and their ability to teach."

"Just this week, three teachers came by the mail room wondering if I'd heard any rumors."

"Omigod," said Ravi, "my English teacher said in class today she was afraid she wouldn't be invited back next year."

"She can't even say that unless she completely trusts each and every one of the students she's saying it to."

"We have to agree on one thing," said Kris, Student Council president. "This meeting is confidential."

"You may not realize what you're getting into," said the old slave.

"What do you mean?"

"Protest means action. Actions have consequences. I've done protests before and I'm here to tell you, the powers that be don't like them."

"Will they expel us?"

"Nobody knows the future."

"We would like to have a say in our future."

"Absolutely," said Kris. "It is our future. It's our school."

"It would just be nice," said Jack, "to know what's going on."

"What's going on," said the old slave, "is a corporate mentality spreading out from private enterprise and taking over institutions, agencies, and schools."

"Including our school?"

The old slave nodded. "Unfortunately, yes. Worse, it's a regressive mentality that actually believes corporations are people."

"Meaning?" Hogan already knew the answer.

"It doesn't care about your future or anybody else's as long as it stays on top."

Demi piped up, "Power?"

"Power in the hands of the few. Plutocracy. We are living in the shadows of democracy. Democracy only works when we, the people, are informed, when we understand the causes of our problems, when we distinguish between policies and practices that are in our interests and those that aren't, when we use our voices and vote our conscience and not our wallet."

Jack said, "I still don't know what's going on."

The practice-room door opened. "Can we come in?" Kylie and Moira had been playing ping-pong. They'd noticed the crowd in the practice room and now stood, waiting for admission. Kris nodded, and two more student conspirators scrambled in and squeezed into a corner on the floor.

The old slave said, "At Occupy Front someone will shout, 'Show me what democracy looks like!' and everyone responds, 'This is what democracy looks like!' Democracy is people acting together, in the street, in the workplace, inside the classroom. Sometimes it's dangerous. Sometimes you go to jail."

"I really, really don't know enough," said Jack. "What does this have to do with Bernie and Dustin?"

"It has to do with power. Who's your favorite teacher?"

"Ms. Gordon."

Several students nodded.

"Put yourself in Ms. Gordon's place. The boss says you can't teach something. Do you teach it anyway or modify your lesson plans? Imagine losing Ms. Gordon, a teacher with the courage to speak out."

"I don't see how it's in my interest to do something about it," said Jack. "I'm here to get my diploma."

"What is in your interest?" Tom looked around at talented teenagers with interests ranging from a mild curiosity about politics to a total dedication to their art. What was the common denominator?

"My interest?" asked Molly. "Or ours?"

Kris jumped to her feet. "This is about us, not just about you!"

"For some reason," said Jack, "I thought this meeting was about Bernie."

"I think," said Demi, "it's about fear."

"We're all in this together," said Kris. "Yesterday Humpty Dumpty called me into his office again. I asked him why Bernie was fired. He said

I shouldn't care and didn't need to know. He's such a lame excuse for a president, a businessman."

"But you're Student Council president," said Kylie. "If he's not listening to you, he's not gonna listen to us."

"It's that we're afraid of him," said Demi. "He has all the power. He could destroy our careers before we've even started. I just want to get my diploma and get out of here."

"You're not the only one."

"I can't take a chance on getting expelled."

Bruce asked, "Why is keeping a job all that important?"

"It's as important," said Tom, "as staying in school. School is preparation for a career in slavery. Instead of money, you get paid with grades. Can you tell me the secret to getting an A?"

"Shut up and listen?"

"Do your homework?"

"Don't fall asleep when I'm giving a lecture?"

"None of the above. It's please the teacher." The old slave had been good at that. "Training for kissing the boss's butt."

"I think we should have goals," said Ravi.

"Me too," said Barb. "We could blockade Z's office."

"How about practical goals? Realistic ones?"

"I can make a poster."

"I think we should write the trustees! Go over Humpty Z. Dumpster's head."

"They're the ones who hired him."

"Actions," said the old activist slave, "speak louder than words."

Kris was drawing on a scrap of paper. "Hogan and I have been talking about making a badge to wear, as, you know, a kind of symbol of solidarity." She held it up and said, "It's a variation of the original school logo."

"I like it," said Barb.

"We've started a petition too, supporting Bernie and Dustin."

Molly joined in, "When all those alums arrive in May, we could put protest posters in dorm windows."

"How about an old-fashioned sit-in?" suggested Moira.

"How about walking out of class?" Hogan mimed walking out the door.

"I wouldn't," said Bruce. "How many teachers are going to look the other way? Not flunk us?"

"We don't know unless we try."

The old slave did a quick mental survey. "All but a few, I think."

"We should," Hogan took a breath, looked around the room, then said, "we should ask our teachers whose side they're on."

We should overcome. It wasn't civil rights marches or anti-Vietnam War protests or the Arab Spring, but the old slave could feel the ground moving. Then he heard the balls bouncing. It was time to play ping-pong.

O

The secretary had put the finishing touches on a sandwich at the salad bar. Tom touched her arm and steered her toward his table.

"You should know, Darlene. Students are asking their teachers to support them."

"Support them?"

"Walking out."

"Of what?"

"The community meeting."

"For what purpose?"

Change, meet status quo.

"Look, Darlene, I know how you feel about unions and those old union bosses, but these are students you see every day."

"Students who will graduate and move on and never make any difference."

"Never?"

"Not in the next little while anyway."

"Hamilton Z. Dempsey only cares about the next little while. Do you agree that the school is being run like a corporation?"

"This isn't a corporation."

"Do you think employees are afraid of losing their jobs?"

"I know I am."

"Do you agree firing is a strategy of the administration?"

"I haven't seen that much of it."

"Bernie. Dustin. Weren't you ever fired?"

"And told to shut up about it or forget about the reference."

"Do you agree Humpty Z cares only about power?"

"I think that's obvious."

"Do students have any power?"

"Very little, if any."

"If the Student Council president came up and asked for your support for students walking out of class in protest, what would you say to her?"

"How many students are we talking about?"

Inspiration, meet number crunching.

"I don't know—yet." The old slave headed back to work.

48

Sven usually stood silently outside the window, waiting for the old slave to give permission to enter, but today the acting major walked in and sat down. Finished sorting, Tom pulled up a chair.

"I don't know," Sven said. "I just don't know what they're thinking, walking out of class. There's a guy down the hall trying to hack into Z's email." He bent, put his forehead on his knees "I think I'm gonna be sick."

A tray of envelopes slipped out of the old slave's hands and landed on the floor, and he bent to pick one up. The letter slid just out of his reach. Slowly, one piece at a time, Tom gathered the mail.

"I just want to graduate," said Sven, "and get out of here."

"Are you hitting the books?"

"I'm trying. It's the same old problem. I can't read. I stayed up all night reading eighty pages. That means four hundred more by tomorrow."

"Is that why you haven't been coming out to play?"

"Yeah. I'm way behind." A year ago, Sven was a raw beginner, one of Tom's original table tennis students, but these days in head-to-head competition, the acting student often came out on top.

"Worried?"

"I don't understand what I'm reading." Sven pulled a magazine out of the incoming mail. "Take this headline: 'Neocon hawks learned nothing from Iraq.' What the hell does that mean?"

"A bobble-head spinning politics."

"What the hell does that mean?" Sven glanced at the clock. "Oh, shit and yi yi," he said, jumping up and sprinting for the door. "I'm late for rehearsal. Oh, sorry, Molly."

10

"The only thing necessary for the triumph of evil is
for good men to do nothing."
EDMUND BURKE

Molly motioned the old slave into the hallway. "We need to talk. A
lot of students are getting ready to walk out—at least a hundred. A few
are pushing for a full-campus sit-down protest."

Riot police, body armor.

"But the whole thing could fall apart," said the girl. "Someone hacked
into Z's email."

"I heard."

"Whoever did it forged a letter from Hamilton Z. Dempsey to the
trustees. That was criminal. The rest of us could pay."

"What if the rest of us is nearly all of us?"

"What do you mean?"

"It's a numbers game, Molly."

"Whoever did it was evil. It's illegal."

"It may be illegal but that doesn't make it wrong. Breaking the law
doesn't make me evil, not when I choose to do so. What Humpty Z did
was both legal and evil."

"It could undermine the whole thing. They can portray us as a bunch
of kids who can't tell right from wrong."

More doubts appeared. The old slave had received an email from
Bernie's former department head. "Sorry Tom," wrote Durwood, "you
need to butt out. Yes, they'll stumble and maybe fall, but if you're involved,
the students will lose the group identity they've worked hard to develop.
Without that youthful identity the whole effort will be a waste of time.
When I was an undergraduate in Arizona, no liberal bastion, we kicked
ROTC recruiters out only because we did it by ourselves."

Tom remembered his college days differently. Without faculty support, the student movement he'd been a part of would never have gotten off the ground.

Durwood went on. "I appreciate your good intentions, but I know Kris, she doesn't want you meddling. I'm pulling for the students too. Heck, I'm almost sixty. Like as not, I'll be Z's next victim."

Julie agreed with Durwood. "They're just children, Tom. Kids. By the way, how old are you anyway?"

A cavity opened in the old slave's chest and there was nothing he could do to fill it. "Seventy-two next month."

"Are you just looking to get in one final shot? One last hurrah?"

Two hurrahs for the cavity.

○

On the day of the community meeting, the old slave had just grabbed a sandwich and coffee when, carrying a tray of salads, Darlene came up and asked, "Well, Mister Know-it-All, is something going to happen?"

"I don't know. Students are calling the shots. Gotta get back. Bulk mailing."

Yu Liu walked up. "Can I work?"

"You can join me," said Tom, "but can you work?"

"I can."

Yu Liu was a prize, filled in everywhere, helpful with the heavy lifting and efficiency itself when delivering packages, especially to Humpty Z. Dumpster's office with its vaulted ceiling, views of campus, and aura of power.

"Molly said we were doing a walking out. What is walking out?"

"It's like stopping work. A protest. You know protest?"

"Yah. Like Tiananmen Square."

"Not exactly like Tiananmen, more like Vietnam."

"Ahh. Many Chinese die there."

"Many more Vietnamese died. I meant like Vietnam protest in the U.S. Walk-outs, sit-ins, lie-ins, be-ins."

"What are those? Beings?"

○

The bulk mailing was ready to go onto the belt when Molly stormed up to the mail room window. "I'm never going to another community meeting! What a total waste of everyone's time. Karaoke. We should have walked."

"But," the old slave asked, "were you ready to face the music?"

○

That night, at the ping-pong dorm desk, "You're late." Moira was never late.

"You're early," he retorted, and headed downstairs. "We can drill for a while." They looped topspin forehands until balls were strewn all over the floor.

Unsmiling, two students approached the table.

"Kris!" said the old slave. "Glad you could make it. You and me against Moira and Hogan."

The Student Council president shook her head. "We're not here to play ping-pong." She motioned Tom and Moira into a practice room. "We showed the petition to the dean."

"What did she say?"

Hogan said, "She gave us the green light to run with it."

"Fifty signatures so far," said Kris.

Moira asked, "Can I sign it?"

"Sure, right there," said Kris, pointing. "Another thing, Tom. Can you write something for the *Blue Comma*?"

The student lit magazine.

○

In the middle of the night, the old slave sat up. What do we believe in? What must we fight for? Where had he seen that? Oh yeah, an excerpt from Steinbeck on the alumni Facebook page:

"Monstrous changes taking place, pouring outward like a torrent ..."

He grabbed a pen and started writing on the pillow, the words coming faster than he could get them down, his pen like a fuse setting paper on fire, burning toward dynamite. An hour later, he went into the kitchen, made tea, and fired up the word processor. There would be no more sleep this night.

Next morning, as he was pulling into his usual parking spot the interim theater director pulled in and parked right alongside, a mile from his office.

"Good morning, Boyce."

No response.

Boyce was normally sociable, and had even put his signature on the armband petition, but in his new position of temporary administrative authority he acted more like a slave every day. They crossed the lot and entered the administration building. The hatchet man came out of his office, and he and Boyce went into a private room.

In the cafeteria, Tom approached the student sitting alone, having a late breakfast. "Hogan. Something's up. The big cheese is beginning to smell. Maybe they found the hacker."

The boy's eyes widened.

"Or maybe Humpty Dumpty figured out who started that petition."

"Aagh!" The Vice President of Student Council choked on his toast.

Glancing around quickly, the old slave pulled out his rewrite of the Steinbeck excerpt. He set it down on the table. "Don't tell me what you do with this."

Tom finished his morning routine, wrapped up some last-minute college applications going out Express Mail, sent an oboe on its way to the repair shop, and a box of dirty laundry home to the mother of a student. He caught up with the history teacher at lunch.

"Hey, Lynn. Counting down the days?"

"Twenty-nine. I am so out of here, Tom."

"How'd Jim's reading go last night?"

"A full house. We sold two dozen books."

"Great! I'm just curious. Is it true Jim shows you his rough drafts for your advice before he starts rewriting?"

"Well, not quite every rough draft."

"Save a copy of his book for me." As Tom reached, he saw the copy paper beside the napkin dispenser. He turned. Every single cafeteria table had a sheet of paper in the middle of it.

"Excuse me, Lynn. Got a meeting."

At the mail room, he stood like a sentry in a German Army greatcoat and Prussian hat. Hard-working, nearly normal, Norm had hit his psychological brick wall. An abundance of musical skills and his clarinet had delivered a full scholarship; he seemed on a paved road to a lucrative professional career. Then he suffered what sooner or later every teen suffers: a change of heart. To the consternation of his teacher, Norm was now bent on a military career.

"Come on in, ex-clarinetist."

Holding attention, the boy stood in place while Tom resumed sorting the mail. Deliberately, Norm reached into the pocket of his greatcoat and pulled out a sheet of paper. "What is this, Tom?"

"I didn't sign it. My name isn't anywhere in it. How'd you know it was me?"

"Your odor was all over it."

"Hogan didn't tell you?"

"Hogan's my hero. He'd never break confidentiality. I haven't told anyone either. Will you be fired like Bernie?"

"Who knows?"

"If you're fired, I'm out of here, and I'm taking someone with me."

"Not a good idea. Did you get accepted?"

"Accepted and offered a full ride. With ROTC."

"Congratulations." The old slave didn't mention his own ROTC experience. He didn't say anything about going to jail for protesting the war in Vietnam. There was a time and a place for everything.

John Steinbeck Attends the Alumni Reunion*

Our grandfathers' grandfathers lived all their lives in the gray. The earth they worked was dark and somber. Day after day trooped by faceless and pale. The forces marshaled around them had declared war by disparagement, by starvation, by repression, by forced direction, by the stunning hammer blows of conditioning. The song they heard in their hearts was a lament for lost freedom, a song burning like a fuse toward dynamite. Monstrous changes were taking place, forces shaping a future whose face they could not know.

But we recognize that face. It appears on billboards and on television and in the bright lights of Times Square. It is the face at press conferences and photo ops, on marquees and packages and labels, on front pages and hood ornaments and glossy ads.

The face has taken over our classrooms and our bedrooms, our aisles and the halls we walk, the cockpits of discourse and the driver's seat of this poisoned planet. Question the face and it flaunts a title deed, confront it in court and it buys the judge and the jury, and the courthouse too. If the face doesn't like the rules, it changes them, calls them insubordinate. If provoked, the face strafes and clubs and fires at will.

We mourn our grandfathers' grandfathers and the dark and somber world they lived, loved, and labored in. We mourn a world where they knew when the master arose and when he went to bed, a world where they knew his daughters and sons and the songs they sang, the songs of the field, the songs of hope.

We mourn the last eight years of searching and destroying the songs of hope in the name of art. We mourn the loss of past, present, and the future while the face dwells among us.

What do we believe in? Art and art alone. What must we fight for? It will become clear when the cricket's song sweetens our ears, when the smell of the earth rises chanting to our nose. We will see when the dappling light under a tree blesses our eyes and we will remember our grandfathers' grandfathers in a moment of freedom pouring outward like a glorious torrent.

Freely and extensively modified excerpt from East of Eden *(1952), chapter 13.*

○

On his way to Armband Day 59, the old slave stopped at Melinda's.
"Tom! So good to see you."
"What's new?"
"Oh, just everything. My lawsuit has arrived at the negotiation stage. The board is circling the wagons around their most unpopular dictator. And, I just heard from a reliable source that she'd like to retire but her bosses won't let her."
"The board? Or city council? Or the county commission?"
"All of the above. What a comedy routine. I also heard a county commissioner just appointed himself to the library board."
"The scumbag."
"Tom, the director violated your First Amendment rights. Get a lawyer. Two lawsuits at once! It will finish her! You can put those armbands into your wood heater."

"It's just beginning."

"You always say that. Are you still working at the art school?"

"Hard to believe. Every day I pinch myself."

"What? Are you in trouble there too?"

"Trouble? I'm doing a little mentoring under the radar. The natives are restless."

"Those rich kids at the art school? You must be kidding."

"I told you about Bernie?"

"I suppose you're helping them protest."

"Couldn't help myself.

"Don't you dare get fired."

"I'll try not to. Hey, Mel, gotta run. Oh, yeah, almost forgot." Tom handed Melinda a bundle of armbands, each with her name on them. "Your daughter knows what to do with these."

"She does indeed. I like these. 'Lest We Forget.'"

11

"Cold comfort is the midwife of sad beginnings."
OLD-SLAVE PROVERB

The email had urgency written all over it. "I've got cautionary advice and promising information. Meet me at Buddie's tomorrow morning at eight."

Dana's impressive intellect and outstanding communication skills had landed her the job at the art school, but fifteen years of reconciling creativity with self-censorship had taken its toll. To the old slave she'd complained about the oppressive atmosphere in her department until one day, without warning, she walked up to her boss, turned in her keys, and walked out the door.

In the favorite student hangout, the former administrator grimaced. "I just hope," said Dana, "you're being careful. Yours is the only current employee name on that Facebook page."

"Others—Bernie, Juergen—have noticed too."

Her lower lip obeyed a tremor. Dana lowered her gaze. "You could lose your job."

The old slave looked around the little restaurant. At eight o'clock on a Monday morning Buddie's was empty, no one within twenty feet.

"Dana," said Tom, "it's a job." He went silent, watching her tears well. "A j-o-b."

They overflowed; he offered a napkin. Gathering herself, Dana said, "I couldn't sleep all night. My stomach hurt. My head hurt. I thought about telling you our little meeting was off, but it wouldn't have done any good, changed anything. There's so much at stake."

"I know."

"If my daughter wasn't a student, it would have been easier. I'd have joined you and those other students, written letters, carried signs, used every ounce of my credibility and resources to make this protest happen. But I can't let this or anything else get in the way of her graduating, and I'm telling you here and now that this had better not have my name connected with it in any way."

Dana placed a list of names on the table.

○

Outside the mail room, two girls he'd never seen before stopped. "Did you write the Steinbeck piece?"

"What Steinbeck piece?"

"I'm Jackie. I think it's great."

"My name is Tom. I'm the mailman."

"This is Elie. We have to do something, and soon, before we waste everybody in this building."

"That would not be a good idea."

"What can we do? Elie and I have been wracking our brains. We aren't afraid of them."

"Talk to your friends. Quietly. Ask them how they feel about Bernie and Dustin."

"We'll start today," said Elie. "What else?"

"There's a little issue; I could be fired."

"What? Why would they fire you?"

"Look behind you. One at a time. Slowly."

The girls turned to view the somber windows of the top floor of the administration building.

"That's Hamilton Z. Dempsey's office," said the old slave. "There. Next is the office of the Vice President of Corporate Relations, who happens to be my boss. Next is the office of the Vice President of Human Resources. What if they looked out their windows right now? You two are not on their radar, but if you were Kris and Hogan and any of those administrators or their lackeys happened to look out the window right about now, I'd be fired tomorrow."

"Tell us what we can do."

"Like I said, talk to your friends. Would they put their diploma ahead of their school? Talk to your teachers. Would they put their paycheck ahead of what's right? Take notes. Pay attention."

Buzzing like bees, the two girls walked away.

○

"Tom?" A familiar voice on the phone. "Where've you been?"

The old slave could hear the balls bouncing, and his old competitive juices began flowing. A few years ago, Roger and he had driven balls with the U.S. Olympic men's table tennis team coach. Suddenly clinics, matches, and tournaments were spinning through his mind-muscle memory.

A polio victim, Roger had been on crutches most of his adult life. To play ping-pong, he crippled up to the table, laid one crutch on the floor, and then, leaning on the other, he'd spin forehands and wicked backhands past opponents.

"How about if a few of you side-spinning geezers come out here to play the kids?"

"Let me ask them."

At the dorm, Moira tackled the old slave at the door. "I've got it!" She joined him on the stairs leading down to the basement, her green eyes sparkling. "I know! I know!"

"Know what? How to beat me at ping-pong?" Tom plopped a bag of paddles and balls on the floor and put on his game shoes.

"Let's go in there," said the girl. Her finely detailed eyebrows stabbing the air, Moira led the way into a practice room. "Thank you for the assignment. I've been working on it all week. Today, I finally know who did it."

"Who did what?"

"Hacked into Humpty Z. Dumpster's email. Larry is the only student with the computer skills who hated, and I mean *really* hated, Z."

Of course. A bright, outspoken, four-year senior, Larry had been expelled the year before. He'd apologized, been forgiven, and allowed to re-enroll the next semester, but when his favorite music teacher was fired, he reacted. At a meeting between the seniors and the president, Larry had stood to ask, "Aren't you concerned about teachers being afraid of losing their jobs?"

"Not at all," Hamilton Z. Dempsey replied. "Some of our faculty have been here over twenty years, a few thirty, and two are approaching forty."

"How many have fled?" Larry persisted. "How many teachers have left in the last eight years?"

"I don't know exactly. There have been several retirements."

"Several early retirements, you mean. Why is it that only one department head has been here longer than you?"

"No comment. That would be information of little or no concern to you or to any student."

The old slave caught up with him outside the mail room. "Hey, Larry, how're you doing?"

"Better than you," replied Larry. "Z is on to you."

"It's a reciprocal arrangement."

"I know," said Larry. "It all depends on what they know and what you know—the money trail, for instance."

"You know about the money?"

"I know," said Larry, "how many donors gave the school twenty grand last year."

"Quite a few."

"Four hundred and twenty-three."

"I know," said the old slave, "of one Wall Street dude who donated three quarters of a million bucks last week, no strings attached."

"Knowledge is power."

"Knowledge is money," said Tom. He invited Larry to the next ping-pong night.

○

"Hey, Dustin," said Tom, rolling down the window of the mail van. "Are we still on for next Sunday?"

"For the library? Sure. As long as I don't have to play ping-pong with you. Anything new with your book?"

"Two chapters today, courtesy of the ping-pong club."

"Congratulations."

"Congratulations yourself. They tell me Z liked the Martin Luther King Day show. Sorry about your job here."

"I was hoping to be working on next year's—inviting Obama. Do you know who Valerie Jarrett is?"

"Obama's senior advisor."

"Once upon a time, she was a classmate of Hart's."

Hart came to the door. "Just took the dog for a walk. Come on in, Tom."

A group carrying instruments was crossing the street.

"The orchestra," explained Hart. "Their concert's in a couple hours."

"By the time we get back," said Dustin, "there'll be cars parked up and down the street here."

"In the mud." Hart handed Tom a cup of coffee. "Quite a little downpour last night."

"For sure. Did you really have Valerie Jarrett in your class?"

"I met her. Intelligent, inquisitive. A force. The omelet must not have been very good."

"Why's that?" asked Dustin.

"You've got catsup on your shirt. You never put catsup on a good one."

"It was the best omelet I ever had."

Hart laughed. "Well, are you two protestors ready to go?" She grabbed her purse, Dustin collected armbands. In town, they dropped Hart off at the grocery.

Pulling into the library parking lot, the old slave announced, "Today, I'm not wrapping arms."

"Oh? What are you gonna do?"

"I'm going inside to read. All eyes will be on me with a book in my hands while you plant those seeds."

Tom enjoyed a new author. Dustin sowed. Fifteen minutes later, they sashayed from the library, picked up Hart, and drove home.

Tom helped carry in the groceries and was on his way back to his truck when there she was, all dressed up, a foxy, sixty-nine-year-old in heels, hat, and scarf.

"Tom! Is it you?"

It's me, all right. It's me standing in the street close enough for a fist bump, for a staredown. It's me looking into the eyes that saw Melinda leave the library she helped build. It's me reading the lips that lied, telling the reporter Melinda was insubordinate. It's me facing the face of fear, the face that has taken over the driver's seat, the face behind the memo "If any staff is caught placing armbands in the library it will be cause for immediate dismissal." It's me thinking, such a little thing, an armband. It's me picturing a new employee reading Lest We Forget, then looking to see if anyone is watching and putting the armband back in the book, or, more likely, dropping it on the floor and stepping on it.

A stranger to high heels, late for the concert, the director slipped and threw up her arms. Her purse took flight, and with a splat landed in the mud on the shoulder of the road.

"It's me, all right," said Tom. "Going to the concert?"

○

Sven was at the window with another late college application. "Express, Tom. It took me a week to burn a decent CD."

The old slave put the postage on the envelope and counted back the boy's change.

61

"Thanks, Tom. Let me know if I can help."

Help? With what?

"We should talk."

"I was just thinking," said Sven, "about speaking and writing. I know I don't write like I talk. Is it the same with you? Do you sound the same on paper as you do in person?"

"What do you think?" Tom handed Sven a sheet of paper.

"What is this?"

"Page from a book I'm writing."

12

"The ultimate tragedy is not bad people abusing good people,
it's good people remaining silent about it."
MARTIN LUTHER KING JR.

Julie arrived at the window in a sour mood. "This morning, Humpty Z. Dumpster called me into the office. He warned me about taking so much time off."

"To perform?"

"Yes. But it's in my contract."

"Warning's the easy part. At least he didn't fire you."

"He's threatened to. I'm doing my job!"

"I know. Your students are devoted to you."

"They practice when I'm away! You should see my phone bill."

"When you go on trips, Humpty Dumpty power trips."

She smiled at the play on words, something in that smile stirring slave memories. The old slave's daughter, granddaughter, daughters of Eve all, experts at the oldest game, slaves tempting slaves, creating victims of love, blinded to our own downfall.

"I heard you were writing a book, Tom."

"Guilty as charged."

"You must let me read it when I get back. I'm leaving for Wisconsin tomorrow."

"Got a gig?"

"I'm playing the Mystery Sonata."

The Mystery Sonata! Ah, Biber, the inspired composer transposing the gospel of Luke, the physician, into music: "And Mary arose and entered the house of Zacharias and there she saluted Elizabeth."

The mother of God must have said something too. No sooner had she said it than the babe leaped in her womb.

Elizabeth was an old woman who'd many years ago given up ever having a child but who was now six months pregnant with "the voice crying from the wilderness." A teenager, technically still a virgin, Mary had received divine notification that she was pregnant with a special babe, not the voice crying from the wilderness, but the voice of God. Biber had set the mystery of this moment in three movements, slow, medium, and fast, and whenever God delivered His message, the violin was called on to speak like an angel, with authority and joy.

At ping-pong that night, Sven and the old slave were tied two games apiece and had just arrived at deuce when Larry walked in. Reluctantly, Tom put his paddle down. "I'll only be a minute," he apologized, leading Larry into a practice room.

"I guess," said Larry, "you know. Everyone's talking about it." He slumped to the floor.

"Go on."

"Somebody hacked into Humpty Dumpty's email." Six words. Icicles to spear the heart.

"I heard about it."

"I'll never graduate. The administration is a pack of hyenas, a dream team of carrion eaters."

"Did you sign the petition?"

"Not yet." The young man almost whispered, "I've been so damn busy with homework and practicing. I'm a loser."

"To be a winner, you have to think like a winner."

"This is my fourth year. I've been expelled, I'm being tested for drugs, and now this. It's killing me."

An African-American boy opened the door. "Oops, sorry."

Tom gave Larry a questioning look.

"Don't worry," said Larry, "he's okay. A voice major looking for a room to rehearse in."

There was no one on the tables. Sven must have gone back to his room. The old slave dug into his bag. "Come on, young man." He handed Larry a paddle. "I'll spot you five points."

Valentine's Day the mail room was swamped with packages from parents, grandparents, girlfriends, boyfriends, cousins, brothers, sisters, and best friends, sending cards and flowers and candy and clothing. Under a head-high stack of parcels, the old slave filled a dorm bin to overflowing.

Yu Liu was at the window. "Hmm," mused Tom's most valuable mail room helper. "Lots of packages."

An hour later, all packages had disappeared into the van, all cards and letters had been sorted into mailboxes and bins, and the outgoing mail had been posted.

Settling into her favorite chair beside the conveyer belt, "So," said Yu Liu, "how is Mister Tom?"

"Fine and dandy. How's the fiddle?"

"Miss Judie not happy with me. President Dumpster not like Asians. Fine except for that. I'm just glad to graduate and getting out of here."

"You're not the only one wanting out of here."

"I think I know."

"Humpty Z. Dumpster didn't like Julie taking off to play a concert."

"She told me."

"Listen, Yu. Can you keep this under your hat?"

"Where?"

"'Under your hat' means don't tell anybody."

The girl nodded.

"Lorenzo is applying to different colleges and conservatories."

"I know! He has many opportunities for conducting. Europe. Wisconsin. Spain! But he can't go. It's like, what you say, pulling teeth, to get away from here, unless he quit."

"Or gets fired. Lorenzo isn't alone looking for another job." Tom pointed to Human Resources. Letters, applications, and references filled the mailbox to overflowing.

"Lots of teachers needing jobs."

"Every day it's the same."

"I can come back tomorrow." Yu stood to leave. "Orchestra in a few minutes."

"Great, see you then. Remember, mum's the word."

Yu looked puzzled, then smiled, nodded, and headed off for orchestra rehearsal.

He was driving home when the call came.

"Tom? It's Julie. I forgot to lock my door—we were in such a hurry."

"You lock your door?"

"Yes, I do. Can you go by on your way home from work? Please? Just go in and lock the door?"

First dusk comes early in February. The stars were out, the western sky glowed orange as the old slave drove up to the little surfer's lakeshore cottage. He noted the fresh tire tracks, the footprints. Someone, most likely her "friend," had joined her and together they'd driven the red Jeep across the bridge and about now were in some motel in Wisconsin.

Tom went down the stairs and opened the door. A drone? Or was it a fan humming? "Hello?" He heard it again, like a boat out on the dark lake, or a bow caressing a string. With snow melting in his hair, nature's tears trickling down his forehead, Tom closed his eyes, turned the lock on the door. And closed it.

He climbed back up the stairs, pausing at the top. The silence was ominous.

○

The old slave motioned the newest member of the ping-pong club inside the mail room and closed the door.

"They think I did it," said Larry, "which is fine with me. I can prove I didn't. I was with my dad that whole weekend. We weren't even in this state. What do you think about this? I'll tell Humpty Dumpty I want to meet with him. Tell him I'll take a lie detector test … then, I can ask him if he wants me to spy on you and the ping-pong club. I can do it."

Larry may have the stuff to pull such a crazy scheme off.

"Well?"

"If you did nothing wrong," said the old slave, "there's nothing to worry about."

"I appreciate your advice." Larry turned to go, stopped. "Oh, hey. I almost forgot. In class today, Dustin came out firing on all cylinders, blasting the administration. Everyone cheered."

Tom wrote: "Dear Sam, All my life I've played ping-pong. It's a great sport that builds the entire body, increases strength and speed, develops hand-to-eye coordination. And, it's fun. I'd like to help more students learn it, set up a clinic and run a demonstration. I've invited a couple of my old club members to help. Okay with you?"

It was okay with the vice president.

Survival depends on awareness and perception, noticing the little differences, the glitches in daily chitchat that pass for conversation. The old slave imagined a formless being with tentacles around every corner and ears in every device. He scoured every corner, nook, and cranny in the mail room. If someone mentioned Humpty Z. Dumpster by name he couldn't help himself. He glanced over his shoulder.

"Liking" a comment on the alums Facebook page brought sweat to his palms, sent shivers down his spine, completely trashed his mood. Those uppity slaves who'd joined hands to create the forty-hour work week, minimum wage, sick and vacation days, workplace safety, and child labor laws, benefits we take for granted, must have known the same sweaty palms, felt the same shivers.

Then it arrived: "Sorry," emailed Dustin. "I've changed my mind. They're looking for another adult to pin this on and now that I've been given my notice it would be convenient for them to do that to me. But I'd like to get another job somewhere else someday. Sounding off in the classroom is one thing, meeting with the ping-pong club is quite another. It's too risky. I'm too scared."

Naomi did, however, agree to meet. "Tomorrow?"

Tom wandered the aisles of the natural food store, until the diva came up and gave him a hug. She pointed. "I put my coat over a chair in the deli."

Her red coat. Of course. "Should have recognized it. Haven't seen it in a while."

Over tea, Naomi said, "It took me over a year to stop crying, to get over the trauma."

"You were great," said Tom. "You shouldn't have been fired."

"I'm fine. Some of my new voice students even attend the art school. Two are daughters of department heads."

"You haven't been banned from campus?"

"Well, I'm not exactly welcome, but I venture onto campus, just not wearing this particular coat."

"Would you meet with the ping-pong club?"

"How about next Saturday?" suggested Naomi. "Buddie's?"

"It's a date." It's a first. "By the way, have you checked out the alumni Facebook page?"

"I have. Are those alums ever speaking up!"

"Students too," said the old slave. "It's time the faculty spoke up."

The diva remembered the old days, happier days before Hamilton Z. Dempsey. "Mark," she announced, "had been there fourteen years. He was simply the best orchestra director the school ever had."

"No argument from me."

"These days, five years is an eternity with that position." Looking up, Naomi did a double-take. "Uh-oh. Don't turn around, Tom. The dean of students just walked in."

At the ping-pong dorm five students went into a practice room. Through the little window in the door, the old slave could see Molly's hands in the air and Ted waving something. A student momentarily covered the window with his back then moved out of the way. The door opened and Hogan walked out with Jack.

"Why posters," asked Jack, "if we're gonna walk out of class?"

Molly came up. "We've got to stay under his radar."

"Think hard," said the old slave, "about walking out of class."

"We are not under his radar," said Hogan. "Not any more. Humpty Dumpty had me in the office for a one-on-one yesterday. That man is a master manipulator. He asked how much I knew about the hack job, wanted to know who wrote the Steinbeck piece, threatened me with expulsion. He said he'd sue my parents. It was all I could do to look him in the eye."

Molly was adamant. "The only way we'll ever succeed is if we keep the ping-pong club secret."

"The consequences," said Hogan, "could be severe."

O

Drake and his wife, Jorna, had been on the art school faculty for forty years. Their beautiful new home on the hill overlooking the school featured a ping-pong table with a view.

On impulse, the old slave called the viola teacher. "Care to meet?"

"Sure thing, Tom. How about in ten minutes?"

The old slave put up the Ring Bell for Service sign, grabbed his jacket, and hurried to Drake's studio.

"This is a surprise. How are you?"

"Fine and dandy."

"How's the ping-pong coming?"

"Twenty to thirty students, faculty, and staff, playing three times a week. We're just outside the door—join us."

Professional certificates, college diplomas, posters of performances, and letters from world-famous soloists and major orchestra conductors covered the walls; alongside photos of former students and revered former faculty. "It'll be tough," said Tom, "leaving this place."

"No doubt."

"You'll be missed. Any misgivings?"

"The decision has been made."

What an interesting psychological study the man presented. The epitome of affability, agreeable with everything and everyone, the violist had perfected the art of noncommittal understatement. It was enough to drive a progressive activist crazy.

"I'll level with you, Drake. I'm a newcomer, don't know the place like you, but your students love you."

"One or two possibly."

If one or two students possibly loved him, his job would be on the chopping block. Tom couldn't imagine his old friend getting fired. He changed the subject. "Thanks for signing the armband petition."

In abstract meditation, staring at the ceiling, Drake put his fingertips together, unaware of the dollop of saliva on his lower lip.

"Just out of curiosity, what's your reaction to Bernie's termination?"

"Actually," said the abstracted viola teacher, "it was a non-extension of a yearly contract."

"Same thing."

Dollop swiped, Drake shook his head, straightened his shoulders, raised his hands as if surrendering. "What was my reaction to it? I went up to Hamilton's office and asked him why he did it."

"What did he say?"

"He said, 'I'd tell you if I could.'"

"Claptrap. He cites legal reasons, meaning the reason he won't say anything is because he's afraid of being sued."

"In due process, the legal system would work it all out."

"If the institution and Bernie had the desire to do so. Drake, I told you Melinda sued. For over a year now, she's been unemployed as her suit meanders through the legal system. Meanwhile, she's approaching social security age."

"Things happen in a nation governed by laws, Tom."

Things happen. Wars happen. Wealth and power happen. Crimes against humanity happen. Enslavement of minorities, homelessness, impoverishment, imprisonment in the name of profit by this law-abiding nation happen.

"Old friend," said the old slave, "I want to tell you something about Bernie's termination. Many students are upset. There's a protest underway. I'm proud to be a part of it, and by now, some of my choicer words will have fallen on significant ears. This is your last year, but I'm thinking I'll be lucky to still be here when you come to the mail room to buy your last stamp. Hamilton Z. Dempsey is a bully boss with a temper."

"He's a decent enough chap. There are two sides to every story."

"There are two sides to every ping-pong table too. Come play tomorrow night. I'll spot you five points."

13

"Beware the Ides of March."

WILLIAM SHAKESPEARE, *JULIUS CAESAR*

On opening night for *Julius Caesar*, before the performance, Tom fed forehand chops over and over to Moira's loop. Four boys in gym strip, shoes, each with his own paddle, came looking for some serious pong.

"This should be fun," said Moira. "Let's watch."

The old slave took a chair beside her and they enjoyed the match. Slamming, smashing, fist bumping, the four put on a Shakespearean performance, complete with triumphant chest bumps and dying gasps. The old slave picked up his gear.

"Where are you going?" Moira asked.

"To render unto Caesar."

"But it's not over here."

"It's just beginning there."

In the theater, Tom found a seat.

"Hello, Mr. Mailman!" came from the row above. "Tom! Where've you been?"

"Oh, hi, Jackie. Just got out of ping-pong."

"Damn, missed it again," she said. "It's so thoughtful of you to always invite me, like a secret guy asking for a date."

"I invite you because I know you; invite a lot of others too."

Elie leaned forward. "You don't invite me."

"I will next time. Not to play ping-pong."

"Am I missing something?"

"You both are. Some of those invitations are to play ping-pong, but I also invite students to ping dot pong. Two different things."

Tom checked the program. Kris would play the role of Caesar …

perfect. The audience hushed. A few audience members stood as Hamilton Z. Dempsey and his wife located their seats in the front row. The president glanced up, and, smiling, the old slave waved and sang out, "Beware the Ides of March!" Z did not smile in return.

After Caesar met his end, Kris taking the cruelest cut of all, there was still time to catch the end of Demi's senior concert. In the old dance hall, a carpet of students jammed together, sitting on the floor. Tom leaned against a back wall. It was quite a show. Partially clad youths leaped and cavorted, exploring the limits of acrobatic exhibitionism, playing to their peers.

Their peers loved it, but the old slave didn't. Teenage titillation. Tots with tits. Too many staff and teachers alike had crossed the line, and too many had been terminated for the right reasons. He didn't like it but he stayed to the end.

The old slave was glad he had no Anita Hills in his closet. He'd never forget Hill, standing tall and strong, accusing her sexually abusive boss at those Congressional hearings, where he'd been confirmed as the newest Supreme Court justice. Twenty years later, her old boss was still on the bench, legalizing the corporate takeover of America, and Hill was writing, "We have moved from an American dream, as community, to an American dream, as opulence."

Demi and her artistic exhibitionists took their bows, the audience jumped to its feet screaming approval, and Tom headed for home, hoping these talented kids would never have to fight the battle Anita Hill had fought for freedom from intimidation and personal security in the workplace.

O

Smiling innocently, Molly dangled the sheet of paper over the mail room window.

"Whooee," breathed the old slave. The poster. A face innocent as a child, flowers in her hair—the poster was straight out of the sixties. And framing the face, an imperative four words: Make Art, Not Fear.

"How many did you guys put up?"

"Over a hundred. They took them down right away. We put more up."

"What if they take those down too?"

"We'll put more up. Where they're harder to find."

"If you get caught, you could be expelled."

"We'll be careful."

An old friend and former mail room helper appeared at the window. "Yang!" the old slave laughed and opened the door. "How's college?"

"It's good," said Yang, "but I miss this place, the mail room especially."

"You liked the art school?"

"I did. But my friends here don't. They ask me, 'What are you doing here? Why did you come back here?'"

"Your Korean friends?"

"Korean and American. People getting fired."

"Students are speaking up about their teachers being fired. Remember how to do the upstairs run?"

"I can run."

Yang gathered the administration mail and organized it for delivery. She held up the latest issue of the student literary magazine. "Is this all for the president?"

"Let me see that."

The *Blue Comma* had been censored—no sign of the Steinbeck piece—yet there on page one was "A Call to Action." The editors wrote: "We are against the firing of our teachers and we will not be silenced."

On page three, an article by Freddie and Georgie: "The school is moving away from a focus on art," it said. And a quote from Kris: "The administration may have felt threatened by Bernie. Student anger has grown to encompass other faculty departures." There was even a photo of Bernie with a quote: "If two thousand signatures on a petition don't matter to the administration, how many do?"

At Hamilton Z. Dempsey's office door, Yang stopped. "It smells funny."

"The administration building is a construction zone," said the old slave. "Carpenters, plumbers, dry-wallers, painters, all getting ready for the big fiftieth anniversary celebration."

Inside the inner sanctum Tom said, "Yang is delivering your mail today."

"Here you go, only this *Blue Color*."

"Thanks," said Z. "I'll read every word."

Back in the mail room, Yang looked puzzled. She asked, "Read every word?"

"Well, in the first place, it's the *Blue Comma*, not the *Blue Color*. Secondly, he was kidding. If he read every word, he'd learn something about his school."

"Tom, excuse, please." A new student, Ari had a wide catalog of skills and strengths, so wide, in fact, that in a school of creative specialists, he'd chosen General Arts as a major.

"What's up?"

"Can you make notes, please, and distribute them?"

"Notes? What notes?"

"Beware The Ides Of March notes. Students are in official revolt, protesting against this firing of our teachers. We know right from wrong. We are many, hundreds."

○

Tom caught up with the two girls and led the way to the basement.

"So," said Jackie, "this is the ping-pong club?"

"It's a practice room, actually."

Elie laughed. "You'd never get a ping-pong table in here."

"Thanks for inviting us," said Jackie. "My dad wonders about the money. Like, by firing Bernie, was Humpty Dumpty trying to save payroll?"

"He'd never admit it if he was. In fact, he'd never admit to any reason for any termination that could lead to a lawsuit and negative publicity. It has nothing to do with money."

"What does it have to do with?"

"Power. Intimidation. One termination does the trick, frightens the rest of the slaves. Consolidates the boss's power."

"How many has Humpty Z. Dumpster fired?"

"Almost a hundred teachers."

"I told my dad the same thing. He supports us."

The old slave opened the door for a student with a scraggly beard and long hair. The two girls looked at each other. The boy walked in and leaned against a wall, casual as a hipster at a white sale.

"I'm worried about you, Tom," said Larry. "The administration has you in its sights."

"Probably."

"We don't want to lose you. Students need you."

"Yeah," said Elie. "You're our mentor."

Jackie said, "I can't get my head around why you're risking your job like this. Are you independently wealthy or something?"

"I guess the old slave is just stubborn about right and wrong."

"My dad has written to the Board of Trustees," said Jackie.

"Writing to the trustees is a total waste of time," said Larry. "I mean, forget it. All those guys are in the same boat."

"A pretty small boat," said Tom. "A one percent boat."

"A penny boat!" exclaimed Larry.

73

"A penny gunboat," said Tom, "with cannons."

Elie squeezed her head between her fists. "But we've got to do something! Can't we wrap the campus in yellow caution tape, like, you know, 'Don't enter the zone'?"

"I think we should start a petition," suggested Jackie.

"We've already started one."

"We could burn Humpty Dumpty in effigy."

"How about an ominous warning?" said the old slave. "Little notes that say 'Beware the Ides of March'?"

"Oh, I love it," said Elie.

"What if nothing happens on the Ides?" Larry argued.

Gordon peered through the little window and spotted the old slave. "When are you coming out to play?"

"Go away, Gordon," said Jackie, senior pulling rank on freshman. "We're almost done."

"How many notes should we make?"

"I put up thirty this morning," said the old slave. "They're all gone now."

"So, let's try a few hundred."

"But what's gonna happen," Larry asked, "on the Ides of March?"

○

"You wanted to speak with me?" The Student Council president almost never visited the mail room.

Durwood warned you. Humpty Dumpty threatened to expel you, to sue your parents.

"I'm done with the ping-pong club," Kris said. "Please, no more invitations."

"Got it."

"Good luck with everything, Tom. It was good working with you. But you know, he's just waiting until us seniors are gone to fire you too."

"Look," said Jackie, opening her bag. It was filled to the brim with hundreds of tiny Beware notices.

"That was a lot of work."

"Took us all night," said Elie. "We're taping them everywhere, bookshelves, desks, even on the toilets in the boys' restrooms."

"How many?"

"Three hundred so far," said Jackie. "We could use some help. How many students are there in the ping-pong club?"

The old slave named a dozen students. "But don't call it a club. The deans want to know about any club. IT is watching every word we write, for Humpty Dumpty. Even Kris has quit."

"What happens in the club stays in the club."

"From now on, it's strictly word of mouth."

"How about starting a closed group on Facebook? Like the alums have. The ping dot pong club."

○

Two days before the Ides of March came a blizzard warning. Would the old slave's friends drive thirty miles through a snowstorm just to play ping-pong? He was finishing counting down the cash register drawer when the phone rang.

"We'll be there in an hour," said Roger. "How deep is it out there?"

By the time they arrived it was almost two feet.

Tom greeted his old friend, "Hey, old-timer, when was the last time we played?"

"I dunno. I'm getting so old, half the time I can't remember how old I am."

"Need a hand making it down the stairs here?"

In the basement, students had already warmed up. While Paul gave Sven tips, Roger began a match with Gordon, and Tom worked with Moira's backhand. A doubles match was getting underway when in walked the vice president, in jacket and tie.

"Welcome, Sam," said the old slave.

"Congratulations. A great turnout! All four tables are full."

"Meet Paul, the father of table tennis in the city. And this is Roger."

Roger picked his crutch from the floor. "I'll sit for a while," he said. "Sam, you play Gordon. He's pretty good."

Sam looked at Roger leaning on crutches. "Who won between you two?"

"I did, Mr. White," said Gordon. "But it was close."

"How long have you been playing on crutches?"

"Since I was fourteen," said Roger. "The vaccine came along a year later."

75

Sam scratched his head. "You're over seventy?"

"Seventy-two, same as Tom here. Paul there, he's seventy-six."

"You gonna play or not, Mr. White?"

"I'm not dressed for it tonight, Gordon. Got a meeting."

Heavy, wet snow continued the rest of the night. All over the northern part of the state, branches and trees fell on power lines and home after home went dark. The sun rose on wet snow over two feet deep. Plows, shovels, and snow blowers went to work, and the old slave spent all day digging a tunnel where only two days before there had been a driveway.

Power was still off on Monday. Dodging around trees bent over the road, plowing through mounds of piled snow, the old slave finally arrived at work. The mail room had gone bonkers, lights coming on and going off. Computer and postage meter emitted mechanical sounds, buzzing and clicking, a short buzz and a soft click going off and coming on again and again in sync with the lights.

Apparently, a fallen branch was shorting circuits and cutting power, causing the backup generators to kick on over and over, again and again. The cash register played along keeping a mechanical beat, printing tape after tape, spewing paper all over the floor.

The old slave unplugged computer, postage meter, and cash register; switched off the lights and jumped in the van.

The mail must go through.

The sun came out announcing the end of the hundred-year storm. As he turned onto the main highway, tuning the radio to the school's classical music station, he cruised along to Bach. There was blue sky overhead. He'd pick up the mail, drive back to the mail room, sort, and deliver it. In a day or two, everything would be back to normal. He stopped and put on his left turn signal to turn into the post office, and waited for traffic to clear.

Like an old friend, a fragment of song, a forgotten memory coming back, in the opposite lane, coming home, was the red Jeep.

14

"Do you think this country was hatched from a soft-boiled egg? Look around you. What do you see? We have become everything we protested against."

JEROME LAWRENCE, *THE NIGHT THOREAU SPENT IN JAIL*

In the cafeteria, Ron wanted clarification. "True or false?" he asked. "Express Mail is extremely urgent."

Tom tried to explain. "Express does mean special delivery, but also accountability because Express Mail is scanned into a data base at every stop along its way. The postmaster signed for your package, then I did, and put a notice in your mailbox. If I deliver it into your hands, it's not special delivery, it's extremely special delivery."

"But on the package it says extremely urgent. Why wouldn't you call Security whenever an extremely urgent parcel arrives for us?"

"It's a difference in priorities. Your priority is one piece of mail. My priority is getting all the mail delivered."

"Talk about weather," Julie said. "Looks like it snowed for a week."

"Saw you coming in on the highway. Welcome back."

"We drove all night. Can I buy a stamp?"

"Sure thing, boss. How'd the Biber go?"

"Fine." The violin paid for her stamp. "How long will this take?"

"Two, three days."

"So, Tom, how've you been?"

"Fine and dandy."

"I still want to buy you that lunch."

"You don't need to."

"I want to. How's the book coming?"

"Two chapters yesterday. Almost up to today, the first anniversary of Armband Days."

"Are you still wrapping arms at the library?"

"Yep. And making another movie."

Three days after the hundred-year storm struck, it retreated as quickly as it had arrived. Snow melted, the ground reappeared, and students with spring fever were out wearing shorts.

On the movie set, Matty directed, "Run! Start slowly, then faster and faster."

The old slave trotted slowly down the beach. Matty ran alongside, aiming a hand-held camera. "Faster!"

The old slave ran faster.

"Faster!" yelled Matty.

A mile later, the old slave stopped. "Cut!" shouted Matty, a hundred yards behind. "Sven! You're on!" He was looking off toward main campus. Someone was yelling.

Kylie came up breathless. "Lorenzo just told the orchestra!"

"You're breaking up the shot," said Matty. "Cut!"

"Everyone's talking about it!" Kylie said. "His wife's leaving too! Orchestra director and band director, both leaving."

Matty was busily gathering equipment and packing up. "All right, Kylie B. Let's go. We're moving the movie to Health Services."

To shoot the most extreme close-ups, the two young filmmakers had confiscated a medical clinic room—lighting, atmosphere, even a pillow.

"Quiet on the set— Action!" said Matty. "Tom, stop blinking. You're dead."

Kylie saw a problem. "Shouldn't Kendra have real tears?"

"How about it, Kendra?" said Matty. "Sad, sad. Your grandfather just died."

"I can do it," yawned the co-star. "It's an old theater trick."

"All right, then. Action!"

The old slave had gone through his supply of practice balls serving against the wall and was picking them up, when here she came, ready to party in high-heeled boots and lacy white mini-skirt over black tights. Yu Liu briskly walked past, slipped the violin case off her shoulder, and opened the door of a practice room.

"Yu! Play with me."

She stopped. "What?"

"Play. Just for five minutes."

Yu Liu's smart, cool indifference disappeared. She smiled and picked up a paddle. "I'm not very good."

Chasing after loose balls, laughing, and running them back to the table in her high heels, Yu bore little resemblance to his mail room helper, but she did bear a striking resemblance to her teacher.

"You know," said the old slave, catching the ball and holding it, "Julie and you could be sisters."

"Thank you."

"She played ping-pong with me, too, right here, on this table."

"She did? When?"

"A few months ago. She's pretty good."

"I can believe it," said Yu Liu. "Miss Judie is an amazing athlete."

On an inauspicious Saturday afternoon, the old slave drove three seniors to Buddie's where Humpty Z. Dumpster's most egregious termination was waiting. The ping-pong club had arrived in the past.

The old slave noticed it too late. "What are you going to do with the laptop, Jack?"

"Record the meeting."

"We didn't talk about that. What do you think, Elie?"

"I think it's great."

"Jackie?"

"Fine with me."

In loose black slacks, casual heels, an orange-and-black tunic, the diva stood in the sun on the deck of the restaurant, smiling radiantly. "Hello, fellow artists!" she sang out. "Thanks for coming."

OUR NEIGHBORHOODS, OUR FUTURES, OUR VOICE. The old slave's weather-beaten handmade sign had survived the winter. Occupy Front oldsters didn't miss the snow and were eager for younger folks to rejoin them now, in the spring.

Right on cue, a family of four arrived—father, mother, and two boys about five or six, each carrying a handmade sign. PEACE said the older boy's sign. I LOVE YOU said the younger one's.

"Welcome to Front. I'm Tom. Love your signs."

"I'm Sarah."

"Heckuva job, guys. You're never too young to Occupy."

"And the best part is, this is an experience they'll never forget."

"I like your sign too. STOP FRACKING NOW."

"It's so important. Do you heat with natural gas?"

"Wood. Natural gas is my backup, but it only kicks on once or twice a year when I'm gone for a day."

Dad stepped away with the boys to be baby-sitter.

"Hey! You there!" A guy yelled, pointing a finger at Sarah's sign. "What do you know about fracking?"

"Enough to know it's dangerous."

"Dangerous? You don't know nothing about it! Fracking isn't dangerous, it's a technological miracle!"

"It contaminates water tables," said the old slave.

"That hasn't been proven in court!"

"Not yet," said Sarah. "It will be. There are excessive, dangerous emissions. More than anything, I care about my kids' safety."

"Safety!" the man screamed. "What do you two know about safety?" People up and down the street turned. "Do either of you have a degree in engineering?"

"I'm just concerned about the future for my kids."

"I'm an engineer!" screamed the screamer, "and I'm concerned about ignoramuses like you."

"Are you concerned about the future?"

"Engineering is building the future!"

"So, you are concerned." Sarah held her sign higher. "Join us, we won't bite."

The screamer had had enough of two ignoramuses. He stomped away.

"Nice," said Tom, "inviting a screamer to join us."

During World War II, the screamers were virtually alone, speaking up against Nazi atrocities. As the Holocaust took its terrible toll, they railed against apathy and indifference, calling silence a crime against humanity; they awakened a few puppies, who, having gotten their fur wet, shook themselves dry and returned to their kennels, wondering what all the fuss had been about.

"We're all in this together."

"Occupy knows no boundaries."

15

"If you agree to not fire me, I will agree to not sue you with some bogus employee claim. My mere existence will make your empire seem larger and stockholders will get stuck with the bill for my paycheck."

DILBERT, COMIC STRIP

Daryl leaned in the mail room window. "What are you doing at four?"

"Delivery to the post office. An Express to Admissions."

"When you're done, can you come by my office for a little chat?"

Tom loaded the van and drove to the post office. It had been four years since Naomi's termination, but there were still folks around who knew who she was. It had been a week since she'd met with the ping-pong club … he tried to picture the faces at the restaurant, and was so preoccupied he missed his delivery to Admissions. He had to turn around and drive back.

At four o'clock he closed the mail room door, walked past Daryl's secretaries, and knocked on the boss's door.

"Great." The boss closed his laptop and led the way to the parking lot. "How do you like this weather, Tom? Isn't it amazing? You could be playing golf instead of ping-pong."

"A little on the warm side."

"I suppose it is, for the last day of winter. Wouldn't you say?"

"Yeah."

Daryl jumped into his new Rav. "If it's okay with you, we're going over to the other side of campus."

"Mary Towney?"

"That's right. Seen it lately? Fabulous renovation, all new, inside and out, the whole building. Wiring, plumbing, lighting, the works."

"I've been in it."

"What do you think? Isn't it great?"

"I liked it the way it was, when I volunteered there, building sets. For one performance of *Our Town*, we built a whole house ... walls, windows, doors, stairways, the works."

"Great." Daryl started the engine. "I heard some tales about that old theater." Baking in the sun, Daryl lowered the windows, and out of the blue, said, "I have to roll the windows up and lock my car. A couple weeks ago it was broken into, right here in this parking lot, in broad daylight."

"That is crazy."

His boss stared at Tom, then drove to Mary Towney and led the way inside to knock on the door of the Vice President of Human Resources.

"Hello, Tom! And Daryl! Come in."

The "little chat" lasted ten minutes. Queen Off-With-His-Head handed the old slave a letter listing his transgressions. "Get a lawyer," she advised.

"Would you like a ride," Daryl asked, "back to the mail room?"

"No, thanks. I can use the air."

In the ping-pong dorm, all the tables were empty, nobody in the practice rooms. Pondering the future, Tom mimed an under-spin slice serve. *Why didn't she fire me?* Then he remembered. Daryl knew, and surely had told Queen Off-With-His-Head, what the ping-pong club had known for months: the old slave was writing a book.

The five-bus, five-city tour had returned and two hundred tired music students were sleeping in. First one back to the mail room, Norm took a chair. "What a farce! Stupidest week of my life."

"Oh, come on," said the old slave. "Washington, New York City—stupid?"

"Insanely stupid. The administration coughed up half a million bucks to ship us out on stupid busses and bore us to death so we could play insanely stupid music in front of way too few stupid corpses. I move we adjourn Humpty Z."

Next to arrive, Yu Liu seconded Norm's motion. "The only good thing," she said, "was I got to see Jae."

"You left the tour to go to Columbia?"

"Ha, ha. Yes. I spent the hundred dollars you loaned me."

"How is she?"

"College is good. She's still upset though.

"What about?"

"With Z. She's just glad for being gone from here. She asked why teachers are still getting fired. I told her I will ask you."

It was a familiar furrow for an old plow horse, and the old slave plodded forward. "Do you remember," he asked, "commencement last year?"

"Of course," said Yu. "Do not ask what your school can do for you. Dumb."

"Imagine a football team gathering around the coach for a few final words and hearing that."

Yu frowned. "The school is a football team?"

"No. But shouldn't it be like a team?"

"Why?"

"I know, I know!" said Norm. "What if everyone in the orchestra just played their parts? Separate sounds. Noise. Even if they played brilliantly, it would just be notes. The director brings it all together."

Yu Liu's eyes widened. "Ah, so."

"When every member of the team is in tune with the coach," said the old slave, "it's music."

Yu nodded. "This coach is not doing his job."

Elie arrived at the window. "I never thought I'd miss this place," she groaned, "but I'm glad to be back. I'm so tired of little people telling me what I can't do."

"Worse," said Norm, "was them telling us what to do. 'Everyone smile! Look happy! Get in line, go to bed. 'Stand up.'" He stood up. "'Sit down.'" He sat down. "'Fight, fight, fight.'"

The old slave looked from one senior to the other. "Graduation's coming up. It means good-bye, maybe good-bye forever. How will you three feel? Sad?"

"Nah," said Norm. "Overjoyed."

Yu nodded. "Glad."

"Getting my diploma and getting out of the bubble will be the coolest and most unbelievable moment of my life," said Elie.

"Hey, hey, mail room!"

They all turned. Morgan stood at the window, silently moving his lips. "I just talked to Rowana," he finally squeaked.

"Big whoopie."

"I talked with her yesterday."

Tom inhaled, tried to stop his hands from shaking. "And?"

"Sve, Sve …" Morgan collected himself.

"Oh, no," said Tom.

"Sven tried to kill himself!"

"Oh, no!"

Norm jumped up. "What? What are you talking about?"

"They found him under the bridge!"

"Morgan!" Norm raged. "Don't you dare kid us about this!"

"It's true," said Morgan in a whisper. "He tried to commit suicide. This morning. Rowana helped the EMTs find him, where they used to go, down by the river. With, omigod, with an empty bottle of sleeping pills beside him. On the ground."

You are nothing, so this couldn't be your body. You've never been here before. Don't believe a word they say, they don't know you, don't know what they did, don't care, and anyway this is not your body. Here, lie down, feel the body, the actor doing the best work of his life. Out of sight, out of mind. The silence before the storm. Have another.

Holy mama, that's better.

This is nothing. What is that bird looking at? Careful loony, crazy bird, making a nest of grass and leaves. Did you forget your pillow? You should have brought a bedtime story. The book's the thing, the conscience of the king, lying king. Liar, lie over there. Here have another. Easy. Child's play. Acting's the hard part. Oh, tell me a ghost story, Mama. I love your taste in my mouth, sweet chocolate, evil bacon, the best shit shouldn't eat. Good night.

Effing dean bitch, roast in hell. School making someone else sick, someone lying down in green pastures. Don't forget your lines. What? In what we'll catch what? Til death do us part for good measure.

Opening lines, don't be afraid. Hello, good-bye, audition, nice knowing you. Good-bye, everybody. Thanks for coming. Here, have another.

Where to, in the water? No, right there. No, under the bridge. No one finds when they call. There. You're not here, you're over there.

Will be not, thy. Done. Et tu brute book. The play's the thing. Eat me Brutus. Ain't gonna work no more. No more.

"Saturday I visited Sven. At his home."

"We can't talk here," said the old slave, motioning Larry to a shady spot near the outdoor auditorium. "How is he?"

"Alive, at least. Humpty Dumpty just agreed to a voluntary withdrawal."

"With his diploma?"

"The lawyers are still negotiating."

"What a way to graduate." Tom stepped aside to let a maintenance vehicle pass. "Trying to kill yourself, I mean." He waved to the driver.

"If Sven gets his diploma," said Larry, "maybe I'll get mine too! But Tom, would you believe, an hour after I got back to campus, they took me to the clinic to test for drugs?"

16

"The founder was a human being who happened to be a visionary. Hamilton Z. Dempsey's predecessor was a human being who happened to be boss. Humpty Z. Dumpster is a functionary who happens to be a human being."

JUERGEN

"What kind of trouble have you made for yourself now?"

"Queen Off-With-His Head has put me on notice."

"No way!"

"If I mention it to anyone, like I just did, I'm disclosing confidential information. It's curtains."

"Oh, curtains. Is that all?" Jeanette's dry sense of humor had made her one of the school's most popular teachers. The ping-pong club loved her. She listened to the story of Tom's little tea party, then said, "A few folks are coming by after dinner tonight."

The century-old house had a curving brick driveway, a quarter mile of beach frontage, and a peek-a-boo view of the greatest lake. Jeanette had just finished grinding freshly roasted coffee beans. Bernie didn't waste his breath on extracurricular details. "Humpty Dumpty has installed lackeys to do his bidding. He's got the go-ahead from trustees, multibillionaires in his hip pocket, and, listen to this, there's a photo of George W. Bush on his wall."

"We've become a boarding school in the boonies," said the ESL teacher, "being taken over by big-business bosses. It's like losing the lottery by a little."

Jon, the English teacher, grimaced. "So, who," he wondered, "really, is in charge?"

"That's a good question," said Bernie, "and it's important because of the brand the school is selling. Interotten's power lies in a deliberately murky swamp."

"The trustees are in a murky swamp?" Jeanette sipped her coffee.

"The trustees have a little power. They hired Hamilton Z," said Bernie, "and are the ones who can fire him, but he's had a hand in selecting many of them. Then, there are the shadow trustees, and below them the shadow chairman of the board."

Jon said, "I knew somebody had to own us."

"I'd like to meet that guy," said Jeanette.

"Good luck," said Bernie. "He has plenty of cover and a legion of lawyers. I've been thinking about this. It seems to me there are two issues on the table."

Tom guessed, "The school or Hamilton Z. Dempsey?"

"Those are certainly issues."

The ESL teacher thought a moment. "Bottomless buffoonery or businesslike burlesque?"

"Which you're pretty good at," said Bernie. "No. As far as I'm concerned, the issues concerning us here are art and business. Which side are you on?"

"The students," said the old slave.

"I am definitely on the side of the students," said Jeannette.

"They're putting up Make Art, Not Fear posters now," said Tom. "They've started a petition. They're still talking about disrupting that minute of silence at the beginning of every community meeting."

"How in the name of Dr. Seuss did that stupid minute of silly silence start?" wondered the ESL teacher.

"It was the hatchet man's idea," said Jeanette. "He must have needed a little extra shut-eye."

"Then made the Student Body President announce it."

"Poor Kris."

"I say we put our heads together," said Jeanette, "and write to the trustees."

"I'm for that," said Jon.

"Also," said the ESL teacher, "am I."

"You know," Jon said, "at a faculty meeting last month we were talking about the founder. Guess what Z said about him."

"The founder was an effing free-loading freak?"

"'The founder didn't have a pot to piss in.'"

"Just a heads up, Tom," said Daryl. "There'll be no more student help in the mail room. I'm sorry. I've informed the rest of the office."

The old slave groaned. "Okay if I still play ping-pong?"

"I suppose."

The news spread quickly.

"What he's doing," Norm said, "is trying to silence you."

"Is it okay," asked Morgan, "if I volunteer? I know you can use the help."

Demi dried her eyes, did a little toe-point, and followed it with a finger kiss and a hug. "I'll miss you so much."

Yu Liu was angry. "Why? It's not fair. Why?"

"I can't tell you," said the old slave, looking over Yu Liu's shoulder. "But your teacher might know."

"Miss Judie?" Yu turned. Julie was at the window holding a parcel-delivery notice.

"I'll deliver this," said the old slave. Turning an imaginary key in his lips, he handed the parcel to the violinist.

Julie nodded and walked away.

"Why is nobody speaking?" asked Yu. "Tom, talk to me! I'm your friend!"

"I can't."

"Why not? This is free country. You have a right to speak!"

"That depends on what I say. And to whom."

"Who did this? Tell me! I go punch him in the nose."

"Then you'd be in trouble too."

"I'm already in trouble. Today, with Lorenzo. I want to quit orchestra." She crossed her arms.

Posting another application letter to another potential employer, Tammy leaned over the window and winked. "Come to Medusa tonight. If the face-changes don't get you, the music will. Live-performance art, live music—what's not to like?"

"Maybe," said the old slave.

Standing behind Medusa, a student learning political-performance art waited.

"If you come," said Tammy, "I'll take you out for a drink after."

"Sure thing." The old slave motioned to Elie.

Tammy got the message and departed. Elie dashed in, opened her laptop, and went to work on an idea of Tom's. In five minutes, she had her own version. "We are not children," she read aloud, "to be seen and not heard, etc., etc."

"Is it a broadside or a petition?"

"A petition. I'll get fifty signatures tonight."

Medusa filled the school's art gallery, a single empty chair remained in the back. Tom stood against the wall as the four young musicians finished warming up. The audience stilled.

"Thank you for coming!" said Julie. With a serious tone, she continued. "Tonight's performance is based on a mythological experience I feel truly passionate about. It has a special place in me, and, I hope, a special place in you."

According to the program: "The Medusa myth describes a young woman of great beauty. Her enchanted countenance attracts the attention of a god, Poseidon, who rapes her in Athena's temple. The jealous Athena becomes enraged, and turns Medusa's most stunning feature, her hair, into a nest of snakes, and makes her face so horrible to gaze upon it turns men to stone."

The lights dimmed and one last audience member came in: Yu Liu. Tom pointed to the empty chair.

"It's okay," Yu whispered. "I'll stand here with you."

Wearing a painter's smock, Tammy strode out, put a mask over her head, and began the transformation. Elie's cello called up ancient spirits from Bach's Suite in G.

"I've never heard her play soli," said Yu Liu.

Tammy pulled a skull cap over the mask, rolled out snakes of surrogate hair, and applied them to her head and face. The cello increased tempo, the piano punctuated with atonal chords. The violin came in, at first softly, then louder, augmenting Bach's eloquence with rhythmic monotones.

Yu Liu leaned over, "What is it about?"

"Change."

"Change what? Her face? Her hair?"

"Change everything."

The essence of life. Reaching down into the darkest days of human history. The instrument of slavery, the roots of jazz. The bass laid down a floor for change—drums rolled, cymbals crashed. Saxophone wailed sad change, cello droned Bach change, violin chirped tragic change, jabbing and etching, center stage changing. Change taking over, occupying.

Yu Liu asked, "No music stands? No music?"

"They're ad-libbing, all except for Elie."

Swelling and straining against some hideous interior prison, the violinist conducted her four co-conspirators, leading them up to the edge, then diving down, immersing them in change, searching in the primordial muck where transformation ruled and Bach's pearl shone like a beacon.

The gruesome transformation was finally over. Medusa stood. In stony silence she walked off.

Outside, Yu Liu's dark eyes glowed. "Tom, do you suppose something like that, like Medusa, happened to Miss Judie?"

"Of course not. Julie's a beautiful woman."

"I'm older than I look, Tom. I'm eighteen. You can talk to me." In the moonlight, the girl looked like an Eastern goddess with the power to change everything.

On Front Street the following morning, "Do you feel as exposed as I do?" Sandra waved to a driver with his middle finger in the air.

"Couldn't be much more exposed," said the old slave.

A car cruised through the crosswalk, horn blaring. "Thank you!"

"Nice to get honks," said Sandra. "I guess they're a sort of safety net. Some nut cases are driving through wearing their hate loaded in a shoulder holster."

"Like that guy in Oklahoma shooting black people mowing their front lawns and raking leaves?"

"Free publicity for the largest lobby in Washington," said Sandra. "As far as I'm concerned, the NRA is a hate group."

"Certainly a growth industry. Before Obama, there were less than five hundred hate groups in the country. At last count there were twelve hundred."

"How many taking aim at him?"

"I'm older than you, Sandra. I remember protest as a proud political activity, people putting their lives on the line."

"I guess I'd take a bullet, as long as it was fatal. As long as it didn't leave me crippled like that congresswoman from Arizona."

"Giffords. Some wackos aren't much good at firing a gun."

"Speaking of firing, are you still working at the art school?"

"We'll see what tomorrow brings."

"I don't understand why your faculty hasn't spoken up. They're missing the boat."

"I understand why. They're afraid to speak up."

"Well," said Sandra, "they should know that a dozen years ago, a majority of faculty here took a stand against the college president. A few months later, he was relieved of his responsibilities."

17

"You say that for us to become a global model for excellence in the arts we must change. Mr. President, will you tell us seniors what we were doing wrong before?"

LARRY

The nightmare always begins with a starless night, a lonely moon rising over the wounded city's skyline. You hurry along, from street light to street light, as fast as you can with the pack of books and the violin strapped to your back. That old professor, always running late, rambling on as if nothing in this world mattered but his own personal illuminations—last week it had been Freudian theory, tonight Jungian theory—where was the music theory? And what did Dr. Chung mean, "practice is the way to perfection"? You practice six hours a day. "More perfect practice—to be a musician, you must practice more perfectly. Tell me, my dear, do you love your violin?" Of course, you do. "Music," he said, "is like love. Marry your violin."

The drugstore is still open, windows a friendly glow. You hurry past, looking straight ahead. The sidewalk widens a block ahead and you can see the dormitory with the light still on in your window. You take a deep breath. The burning, the ashes, are history. Tonight you will practice the Bach, call your parents, read a chapter, and get a good night's sleep.

A small cloud of ashes rise. From under a parked truck a shadow moves into your path. A rat? No. Only the neighborhood cat, rubbing against your ankles, looking for a handout. You shift the violin to the other shoulder.

And everything changes.

He comes out of the alley beside the drugstore and clamps a hand over your mouth. Cursing, he pulls you into the alley, wrestles you to the ground on your back, and there is an animal eating you, hot breath covering you with curses, stinking of whiskey. Groping, tearing at you, hands fouled with disease rip at your shirt and scratch you. You open your mouth, trying to breathe, trying to scream for help, and taste his palm.

The strap of the violin harness stops his hand and for an instant he looks down. You thrust your knee up sharply. He yelps, lifts his filthy body. You roll out from under, jump to your feet, and run.

You're a good runner. Halfway through a red light you stop—the violin! It's still on your back. Up the steps of the dormitory two at a time. The door is a different color.

In the lobby everything—lights, furniture, desks, stairs, paintings, walls—different. You open the door to your room. Someone is in your bed. Places and people have moved into another dimension. An alien furnace has fused the pieces of your life together and they no longer make sense. You look in the mirror and see ... what?

In the heart of the city a ghost of yourself descending into the sleep of the dead looks and looks in the mirror.

Every morning for the last few months the old slave had showered and shaved, driven to work, punched in, and pinched himself. When every day could be your last, you pinch yourself a lot.

On Easter, he was leaving church with his sister. "You're sure?" he asked.

"I am."

"There's life after death?"

"You always were the doubting Thomas," she said. "Have more faith."

"I have faith. I truly believe I'm going to be fired."

"Oh, you always say that," she chided him. "Stop crying wolf."

Next morning, he wrote Stop Crying Wolf on a scrap of paper and taped it to the cash register.

Mondays were always heavy lifting and this Easter Monday morning boxes of chocolate bunnies, giant candy eggs, and other gifts from parents and grandparents covered the floor. The old slave could hear the kids.

"Did you see my package?"

"Where is it?"

"I know it's here. Mom sent it a week ago."

Molly wasn't looking for a candy heart. "I heard a rumor, Tom. Are you trying to get fired?"

"Why do you ask?"

"Because I need to know. Do you like your job?"

I could hug you.

"I love my job."

"Students need you. Last night, at the meeting, we talked about it. Tonight there should be forty students, or more."

"I'll be at ping-pong. Did you get the fifty bucks I put in your mailbox?"

"I made five hundred more stickers. I'm hanging on to them."

"We'll need a thousand," said Tom, reaching for his wallet.

"I'm not taking any more of your money."

"It's not my money, Molly."

"Whose is it?"

As long as I'm drawing a paycheck. "It's the school's," he said.

Finished with the administration run, Palma set a full bin of outgoing mail on the floor.

"Looks like I'll be here all day. This will take an hour and then there's all that." She pointed to a bulk mailing.

"A long day," said the old slave. "Can you come in tomorrow too?"

"Guess I can, for a while anyway." She noticed the scrap of paper taped to the cash register. "Stop crying wolf? What's that mean?"

Kylie and Matty had commandeered one table, Alex and Merci another. Tom, Gordon, and Moira worked on forehand counter-drives.

"Not so much arm." The old slave demonstrated the stroke. "Body in the ready position, knees bent, hips on a swivel. Then your arm is merely the extension of a pendulum."

Moira spun the ball past him.

"Great!" said the old slave. "Again."

She did it again, and again.

"Bravo, Moira!" said Danny, stepping out of a practice room. "You're getting too good for me."

"Bravo yourself, Dan," said the old slave. "You were a great second fiddle to Yu Liu last night."

"She's a virtuoso."

The old slave hit a topspin to Moira's forehand; she looped it back, low and deep. "By chance, Dan, have you checked out that alumni page on Facebook?"

"No, I haven't."

"How do you feel about Bernie's termination?"

"It's crazy!" Danny picked up a paddle and began trading backhand loops with Moira. "It was the same thing at my old school," he said. "One good teacher got fired and dozens of other teachers quit."

"Your loops are too high," corrected Tom. "Go down more, almost to the floor, then snap the paddle up through contact. More wrist."

A good player and an excellent student, Danny's loops started coming low and fast. "When they fired my favorite teacher," he said, snapping the paddle up, "I decided to leave. I thought this place would be different."

"It is different. At this place, we play ping-pong. Keep your grip loose."

The old slave had worked up a good sweat when Elie walked by, set her cello inside a practice room, and then came back out to watch for a minute. "We're meeting in an hour, Tom."

The old slave snapped a backhand loop. "Let me know how it goes."

"We had twenty students the other night. I expect fifty tonight." Elie turned to Danny. "How about you?"

"I'll try to make it," said Danny. Changing strokes, he began hitting backhand chops, alternating them with forehand loops.

Next day, after they'd finished sorting the mail, Yu Liu took up residence in her usual chair next to the conveyor belt.

"Thank you, Tom, for coming to my recital."

"Danny calls you a virtuoso."

"Everyone talking about that meeting last night."

"What about it?"

"Not sure. They're talking about walking out. Or something."

A leading student revolutionary was leaning in the window. "Thumbs up, people," said Elie. "Forty-seven students and a dorm counselor last night."

Jackie said, "We need a bigger space."

"We've broken into subgroups," said Elie, "each with a different focus. Media and advocacy groups will be in touch with you soon, Tom."

Jackie raised a fist. "Look out, Humpty Dumpty, you're headed for a fall!"

The old slave stopped running envelopes through the postage meter. He turned. "Jackie."

"What?"

"This is going to get worse before it gets better."

"What do you mean? We're just getting started. Forty-seven last night. How can it get worse?"

"Karma," suggested Yu Liu.

"Power," said the old slave. "So far, power hasn't winced. Nothing but empty threats. Humpty Dumpty is shooting peas."

"He took your community service students away from you," said Elie. "That's not shooting peas."

Tom handed a tray of mail to Yu Liu, who moved it onto the conveyor belt. "Most students care only about their academic major. Not about community service."

"We care," said Yu Liu, loading the belt.

"Most don't. It's a slap on the wrist. The vast majority don't have a clue about community service. Students are apathetic."

"They are pathetic," said Yu Liu.

"Apathetic," corrected the old slave.

"Like me?" asked Yu.

"Well, if you feel separated from decision-making and powerless to make a difference, then you are."

"I'm not apathetic, I'm angry," said Jackie. "I could off Humpty Z."

"Another bully boss would take his place." Tom had been over this more than once. "It wouldn't matter if you offed the new one either. This is about power—getting it and keeping it. This country used to be of the people, by the people, and for the people, but the people have given up, and turned the reins over to a handful of brigands whose only mission now is to hang on to them."

"We should make demands."

"Hire Bernie back?"

"No more five-bus concert tours?" asked Yu Liu.

"I'm not in it to make demands," said the old slave. "I'm in it to make changes."

"I'm in it," said Elie, "to find out who's willing to go to the wall."

18

"Ain't nothing gonna hurt you if your head's in the sand."
OLD-SLAVE PROVERB

The old slave pulled up alongside the girl hurrying to class. He rolled down the window of the mail van.

"How is he doing?"

"Fine." Rowana's expression was that of a deer in headlights. "How—how did you know?"

"His father's a friend. I just spoke with Larry."

"It's really hard to talk about."

"He's alive. He'll graduate."

"Yes! He just got into the Royal Academy."

The old slave turned off the engine. "He'll graduate from there, the Royal Academy. Then he'll land a role with a traveling Shakespeare company. From there, it's just a short step to Broadway, or becoming a famous movie star."

"It is? He will?" Rowana's eyes opened wide.

"I'm sure of it."

"Thank you, Tom! You know, he still talks about those student movies you guys made. You two were stars."

"We were a good team. Things have changed."

The girl's lip quivered. "Yes."

"He has a bright future. I can see the marquee now: *Escape from Hell*, starring Sven Smith."

"What happens after he's a movie star?"

"He'll ask you to marry him."

"Omigod!" Rowana leaned through the window and gave the old slave a hug. "You just made my day."

95

"I'd love to see him. Ask him to come back—we can play one more set. Two out of three, and I want five points."

"I will," vowed Rowana, bouncing off to class.

The old slave finished deliveries, returned to campus, and was on his way down the stairs when he heard the hum. She was at the window.

"Hey, kid," he said. "What's up?"

"I don't understand." The voice of God was mailing an envelope. "I just need a stamp for this."

The old slave checked the weight. "That'll be a dollar sixty."

"What?" Julie said. "I haven't got that much. Here." She put a dollar on the counter. "I'll be right back."

He taped the dollar to the cash register, and was posting outgoing mail when Palma returned from the upstairs run. She looked around.

"What's up with the dollar?"

"Down payment for a flat. She said she'll be right back."

"Who said?"

"The voice of God."

"Who?"

"My granddaughter."

Palma laughed. "Ha, ha. That's a good one. Your granddaughter lives in Canada. This here's a U.S. dollar."

"Glad to meet you folks," said the stranger. He had a clergyman's collar, a warm smile, and a warmer handshake. "My name's Jeff. We Unitarians have been Occupying Centreville all winter."

"And what a winter," said the old slave.

"That storm in March! It was something else. We almost gave up, but I guess you know all about that."

"We made it through the winter," said Sandra. "Let's build on it, onward and upward. Occupy spring!"

She stepped aside as a stout, broad-shouldered chap came through the crosswalk. "I am the one percent!" he shouted.

"Hey, Delusional," said Sandra, "don't brag about it."

"I'm an American patriot! I work hard! I pay my taxes! And I've got better things to do with my time than stand on a sidewalk waving a sign!" He hurried off to do better things with his time.

"You know," said Sandra, "sometimes I feel just like him. Then I realize it's people like him that keep me coming back."

"He's searching for something to pin his hopes on."

"His high hopes, apparently. But we can only take one small step at a time."

"For mankind," said the old slave. "This is what democracy looks like!"

The chairman of the library board and his famous author wife were crossing Front. A compact car crawled to a stop, half-in and half-out of the crosswalk. It would have been child's play, easy as pie, to walk around. The chairman let go of his wife's hand and slammed his fist against the driver's door. "Stop, damn you!"

Wide-eyed, the girl behind the wheel froze. The chairman steered his wife around the car, swore, and took a swipe at the fender.

"Confrontation assumes many forms," said the old slave.

"We need change," said the Centreville minister, "not confrontation. But the message of our society is that there's no viable alternative to the present."

"Didn't Maggie Thatcher say something like that?" the old slave asked.

"C. Wright Mills, I believe."

Sandra chimed in. "As long as we go along without ideals or an idealistic future we're all alone."

"I know that one. Ronald Reagan."

"Camus," said Sandra.

"Hey, there's my ride," said the old slave. See you next Saturday." He was climbing into Dustin's Subaru when the group of students arrived at the curb.

"Yo, Tom! Mr. Agnew! Where are you going?"

"To the library. What are you guys doing here?"

"We're here to Occupy Front."

Although many art school students had offered to join the old slave at Occupy, this would have been a first.

"We're done here for now," Tom said, wishing they weren't. "Dustin and I are off to plant armbands."

Dustin started the engine. "Do you want to stay, Tom?"

"I did." He waved good-bye to the students.

Driving away, Dustin wondered, "How long do you think the library director will hold on?"

The old slave imagined a new library director. "No," he said, "that's not it."

"What's not it?"

"A new director. Oh, wait."

Dustin put on the brakes.

"No, don't stop," said the old slave. "Yes. That's it. What the library needs is a new chairman of the board."

"Easier said than done," said Dustin, steering into the library parking lot.

"That's not what you were supposed to say," said one fledgling author to another.

"What was I supposed to say?"

"New chairman? Piece of cake. How about a whole new board?"

"That's ridiculous. A whole new board? Never gonna happen."

"You weren't supposed to say that either."

"I'll say what I want to say."

"No, you won't."

"Why not?"

"Because this isn't your book. You say what I say you say."

Every slave knows the taboos. Don't speak up. Don't piss off the boss. Don't complain too loudly. Most importantly, do not, under any circumstances, organize a protest—caution flags will wave, alarms will go off, the earth will open.

It seemed the old slave no longer had a choice. Or had he already chosen? It was confusing. Where was the line dividing a future of choice from one of choosing not to choose?

When the boss dropped by for another little chat, what options were still available that would allow the old slave to hang on to his job? An endless train of opportunities and failures was careening by. Taking the wrong track, choosing wrongly, would throw him under the train. He needed to dig deeper into this whole notion of choice and change. He consulted the experts.

Yesterday twisters touched down in Oklahoma, Kansas, and Iowa.

Escaping the house, the old slave went out to the garden, picked up a shovel, and loaded compost into a wheelbarrow. He would raise a bed for carrots, beans, broccoli, tomatoes. It was a normal April afternoon, temperature in the sixties, a light wind, the sun playing peek-a-boo. In the corner of the eaves on his shed a robin was building a nest. The silence before the storm. A drop of rain blessed his arm.

The old slave planted his shovel again and again into earth soft as a pillow, pliant as a caress, sweet as a song. Kicking off his shoes, he turned, forked, lifted, then raked the tops of the beds level; and sowed. Awaken carrots, broccoli, tomatoes, he exhorted, at your appointed time! Reach roots deep into the earth, speed your leaves and flowers toward the sun! He patted down seeds and moistened and listened. The silence before the storm tells a story.

Cold as Medusa's breath it came, raising the hair on the back of his neck—a stirring of sap, a rising of spirit, a scattering of dry leaves. He leaned on his shovel and listened. Then was now, in the beginning, one word was many, here and gone as the past inseminated the present to beget the future.

The revolution would come from the west and wouldn't look back.

It would spill over the prairies, churn the greatest lake, kiss swooning saplings, embrace the pollen of today, lift it into the unknown. It would sweep the sky, shake the hills, turn his soil to dust, and tear the roof from his house.

Or it would not. The clouds thinned, broke apart, and a hole opened in the sky. A blue eye gazed through, echoes of dying thunder rolled northward to the edge of sound, and Tom suddenly knew. There would be no revolution. Taking a breath, he turned the page on change and closed the book at the end of a chapter writing itself.

Directly overhead, soaring between sun and earth, between the giver of light and the seekers of light, hanging like a kite with no strings, a hawk had locked him in a staredown.

19

"There is a cure for everything, what ails us, and what fails us."
ANNE D. LECLAIRE

"Haven't you talked to her yet?" Dana handed him an address. "Dude, you have got to get in touch with this woman."

The beach manor was at the end of a long, paved driveway. Tom knocked on the door and woke a pack of dogs. From the back, a man came out in his underwear, corralled the dogs. "Yes?"

"Sorry to disturb you. I'm looking for Candy."

"Oh, for god's sake," he said to the dogs, "will you shut up? Have a seat. If you'll just excuse me for a minute."

He came back with pants but no shirt. "I'm Mike."

"Tom."

"Tea, Tom? Coffee?"

"No, thanks. Only got a minute. I'm the mailman at the school. You may have heard that students there are upset."

"I've heard. My daughter was Student Council president last year."

"They're organizing a protest."

Mike raised an eyebrow. "Protest? Protest is ineffective and inefficient and student protest is useless. It only helps the president's image. Makes him look better."

"How's that?"

"Hamilton Z comes off looking like a poor, besieged victim."

"Unless he reacts inappropriately."

"He won't."

"You're sure about that?"

"I'm sure," said Mike. "He has goals."

"What goals? Wrongfully terminating more teachers?"

"That's possible, even likely. He doesn't care."

"You got that right."

"So, tell me, what is the students' goal?"

"It's their show. They're working on it."

"Tom, you're playing with fire. I run a large company with offices in forty countries. Five hundred employees. We're successful, in spite of the fact that not every employee is a happy camper, and I'm here to tell you, success depends on having a goal. What's yours?"

"Awareness."

"Hmm. What else?"

"Inform the trustees there's a problem on campus. Involve the media."

"That wouldn't be in your job description."

"Changing things. Opposing the exploitation of workers."

"Also not in your job description."

"It isn't a job. It's a duty."

"So, tell me, how do you plan to achieve your goals?"

"Writing, phoning, petitioning, making posters. Knocking on doors, like I just did."

"That's a big job." Mike paused, chin in hand, thinking, then made a decision. "You should know something else about me, Tom. The other day, I walked into Z's office and told him to stuff it. He'll never get another dime from me as long as he's president."

"Would you tell that to the ping-pong club?"

"Let me think about that."

One of the dogs wandered over; feeling like the stranger was standing too close to the leader of the pack, it started yowling.

Mike scratched the dog behind her ear. "Shut up, Jessie."

Ping-pong three nights a week! New players showing to find out what all the fun was about! The old slave was busy planning another tournament, imagining drills, even figuring on another table, and he almost missed it. Slamming on the brakes, he backed up.

It was right there, in plain view on the 15 MPH sign in front of Mary Towney lying across the horizontal line in the H: **Beware the Ides of March**. Perfect location for a warning sign.

Danny and the old slave drilled serve and return. Lee tried out the penholder grip against Gordon. Merci argued with Alex. Moira and Kylie settled into cross-court counter-drives. And then a practice room door opened and the trustee's daughter came out. Doreen stood watching for a moment. Moira had invited Doreen to play many times before, she'd always said she had to practice, but this time the freshman violinist picked up a paddle. She held it upside down like a headless bird. "Which end do you use?" she asked.

101

Moira served an easy one. Doreen uncoiled, swung mightily, and missed.

"Easy does it," said the old slave. "Let it bounce, once only, then stroke it over the net."

"Face me," Moira instructed. "Keep your eyes on the ball. Relax."

"I think we should play cutthroat," said Tom. "Moira against Doreen and me."

Cutthroat uses the dynamics of team play on one side, the doubles, and solo strategy on the other. One doubles player must hit the ball and then get out of the way for her partner to take a turn. Moira laced forehands at the old slave, then hit lobs to Doreen, and before long all three were laughing. Doreen promised to practice every day.

Lee gave up on the penholder grip. "It's all shake-hands now for me."

"No more bumping hips for me," Merci said to Alex. "Next ping-pong night, big boy, we're bumping belly buttons."

"I'm not playing again," said Moira, "until you buy a new paddle, Tom. I want your old one."

A dream of sand, sky, and sea; with the violin's small arm behind, her hand playing over his ribs. He raised his arm and she cuddled into his chest.

"I like tan lines," he declared from his bully pulpit in the back of the red Jeep. His daughter frowned in the front passenger seat.

Spinning tires, humming "Good Vibrations," Sven turned off the beach to climb a dune.

"This is not the way," said his daughter.

"Oh, yes, this is the way." A cloud of gulls lifted from the sand, scudded out of the way, and out to open water. "I've been here before. What's with the tan lines?"

"I do everything right. I use block and watch the clock. I get them anyway."

"A natural result of time in the sun with your clothes on."

"We should have turned at that boardwalk," said the violin, shifting to a more comfortable position and running her fingers over his chest. The Jeep flew over the beach, chasing a sun falling into the ocean.

"I move we start a new party," he said. "The Tan Lines. The party without pretensions. The only party that doesn't care what it looks like."

"Oh, stop it."

"I'm serious. Let's show our tan lines, show the world what honest work in the sun looks like. We'll challenge Obama with verity, not vanity."

"No more!"

"No more darkies, how my heart grows weary. Button up your

overcoats! Down with brown as a berry! Throw away your blocks, blues, and hues! It's Tan Line time!"

Hearing a happy deluge of silly slogans coming on, his daughter took over the wheel of a Jeep changing color, turning blue; as the warm comfort under his arm evaporated.

Tammy was at the window to mail another job application. "I'm giving up. I'll never find another job."

"Don't give up," Tom advised, "until you're done."

"I'm not done," said Medusa. "Got my life. Got my art."

Got my Gorgon. Got my muse.

"Would you like this to go overnight," asked the old slave, "like the others?"

"Yes, Tom, dear. And can I have a receipt, please?"

"Sure thing, boss."

The performance artist stuck out her tongue.

"What's up?"

Something certainly was up. Jackie grimaced and moved close enough to see herself in the old slave's eyes.

"Z is calling everybody into the office," she said through taut lips. "First it was Kris and Hogan. Now me and Elie."

"Standard bullying tactics. Empty threats."

"I could have punched him in the nose."

"Counselors are feeling the heat too. Carol was called into the dean's office. They want to know who's behind the posters, the Beware the Ides of March notes. Who hacked into Z's email."

"He also asked us about the ping-pong club."

"Hey, guess what? I'm still here."

"Guess what else?" said Jackie. "I've been asked to speak at graduation. The valedictory."

The rest of the afternoon the old slave's thoughts were winged blurs, wheels of a valedictory spinning his brain until he had to sit down. He mailed Tammy's application Express, finished deliveries, and labeled some trays, but his mind was fully occupied composing a speech that would never be delivered.

After dinner, he showered, put on a clean shirt, and drove to campus, arriving at the chapel just as the students finished tuning. An exchange of glances. Jackie nodded, Elie lifted her bow, and the young string quartet raised Mozart from the grave, circumnavigating the earth to pick the old slave up and carry him out of the chapel on wings of resolution to an aerie perspective high above it all.

From here, friends, fellow slaves, bosses were incidental, temporary. From this perspective, his family, children and grandchildren were ideas he'd almost forgotten. There was only one problem needed attending to, one crime as old as the original garden afflicting everyone on earth, one cause of wars, poverty, recession, and global climate change, one threat too large and too advanced for one old slave to tackle.

The glitch though, of wrongful termination, that was another story. Those four doves would graduate and fly away, carrying messages in their beaks the future would have to listen to.

At Occupy Front, the crosswalk signpost didn't provide any shade. "Hot." The old slave mopped his brow. "And nice to see new faces."

"I told you we'd grow," said Sandra, "once the weather warmed up."

"Which is why we kept this going all winter."

Jacques, the old drummer boy, rejoined the old fiddler and the old bottle tinkler on the bench in front of the bookstore. He stopped a passerby, "Hello, Ma'am. What's your favorite movie?"

The elderly lady thought a moment. "*West Side Story*, I guess."

"Gotcha," said Jacques. "Where, oh where, but in America does the money grow but in America?" Hand-drumming a conga, accompanied by fiddle and bottles, the old drummer boy improvised verse after verse. Occupy Front sang along.

"Hellooo, Tom!"

"Well, I'll be," said the old slave, "if it isn't Queen Off-With-His-Head."

"Looks like she wants help crossing the street," said Sandra.

The old slave leaned Our Neighborhoods Our Futures against a lamppost and stepped into the crosswalk, stopping traffic.

"Beautiful day."

"Sure is." The queen extended an elbow.

Haltingly, they started across Front. Tom leaned over, "May I ask you a question, Alice? Are you one of the ninety-nine percent like me?"

"I sure am," said the queen, limping, struggling over the curb. She paused to catch her breath. "Thanks, Tom."

He waved, watched her hobble away.

"You are crazy," said Sandra. "I can't believe you escorted her across. I'd have punched her in the nose."

"You would have punched one of the ninety-nine percent. Anyway, she's still my boss."

"Delusional old slave."

20

"Demons run when a good man goes to war."

DOCTOR WHO

The old slave tried his hand at writing a speech that turned the president's commencement speech to the previous graduating class on its head:

Once I was a happy freshman. Then my teachers started getting fired and other teachers quit. The dream of the founder became a nightmare of fear, and I am now an angry graduate. How ironic it is for the man responsible for the nightmare to invoke the words of Robert Louis Stevenson: "It is not likely that posterity will fall in love with us."

This is no time to look backward; it is time to awaken from a nightmare. We look into the future with a spirit that comes from a combination of hope and energy, a spirit that has the brilliance of a rare star, a Betelgeuse in a universe of potential, because we are desperate to get away from here.

Posterity will not fall in love with a nightmare, and we will certainly not come back to it. We will not nurture our spirit nor share our talent here. We will not ask ourselves what we can give so that he who builds nightmares can spend. Our alma mater doesn't need our money; it needs our prayers.

Art has moved on. The battery of the Energizer bunny of art schools is dead. Here lies a broken, abandoned robot, an employment cul-de-sac, a curriculum looking over its shoulder. Here are only monuments of concrete and brick.

"Two vast and trunkless legs of stone stand in the desert. Near them on the sand, half sunk, a shattered visage lies with frown and wrinkled lip and sneer of cold command. On the pedestal these words appear: 'My name is Ozymandias, king of kings, look on my works ye mighty and despair.'"

You showed us no respect, o king of kings, and now we have none for you. It's your nightmare, not ours.

"That should thoroughly piss him off," said Tom.

"What?" Dustin arrived at the mail room window to buy a stamp; placed a three-ring binder—his novel—in the old slave's hands.

Earth Day was Armband Day and the old slave entered the library with seeds to plant. He waved to circulation librarians, headed into nonfiction, and was bookmarking Bill O'Reilly when Michelle came around the corner and stopped dead in her tracks.

"Oh! Hi, Tom."

He put the bookmarked book back. "Howdy. Didn't know you worked Sundays."

"The concert in the community meeting room today is a little project of mine. Are you coming?"

"I'll try to make it."

"Looks like you're catching up on your reading?"

"Bill O'Reilly's a gas. Irony with a sledge hammer."

"You are not reading Bill O'Reilly." You got it, girl.

"And you're not reading my book."

"No, I'm not. I'm going to a meeting."

The old slave planted a few more armbands, put another Armband Day in the books, and was on his way out when the former director, now a volunteer, came up.

"What's new, Tom?"

"Same old, same old."

"Still full-time at the art school? How's that going?"

"It's going to be a book. Today's another chapter."

"Nonfiction? Are we in it?"

"The library's in it. Your legacy and your character play a role."

Norm plopped down in a chair, crossed his arms over his chest, and laid his forehead on one tight fist. Sorting done, nobody at the window, somebody with something on his mind. The old slave settled in for a chat.

"How are things, future tank commander?"

Norm looked at the ceiling, every muscle in his face ready to leap into action. "Tom. Am I a coward?"

"Certainly not."

"I'm being accused of being a coward."

"You're volunteering for the Army. That's not being a coward."

"There are some things—like what students are talking about."

"Protest?"

"There's this meeting tonight. I'm not going. I hate Humpty Z.

106

Dumpster more than any of them and I understand why they're doing it. It's obvious. But I can't get on board."

"What are you gonna do instead, practice your clarinet?"

"Work out at the gym. Gotta get to a hundred push-ups in two minutes before they test me this weekend."

After a set of doubles, Tom was changing shoes.

"How is the book coming?" asked Moira.

"Another two pages yesterday. Should be finished by graduation."

"Did you change my name yet? I hate Moira."

They climbed the stairs from the basement together and stood outside in first dusk. "You know," said the old slave, "I'm starting to think the book is the only reason I've still got my job."

"Why's that?"

"Z knows about it. Power knows about free speech."

"You mean the book?" asked Moira. "Can I read it when it's done?"

"Your copy's reserved. Are your folks coming to graduation?"

"Yep. My kid sister too."

"I'd like to meet them, your sister too."

"My dad wants to play ping-pong."

The old slave had finished lunch and was lingering, waiting for Bernie in the cafeteria. "How's the new movie coming?"

"Great!" Kylie said. "We just shot the rest of the scenes at the same location we used for yours. At Mr. Agnew's. I was so sorry to hear he was fired."

"Guess the actors won't be running for miles this time."

"Nope. Just fist-fighting."

Bernie arrived out of breath. "Sorry I'm late. Had a meeting with my one-actors and, as usual, it ran over."

"Did you bring them?"

"In the shoebox."

Tom took one look. "Wow."

"His daughter put a lot of work into them," said Bernie. "She also insisted that they all be distributed at once. On May Day. Apparently, that's a favorable astrological moment."

"To fire Humpty Z?"

"To make progress."

"This subtitle," said Tom, "A Value System, what's that about?"

"The founder wasn't just an organizer and musician. 'The major tragedy of civilization,' he wrote, 'is its failure to guide youth into appropriate channels for service to humanity.'"

"Service ... what a laugh ... to the few for the enrichment of the few?"

"The founder meant service to the many for the greater good."

"The founder was a philosopher."

"Good luck with these. Remember, seniors first. May Day."

Cradling his treasure, the old slave hurried back to the mail room and sent off an email.

Ten minutes later, Elie dashed in. "I'm between classes. What's up?"

"You're always saying you want something to do."

"Omigod! Is this cool or what? How many do we distribute?"

"The whole box. Start with the seniors. You'll have to organize carefully and time everything. They all have to go in on May first."

"We can do it."

"How'd the meeting go last night?"

"We were all set, reserved the room, got an adult supervisor. Fifty students said they'd be there. Then some junior told everybody the meeting was off."

"Personality differences?"

"Just stupidity. Still, nine showed up."

"One step at a time," said the old slave.

That night, Matty and Gordon teamed up to challenge the old slave and Moira. After another lopsided loss, Gordon said he felt tired and was going to his room to read the Bible.

"That line's in the book," said the old slave. He picked up his gear and hurried across campus to Drake's final recital at the art school.

"This is a man," the program read, "with forty years on faculty."

The audience exploded in laughter. Tom looked up. Three members of the quartet were holding enlarged photos of Drake in front of their faces.

"We've been waiting forty years for this," said Cam.

As concert mistress, Julie made eye contact with her fellow musicians, nodded her head, raised her bow. Dvorak's and Beethoven's romantic message trumpeted: Awake, slumberers! A new dawn is upon you! And one awakened girl led her ensemble with body English, raised eyebrows, smiles of encouragement, and a bow that seemed to strike sparks from strings, Julie in her element, poised upon the high-performance wire between conducting and playing.

A rousing standing ovation and the old slave felt a tap on his shoulder.

"I thought," said Tom, "that you were going to your room to read the Bible."

"This is the Bible," said Gordon.

Tom reached for his keys. What do you know, a lost ping-pong ball.

Without a word, the old slave looked around at the standing crowd in the audience and put the little white sphere in the palm of the nearest hand. Yu Liu's.

Palma had been selected over ten others to work nights at the switchboard, a job she really wanted, and needed. Her twelve hours a week in the mail room would continue and she'd still cover for the old slave until the end of the school year. When summer camp began, she'd work longer hours at the switchboard, possibly eventually getting to full-time. Then, one day before she was to begin training, Queen Off-With-His-Head canceled the switchboard job, calling it a conflict of scheduling. Palma was fired before she started.

"What conflict?" cried Palma. "Nights at switchboard, days in the mail room. I can do two part-time jobs!"

The old slave explained. "It was Humpty Z. Dumpster's call. He's trying to make you as miserable as he's trying to make me."

Palma wrote the queen: "I love working here at the art school! So when I was hired to work the switchboard too, I was excited. Recently divorced and trying to raise my four sons to the best of my ability, I really needed a year-round job. Please reconsider hiring me for the switchboard."

At the window, the Bible was upset. "This weighs next to nothing."

The old slave placed the envelope on the scale. "It weighs a little over half a pound, not next to nothing."

"I put a stamp on it. It's only a card, has to go out right away!"

"Hmm. Too thick to be a letter or a flat. It's a parcel."

"It's a musical card. My brother's birthday is tomorrow."

"Hold on," said the old slave. *Little brother, big brother?* "What's the zip code? It's missing a digit."

"Let me see." Julie opened her phone. "The zip code is wrong. Can I borrow some Wite-Out?"

"Sure." He opened the door.

"You shouldn't be letting people into the mail room. Especially now."

"I let the kids in all the time."

"I'm not a kid," she said, closing her phone. "I'm almost thirty."

"Here's your Wite-Out. By the way, nice job conducting the geezers last night."

"What?"

"I said nice job last night."

"Just tell me how many stamps to put on this."

"It'll be a buck eighty, First Class mail."

"That's ridiculous! I haven't got that many stamps! And, please, stop calling me a kid."

"Just hoping you'll start acting like an adult."

"I am an adult."

"An adult who doesn't know which side of the fence she's on."

"I know exactly which side I'm on."

"Me too."

"That is why, Tom, you lost your community service students."

"Was your name on that faculty letter to the trustees?"

"No, it wasn't."

"Would you like to know what the letter said?"

"No, I wouldn't. I don't want to hear about the trustees, the president, or your problems with Human Resources. You've gone too far overboard."

"Dempsey just fired my part-timer."

"Palma? I had lunch with her today."

"She's still working in the mail room; she was fired from her new job at the switchboard. I'd say she deserved that job as much as you or I deserve ours."

"You don't know what you're saying."

"Like I said before, this is just the beginning."

"I would call getting fired the end."

"Depending on who, where, and how, it's the end that justifies the means." The old slave loaded outgoing mail onto the conveyor belt. "Where've you been? Haven't seen you lately."

"I've been in town, at a friend's."

"You say the envelope is for your brother? Older brother?"

"Younger. He's twenty-six."

"My kid brother was also three years younger."

"Was? I'm sorry."

"Help me get these packages into the van."

The violin hesitated. "I really am sorry about your brother, Tom."

"Please." The old slave stood in the door.

"Help me get this inner tube down to the lake, Landon."

"Are you still going to the library, Tom?" asked Julie. "For armband days?"

"Are you still gonna swim, Tom, all the way across?"

"Yep. I'm throwing off the bowlines. Once you get aboard, you're good all the way to the other side."

"Yes."

"You know, I still support you, and the armband."

"Thanks."

"And I still want to give you that lunch."

The old slave walked out, leaving the voice of God standing there with her mouth open. Outside, he flipped the switch and the belt began crawling upward.

Through the hatch door, he said, "You can help."

Driving a conveyor belt requires a certain mechanical aptitude and a dollop of common sense, neither quality in abundance in Julie's repertoire. Nevertheless, she managed to get most of the load to the top of the belt before the load started slipping sideways. The first package hit the floor, another, and then a full tray of envelopes, a Niagara of mail cascaded down the moving belt to splash at her feet.

The old slave turned off the belt.

"I hate this," said the virtuoso. "Get a student to help you." She turned on her heels. "I'm going home."

"Don't let the door hit you on the way out."

21

"Thy life's a miracle. Speak yet again."
WILLIAM SHAKESPEARE, *KING LEAR*

"They're trying to expel me again." Larry caught up with the old slave in the street below Hamilton Z. Dempsey's window.

"This isn't the best place to talk. Over there." They moved to a bench behind a tree. "What for, this time?"

"Everything. Hacking into Z's email."

"You said you were off campus with your family."

"That's what I told them too."

The old slave closed his eyes. "So, my friend, did you do it?"

"Like I told you before ..."

"If you didn't do it, there's nothing to worry about."

"But Tom, how do I know everything that's on two computers? I'm always online, I'm doing research. I love Facebook."

"You had two computers?"

"The deans walked into my room, didn't even knock, and these two IT guys grabbed my computers. Isn't that an invasion of privacy?"

Strange times we live in. A glitch in a kayak knocks you out of kilter, a fawn freezes in your path, a hawk hangs overhead like a kite.

Occupy Front started out quieter than normal—a flip-off, a few honks. The old slave complimented Sandra on her newest handcrafted protest sweater embroidered: Break Up the Banks.

A girl with orange hair sat down on the curb. Tall, almost emaciated, she could have been expelled from Interotten.

"Would you like a sign?"

"Okay." She picked up a sign, WE ARE THE 99%, and sat back down with it on the sidewalk.

"How about an Occupy cookie?" asked the old slave.

The girl shook her head. "I'm allergic to everything."

"Where are you from?"

"I've been in town a month, staying at the Whitmore, that old hotel down the street, but I'm gonna have to move. There's nothing here I can find to eat."

"You can't buy groceries?"

"There are no grocery stores downtown."

"You don't drive?"

"Mom never let me."

"She wouldn't let you?"

"She called me retarded. I ran away."

"Looking for a job?"

"I had one, at Burger King. Then yesterday I got sick and left early. They fired me this morning."

"Do you have email?"

"I blog."

A blogger? This embodiment of destitution? This jobless, homeless, probably abused child, whose mere presence on Front Street should open one-percenter's hearts, minds, and wallets? The old slave folded a twenty as small as possible and put it in her hand.

She mouthed a thank you and handed it back. "I don't beg."

Suddenly around the corner came a clown pedaling a huge orange fish. Right behind him a dozen kids in balloon hats playing kazoos and waving flags, followed by a costumed drum line. The Earth Day parade! The homeless waif waved good-bye and ran off with the kids and clowns.

Tom's cell phone rang. "Bernie here. I just learned Humpty Dumpty has IT monitoring everything, probably even my email and phone."

"What? Wait. You're calling to tell me they might be listening to us now?"

"Just a warning. And to tell you we need you to keep your job."

"Probably too late for that."

"At least stop posting on the alums' page, Tom. You've already done more than your share, kept the momentum going, taught the kids the right way to do it. But we have no guarantee of success. If this effort falls short, we need you there on the inside to continue helping students."

At the mail room window, Dustin had another job application. "I just got back from an interview in Durham," he said. "Discouraging. Forty others lined up for the job."

"It's only May."

"So, Z fired the new science teacher. And Carmina's leaving."

"She's only been here a year. Her predecessor had been here fifteen."

"I call that another termination."

"The official reason," said the old slave, "was a 'mutual understanding.'"

"Hello and good-bye, round and round we go."

"Five this year. We're just pawns in their game, frightened pawns, at that. Whatever happened to bold and courageous?"

"Can't remember ever feeling bold and courageous. Must have been deleted from my genetic makeup."

"You're the history teacher, Dustin, not me. Frightened pilgrims found the courage to set sail for the new world. Unarmed, Gandhi and Martin Luther King stared fear down."

"What's your point?"

"Courage is as much a part of our genetic makeup as fear but we're all creatures of habit, victims of routine—silent, obedient, corporate and nonprofit slaves. We can hate our jobs, never considering what they're doing to the earth, but we're always afraid of losing them. It's how we deal with fear and courage that makes history—or doesn't. Ever think about leaving teaching history to take part in making it?"

"No."

Elie and Jackie arrived. "May Day tomorrow. Can we come in?"

"Everyone else does."

"We like the idea of a booklet mark," said Elie. "But instead of 'Compliments of the Ping-Pong Club' can it say 'Courtesy of' and then the original school symbol?"

"You're the bosses. Dustin, do you know Elie and Jackie?"

"I've seen them on stage with the orchestra."

"They're here for these."

The history teacher took a founder booklet and flipped through a few pages. "This is impressive. Who's the editor?"

"The founder's daughter."

"When Z sees it, he'll shoot you and sue her."

"He may fire me, but he won't sue anybody. Public relations matter."

"You know," said Dustin, "Z and I were on the same flight coming home. As a matter of fact, I walked right by him. He looked the other way."

"To Humpty Dumpty, you're a dead man walking."

Elie tucked the box of booklets under her arm. "Bring it," she said, "bring on the wall." And the student revolutionaries went off to battle.

"Tomorrow, Dustin, the ping-pong club is planting those booklets in every mailbox on campus."

That night, Merci flirted with Alex, Dan and Norm blasted forehands past each other, Gordon worked on backhand chops while Moira looped to him, and Matty and Kylie warmed up in their own little world. Merci wanted to play doubles—"But only if you hit easy to me. You can hit hard to Alex." Dan and Norm stepped up.

At table two, Moira suggested Matty and Kylie team up against Gordon and her. "Come on, Matty," she said. "We'll hit easy to you."

"No, no," said Matty. "Just singles."

"You like doubles," Moira insisted.

"You know you do," said Gordon, coming up from behind and grabbing Matty in a headlock.

It seemed all in fun. But the old slave remembered that free-for-all a month ago in P.E. They'd been playing dodge ball, a game where young men throw balls as hard as they can at each other, and a few boys had started throwing too high and too hard at a certain senior.

"Stop throwing at my face!"

"Yeah? What are you gonna do? Hit me?"

The teasing went on until it got under the senior's skin. He soccer-kicked the face-thrower in the back of the head. Next day, the senior was expelled.

It wouldn't happen during ping-pong.

"Gordon." Stress on the first syllable, slight lift on the last. The old slave leveled his gaze at the boy, and he let go. Matty hurried from the room.

"What'll we do now?"

"I guess," said the old slave, "you play cutthroat."

Moira said, "I'd rather play doubles. You and me, Tom, against anybody."

Cam appeared at the window lugging a large box. "My sister's computer," said the cellist. "Can you Express it?"

"Where to?"

"France."

"Give me a few minutes." The old slave weighed the parcel and punched in a few numbers. "It'll take six to eight days, and cost, let's see, forty-seven fifty."

"That's good!"

"Just wondering, Cam, how long have you been teaching here?"

"Twenty-three years."

"Not quite long enough for tenure."

"No, that would take a lifetime."

"Ever think about looking for another job?"

"Think about it, yes, all the time. I can't afford to take the chance."

"No pain, no gain."

"It's all pain these days, Tom. There's nobody around stepping up to help out a fellow musician. I'm keeping a low profile."

22

"The distinctions between human and non-human are inconsequential attributes designed to support self-serving theories."

JOANNE STEPANIAK, *THE VEGAN SOURCEBOOK*

Keeping a high profile, Palma returned from lunch talking at the top of her lungs. She'd attended a sing-along the night before. As she opened the door, she was still talking over her shoulder. "Everyone knows the words!"

"Words to what?" asked Tom.

"'I've Been Working on the Railroad!' There I was yelling, 'Come on kids! Parents!'"

"I'd have stood to sing along with you," said the old slave. "I was song leader in my Boy Scout troop."

"It was a total blast! And then this guy got down on the floor and started taking pictures of me. What do you wanna bet, to post on his Facebook wall?"

"That photo could go viral. You could be famous."

"Oh, yeah, for singing 'I've Been Working on the Railroad.'"

"You never know. Sharon was just another fired teen when the newspaper came out and photographed her in front of the store."

"Sharon? Your bagger?"

"At Hank's. The girl fired with a lie who fired the liar back."

"I remember you telling me about it."

"Your picture could be in the paper."

"No flipping way! How?"

"Help me plant armbands Sunday. I'll try to arrange a photo op. Page three good enough?"

"The local news? What time at the library?"

"Noon."

Armband Day 79. The sun came out and Palma too.

"You came!"

"Sorry I'm late. Just got out of church."

"I called the newspaper," said the old slave.

"Who cares about that two-bit rumor rag?" Palma eyed the steady crowd of incoming patrons.

A lady stopped to read the petition. "Armbands are free speech?"

"They sure as hell are," said Palma. "It'll get you into every department inside, and even better, start a conversation."

"I guess I could put one on."

"Here, let me help you. Mmm, nope, that's upside down. There you go."

Parading back and forth in front of the library, Palma shouted, "Free armbands! Get the grief right here! Wear your mourning with pride! Remember the ones who've gone before you!"

The old slave shook his head. "Where have you been the last few months?"

Palma was stuffing her pockets with armbands.

"What are you gonna do with those?"

"Plant them," said Palma. "Shoot, I almost forgot to tell you, Tom. Last week, I tried to get into that meeting on closing the Library for the Blind. Couldn't. It was packed."

Tom knocked softly, as always, on the door.

"Come in." Z's secretary looked up from her computer.

"Three personal letters for him," said Tom. "And a few mysteries."

"Thank you so much. I'll open them right now. And please, if you have a few minutes, I've got news."

"About the grandson?"

"I'll see the 'terrible two' tomorrow."

"Is the proud papa still parading his firstborn all over town? I haven't seen him on campus in a while."

"He is very proud. The news concerns me." The secretary opened each envelope, noting which department should get which letter, and moved the little pile forward. As the old slave reached to pick them up, Darlene covered his hand with hers. "I haven't told anyone else, Tom. I'm retiring in July."

"A young chick like you? You didn't ask for my permission. After how many years?"

"Almost thirty. Finally, I can be a grandma."

"You're a much better grandparent than me. I never see my grandkids."

"Of course you don't; they're thousands of miles away. You should visit them more often, or move back to Canada. Are you planning to work here forever?"

The old slave pulled his hand away.

"Tom."

Darlene wore too much perfume.

"We've worked together a long time." Darlene came around to the front of the desk. "You're the luckiest employee. A month ago, the decision was made to give you another chance." The woman reminded him of the library director. "It could be your last chance."

"Thanks for the warning."

"You know Dempsey reads every post on that alumni Facebook page. If you care at all about your job, don't post any more comments."

"Can't promise you."

"He's getting angrier every day."

"The page is achieving what it set out to do."

He turned to go, but Darlene clamped a fist on his arm. "He's contacted our lawyer, just in case you try something stupid, like those protests you've tried in the past. He's serious."

"The students are serious."

"Tom." Fluttering her eyelashes, Darlene moved close and looked in his eyes. "You've got years ahead of you. Let it be. Retire with me."

His blood froze. Spasms rose in his throat, nightmares ricocheted down his spine. He clasped a handful of mail, staggered out of the office, and plunged down the stairs. In the mail room, blood began returning to his extremities.

He notified Daryl's secretaries of the news. "Anybody wanna move upstairs?"

"Are you kidding?"

"No way!"

"Not into that office!"

"A new paddle changes everything! Ping-pong tonight!"

"You bought a new paddle?" asked Moira. "Where's your old one?"

The ping-pong players gathered around to argue about paddle design, sponges, grips, rubber sheets.

"I want pips out," said Gordon. "Smothers your opponent's spin."

"Pips are for losers." said Norm. "I want spin."

"Speed rocks," said Lee.

"Spin!"

"Speed!"

Moira pulled out the little bar in the handle of her new paddle.

"Where are you putting that balance weight?"

"Right there, in the middle, where you had it."

"That's good. Perfect for your all-around style."

"How much for this little beauty?" asked Dan.

"The 900? Fifty bucks."

"I just want new rubber for mine," said Gordon.

"I just want a new paddle!" whined Merci, grabbing Alex and going off to play their own game of doubles.

Business was slow in Buddie's. The old slave looked forward to meeting the art school alum whose comments on the alumni page seconded his own. Grabbing a coffee, he found a seat. The hatchet man came in, took a seat, and Tom moved a few tables away.

Dr. Louis Penfold walked in and looked around the restaurant. "Tom Freeman. I recognized you from your Facebook photo."

"Nice meeting you, Louis."

"Such a good job you and the students did, getting those founder booklets out. Thanks."

"Thank the ping-pong club."

Louis had a long history with the school and the local music scene. "I know very little about Dempsey," he confessed. "He's new."

"And ambitious."

"Maybe too ambitious for this school. I may not know much about him, but I know a little about the system he's part of. I was part of it myself for decades."

"Likewise, I'm sure. I'm writing a book about the system now, looking at it from the bottom. With your permission, you're in it."

"Be my guest."

Louis named a few former presidents who'd worked to get the students and teachers on their side.

"I only knew Irv Delaney," said Tom. He glanced outside. On this cool spring day, Molly had walked the mile from campus in short shorts. "Excuse me, Louis."

Greeting one of his favorite ping-pong club members, the old slave pointed out the hatchet man.

"Gotcha." Molly paid for her sandwich and folded her long legs under the table.

Louis asked, "So, Molly, what are the key issues for the students?"

"Secrecy and intimidation. For me, as a visual artist, the most important thing is censorship."

"They're censoring you?"

"Oh, yes. Our exhibits, shows, publications. Everything we say or do."

The hatchet man pricked up his ears.

"What about that nice, new visual arts building?" asked Louis.

"It's okay, if you like monuments."

"I heard," said Tom, "that when Humpty Dumpty made the decision to demolish the old building, some V.A. students chained themselves to it."

"It's true," said Molly, raising her voice. "Where did all the visual arts money go? I have to buy all my materials—fabric, oils, wire, charcoal! We need canvas, not concrete!"

The old slave nudged her. The hatchet man had stopped eating, mouth full, beady little eyes fixed on the tall teen with the torrid tongue and mind of her own.

"I've taken on some large projects," said the girl, "that cost a lot of money."

"You are what an art school is about," said Louis.

"I just got into MICA. Large projects can mean large scholarships. I've been offered a full ride."

"Congratulations."

"It's not easy," said Molly, "for students, or staff." She looked at Tom. "Humpty Dumpty pinches pennies on payroll while he builds monuments to his ego."

Louis noticed the girl's glance. "The mailman's rolling in money, right?"

"This mailman," said Molly, "has contributed more time and money to the students than anybody."

"I'm as concerned," said Louis, "as you two about the direction we've taken—the school, the country, and indeed, the world. It's a slippery slope you've inherited, Molly. Are you as concerned about the future as you are about students? What about those who will be here after you're gone?"

"Students need leadership from people like you."

Louis said, "I've been teaching for twenty years, managing institutions for thirty, and I still don't have an answer."

It was spring and romance was in the game. In low-cut top and shorts, Kylie played coy, leaping into a game with Gordon while Matty stood by whistling Bach sonatas and watching Kylie's every move. Doubles partners Merci and Alex spent more time bumping and grinding each other than they did returning the ball.

Out of nowhere, a new doubles team was developing. Norm and Moira had opposed each other many times but tonight they teamed up to play Gordon and the old slave.

"Watch your backhand," kidded Norm.

"My backhand's better than your forehand," retorted Moira.

Gordon served first; Moira returned it with a winner.

"Lucky you," said Norm. "It caught the edge."

Moira already had her forefinger in the air, ping-pong symbol for "Lucky me."

Norm stuck out his tongue.

Moira laid her paddle on the table. "I'm not gonna be your partner."

"Get back here, it's your serve."

She grabbed the ball and served a fast top-spin. The old slave returned with a high lob—cheesecake—that Norm attacked, driving the ball for a winner.

"That's better," said Moira. "Watch your backhand now." She served again, but this time the ball spun long and off the table.

"I watched my backhand," said Norm.

She stuck out her tongue.

"Four to six," said the old slave. "My serve." He dished up another piece of cheesecake. Norm jumped, smashed, landed awkwardly. He curled up on the floor and stayed there.

"Omigod!" Moira clapped her hands to her head.

"What happened?" shouted Kylie.

"Are you okay?" asked Moira, leaning over, modest cleavage on display.

From a practice room, a piano could be heard practicing Beethoven. Farther down, a soprano broke into an aria from Don Giovanni.

Norm opened one eye, then jumped to his feet: "Five to six!"

"Oh, you—you!" Moira punched him on the arm. "You idiot. I hate you."

The score bounced back and forth as the two new lovebirds brushed wings over and over, exploring the ancient charm of physical contact. When they lost a point, they took each other by the hand, turned away, and whispered strategy. When they won a point, they gave each other fist bumps. As the score neared eleven, after every point Norm took Moira by the waist and spun her around. At deuce, he dashed around the table to give both Gordon and the old slave high fives.

The final score was 20-18. Moira applauded as Norm lifted his new friend to his shoulder and twirled her around, yelling, "U! S! (beat). U! S! (beat). U! S! (beat)."

Tom picked up paddles and balls and left the dorm musing *that is no country for old men.*

At the window, Julie was silent, her attention focused on her phone. Tom set her envelope on the scale. It was the same envelope that a week earlier would have been late for her brother's birthday.

"I was just wondering," he said, mumbling like a bee bumbling around a petal, "would you like to join me tonight? Planting armbands, I mean, in the library?"

Drawing a breath, letting it out, Julie opened her bag and put her phone away. "I should have finished this last week."

Outside, on their way to the community meeting, a group of students jabbered like jays over the latest juicy gossip, screeched like starlings over whose nest to next steal an egg from. The old slave recognized a few of the nestlings spreading their wings, courting as they learned to fly. What if they had to learn by watching every failed attempt? What if they spread their wings and nothing happened?

"I heard a rumor," said Tom, tripping over his tongue, "about the community meeting. Do you suppose there'll be a minute of noise? I mean, do you think the minute of silence will be silent?"

The violin finished correcting the address. "Last week, this would have been there on time."

"Last week, you said you hated the mail room."

"I also had a meeting in town."

"With your friend?"

Silence.

"I see you're playing the Bach this weekend."

"How'd you know that? Have you been peeking at my Facebook page?"

"No. Well, yes. Are you going to the community meeting?"

"I don't have any choice."

"Sure, you do."

"No, I don't. We were warned."

"Everyone has a choice. It's called free will. Do you think Humpty Z. Dumpster would dare fire you for skipping a community meeting?"

"I was hired to do a job, and that's what I'm doing."

"You certainly are, but you're not a slave."

"No, I'm a teacher."

"Did you ever think about directing? Conducting?"

"That is not my goal."

"What is your goal?"

"That would be a subject for another conversation. At the moment, I'm mailing a letter, and I'm late."

"For a community meeting?"

"I meant late with that." She pointed at the envelope.

"I never go to meetings," said the old slave, weighing the envelope. "Last time Daryl called a meeting I said I needed to finish writing the book."

"You'd better not put me in that book."

"Have you been peeking at my Facebook page?"

The silence in the mail room was deafening.

Somewhere in Syria, a teenager was killing himself, fifty-five soldiers, and injuring hundreds of others. Somewhere in Russia, workers were "going for a walk," defying their autocratic owners and risking their lives. All across America, hundreds of thousands were taking to the streets, Occupying parks and public buildings and crosswalks.

"You should be teaching at a university next year, like Lorenzo. Humpty Dumpty pays you next to nothing here."

"My salary is enough."

"Enough to make your student-loan payments?"

"How do you know that?"

"Your statements come through the mail regular as clockwork."

"You know too much about me. Just mail this letter."

"Are you coming back next year?"

"Not if you're still here."

"If you come back, it's a thousand dollars for postage and I guarantee it arrived one week ago, just in time for your brother's birthday."

"Stop it. I just want to get it out of your mail room."

He looked at the meter. "If you decide not to come back, it will cost a dollar eighty. Now, you've already put a dollar down, and a stamp on it, so it will cost you thirty-five more cents and it will arrive in two to five days."

"I don't know what you're doing, or what you're talking about. Give it back. I'll mail it at the post office!"

He zeroed the scale and punched in a few more numbers. "Oh, wait, Julie!" He put a finger in the air. "My bad. It's a dollar eighty, plus fifty cents for handling."

"Give it to me!"

Words are such a waste of time. Sanity is such a system of slavery.

"How about lunch?"

23

"Labor is prior to and independent of capital. Capital is only the fruit of labor and could never have existed if labor had not first existed. Labor is the superior of capital and deserves much the higher consideration."

ABRAHAM LINCOLN'S FIRST INAUGURAL ADDRESS

"In the library," asked Yu Liu, "where is your book?"

"I'm still trying to figure out where. Fiction, I guess."

"It's not fiction."

"It's not finished either."

"When will it be finished?"

When? When you take a stand other than a music stand. When I stand holding hands with you and Norm and Kris and Bernie and Dustin and a hundred others.

"I want to buy your book," said Yu Liu. "How much?"

"Five hundred dollars."

"Why only five dollars?"

"Never mind. Are you playing the orchestra concert tonight?"

"Yes. Are you coming? I pray solo Bach Adagio. Come! Tom. Preez!"

At Occupy, a young woman crossing Front caught the old slave's eye: "Hey, Stephanie! You're a ninety-nine percenter. Join us!"

"You know I can't, Tom."

"The 'objectivity' of the media?"

"That's right."

"Occupy Front is a story you should cover."

"We're ready whenever you are."

"Tom!" said John. "Wasn't that Stephanie Dane? The radio announcer?"

"She's so young," said Linda. "If only more young people were here. What if we don't get any more kids?"

"It's a time warp," said John. "In the sixties, kids led the way. Now, they're too busy."

"Let's hope they get the message soon," said Marcia, stepping aside for a heckler to walk through, "before it's too late."

"Good afternoon, communists!"

"Good afternoon to you, too, Fox News," said Sandra.

"It could be too late already, said Tom, "with our dear governor trying to privatize every public school and university."

John flipped his sign around to WHERE ARE THE REST OF THE 99%? "Remember in the sixties, how slowly it started?" he asked. "A few civil rights workers. Then the anti-war protests. It took me two years to climb onboard. My wife watched me marching for years before she picked up a sign and joined me."

"We're not getting any younger out here."

"Just the man I need," said the physics teacher. "Has the mail room got any of those triangular mailing boxes? I believe they are Priority. You know, the ones that are about four feet long, or a little longer."

Tom dug out several Priority/Express tubes.

"Perfect! A camera obscura! There will be a total eclipse of the sun on Sunday, and we will be watching. Of course, you can't observe a solar eclipse without harming your eyes. Therefore, I have students make light absorbers. You put a pin hole here, observe over here, and trace the moon's path across the sun. Can you believe this is the first solar eclipse I've witnessed in forty years?"

"What an opportunity."

"Yes, indeed. So, Tom, how much do I owe you for providing my class with these astrophysical experiments?"

"Thank the postal service, Ashqar."

"Thank you, United States Postal Service!"

Thank you, sun. Thank you, moon.

"It's a slave market," groaned Dustin, holding another job application. "The one percent is fully in charge."

"Qualified folks lining up for every job as soon as it appears?"

"Oh, yes. The labor market is loosey goosey. A buyer's market. Everyone will now do the bidding of the mega rich."

"Hey, as an Occupyer, I resent that," the old slave protested. "I don't do their bidding. Me thinks, however, Occupy could use a goose, even if it's a loose one."

"I admire your idealistic work play," said Dustin, "and I support the movement, but Occupy is a complete waste of time. The inequality between rich and poor is now so endemic and pervasive that dissent will do nothing to change it. We're at a crossroads between idealism and reality, and, like most people, I'm choosing reality. I advise you to do the same."

"Abandon hope, all ye who enter here?"

"Simply resign yourself to smaller ambitions."

"And not pursue your dreams? Not chance changing things? Inequality is un-American."

"It is primitive and barbaric, but hardly un-American," said Dustin. "And your protest is too little too late. The preconditions for revolution are firmly established."

"What about the Arab Spring?"

"The Arab Spring was a mostly nonviolent gesture that caught a few petty tyrants off-guard. The plutocracy has taken notice and is now ready and able to bring out the heavy artillery. Libya. Or look at Syria now. Nonviolence will not succeed in the Middle East. Neither your protests nor the Occupy movement are broad and violent enough to change the world's economic pattern."

"The one percent don't want to kill us. We're their bread and butter."

"We are their maids and chauffeurs, mailmen and book pages, art school presidents and district librarians, and there are lots more where we came from. The one percent will keep their stranglehold on power even if it means mayhem, incarceration, and genocide."

"Ronald Reagan lives?"

"Alzheimer's lives. History repeats itself."

That night, after a grueling match, Gordon asked, "If you're fired, will you still come back to play?"

"Yeah," said Norm. "Students need you, Tom."

"I need a cover for my paddle."

The old slave tossed Gordon one of his old covers.

"I already need a new paddle," said Moira.

"What? You just confiscated my old one."

"And look what happened tonight." A piece along the rim of the blade had broken off and part of the rubber surface had separated.

"I'll buy you a new one," said the old slave. "Offense or defense?"

"Offense," said Norm, driving top-spin counters.

"I know you like to keep the ball in play," Moira said. "And I agree, it makes for great practice."

"Practice makes perfect," said the old ping-pong teacher.

"In a game, though, do you do the same thing? Just keep hitting the ball back, watching for your opponent to make a mistake?"

"Yes."

"Then what?"

"Then you kill your opponent."

"Wait," said Gordon. "Are we your opponents? Students?"

"In the game of life, it's wise to consider everyone your opponent."

The little group of ping-pong players laughed out loud.

"But wait," said Moira, "if you're fired, two of these tables are yours."

"They're yours now."

Norm wondered, "You didn't say if you'd come back after."

"After?"

"After you've been fired."

"If Humpty Z bans me from campus, I shall return."

24

"In a closed society, power silences critics rather than engages them."
GEORGE SOROS

On what should have been his brother's sixty-ninth birthday, the old slave sat up in the middle of the night. A long day loomed, a bulk mailing, packages to be shipped to China for a student, the usual sorting and deliveries, and graduation right around the corner. He flopped back down, pulled up the covers, and the dream returned.

He was swimming across a lake, the tree-covered peninsula jutting halfway across, the school auditorium in front, the hills above his home; and then the sun disappeared behind a cloud and the wind picked up. Whitecap commas were curling over his head.

"Tom!"

He and Landon had not told anyone they were going to the lake to swim all the way across. Landon in the inner tube. But where was that boy?

He shouted, "Landon!"

Silence.

Then, "I'm dead."

Routine had abandoned the mail room since Daryl cancelled regular student help; any and all were welcome. At the meter, Gordon figured bulk-mail postage. Norm was writing in his journal. Yu Liu calculated the stamps she'd need to mail her residency form to a West Coast conservatory.

"I've got it!" Gordon said. "The difference between first-class and priority!"

Yu looked up. "What is it?"

"Who cares about priority? Poetry rules." Norm began reading aloud from his journal; Gordon and Yu plugged their ears.

"Time to load up, guys," said the old slave. "Dorm run."

"I'll help," said Gordon.

"Me too," chimed in Yu.

"Art," said Norm, "you don't live here, not anymore, so get your butt on the bus." He threw his journal onto the conveyor belt. Everyone watched it ride up to the mail van.

The old slave put his Ring Bell for Service sign up and they all piled into the van. He dropped the students off at their dorms then delivered to the radio station and Admissions and the post office. Finally, at Tom Jefferson dorm, he filled his arms with packages, entered the lobby, and found a full-scale harp.

Charles stood by as a lucky voice major, delighted with her brief investment in angelic power and glory, drew strange combinations of sounds from the stringed giant. Behind the desk, the dorm mother clapped her hands. The girl gave the harpist a hug and ran off to class.

Charles tuned the instrument of the gods; Tom ascended the seventh step to heaven. Death of unions? Rise of top-heavy economics? Mystery sonatas? What ancient myth turning whom to stone? He pulled up a chair and took a front row seat, an audience of one.

"Where's your home, Charles?"

"Centerville."

"I was born and raised in Centreville. What's your full name?"

"Charles Martin Dewey Washington."

"Two middle names. Are you Catholic?"

"No, sir. Southern Baptist."

"There are no Southern Baptists in Centreville, Michigan.

"Centerville, Virginia."

"I see. Are your parents coming to graduation?"

"They sure are, Mister Tom."

"Great. Thanks for playing for me. Ask your folks to drop by the mail room."

"I'll see they come by."

Three days before graduation, the old slave drove to campus for a special session of ping-pong. Moira's father couldn't get a point from his daughter. Gordon and the old slave practiced loops. A young man in a white shirt and Angora turtleneck came down the stairs and stood watching.

After a minute, Tom caught the ball. He held out a paddle to the boy, "Wanna play?"

"Sure."

"What's your name?"

"Eli."

A woman came down the stairs into the basement and found a chair. They watched Eli and Gordon play a set of competitive table tennis, dancing, diving, slicing, and smashing, every point fought over as if their lives depended on it.

At two games apiece, the old slave said, "Maybe it's time, Gordon, to consider Eli your opponent."

Gordon laughed, Eli too. When it was over, the boys shook hands, loser congratulating winner.

The woman turned to Gordon. "How old are you, young man?"

"Fourteen."

"My son here is twelve. What is your name?"

"Gordon."

"Where do you live, Gordon?"

"My home is in Florida, but I live here, in this dorm. How about you?"

"We are from Israel."

"In Israel," asked the old slave, "are people fired for no reason?"

"Sometimes. Not as often as here."

The school's fiftieth anniversary celebration provided a feast of performance options. Tom stopped at the chapel to hear an odd combination of instruments—violin, viola, cello, clarinet, bongos, bass, and marimba—playing an original composition by the clarinetist, who, at Medusa's transformation, had played tenor saxophone.

He visited the indoor auditorium where Julie took center stage in her bare feet, accompanying Demi and a dozen dancers in a daring performance imbued with sexual innuendo.

He stood outside the outdoor auditorium, listening to Lorenzo rehearsing "Pomp and Circumstance" in preparation for his final concert.

At the concession stand, the old slave was ordering a glass of juice when a tall woman walked up and set a box on the bench. "Hello, Tom."

"Karrie? Welcome. If those are what I think they are, I'll take one."

A redheaded girl took a seat. "Hey, Tom. Long time no see."

"Chandra! How about a t-shirt?"

"Of course!"

Four students arrived. "T-shirts, please."

Tom recognized a familiar face. Harman had taught for forty years at the art school. "Old friend, can I offer you a free founder t-shirt?"

"I guess so. Are you still working in the mail room?"

"I love my job."

"What is this Facebook address on the back?"

"A group of alumni. Concerned alumni."

"And the purpose of the group?"

25

"The purpose of education is to bring forth a child's innate possibilities, to guide him toward spiritual, moral, physical, and intellectual maturity, to equip him with something more than the knowledge of how to make a buck or build a rocket."

THE FOUNDER

Thousands of students, alumni, guests, parents, and faculty strolled by on the last day of the academic year.

"I just checked the program," said the old slave. "The president has chosen not to address the graduating class. Has that ever happened before?"

"Never. I'd call it a victory." The mother of an alumna and a long-time donor to the school, Karrie understood the importance of tradition at commencement.

"How many t-shirts yesterday?"

"I counted one hundred twelve. It's just beginning."

The hatchet man walked up and sat down.

"Good afternoon, sir. I'm Karrie."

"Shawn."

"Do you work here, Shawn?"

"I'm in Education. What's in the box?"

"What a coincidence!" said Karrie. "Me, I've been in the school system most of my life. I was a counselor for years and years; then changed schools to take a position in the admissions office in the southern part of the state. Do you know Little Big Rapids?"

"There is no such town as Little Big Rapids."

"Oh, but there is. It's just outside Shale City, where my daughter went to junior high. Freda was in the theater department here. Oh, Shawn, she loved the art school so much! If she weren't working on stage right now, she'd be here for this special reunion."

"Shale City doesn't exist."

"I'm sure if you look closely at a map you'll find it. Can you believe, Freda just got the lead in *Annie*?"

"That's a good play," said the hatchet man, craning to read the back of Karrie's shirt. "What's in the box?"

"She was so fortunate to get the part. Freda gives all the credit for her success to Bernie, and no wonder, he was such a dedicated teacher. All his students felt the same. Unfortunately, the Theater Department is undergoing some changes."

"Why do you say 'unfortunately'?"

"It's just my way of talking. Fortunately this, unfortunately that. Fortunately, you sat down to chat; unfortunately the Theater Department is changing. You know, Shawn, I don't talk like this every day. Most of the time, I have almost nothing to say. I'm silent as a bump on a log, sitting there in my empty nest. Then someone knocks at my door to sit down and listen to me. You're such a good listener." Karrie reached for her thermos. "Can I pour you a latte?"

"I'm good."

An old friend walked up with his graduating daughter. Cordell had been orchestra conductor, and his wife, a violin teacher, before becoming two of the fifty-three victims of Humpty Dumpty's Thanksgiving Massacre. "Hello, Tom. Any shirts left?"

"How many would you like?"

"We'll have three. Right, Lena?"

Shawn observed this short exchange, stood, and strode away.

Laughing, leaning against the box of t-shirts, Karrie asked, "How'd I do?"

Commencement was over. Students and faculty had gone home.

At the mail room window, "Got a minute?" Daryl asked. "We'd like to have a little chat."

"Just finishing printing the end-of-day reports. A few more minutes."

It had been a busy day, dozens of boxes and personal belongings going out, mail for employees to be held for later delivery, notifications of job application approvals, in addition to the usual sorting and deliveries.

The old slave followed his boss upstairs.

"Nice weather, Tom. Eh?"

"It'll do."

It'll do in the office of the vice president. Joining Queen Off-With-His Head was another vice president. The old slave had drawn two vices.

"We are truly sorry to have to do this, Tom," said the queen.

"Involuntary termination," read the pink slip. There was also an official-looking letter from Dempsey's lawyer banning the old slave from setting foot on the premises for any reason, effective immediately.

Tom stood. "If Palma needs anything, ask her to give me a call." The Director of Security accompanied Tom back down to the mail room, then watched as the old slave gathered family photos, thank-you notes, cards of appreciation, and table-tennis trophies.

"The evil part of my job," said Ron. "I hate it." He escorted the old slave to the parking lot.

"It's a job at least," said Tom.

"Yeah," said Ron. "A job I'm ready to quit."

"It's been great working with you."

"I'm so sorry, Tom, that it had to end this way. You've always been good to me."

Former Orchestra Director Dead. News of the death appeared on the front page of the local newspaper and beside the article was a photo of Venus transiting the sun.

At the memorial ceremony, the former orchestra leader's son took the stage to receive his diploma and the auditorium erupted with cheers. "It was pretty emotional," said Tom, sending his condolences, "to hear that kind of support from the school community."

"That's very kind of you," said Connie. "It's hitting me really hard right now."

"He was a bold and courageous man. One of my heroes."

"Mark never made it to our son's commencement."

"Your husband was much too young," said the old slave.

"I know. The children and I are leaving for Colombia tomorrow."

"Juergen! Welcome to Occupy Front!" said Tom. "Would you like a sign?"

The administrator of the alumni Facebook page held I Am the 99% high. "Sorry to hear about your job, Tom. I'd have joined you handing out t-shirts, but I've been outrageously busy. And now it's full-speed ahead on *A Midsummer Night's Dream*."

Tom introduced Juergen to the other oldsters Occupying the busiest corner of the city and the newest candidate for sheriff, Jack Armbend, who just happened to stop by the modest demonstration.

"You've got my vote, Jack," Tom promised. "I don't know about Juergen's though. Care to give us your stump speech?"

They were all gathered around the candidate, chatting about the primary election, when the red Jeep drove through the crosswalk.

"Just drove by Occupy," Julie texted. "Looks to me like you are exactly where you belong, in uncharted waters. Congratulations, Tom. You're a free man."

PART TWO
UNCHARTED WATERS

26

"Mark, your views about what might happen to the school in the future are conjecture and supposition. When expressed publicly, they constitute an act of slander."

HAMILTON Z. DEMPSEY

The end of May. Students had flown home. Faculty was busy cleaning out files and drawers, packing the year up; some were already nestled in their little lakeside cottages.

Tom vacuumed out the delivery van; then worked inside, changed the calendar, recycled the rest of the old magazines, finished his filing. He brought in the oversized sorting rack and re-labeled a few mailboxes. At last, he looked around and took a deep breath. The mail room was ready for summer. He printed the daily reports, counted down the cash register, and glanced at the alumni Facebook page.

> I wanted to let everyone know that today we have lost an incredible arts leader. Mark died this morning on the podium in Bogota. He will be remembered for his passion for music, and for communicating that passion. His students will remember him as a consummate educator. He will be missed.

Tom stood, his knees wobbling. He grabbed the back of his chair, his hands shaking like a mourner in a funeral procession.

At the window, "Got a minute? Can you come up to the office? We'd like to have a little chat."

"Um ... sure thing," said Tom, choking the life from a chair. "In five minutes?"

"That's fine. I'll be right here, across the hall," said the boss.

A spasm shot through Tom like a bullet, jerking his head back. He felt like a jack-in-the-box with tears. His hero! Dead! At least he was doing what he loved. Poor Connie! And the children—Juanita in college, Hal still in high school! Turning off the computer, Tom turned to face the music.

"Are you okay?" Daryl opened the mail room door. "You look kinda pale."

"I'm okay, I guess. A friend just died."

"Really? Well, then, I'm sorry." Together Daryl and Tom walked upstairs. "They're waiting for us."

Chaired by the Vice President of Facilities and Human Resources and witnessed by the Vice President of Corporate Relations and Financial Development, Tom's "little chat" had drawn two vices. He took a center chair at the table.

Queen Off-With-His-Head handed him his pink slip. "We are truly sorry to have to do this."

Tom's lower extremities turned to birds' legs, with claws for feet. His head was a crowing rooster's left on the chopping block with its mouth wide open. From somewhere somebody was speaking half crow and half dodo. Balance flown, reality was the ghost of migratory ideas.

"Please," said the queen. "I can see you're upset so we'll be brief. This is a letter from our lawyer that explains why we're doing what we are doing. You should read it now. As a matter of fact, I won't feel right until you familiarize yourself with our legal position. That is, the *school's* legal position."

He tried and failed to read a few sentences. "Legal schmegal."

"Lawyer talk," agreed Daryl. "Try to read it, you know, at your own speed."

"Please," said the queen, drumming her fingers on the table, "help me here, Tom."

"Okay. 'You have knowingly and willingly engaged in activities that constitute …' What's this? Insubordination?"

"It means you went outside the lines," said Daryl. "You'll be fine."

"I was playing ping-pong."

The Vice President of Corporate Relations and Development put in his oar: "You were using ping-pong."

"Yes, Keith. Using it to have fun. *You* played ping-pong with me in the basement. You too, Daryl."

"Ping-pong was a ruse for you to raise an insurrection," said Keith. "That is a clear definition of insubordination."

The queen said, "Organizing students, encouraging them to protest, is not exactly a model of *subordination*, Tom."

"What does that mean?"

"It means," said Keith, "that you, like everyone else, must submit to authority. Students and employees must submit to the authority of the administration."

"Just stay out of trouble," said Daryl. "You know—as best as you can."

"Stay out of what trouble?"

"Well." Daryl scratched his chin. "For one thing, don't go out and break a bunch of laws. Stay off campus. Don't use Buddie's for meetings."

"Buddie's is off campus. I like their coffee."

"So do I," said Daryl. "Couldn't make it through a morning without their coffee."

"Teachers like it too. Students go to Buddie's all the time; my old ping-pong players included."

Queen Off-With-His-Head rhythmically drummed the table with ten fingers. "Daryl means, behave yourself. Watch what you do. Be careful what you say—and to whom you say it."

"Don't go flapping your lips," said Keith. "To students, in Buddie's or anywhere else, about this little chat. Same with faculty and staff."

"No one," said the queen, "needs to know what was said here today. We are sorry to have to put it to you this way, but you've violated our trust. It's been difficult, under the circumstances."

"Mum's the word."

The queen didn't smile. "The letter from our lawyer is a legal notice banning you from campus and ordering you in careful language to cease and desist from engaging in any more protests like these."

"Okay."

"Okay?" Queen Off-With-His Head looked blank.

Tom looked her in the eye. "Who fired me?"

Waving her hand, the queen cleared her throat. "Read the last part of the letter, please."

"Looks like somebody's threatening—what? To sue me or something?"

"That would be correct."

"If I set foot on campus."

"No. That is not it at all. Coming on campus would constitute trespass, and you will go to jail." The queen paused. "That is one of the legal avenues we could pursue—are pursuing."

"Pursue away. I'd like to go home now."

"If you're serious about behaving yourself," said the queen, "it will make it much easier for everyone as we go forward."

"What can one old man do? The ping-pong club graduated. They've all gone home."

"We are concerned about the effects of your actions on other students next year, especially those who are returning."

"I guess there were a few juniors."

"There were twenty-one underclassmen participating, twelve from the junior class. Far too many students. Protests went on almost the entire academic year."

Tom shook his head. "No, they didn't. Not almost the entire year. Bernie was fired in late December. The first meeting of the ping-pong club came in mid-February. Three months."

"Three months of trouble. It seemed longer."

"Did you listen to Jackie's valedictory?"

"She could have more carefully couched her criticism."

"An alumnus helped her with the final draft. You know, the students really hate Dempsey. They are not at all upset with you."

"Yes." The queen leaned back in her chair and her feet came off the floor. "Yes," she sighed, "that is a comfort. I pray for them all."

"It must be difficult, with your son a student."

"Bradley is a believer in the goals of the founder. Did you know, Tom, my husband and I have together given over eighty years to the school?"

"How ironic. Eighty is the number of faculty Humpty Z. Dumpster has dismissed."

"Oh, I'm sure it's much less than that," said the queen.

"The number of faculty terminations," said Keith, "during Hamilton's administration is more than eighty. Dustin was one hundred and seven." He peered at Tom. "If you were faculty, you would be one hundred and eight."

"Twelve a year, on average."

"The average is eleven point seven."

"Out of forty teachers," said Tom.

"There are forty-six current full-time faculty."

"Details," Tom said. "I'd still like to know, Keith. Did you fire me? And if you didn't, who did?"

Keith pretended not to hear; Daryl was absorbed in his laptop. Tom nearly screamed, "Who made the call? Who fired me?"

After a long silence, Queen Off-With-His-Head sighed. "Hamilton," she said. "Hamilton Z. Dempsey made the call."

○

142

At eight in the morning, Buddie's was always crowded with faculty getting their caffeine fix. The organ teacher said hello; the dance teacher waved. Cam thanked Tom for his service. "My sister's computer arrived in Paris in three days! The mail went through!"

"Sorry about your job," said Jeanette. "Now I'm worried about mine."

"You're the most popular teacher in school history," said Tom.

"It was a popularity contest? Nobody told me! And here I was trying to educate the brats."

Tom showed her a large envelope.

"What's that?"

"Rough draft. *The Ping-Pong Club*."

"Really? I've heard about it!"

"I'd feel better about submitting it to a publisher if you gave it your considered opinion."

"Thank you, Tom. I'll do my best. By the way, did you hear about the trustees' emergency meeting? The Accreditation Committee gave the terminator a thumb's down."

Tom had just poured himself a celebratory cup of coffee when Rolph came up and gave him a fist bump.

"Long time no see, Mr. Mailman."

"Mr. Former Mailman, as you well know."

"Yeah. Shit happens."

"Congratulations, Rolph. Palma's a good mailman."

"She's a little wild cat."

"Keep a handle on her for me, will you?"

27

"Though we have life, it is beyond us."
WENDELL BERRY, *LIFE IS A MIRACLE*

*N*o one at the desk. A fine day for planting. The former mailman left fiction and strolled over to the atlas stand. Let's see ... the Arctic? Nah, nothing grows there. South to the pole? Nothing grows there either. Turning a few pages, he paused over Polynesia before planting one in Australia. In Vietnam, he planted one for Lyle; and in Korea, one for Julie. May your roots grow deep, your stems be tall, and your progeny fecundate the second floor.

"Tom."

Damn. He'd forgotten about the little chat.

"Can you come with me?" The director led the way into the office, where Gwen joined them, along with a stranger.

Apparently, the director had been doing some remodeling—old bookshelves and file cabinets replaced by computers. Banks of them. Row upon row of monitors. And all covered in lush hydrangea vines hanging from the tables, blanketing the furniture, climbing the walls. Under the floor hummed a high-tech string bass; through the leaves, eye-like cameras peered.

"Sorry. I forgot."

"That's all right," said Gwen. "We won't be long."

"Where's your armband?" asked the director.

"I took it off. In fiction."

"You weren't in fiction, you were in the atlas section."

"I'm going back to fiction right away. Still plenty of fertile books there."

The stranger cleared his throat. "Tom, I'm with the firm."

"The firm? I thought this was the library."

"The law firm. We've got you all over the new security cameras. You're not planting enough armbands."

144

"You're trespassing," said the director. "Give him the warrant."

He woke up. It was just a dream.

Slimy hot on Front Street, a steam bath. Sticky hot. Shorts-clinging-to-thighs-hips-and-crotch hot. Tom looked around at the crowd of adoring fans standing in broiling sun waiting for the limo to arrive. He fluffed his green Film Festival Volunteer t-shirt against his chest and wiped his brow.

"You're wasting your time, bro."

"Max!?"

"She's already inside." The old bottle tinkler came limping up, in pirate costume today. "A guy just talked with her in the alley."

"I've been sweating here for an hour."

"She saw the crowd, and used the back door."

"Why aren't you standing in line like the rest of us?"

"I don't stand in lines." Teetering, Max leaned against a lamppost. "Damn knees aren't responding."

"Sea legs. Where's your land legs?"

"I don't need land legs to watch a bunch of poor suckers walking the plank." Max drew his sword, waved it in the air. "Aaargh! Captain Jeremiah McDowell is aboard! Move it along, mates!"

No one moved.

"Will we see you at Occupy Front on Saturday?"

"Roger on that. Don't you always?" Grabbing his cane, Max toddled off down the street.

His hands sweating, Tom checked the letter in his pocket. Surely if she read it, she'd glance at the book. He walked around the corner to the rear entrance, stood by one of the dumpsters lining the alley, and wiped his brow again.

Crowds, traffic, standing in lines—nothing to like about film festivals. He refused to wait an hour in the sun to sit through a two-hour movie. After finishing his three shifts changing movie titles on the marquees, grappling eight-inch tall letters into place, he just hoped to meet the movie star.

"Excuse me."

Large bonnet, gray sack-like dress, sunglasses.

"I'm from San Francisco. There's an enormous crowd in front. Can you tell me what's going on?"

Sixty-five? Seventy? The woman removed her glasses. Tom revised his estimate. Late fifties, tops.

"Salome," she said, holding his hand in hers for a long minute. "Salome Van Slyke."

"Tom Freeman."

A rental SUV with dark-tinted windows pulled in and parked beside the dumpster. The young driver noticed Tom's volunteer t-shirt: "Hold these for a minute? I'll be right back." Handing over the keys to Susan Sarandon's car, he disappeared inside the theater.

"Are you waiting for someone?" Salome looked fit of body and mind.

"What do you think?"

"To get her autograph?"

"To play ping-pong with her."

"I see."

"Susan's not just a player, though. She's an ambassador for the sport ... an Olympic sport. She started sixty ping-pong programs in public schools, thirty in New York City alone."

"I had no idea."

The stage door opened and out stepped the ping-pong ambassador, a toy poodle draped over her arm.

"Ms. Sarandon!"

"Hello?"

"Thank you, thank you!" exclaimed Tom. "For all that you've done for ping-pong and for the kids in the schools."

She smiled. "You're welcome."

"I've started ping-pong programs in schools too," Tom blurted, voice shaking. "Not nearly as many as you; only three in the public schools but a few years ago, I started a program right here, at Interotten Art School."

At the name Interotten, the famous eyebrows went up. "Really?"

"Yes!" Words tumbling out like a multi-ball drill, Tom went on. "We had a hundred students and staff. Faculty too! And we were growing, adding tables and equipment, and playing three times a week. We even hosted a tournament—I mean, players from the city drove all the way out to the school to play us. Through a snowstorm! A hundred-year storm. And we filled every table."

The poodle yipped, and the actress reached for the cup of water her driver had placed on the dumpster. Kneeling to the pavement, she set the dog down and watched the tiny tongue flick in and out, catching one drop at a time.

"It was great, having the old guys show the kids how to play. And the enthusiasm! We were growing so fast, I felt a bigger space to play in was just around the corner."

"Was?"

"I believed so, anyway."

"Believed? You are using the past tense."

"Ms. Sarandon. Can I give you a letter?"

"Of course."

Heart thumping, letter in one hand and book in the other, Tom waited for the pooch to quench its thirst.

"Hold on here." A muscular guy bumped against Tom's shoulder and stepped between him and the actress. "What's this?"

"A letter. To Susan."

"Give it to me. And this?"

"*The Ping-Pong Club*. A rough draft, I mean."

"I'll take that too."

"Thank you," said Tom, shaking the man's hand, unable to believe his luck. "You're one of my heroes."

"All right, then. Let's go."

The actress gathered the poodle in her arms, stood, and gently placed the dog on the rear seat of the SUV. "I wish you luck, sir," she said, "with your ping-pong club."

As they disappeared around the corner, Salome said, "She's very beautiful, isn't she? But who was that rough character?"

"Michael Moore. I hope he reads it."

"Let me guess. The book isn't about ping-pong, is it?"

"Yeah. Well, no, not exactly."

"It's political, isn't it?"

"More protest than politics."

"What is it protesting?"

"Wrongful termination."

"Interesting. Is this something new?" Smiling, Salome leaned back against the dumpster. She yawned, stretching her arms to the sky. "I've been out of the country for a while."

"It's been going on for thirty years, since Reagan. Where have you been, out of the country?"

"Europe. I've been camping."

"Nice. For how long?"

Salome removed her hat and brushed it off. "I've been camping in Europe for six years."

A new perspective on his new acquaintance. "Six years? Sleeping on the ground?"

"Of course."

"In the woods?"

"Or in a kind stranger's backyard. Or on the beach, my favorite. Or in a park, a cemetery. Many times, I slept in a barn."

Salome had the smoothest complexion—face, arms, and shoulders tanned naturally, by sunlight. No makeup, no nonsense. And the longest neck and brightest blue eyes Tom had seen in a long time. "So, where are you sleeping now?"

"In a room in that hotel there, across the alley. The Whitmore. Where are you sleeping now?"

Where is Susan sleeping now? "Here."

"Here? In the alley?"

"My home," said Tom, "is a few miles down the road. Been here for twelve years. Once upon a time, I lived in the Bay area."

"I grew up in Berkeley," said Salome. "My father was a hipster in the sixties."

28

"When corporations are people, money is doing the talking."
OLD-SLAVE PROVERB

In the sixties, California was building freeways and Tom got a job surveying. As rear chainman, he pounded wooden posts into the Mojave Desert, adding nails to mark the points. As gunner, the tool of his trade was a telescopic transit he plumb-bobbed over the points to project center lines, edges of pavement, and rights of way, slashing rattlesnakes in half with a machete along the way.

Vietnam struck him like a snake attack. He took night classes at the junior college and kept his student deferment, but the war dragged on and on, and at twenty-five he faced a choice. Conscientious objector? Citizen of the world, sleeping in barns and on beaches? Or should he move to Canada?

His conservative Republican father advised, "Stay out of it."

One day on his way to work, the riots began, the first explosion right there in his backyard. Watts was on fire.

O

Salome had her own version of the riots. "The blacks were destroying their own homes and stores. I didn't know why and my father couldn't tell me why. For some reason, though, he supported them. He was enthralled."

"Burn, baby, burn?"

"That's what he said. Burn, baby, burn. He was rooting for the rioters."

"You weren't?"

"I was fifteen. I just wanted to party."

"I went to a party," said Tom, "where they served Molotov cocktails. One taste was plenty for me."

He'd found the Congress of Racial Equality's small office near the Civic Center. Young people were heading out; an hour later, Tom was marching in front of City Hall holding a sign: End Police Brutality.

Hundreds of homes and businesses burned. Thousands of national guardsmen called out. Children and families sleeping in churches. Black men arrested for standing outside their own homes. After work, at CORE headquarters, Tom loaded up his little car with boxes of cereal, powdered milk, and jars of baby food. He took the freeway past the university, turned into the church drop-off, and in growing darkness was headed home.

On a street corner, a few black men were standing.

"Whitey!"

Something came spinning in slow motion toward his head. He ducked, stepped on the gas, spun his tires, and the bottle exploded on the curb.

O

At the City Hall protest, he met a tall girl several years his junior, but knowledgeable and much more confident than he. When he told Jenny about the Molotov cocktail she snorted, "You're nuts. You don't drive through Watts now."

"I was delivering baby food. To a church."

"A white baby feeder in a black man's riot."

"People down there are suffering."

"Suffering? It's nothing compared to Vietnam. Watts isn't a war zone, it's a protest."

"They're not holding signs, Jenny. They're standing on the corner yelling whitey and trying to kill me."

"Those bucks are fighting back the only way they can. Racism rules everything they do. Whites have taken away their every outlet for self-expression, isolated them, stomped all over their human rights."

"We're the aggressors?"

"In Watts, we're the exploiters. It's the same thing in Vietnam. The domino theory is a bunch of ideological pap."

Jenny was a Molotov cocktail aimed at Tom's heart.

"There were civil rights demonstrations in Berkeley," Salome said. "My father even spoke at one."

"He spoke at a demonstration?"

"They needed faculty participation, and Dad was a professor of economics. Unfortunately, he used a few choice words to describe the Los Angeles Police Department."

"He swore? In public?"

"And the university canceled his contract."

"Fired him."

"He never used that word, never admitted he'd been fired. Maybe it embarrassed him. He felt the country had made a terrible choice in Vietnam; Watts convinced him America was a lost cause. We moved to Europe and he never taught again."

"Why didn't he move to Canada?"

"Canada had just opened its doors to draft dodgers—Dad needed to retreat, to get away, to think."

"I would have gone to Canada if my girlfriend would have, but she preferred to stand in a circle, holding hands, and singing 'We Shall Overcome.'"

"Did you sing that?"

"Many times."

"Then civil rights was passed?"

"Yeah. Access to lunch tables and busses is good, I guess—until a new law comes along and denies it. We thought rights were inalienable. Overcoming was more than legalization."

"My dad said we are all slaves."

Tom strolled to the end of the alley and back, wishing he'd known Salome's father. "We thought that someday we'd overcome isolation, discrimination, fear. Maybe employees would even overcome the fear of speaking out."

Brushing her shining grey hair, Salome said, "I've never held a job longer than five months."

"Bully bosses? Jerk bosses?"

"Oh, plenty of each. I've never been afraid of them though."

"They don't own *you*, Ms. Van Slyke. If the owners only knew."

"Thank you, Mr. Freeman. Knew what?"

"Most of us are owned—by mortgages, our food sources, our credit ratings. All the strings on our purses. The owners have bought our privacy and our votes and our futures. The only thing they don't own is our voice. It's a constitutional thing."

"You are an old-fashioned Tom Paine revolutionary."

"I'm just an old slave who sometimes disagrees with the boss. A revolutionary calls a wrong a wrong and shoots the wrongdoer."

"Sure glad I haven't met many of those guys."

"If the boss says jump, a slave asks how high. A revolutionary asks why. Why are you abusing your authority? Why are you firing the people who give you that authority—your slaves?"

"Why," asked Salome, "are you destroying habitat and poisoning the planet?"

"Why are you shooting civilians in Afghanistan with drones? Stealing from farmers in Ecuador? Dehydrating Somali children?"

"Myself, though, I mean personally, I don't support revolution."

"So, you're against change?"

"I am not against change."

"Where is the sun? Right now?"

"I know what you're going to say, Mr. Freeman."

"No, you don't, but you look like you do."

"What does that mean?"

"It means you've taken care of your skin, even out in the sun. How old are you, Ms. Van Slyke? Fifty?"

Winsome Salome coyly smiled. "Actually, Tom, I love change. Seasons, growth, evolution."

"Those are slow changes. Let's get back to revolution. Say you're working for a very ambitious boss. Through the grapevine you learn your boss is about to declare war."

"On what? I mean, on whom?"

"Oh, I don't know. Let's say he's about to declare a war that just might end all life on earth. Do you go home to dinner, go to bed; then get up in the morning, brush your teeth, and go back to work?"

"Okay. I'm against violent revolution."

"So, it depends on the revolution?"

"It does." Salome took off her bonnet, exposing her long neck. "Gandhi is my guru, my kind of revolutionary."

"Your guru knew how passive and submissive his people were. Even if he'd had the guns, the Indian people would never have used them."

The brick walls in the alley behind the theater radiated heat. Salome leaned against the dumpster again—a wild animal comfortable in any bed.

"Unlike the American people," Tom added.

"Guns are for cowards. Gandhi said, 'Look, you're all just sitting there anyway. Why not sit over here?'."

"India was a nearly ideal country for a nearly nonviolent revolution."

"I don't need a nearly nonviolent revolution." Salome turned her back. "I need a roof over my head."

"Are you happy?"

"Happy enough. My dad always said the end doesn't justify the means."

"My dad taught me a nice test for that."

"You're going to ask me to choose between my well-being and the well-being of everyone else."

"Simpler than that," said Tom. "Chaos or order."

"Silly old slave," said Salome, shaking her hair loose. "It's not one or the other. It's a blend. A little chaos, a little order."

29

"It was a mistake in the system that lay in the precept that the end justifies the means. With our sole guiding principle now logic, we are sailing without ethical ballast."

ARTHUR KOESTLER, *DARKNESS AT NOON*

A week after the National Guard had gone home, sporadic fires still burned in Watts. Suddenly, anti-Vietnam protests were breaking out everywhere. As they drove across town to the UCLA campus, Jenny crossed and uncrossed her legs. "It's the end of the world," she said. Opening the glove box, she looked inside, closed it. "Today. Here."

"Or not," Tom said quietly.

In front of the administration building, a crowd of young people were sitting on the ground listening to a fire-breathing speaker. Jenny accepted a joint from a total stranger. Tom whispered in her ear.

"What?" Jennie turned angrily, blowing out smoke. "I can't believe you said that."

On stage, the speaker pounded his fist. Almost whispering, his heart pounding, Tom said, "It would mean everything to me."

"It has nothing to do with me," said Jenny. "We're confronting wars and atrocities and you're putting your tail between your legs."

"Not just to dodge the draft," Tom said, beads of sweat breaking out. "We could get married. Build a log cabin. In the mountains."

The speaker looked over silence as solid as a block of ice. He gave a hand signal; it seemed like a wave of frozen fire spread through the crowd. Wearing a shirt with a peace sign on it, a young black man walked on stage holding up an American flag.

Jenny's lips moved. "I can't."

The black youth raised the flag over his head. A soldier in uniform reached for an edge, the flag burst into shimmering flame, and in an instant it was gone, only a trace of smoke.

The flag-raising fire breather yelled, "That wasn't my flag! I don't know that flag!"

Tom stood. "I want to go home."

"Not yet." Jenny took him by the hand and led him through the crowd to the far side of the stage. "This won't take long."

A few minutes later, the flag burner in uniform walked up. Jenny hugged him. "This is Tom," she said. "A friend. A dodger."

"You set the flag on fire," said Tom.

"That I did, old man. Spectacular, what?"

Douse the firebug.

Jenny said, "John lost his toes to a land mine in Vietnam."

"Only one," said John. "The left pinkie."

Tom raised a finger. "Only one little toe?"

Jenny stamped a foot. "Tom!"

"At least you came back." Douse the firebug.

"Oh, the hell with it," Jenny hissed, and grabbed Tom by the shoulders. "Listen," she said, "John got a Purple Heart!"

"And came back. Alive."

"He's a hero."

"Who burns a symbol in public. Why not burn the damn flag in the incinerator? He didn't have to do it in front of a thousand people."

"He chose to do it. He's dedicated his life to stopping the madness. Isn't it about time you got off the fence and did the same thing?"

John said, "It's okay, Jen. Burning a flag doesn't mean all that much anyway."

Jenny stalked away.

"Tell me, Tom, why did you come to this demonstration?"

"I've got my reasons."

"You know, a lot of Nam vets are against the war too."

"While thousands of American kids are getting killed."

"It's bad over there, but we came home. At least some of us did."

Tom thought a moment. "No hero's welcome. And no end in sight."

"We're working on that. When I was hurt, I swore I'd do everything I could to fight this senseless war."

"Don't you have a job?"

"You mean a full-time job? Damn few vets find those. Older, wounded vets like me, forget it. It'll never happen."

"You don't look older than me."

"When I was drafted I was thirty-three, working on my MA."

"Hey, you almost made it to thirty-five."

"Don't I know it?"

"So, if you're not working, what are you doing?"

John grinned. "Burning flags. Raising awareness and money for peace. Writing and speaking to congressmen. Looking for a job. And hoping to get back into college on the GI Bill. I'll confess, though, I'm not sure of anything anymore."

"Well, I wish you luck."

"Thanks. So, what do you do?"

"I'm a surveyor. Building freeways."

John rolled his eyes, inhaled. "Hate to tell you this, old man: you're part of the war effort."

30

"This night I must enjoy thee; if thou deny, then force must work my way, for in thy bed I purpose to destroy thee."

WILLIAM SHAKESPEARE, *THE RAPE OF LUCRECE*

Part of the war effort! Another Molotov cocktail tossed at his head. The fire, this time, had crossed the Pacific, televised bombs falling in backyards, napalm burning in homes, offices, and churches from sea to shining sea. Tom's loyalty to the state of California turned to ashes; he gave his notice, packed up, and with little more than the shirt on his back, drove north and enrolled in the creative writing program at a small liberal arts college.

He would be a poet.

○

Salome sat on the curb. The sign on the two-story brick wall behind read: ... ZING LEATHER GOODS — 1899. Below ZING a smaller sign identified the current proprietors: Lilies of the Alley.

The sun had turned the dumpster into an oven and something inside was stirring around, trying to keep from being roasted.

"I suppose," said Tom, "this is where I ask if you'd like to do lunch."

"My place," asked Salome, "or yours?"

The Whitmore Hotel was one fire exit away from being condemned. Tom steered through ancient furniture, doors coming off hinges, and derelicts. Mice turd, mildew, and bad plumbing seeped into his pores until his nose abandoned hope.

But Salome skipped through the lobby exuding charm, danced up the stairs, and spun around on the landing, a bubbling fountain of pretense. "I'm so glad you came to my home! This is great! And it's just beginning!" She rattled a doorknob. "Here, hold my bag." She turned the key and tried again. "Oh, wait, I've got it." Turning the knob and the key at the same time, she thrust the door open. "Open Sesame! I've got the golden touch. Bet you can't guess what my college major was. Dance!"

"I never imagined."

Pulling down curtains, Salome twirled from window to window. "Classical dance! Ballet! Once I even danced with the Joffrey!"

"Yeah."

"Yes, sir. Yes, indeed, I did. Can you believe it?"

"Can you believe I once staked out freeways through the desert?"

"I had the lead, Tom!"

"No, you didn't. If you had the lead, it would have been more than once."

"Okay, it was twice." Salome scooted around, picking up clothes and throwing them into a closet. "And guess what? Yesterday I met an elderly gentleman here who fought in the Civil War."

"No, you didn't. The Civil War ended a hundred and fifty years ago."

"I didn't mean the American Civil War, silly. The Spanish one."

"On whose side?"

Tom sat on the unmade bed. Peeling wallpaper revealed patches of discolored plaster. An open newspaper section lay on the floor with the crossword partially filled out. A half glass of white wine or murky water sat on the table.

"Okay," he said, "let's talk business."

"Oh, business can wait," said Salome, patting his arm and disappearing into the bathroom. "I'll be right back."

○

The first time—that awkward, terrifying experience—neither he nor Jenny had a clue what they were doing or why, only knew there was no holding back. Unlike now.

Afterward, Jenny had lit up: "That was great."

"Better than going to jail."

Tom sat down on the bed, reflecting, remembering …

In writing class, he'd been working on another protest poem when there was a knock on the door. No one ever knocked on Dr. Allen's door.

"Yes?" Dr. Allen pulled his glasses down to the tip of his nose and peered over. "Come in."

"Tom Freeman?"

The class froze. Students looked up. Dr. Allen wiped his glasses.

Looking around, the cop said, "Tom Freeman?"

"Here."

"Come along, then."

Three other students and a professor were also arrested. It caused a stir on campus, hundreds of students milling around, wanting to find out what happened. The next day, a photo of the four walking into jail appeared on the front page of the local newspaper.

○

"Almost ready," Salome sang out, whispers of steam eddying out from under the bathroom door.

Tom lay back on the bed, reflecting on those three quiet hours of jail, hugging the memory close. He'd been allowed one book ... Shakespeare's tragic political story of Lucrece, the aristocrat as work of art, the victim objectified as if she were a material possession ... but the guilt of Tarquin was too much to bear, caused too much pain, and he hadn't finished it.

It had been a long, hot day. Tom was bone-tired but happy. *The Ping-Pong Club* had come of age, and was in Michael Moore's hands. With a sigh, he lay back. He'd almost fallen asleep, when, smelling of lemon soap and wrapped in a pink towel, Salome came forth and began to dance.

31

"The use and the abuse of fear are the same."
OLD-SLAVE PROVERB

Lob and get slammed. Chop and get looped. His opponent countered loops by blocking short. It forced him to push deep, which made it easy for his opponent to loop and send the ball out of reach.

"That's it! Game over!"

Shaking with frustration, dripping in sweat, Tom sat up. The dream vanished. Street lights and crowd noises trickled in through drawn curtains. Finger over finger, he walked his worried hand to the other side of the bed. Salome was gone. Whew. He climbed out, threw on his clothes, and ran down the hotel stairs.

Into a mob scene. Front Street blocked off, barricades and police cruisers at every corner, and hordes of adoring Sarandon fans strolling from tavern to bistro to store, taking photos, and standing in line. At the end of the block, the marquee read Occupy Wall Street Documentaries—and Tom began threading his way through the crowd.

He felt a tap on the arm.

"Omigod! Is it really you? The wife and I were just talking about you the other day. You've lost weight, Tom."

"Comes with the territory. How're the kids, Lee?"

"Great! The daughter just got into college here."

"Last time I saw her," said Tom, "she was an itty-bitty thing blowing bubble-gum bubbles."

"She's as tall as me now."

"Are you still shopping at Hank's?"

"The wife goes there once in a while. Me, I haven't been back since you did the deed and fired the jerk boss."

Tom edged away. "Well, it was nice seeing you again."

"Ever since, Hank's has been going downhill. Community hasn't been the same. So, what was the real scoop?"

"The boy's letter. It did the deed. Johnny fired the boss."

"I knew it." Lee pumped his fist. "Hell's bells, if I was his dad, I'd have sued Hank."

"We talked about a lawsuit. There were witnesses to the director wrestling Johnny to the floor. At least four employees saw it."

"Employees! Afraid for their jobs. Me, I might've killed the jerk."

Tom looked toward the movie theater.

"You remember I always came in on Friday nights? Dropping three hundred bucks on groceries? Then, that time you went on vacation and the jerk director wouldn't let me cash my payroll check. Said I needed a check-cashing number. I told him I'd come back when you were in charge. The jerk got right in my face, carrying on like I was a thief, telling me I could take my business down the road. Then and there, Tom, a little pressure on his external carotid artery."

"Are you still teaching martial arts?"

Lee shook his head. "Got a better job. Are you still working at the art school?"

Tom turned. "I'm late for the movie."

"Wait a minute, giant slayer." Lee pulled a video camera from his shoulder bag. "Guess what I'm doing here on Front Street on the busiest evening of the year?"

"Making a movie?"

"Documentary. For WKTC television. How about an interview? Give your old buddy a quote. Ten words."

"No, thanks."

"You're not just some innocent bystander, you know, a tourist passing through. You went to jail and fired the boss."

"And you're still the bull-shitter." Tom began to walk away.

"Fame and fortune await," said Lee, following. "A few words. I'll turn on the mic and you can say whatever you want."

"No comment."

"I see you're working the film festival. How about telling the world what you think about Michael Moore?"

"Still no comment."

"What do you think of Barack Hussein Obama?"

"He's doing his job, like a good slave."

"Hot damn! Let's turn it on, right now."

"See you, Lee."

The documentary maker's shoulders slumped. "Aw, okay." He put the camera back in its case. "You win. Which movie would you be late for, may I ask?"

At the ticket window Tom said, "One, please," pointing at the poster.

"Hah. Occupy. That wasn't a story until the police moved in."

"Are you still stockpiling guns?"

"Yeah, man. Forty-seven in my closet now. Automatic rifles. Handguns. Wanna see what I'm carrying?"

"That's okay."

Lee followed Tom right up to the door into the theater. "An arsenal. Even a few grenades. Me and the wife target practice every week."

Tom entered the theater.

"Mark my words, if Obama's re-elected, it'll be war in the streets— the Second Coming."

The movie had already started.

O

Stevie, the newly elected student body president, emailed: "I'm excited to hear about your plans for next year. Let's meet."

The Ping-Pong Club would have a Second Coming!

But one student was less eager to come aboard. "I can't afford to take a chance," wrote Ari. "We'd have to hand out hundreds of those black shirts."

"We won't know if we don't try."

"Listen, Tom, protest isn't three students in t-shirts. Protest is five hundred students blocking access to the administration building. I'm afraid. Humpty Dumpty could have some undercover cop following us around taking pictures. He'd expel us."

"For wearing t-shirts?"

"You don't know how important staying in school is."

"I think I know. I know how important fear is too."

"But, Tom, my education is my entire future."

"My job, Ari, was my entire future."

"Yes. Sorry. I know you loved your job."

"More than any job I've ever had, and I've had a few. My job was why I wrote the book."

"Am I in it?"

"You're all in it."

"Oh, Tom, I wish you hadn't put me in the book. What if Humpty Dumpty reads it? What if he recognizes me?"

"Do you remember those Beware the Ides of March notes?"

"Like they were yesterday."

"Hold on a minute." Tom forwarded that short chapter of the book.

"Thank you, Tom, for changing my name. I should have trusted you."

"That's all right. Just out of curiosity, Ari, how did you know that a hundred-year storm was coming?"

"Of course, I didn't know. I'm not prescient. I'm an artist."

○

"Hey, I didn't know you shopped at Herb's."

"Grub's necessary," said Scott, pushing a full grocery cart. "Almost as necessary as music."

Tom had played trombone alongside Dana's husband at dozens of concerts. "Music hath charms to soothe the savage breast."

"You still playing?" asked Scott.

"Nah. Pretty much retired these days."

"That's too bad. The jazz band could use you." Scott headed for the checkout lanes. "Hey, man. That's right! Dana mentioned you're writing a book."

"She's been a big help introducing me to people and providing leads. Her character even survived my editor's delete key."

"When does it go to the printer?"

"It's there right now."

"I look forward to reading it."

"I'll see you get a copy. But you know, the book is only a tool, a means to an end."

Scott had a puzzled look. "A means to an end?"

"Like a trombone."

32

"If you play a musical statement that's a truth right there. In order to play truth, you've got to live as much truth as you can."

JOHN COLTRANE

Carrying a special passenger to a special concert, Tom put the truck into third gear, then second, and slowly they rumbled up the spine of the peninsula. From the top, the view of the greatest lake opened up on both sides of the road. Tom turned into a paved drive and parked outside an architectural throwback. The small private concert would take place in a dome.

"I mean, c'mon, Tom. What's up with that? You gotta be kidding," Charlie complained, putting on a pretend pout. "You write a book on my alma mater and I'm not in it?"

"So, do something about it."

"Right on, bro." Charlie hopped out of the truck, grabbed his sax, and together they walked up the winding stone-walled stairway.

"Welcome!" said the woman. "You must be Charlie! I'm Thorna. So glad to meet you." She opened the door wide. "And you are?"

"This here's my old friend, Tom."

"Pleased to meet you too. Thank you for coming." Thorna took them both by the hand and led the way inside. "Welcome to my humble abode." Something about the hostess reminded Tom of his old part-timer Palma.

An elderly lady with a hearing aid arrived with an elderly gentleman in a blue vest. Right behind them came a young man.

"Gary!" Charlie gave his former art-school classmate a hug. "If I'd known you were coming I'd have brought my soprano."

"Dana's here too," smiled Gary's mother. "Surprise!"

Thorna conducted the tour. "It isn't Buckminster Fuller. It's a one-of-

164

a-kind! We bought it from the coolest architect. He built it himself, back in the sixties. Eesn't eet grand?"

"The only piece missing," said Tom, "is a baby." He smiled broadly. "A baby grand."

Open in all directions, its ceiling dotted with skylights, the dome had six bay windows offering views of forests, gardens, vineyards. Off in the distance, the blue waters of the greatest lake shimmered.

Tom liked the modern bidet in the old-fashioned bathroom, and was starting to feel right at home, almost like being back in the mail room where Palma also liked to fake a French accent.

"A pièce de temps! A tour de force! Fifty years old!" gushed their hostess. "Can you believe? And the acoustics, mon Dieu!"

"Pretty good, eh?"

"Frances!" Thorna gestured to a beautiful, dark-skinned woman sitting quietly on the couch. "Sound check!"

Frances squared her shoulders, hands clasped as if in prayer.

"Your attention, everyone! My massage therapist will demonstrate."

The masseuse clapped her hands, once; it was like a rifle going off. A cat jumped up and scampered away, tail erect.

Reed in mouth, Charlie stood gazing out the windows, waiting his turn. Gary joined him and the two young men began making up for lost time.

"Everyone, please make yourselves at home," said Thorna. "The bar is right there, hors d'oeuvres are on the sideboard."

Tom grabbed a beer and joined Dana. "How's life after the art school?"

"Much better," she said. "Not just the pay. I love not being micro-managed."

"Did Scott mention meeting me in Herb's?"

"Yes. Congratulations on finishing the book."

"I still need to get the dedication straightened out."

The hors d'oeuvres disappeared, and one by one the audience found seats on the long, U-shaped, lion-skinned couch.

Sax in its strap, Charlie, suggested, "Why don't each of you give your name and maybe tell a little about yourself?" He went on. "I'll go first. Two years ago, Gary and I graduated from the art school here. He's at Purdue now. I'm a jazz major at New York University."

Gary told a joke on himself, then said, "Yeah, I graduated. Charlie here got the Jonathan Award."

Murmurs and whispers. "Jonathan Award?"

The man in the blue vest spoke up. "I don't know much about music, but I know that award. Named for Jonathan Richter, a former president of the school. It's the only student award for humanitarianism and service. Congratulations, son."

Tom added, "The award was recognition for the most outstanding all-around student."

"Out of how many?"

"Two hundred graduates," said Charlie. "Your turn, boss."

Tom said, "I worked twelve years at the school."

"For both my junior and senior years," said Charlie, "I did my community service in Tom's mail room."

Blue Vest had a puzzled look. "You don't work there any longer, Tom?"

"A month ago, I was fired."

"What?" Gary jumped up. "I hadn't heard."

"Why?" asked Blue Vest.

"He spoke up about all those other terminations," Charlie said.

"One in particular," said Tom.

Charlie lifted his horn. "The president has fired nearly a hundred experienced teachers. Last year, students protested; Tom helped them."

"But the school wasn't founded to fire faculty," said Blue Vest. "Shouldn't student art be the higher priority? My old Princeton colleague, Jonathan, must be rolling over in his grave."

"Termination is only one ending," said Charlie. "I'd like to start off with a song that ends twice, called 'Nuff Said.'"

Putting sax to mouth he worked through chord changes with a primal bluesy tone. It was sad, yet somehow appreciative. Another breath, and off he went, riffing, sending the little group on a tour exploring the mysteries of change. Solo soul, but Tom could hear piano, bass, and drums. He applauded lustily.

Charlie let his sax hang for a moment. "That was a little piece by Nina Simone. Any requests?"

"'Time Out'?" suggested Dana.

"Paul Desmond. One of the greatest sax melodists." Charlie hit the time signature and chords, improvising on the famous Desmond solo, filling the horn with deep tones—rich, meaningful.

Dana led the group in bringing their hands together. Charlie wiped his mouthpiece, and changed to a composition that seemed to come from a frenzied dream of atonal chords and scales.

Solo, Tom applauded. "What was that last piece, Charlie? Bird?"

"Yeah, that's right, Tom," said Charlie. "A Charlie Parker piece called 'Cheryl.' It was first recorded back in 1953."

"Jeepers," said Thorna. "It sounded really modern."

"Bird never gets old," Charlie said. "What else would you like to hear? It's up to you. Anyone have a question?"

"I'd like to know," said Blue Vest, "how you memorize all that music."

"I'll tell you, sir. The answer lies in the roots of jazz. I don't memorize any music; as a matter of fact, I have a terrible memory. When you play by ear, though, you can play the same song over and over and it never sounds the same."

"Dear me," said Hearing Aid. "It seemed like such a nice piece."

"I know you practiced a lot when you were at the art school," said Gary. "Now that you're in college, how many hours a day?"

"Three or four. Mostly, I'm performing."

Thorna asked, "Where's your home, Charlie?"

"I'm from a small town in Maine, close enough to the border that sometimes I feel Canadian. That's why I feel a special bond with Tom here."

Frances turned. "Are you Canadian, Tom?"

"Oui, madame."

"Are you south of the border to capitalize on us? To make a little money?"

"I've got a little unfinished business to attend to."

"Are you in business?"

"Not any longer."

Frances was determined to find out why a Canadian would choose to live in the United States. "My newest friend, Thomas, you intrigue me. It's possible you could be my best friend. When will you be moving back to Canada?"

"The minute President Romney takes the oath of office."

"I don't understand," said Hearing Aid.

Gary and Charlie laughed out loud. "Tom doesn't compromise," said Charlie, "when it comes to politics."

"But," said Thorna, "everyone has to compromise. If for no other reason than to keep their jobs."

Tom chuckled.

Blue Vest said, "Well, I must admit, I'm stunned. I had no idea our little art school here was turning out such talent."

"There's a lot," said Charlie, "that people don't know about my alma mater."

"I'll say," said Tom.

"How much longer will you be here, Charlie?"

"Taking the Greyhound home day after tomorrow."

"Oh, that is such a long bus ride," said Hearing Aid.

"Twenty-two hours."

"Dear me."

"Good luck, young man," said Blue Vest.

Thorna wasn't a happy camper. "So, why, Charlie? Why did you come back today?"

Charlie unclipped his sax and set it on the sofa. He walked over and stood behind his old mail room supervisor.

"You know, this was my home for four formative, wonderful years. The lessons I learned will always be with me. But now, my friends at the art school have all gone on to university, conservatories, symphony orchestras, and my old teachers have been fired or they quit."

"You can't go home again," said Thorna. "C'est la vie."

"That, indeed, is life," said Charlie, putting a hand on Tom's shoulder. "I wanted to visit old friends."

Dana dabbed her eyes with a tissue.

The jazzman looked around. "And," he said, "to play for you."

33

"The odds can only be stacked against this high once."
OLD-SLAVE PROVERB

Mannekin Auditorium, named after a former Governor, was packed. The orchestra finished warming up. Low notes from the double bass vibrated through Tom's bones as he found a seat, his eyes fixed on the violinist on stage. A choir performed an excerpt from the Mozart requiem; the orchestra played part of Beethoven's *Missa Solemnis*. Speaker after speaker came up to praise the former orchestra director, and by the time his two children finished remembering their father's dreams, there wasn't a dry eye in the house. Afterward, in the adjoining art museum, friends, family, and musicians mixed and mingled, munching hors d'oeuvres, sipping iced drinks. Tom waited.

The double-bass player, a big man with a strong grip, walked up. "Sorry about your job."

"Thanks, Gene." Rubbing his hand, Tom kept watch.

"Hello, Mr. Mailman," said Irv Delaney.

Shaking hands with the former Interotten president, Tom felt the envelope under his arm pulse, leaping, almost, like a babe in the womb.

"The last time I saw you," said Irv, "it was at the church. You were playing trombone in a brass quartet. Still playing?"

"Negative. No chops."

"That's too bad. Mail room under control?"

"I wouldn't know."

Raising his bushy eyebrows, Irv cocked his head. Tom remembered an energetic leader, forceful and always friendly. During his tenure, the art school had grown modestly in enrollment and scholarships. The financial base had been secured, and he'd acquired the admiration and support of alumni as well as the surrounding community. He earned a reputation as a statesman for the arts, traveled the world expanding the school's reputation. His most-admired accomplishment, however, was neither economic nor political. For almost a decade every staff and faculty member came to work secure in the knowledge that they weren't about to be dismissed.

"You wouldn't know?" repeated the former president. "Why do I have this feeling you're going to tell me something I don't really want to hear?"

"Dempsey fired me a month ago."

Irv slapped his forehead. "Oh, for crying in the bucket. I'm so sorry, Tom. What on earth was his reason?"

"Your replacement doesn't need a reason."

"It's starting to be an epidemic. The school is looking more and more like a corporation. How long had you been there? Ten years?"

"Twelve."

"There's got to be a story in this. You are implying Dempsey fired you without a reason. Did you two not get along?"

"Guess he didn't like my politics."

"Meaning?"

"I opened my mouth. Like you just did— 'the school's looking more like a corporation.'"

Irv forked an olive from his glass, popped it into his mouth, and smacked his lips. The octogenarian did have beautiful teeth. "Opening your mouth," he said, "can get you into a lot of trouble."

"It depends on what you say. And to whom."

"Whatever happened to the First Amendment?"

"The Supreme Court," said Tom, "has decided employees have no free speech, none at all. Only employers have free speech."

"What did you say when you opened your mouth?"

"Rah, rah, rah. Cheering on students, encouraging dozens of them to protest the termination of their teachers."

"Mark was doing the same thing—encouraging orchestra students to protest Naomi's termination. The evidence is all in now. He was a force-out; Mark was dismissed."

"Mark is my hero. Bernie too, now that he's been fired for talking to students about Jay's termination."

Irv gasped. "Jay was fired?"

"He said boo to a fencepost."

"That's awful. A brilliant music theorist, Jay. I hired him myself. What else can you tell me about Bernie's run-in with the administration?"

"Dempsey instructed Durwood to fire Bernie."

"And Durwood wouldn't take orders?"

"You know Durwood—chair of the department, national awards for outstanding teaching. His own boss. But Humpty Z. Dumpster was determined to get rid of Bernie, and offered Durwood a sabbatical. Boyce did the dirty deed and burned a trainload of alumni bridges."

"Durwood's priorities always were his students." The former president sipped his drink.

"And his alums," said Tom. Over Irv's shoulder, he saw who he'd come to see. Gliding toward the refreshment table, meeting and greeting friends, Julie made her entrance, a daffodil radiating warmth, a comet coming into earth's orbit.

"Excuse me, Irv."

The violin had changed from concert garb into a lavender top with a yellow silk scarf. At the refreshment table, the double-bass player broke into laughter. The envelope under his arm stirred impatiently, growing warmer as Tom waited behind Gene's expansive back. A moment later, Julie noticed Tom, gave the bass player a farewell tap on the arm and walked up, smiling.

"Hello, Tom." Suddenly she was in his arms.

A first.

"It's been awhile," he said. "Great to see you. The orchestra did a nice job with the Mozart. Mark would have loved it."

Blinking back a tear, "I know," she said. "It was his favorite."

"Nice shirt. Or whatever."

"It's a dashiki. Connie gave it to me. Mark loved bright colors." She took a sip. "You know, I still want to give you that lunch."

"It's not necessary."

"I want to do it." Shaking her hair loose, glowing with warmth, she smiled. "So, Tom, what have you been up to?"

"Occupying Front Saturdays. Armband Day 84 is this Sunday. I'm a free man now."

"In uncharted waters. I understand. Really, I do. Weren't you also writing some kind of book?"

The double-bass note took a turn down his spine, climbed back up. Everyone in the room seemed to stop talking at once. The envelope pulsed. Tom drew it out from under his arm. He held it like a newborn and watched it leap into Julie's hands.

"What's this?"

"Rough draft. Of the book. Have a look."

"This?" She took the envelope, held it gingerly, like a bow, between thumb and forefinger. "This is it? Am I supposed to read it?"

"Would you? I mean, would you please, and tell me what you think of it, because, well … because, I'd like to dedicate it to Mark. I mean, to his memory."

Tears broke through the dam and ran down her cheeks. Clasping the envelope close, "Wow." Julie breathed. "You're really into last hurrahs, aren't you?"

"Two hurrahs. But I hardly knew Mark, only met him once in the mail room, and I only met Connie that once in the library when we went to Cam's concert at the art gallery."

"When you called Mark your hero."

"He still is. Will you ask Connie if it's okay?"

"I'm not sure she's ready for this. I'm not sure I am."

"It's a dedication, not a *Missa Solemnis*."

"I understand. I also understand there's some controversy surrounding your book." She held the envelope out, studied it.

"There is."

"Mark is in it, correct?"

"His character comes up in the dialogue."

Julie bit her lips. "You don't seem to realize, Tom, that everyone is not like you. Most of us just want to hang on to our jobs."

"At what cost?"

"What do you mean?"

"Hanging on to your job could cost your integrity. It depends on where you draw the line."

"The line between what?"

"Keeping your job and keeping your integrity."

"Where do you draw the line?"

"Down the middle."

"You know, Tom, there are some who disagree with you about that."

"Including you?"

"I don't know." Julie tucked the envelope under her arm. "Yet."

"Will you ask Connie if it's okay? And, will you read it yourself?"

"I will."

People began heading toward the exit. Tom waved at Irv Delaney. As the double-bass player bustled by, his shoulder bumped Tom just hard enough to knock the former mailman off balance. Tom tried to catch hold of something, groping blindly to keep from falling. On her way, perhaps, to deliver the envelope, the violin turned, and Tom's hand grazed the upper part of her arm, the arm cradling the pulsing envelope. He also made brief contact with something else.

Dropping *The Ping-Pong Club*, Julie bristled, eyes blazing. "What the hell? What do you think you're doing?"

Heads turned. The exodus from Mark's memorial halted.

"Don't you ever, ever, do that again!"

34

"When asked what he was doing, one mason replied, 'I'm carving stone.' The other said, 'I'm building a cathedral.'"

LEIGH BRANHAM, *KEEPING THE PEOPLE WHO KEEP YOU IN BUSINESS*

One day, Tom waited three hours. The pine stump had ceased being a curiosity at a convenient height. Cold, rugged, it spoke of long ago, when times were tougher in the northern forest. Finally, picking up t-shirts and books, Tom sadly headed for home. He was turning onto the highway when the red Jeep pulled out of the school parking lot, paddleboard on top. Honking, waving, Tom watched WAH zip past—not a sideways glance.

He followed. North of Buddie's, the red Jeep's left turn signal blinked; he swerved into Hank's, wove through the parking lot, and was waiting when here she came, burning up the road, eyes straight ahead. Where was she going in such a god-awful hurry? He hit the gas.

A few miles later, that left turn signal began blinking again, then went off; Julie laid pedal to the metal until, at Lake Thelma Road, she slowed and signaled right.

God doesn't speak in thunderclaps; there are no angelic choirs. His ethereal muse doesn't signal left and then go right—earthlings with steering wheels in their hands do, and Tom was pursuing a Danica Patrick WAHnabe, risking lives, signaling WAHtever, hell bent for WAHt the hell? Jeep paradise? How should he know he was about to witness something out of the twilight zone?

After Lake Thelma Road leaves the highway, it continues level and straight for a stretch, then dives down a steep hill. A hundred yards ahead, the red Jeep approached the brow of the hill, brake lights on, right turn signal flashing. So Julie was going to the horse farm. It would be the easiest thing in the world—child's play—he'd turn in behind, hand her a t-shirt, and then surprise her with *The Ping-Pong Club*, in print, finally.

Once Tom had been caught here in a summer downpour. Windshield wipers flailing, he'd pulled into the farm to wait out the storm. Beautifully maintained large red barns, white-rail fences. Over one fence, an old brown mare enjoying the shower had wagged her ears hello. The farm had been for sale at the time. Bruce Willis had even considered buying it when his daughter Rumer enrolled at the art school—big news in a small town.

Easiest thing in the world to pull in and give Julie the book.

Except the red Jeep disappeared. Tom came over the hill, looking down on Lake Thelma, and WAH was gone, vanished like a cloud. Like a dream. Like the memory of a forgotten face.

O

Throughout the winter of the hundred-year storm, Occupy Front held down the fort Saturday after Saturday, a dozen performance artists blending their show of unity and bravado, demonstrating their conviction and faith for locals, tourists, and gun-happy documentary makers alike. They had overcome the mind-killer, fear. They'd inhaled a speck of heavenly dust on the winds of fate, looked reality in the eye, and were no longer afraid of changing it.

New faces arrived. "How's the student uprising going?" asked Tom's favorite former mail room helper.

"The rising could be more up."

"More up than this?" Joanne grabbed an I Am The 99 Percent sign and held it high.

"Much more up. Humpty Dumpty has warned students against speaking with me."

"You've been blacklisted? Woo! Woo! How can I help?"

"Join me in the park tomorrow."

The eleventh anniversary of 9/11, a few minutes before eleven o'clock, Tom knocked on Joanne's door, bent to pick up the newspaper, and sat down on the porch. The front page had a photo of the Statue of Liberty with the Twin Towers still standing in the background.

The door opened.

"Omigod! Sorry, Tom. I forgot. Let me put something on."

On the road to the art school, Tom asked, "Sleeping in?"

"We were out until dawn," said Joanne. "Jeremi found a crystal he thought would be perfect for greeting the sun."

"Your boyfriend's weird."

"Nobody can say that about you."

"Me? Weird? Something weird about giving away t-shirts in the park?" Tom laughed and turned into Buddie's.

"I thought," said Joanne, "we were going to the park. Do you need coffee?"

"Just need to stop for a second." Tom and Joanne walked inside the eclectic coffee shop. A stern-looking woman in steel-rimmed glasses stood behind the counter. "I'd like to speak with the manager," said Tom.

"I'm the manager. How can I help you?"

"I'd appreciate your putting this on the shelf."

Joanne clapped. "Woo! Woo! Is that the book?"

Steel Rims held *The Ping-Pong Club* as if it were a dead crow, scanned the front and back covers, flipped through a few pages. "Mmm ... on page eighty-five, I see there's a reference to a Buddie's. That wouldn't be this restaurant, would it?"

"Of course not," said Tom. "This restaurant is real."

Steel Rims blinked. "I'm sorry," she said, deadpan. "All of our books are food-related. Maybe you should try a bookstore."

Back in the truck, Joanne said, "Well, that was a surprise."

The main entrance to the art school lay directly across the road from the park, which meant that from the stump, they would be able to see anybody approaching or leaving the school. They grabbed boxes of t-shirts, books, and an umbrella just in case. In the little clearing, Joanne sat on the old rugged pine stump, and Tom plopped down on the ground. Picking up a discarded bottle cap, he set it between thumb and middle finger, lifted an elbow, and snapped.

Joanne watched it sail like a kite to the shoulder of the road. "How'd you do that?"

"Woo! Woo! It's like greeting the sun with crystals."

"No, it's not."

"Okay, it's like the pine stump you're sitting on. How old do you think that tree was?"

"Let me count the rings. Mmm ... maybe a hundred fifty."

"Small, tight rings. That white pine was two hundred and eighty-seven years old when it was felled. That was thirty or forty years ago. Today it would be more than three centuries old. The founder walked in its shade."

"This is a special place," said Joanne. She picked up *The Ping-Pong Club* and settled down to read.

A new school year was getting off the ground: changes everywhere, a nip in the air, leaves turning colors, seeds blowing to their new homes. Two boys on bicycles pedaled by on the highway; a forty-foot camper rolled into the campground.

Joanne laughed at a scavenging chipmunk scooting toward her shoe. She clapped her hands and watched it run away. Tom kept his eyes on the main entrance. A new, shiny, black Mercedes approached the exit.

Setting the book down, "I'm not in it," Joanne complained.

"Neither am I."

The Mercedes pulled through the entrance with its right turn signal blinking. In a moment it would be thirty feet away.

"Duck, Joanne! He'll see you!"

"What are you doing?"

"Duck!"

"I'm not ducking," said Joanne. "And neither are you. You're sitting on the ground, dreaming or something. Are you still writing the book?"

"Yes, I am!" But where were the students? In the distance, a clap of thunder rumbled and rolled slowly away.

"If no one's coming," Joanne said, "I'd like to go now."

"Wait."

Two girls were starting across the highway.

"Hello, Tom," said one, running up and giving him a hug. "I am so sorry you were fired. It was wrong. Everyone misses you."

Tears in his eyes, Tom said, "Doreen, this is Joanne, class of 2011."

"I remember," said Doreen. "You were a friend of Larry's. What are you guys doing here?"

"Stevie said she'd meet us here."

"Stevie? The Student Body president?"

"She said she wanted a founder t-shirt."

"Like the ones everybody was wearing at commencement? I didn't get one! Did you, Emily?"

Joanne handed them each a t-shirt. "Do they get books too?"

"Wait." Tom raised a hand. At the main entrance to the school a security car had stopped. Engine idling, the driver watched the little gathering in the park. Deliberately, Tom turned and handed Doreen a copy of the book.

She squealed. "*The Ping-Pong Club*! I've heard so much about it!"

In a minute, the security cop arrived and rolled down his window. "Hello, folks. Hi, Doreen. Tom."

"If it isn't Jack!" Out of the side of his mouth, "Let him have it," said Tom to Doreen.

"What've you got there? Can I see?" Bossily, Jack trumpeted command.

He brusquely flipped through the book, set it down on the passenger seat, and without another word, drove away.

Chattering like chipmunks, the girls returned to campus.

Joanne smiled. "I'm beginning to understand, finally, why you wrote it. And I'm beginning to like it."

"Hey, Tom!" said the students crossing the highway. "Can we have a couple copies of *The Ping-Pong Club*?"

"Matty! Kylie! Good to see you again."

Joanne handed out the books. "Tom. Will you please wipe that smile off your face?"

"Okay, boss," said Tom, picking up boxes of books. "We can go. We have infiltrated campus with t-shirts. The book is back where it belongs. And damn, do I like getting hugs."

"You looked like you were enjoying it. Doreen's a lovely girl."

"Who's nowhere near as lovely as you."

Joanne touched his arm. "Wait."

The Student Body president was crossing the highway.

35

"The tragedy of so-called human resources is that though it is potentially the most significant and rewarding work any manager could want it is usually dismissed as the 'human remains' department."

STEFAN STERN

Flood or drought? Favor or scorn? Always the wind sifts the sands of time, the sun shines here not there, the world turns for or against. Always it seems the operator at the controls of this orbiting bottle cap is having either a good day or a bad day.

Once holding a reservoir full of faith and community spirit, Tom now felt like an old, broken earthen dam being drained of resources.

Ping-pong support slowed to a trickle of mailed founder t-shirts or copies of the book. One day in the post office, the postmaster finished counting back change, asked, "How's the book coming?"

"You're in part two. Can't decide if you're a boss or a slave."

Stiffening, the postmaster said, "I ain't no slave."

"No slave? Selling stamps? Counting back change? Is that what you want to do with your life?"

"Not the only thing."

"What else?"

"Travel. I always wanted to go to England."

"Go. Right now. Go to England."

"Can't do it, Tom." The postmaster flipped the envelope into a bag. "I've got a sick wife."

"Well, for Pete's sake," Palma exclaimed, her arms full of packages. "Look who's here."

"Aw." Tom awkwardly hugged his old part-timer. "Put those express things down, girl. Looks like you got the job."

"I did! Thank you so much, Tom! I had no idea how I was going to make my next mortgage payment."

"You're welcome. I couldn't have done it all alone."

"Thank you, Hamilton Z."

"A slave grateful another slave was fired?"

"Oh, you and your slavery."

"I used to be a slave like you."

"Slavery ended two hundred years ago," said Palma.

"Slavery was made illegal a hundred and fifty years ago but it didn't end. Americans are addicted to slavery. It's our birthright."

"Call it a birthright or whatever you want. I call it a full-time job."

"So, you can pay the bills? Go along day-to-day delivering the mail, selling your integrity for slave-labor wages and a piece of apple pie and some pone, raising four kids, driving a ten-year-old beater that gets seven miles to the gallon. The American dream."

"Dad bang it, you are so pessimistic."

"The American dream is a nightmare that's moved. To China. India. Bangladesh. Pretty soon you'll be fired too, and then it'll be unemployment assistance time, Dad-and-Mom-to-the-rescue time, food stamp time, all over again."

Tears in her eyes. "You sad, old slave," said Palma. "You are missed."

"Humpty Dumpty would fire you in a nanosecond if he heard that."

"He just hired me!"

"In a nanosecond. Before you know it, your boys will be dealing drugs to put food on the table."

Palma reeled. "Oh. My. God. How'd you know? My oldest just got suspended."

"Where to next for you? Slave-mart? McSlave-hold?"

"I know how the system works, Tom. You explained it many times. But dognab it, I'm happy now, happier than I've been in a long time." In front of posters of missing children, Palma threw her arms up, striking a pose. "Yahoo!"

"Yahoo."

"I am sorry, Tom, the mail room didn't work out for you."

"I mean it. Yahoo."

"Yahoo?"

"This is just the beginning."

"You always said that. But there's no ping-pong club. They've all graduated. Nobody plays down there anymore."

"The ping-pong club is alive and well. Do you remember those seniors who met with me in the dorm basement?"

"I remember Kris. Hogan, Jackie, Elie. A few others."

"Not a one ever picked up a paddle."

"The ping-pong club didn't play ping-pong?"

"They were playing ping dot pong and playing for keeps. Even after Humpty called them all into his office and threatened to expel them."

"I would have cried."

"He can be brutal to his students. But they all graduated, and Jackie became valedictorian, pointing the way for this year's students. They'll be coming back in the spring for a little event. By the way, *The Ping-Pong Club* is back from the printers."

"Your book? Am I in it?"

"With bells on. And an armband."

"Are you still planting those old things in the library?"

"Sunday will be Armband Day 115."

"I'll be there. Oh, Tom, do you remember Rolph?"

"Cook in the cafeteria? Yeah, great guy."

"He and I are seeing each other. Rolph's my new sweetie."

And rolph and rolph we go.

○

After following the script for months, it was like punching a time clock. Knock, knock. "Hello, my name is Tom. I'm volunteering for George Mendez for the Senate."

The bumper stickers on the car in the driveway looked promising. The door opened. "Hello, my name's Tom and I'm wondering …"

He was face to face with the author-wife of the library board chairman.

"I'm Tom, and I'm … wondering. I'm sorry, how are you doing today? As I started to say, I'm wondering if you've decided who you're voting for."

"When? In November? For what office?"

"Congress. I mean, the Senate."

"Not yet. Thank you for asking."

"Wait, ma'am. Your last book, I really enjoyed it. But was it fiction or autobiography? I'm just wondering because the voice you used, the tone, made it seem like a novel. But the whole book was so personal."

"It was both."

"I knew it! Just like mine! Can I give you a copy? Because you're in it, ma'am, and so is …"

The door closed. Tom trudged back to his truck.

At his next address, a tall woman shooed the dogs from beneath her feet and leaned her broom against the wall.

"Hello, my name is ... well, I'll be darned."

"I know you! Tom, isn't it?"

"You were a customer of mine at Hank's! Fiona?"

"You always remembered my name; my kids' too ... but lately I've been shopping at Herb's."

"The tale of the parking lots tells me that Hank's is losing the battle of the bottom line."

"I can imagine." Fiona pointed indoors. "Got a minute?"

Over coffee and a doughnut, Tom asked, "How's your ex doing? I heard he broke a rib."

"Bernie will be fine. It was a bruise, mostly to his ego. He's pretty upset still, and no wonder. What in the world is going on there at the art school? He told me others had been fired, even you'd been fired."

"And banned from ever going back. Another day at the office."

"Isn't it the truth? I was just fired too. Again."

"Full-time jobs have become endangered animals. New jobs are seasonal, temporary, or unscheduled with no benefits. A script written by the one percent."

"A script for my acting debut," said Fiona, standing. "Walmart calls. Gotta run, Tom."

"How about a copy of my book?"

"Of course. Thank you! By the way, Bernie told me yesterday. Dempsey fired his vice president."

36

"To live in the minds of the living is never to die."
THE FOUNDER'S EPITAPH

We all have the same chemical composition. One dead looks like another; one cemetery looks like another. From Arlington National to Forest Lawn, graveyards are kissing cousins, Old Town Glades their absentminded aunt.

On an autumn afternoon under ancient oaks, Tom prowled among graves, accompanied by the purr of a lawnmower. He imagined a procession of six hearses, a hundred-car motorcade, each car flying the Interotten emblem. He could hear the thousand mourners weeping, the band of school musicians accompanying a soprano singing "Just A Closer Walk With Thee," the elegy delivered by a black-robed minister flown up from a downstate Unitarian church. Next day, the front-page obituary would have read: Historic Tribute to Art School President.

Zooming overhead, an airplane descended to land on the runway on the other side of the fence. A gray squirrel skittered down an oak tree. "Out! Out! My tree! My tree!" A chipping sparrow flitted to an overhead branch. "Caretaker? Care to call?"

The purring stopped. A moment later, the caretaker strode up. "Can I help you?"

"Directions to a grave."

"Is she in the Catholic section?"

"No, he's not."

"Then you have to go to the city section. Three quarters of a mile that way, over on the other side."

"I'm new here."

The caretaker drew a rough map. X marked the spot.

In fact, there were two stones, one beside the other: the founder's and a slightly larger one. His son's. Tom remembered stopping at the son's studio several years before. Jeffrey had been reconstructing a cello.

"See this veneer? It's the most important part, cut from that grove of maple just across the road there."

"The sounding board, right?"

Jeff ran his fingers across the grain, holding the board up to the light. "Gotta be the same thickness, three and one-half thirty-seconds of an inch, all the way."

"For resonance?"

"Without ninety-nine percent resonance or more, you might as well throw the whole doggoned instrument away."

"Somebody told me you were a camper. Must have been one of the first."

"Mmm. Came in the second year, soon's I turned eight."

"Quite an experience, huh?"

"Experience? I guess. Hand pump for water. Privy. Camp food."

"After that you were a teacher?"

"Camper, to teacher, to staff. Triple play."

The son had carried the founder's torch for half a century and now they lay side by side under unremarkable stones, birth and death dates duly recorded. On the founder's was an inscription: "Where art lives, let renown and fear be muted."

What on earth did renown sound like? Kneeling, listening, Tom laid hands on the stone.

The founder had lived long enough to see his dream come true; Tom's father, not so lucky. In the death grip of the Depression, Tom's father was out of work, needed a job to put bread on the table. A position opened at a J. C. Penney's store in Michigan, and he packed up his family in the old Ford and left Kansas City behind.

It was a six-hundred-mile ordeal, with five-year-old Betty missing her friends and crying nonstop in the backseat. At a cheap motel an hour's drive north of Chicago, they pulled in, took a single room, and, too exhausted at last to cry anymore, Betty fell asleep. Her parents celebrated with a glass of wine, and a little later, in the next bed, Tom was conceived.

The growing family stopped for gas a mile from the founder's dream. It was a small, nondescript camp of young musicians who could not know that in a few decades their little outpost in the northern woods would be an oak in the world of arts education, bearing acorns of creative fruit, multiplying itself by itself, over and over.

Tom remembered the difficult years—his father's dream fizzling into ruins, the loss of earthly possessions, the pain of failure, the years of cold fear—and closed his eyes.

Cold. No, that wasn't right. In fact, he felt warmth. He lifted his hands. Is this a dream?

Something under the fifty-year-old stone was stirring. Tom opened his eyes. There. Carved into the top corner, the same symbol Kris had sketched on a scrap of paper in the practice room. Lifting his hands, he traced the circled letters with his finger.

A glitch?

He put his hands back on the stone. Warmer now, and the warmth was coming in slow pulses, like heartbeats.

Hug.

Hug?

Hug.

Holding the founder's stone close to his chest, Tom shuddered. He recalled his father's relentless pain, the methadone, the talk about the gun in the closet, and the cavity inside his chest erupted. A torrent blurred his vision, tears fell to the ground.

Who's there?

"What?"

I said, 'Who's there'?

"It's …" He took a breath. "It's me. I think."

Are you alone?

"I'm always alone."

Why are you here?

"I don't know. I don't know anything anymore."

There is no deceit.

"Who … ?" Tom lifted his hands.

You know.

"Dad?"

Your father is here. You should know why you are here.

Why was he here, among rows of silent hopes and dreams, buried calamities and destinies? The inhabitants of the Glades knew why they were here. Why was he?

Tom stood. There was life after Interotten; he still had his to live. He gave the stone a fist bump, too hard, winced, rubbed his knuckles, and left the Glades where they were.

Storm clouds were approaching.

In the front yard, Betty was raking leaves.

"Sis! I just talked with Dad!"

"Sure you did." She threw the rake aside. "Stupid weather. It's going to rain. Dinner needs to be started. You talked with Dad. And this darned rake is too small." She collapsed in a lawn chair.

"Maybe it wasn't him." Tom raked leaves onto a tarp. "A voice said he was there."

"What voice?"

"The voice in Old Town Glades."

"Dad's not in the cemetery; we spread his ashes over the greatest lake."

"I found the founder's stone. It felt warm. I heard a voice."

Betty ran fingers through hair dampened by the first drops of rain. "One of the signs of stress is hearing voices."

"And hugging tombstones?"

"What were you doing hugging tombstones?"

Tom folded the tarp. "It asked for a hug."

"Let me get you a blanket."

"This tarp is big enough."

"I mean for you, to cover you up."

"Thinking of Dad, you know, I can hear his voice."

"I know," said Betty. "Sometimes when I think about him, I hear his voice too."

"He said I should know why I'm here."

"He should have known why he was here."

"For you and me. And Landon."

"The only three seeds he planted in his life."

"It's just you and me now, Sis." Tom slung the bulging tarp over his shoulder and turned toward the garden. "I was thinking about Dad, but I was also thinking about the founder."

○

"Tom! It's Doreen. You're not gonna believe this. Dempsey has banned students from the park! It's all over campus."

"Did he say why?"

"He said ... here, let me read it: 'A certain ex-employee who had been banned from campus has chosen that location as a meeting place with students.' Gee, I didn't know you were so important."

"Important as a gnat on his leg."

"What'll we do with the books you sent us?"

"Give them away."

"It's different now, though. Everyone's afraid. There's a lot of word out, you know, about the book."

185

"Then hang on to the books. Work on your grades for a while, like your mother wants you to. Practice the Beethoven."

"What about those Make Art Not Fear posters?"

"That's up to you."

"Moira wanted to know if you had any of those t-shirts left."

"They're for an event in the spring."

37

"If we are attached to our goal of winning liberty
we shall not hesitate to use bad means."

MAHATMA GANDHI

After months of bristling outrage about Bernie's dismissal, the alumni Facebook page had grown suddenly quiet. Then Tom sounded the call:

UNCHARTED WATERS

At my termination and banishment from the campus, I let the two vice presidents know that I was proud to have committed time and energy to the ping-pong club. I said Interotten would remain for the rest of my life one of my favorite places on earth.

Keith and I bowled, golfed, and played ping-pong together. Alice knew that for twelve years all of my performance evaluations were excellent. I told the vice presidents I respected them and their authority. My problem was with the Terminator.

That would be you, Hamilton Z. Dempsey. Alice admitted you made the call. You fired me for disagreeing with your decisions; for encouraging students to speak their minds, express their thoughts, and voice their opinions.

My termination had nothing to do with performance or policy or money, only with refusing to be silent. Your other victims—Mark, Naomi, Ken, Jane, Bernie, Jay, Dustin—

have been silenced but I will not be. Your money-oriented philosophy reminds me of Alan Ginsberg's Moloch, "whose mind is pure machinery, whose blood is running money, whose fingers are ten armies, whose soul is electricity and banks ... Moloch! Heavy judger of men!"

The school is better than that. We are better than that. The world is better than that.

We have arrived, like Robert Frost, at a crossroads. "Two roads diverged in a yellow wood, and sorry I could not travel both and be one traveler, long I stood and looked down one to where it bent in the undergrowth; then took the other as just as fair and having perhaps the better claim because it was grassy and wanted wear."

We're sailing in uncharted waters, Humpty Z, with each way leading beyond our horizons. Let us choose our ways wisely.

O

"Yes?"
"It's me."
"Come in." The Dean of Students frowned. "Close the door."
The president of the student council stepped toward the desk. "You said to tell you if he contacted me."
"Let me see that."

Dear Stevie,

You say students are frightened of me. Every student I've met has been exactly the opposite—glad to see me again, greeting me with a hug. But you're their president; ask them why Hamilton Z. Dempsey is frightened of a little book.

"Thanks for this. Any other contacts?"
"Just that once in the park. That time he gave me and Esther those black shirts."
"All right. Stay in touch."
"Oh! One more thing. Dante swore again today."

O

Every boss has his weakness, his bane. Hamilton Z's was his temper and Uncharted Waters flipped his temper switch. Smoke billowing from his ears, he fumed down the hall, using his bulk like a tailback blocking would-be tacklers, shoving a grant writer aside, picking up steam, swearing at a student standing at a counselor's door. Blowing tornado-like past a clutch of secretaries, spewing curses, he banged open the outer office door, charged by gaping receptionists, and sledge-hammered a fist on the door of the office of the Vice President of Facilities and Human Resources.

"What do we pay you to do, Alice?"

"Excuse me?"

"You heard me! Answer the question. Now!"

Trembling, eyes wide, a receptionist closed the inner office door and moved to her coworker's side. "I'm scared."

"Me too. I've never seen the boss this mad."

The tumult in the inner sanctum grew louder, then fell silent. Hamilton Z. Dempsey roared out, crossed the hallway, and stomped into Keith's office, where the shouting picked up where it had left off. The two receptionists stood, whimpering, holding tight to one another to keep from falling down.

The queen emerged. "It's all right, girls," she said, dry-eyed. "I'll be fine. You are wondering what has happened."

"Yes. Yes!"

"I've been dismissed."

"Nooo …" Her children sank onto their chairs.

"Involuntarily. Well … for all intents and purposes, involuntarily."

"But— but— but— why?"

"Because I could be. I can't tell you the real reason, it would endanger your positions."

Z ordered Uncharted Waters removed from the alumni Facebook page. He threatened a lawsuit, causing many Interotten alumni to start worrying about careers linked to matriculation at the art school. Teachers, gardeners, cooks, mail room clerks, radio announcers, and technicians all began looking over their shoulders, wondering who would be next.

O

Julie frowned. "I don't like it."

"Don't like what, boss?" asked Palma, setting the violin's package on the scale.

"Oh, nothing."

"Hell, girl, you're not another one of them worry warts, are you?" Palma punched numbers into the postage meter. "Because of Alice, I mean? You know, that alumni thing on Facebook? Don't sweat it. That was between Tom and Alice." Slapping a postage label on the violin's package, "There you go," said Palma. "That'll be $5.95, first class. To California, huh? A gift?"

"A friend in San Francisco is getting married."

"Far out! You'll be celebrating, huh?"

"Not exactly celebrating. He's a friend."

"This here's for the groom?"

"The bride."

"Me," said Palma, "I just love weddings, especially big church ones, with showers and receptions and gifts."

"The ceremony is on the beach."

"Soo … what did you buy her?"

"I'd rather not say."

"It's too bad," said Palma, "you're not going to California."

"Oh. I am."

"You are?"

"After the wedding."

○

Sounding nearly professional, nearly a finished product, the student orchestra had been made a team by the sheer will of the conductor. In titanic contrast with his predecessor, Dante's personality lit the music on fire. If Lorenzo personified reason and order, Dante was passion and chaos: ice melting versus volcano erupting. The volcano suited the students—the orchestra had just won *Downbeat Magazine's* major annual award—with one exception.

Shaking his finger at the Student Council president, Dante shouted, "If you're not going to learn your fucking part, you will do us all a favor by dropping orchestra."

Stevie wasn't used to being reprimanded, much less sworn at, and she took her presidency seriously. "I did learn my part! It's just that I can't play it now."

"Now is when we need it. Let me hear it again."

Cringing, the violin played it again.

"Stevie! That is not what Dvorak wrote," bellowed the fireman.

"Damn it, we have a concert in three days, and I've warned you twice! Learn your part before you come to rehearsal! Next time I will suggest to the chairman that you do us all a favor and drop orchestra."

"It's just that I can't play it now," said the girl, fighting back tears, feeling nine years old.

It had been a rough day, her roommate up all night, cramming for a physics test, screaming at the alarm, throwing her book, barely missing Stevie, who was still asleep. The president had an exam of her own, plus a report and an early meeting with her council. When to practice? It was impossible. The last few weeks were impossible. Now Dante was swearing at her! In front of the whole orchestra. Stevie took a deep breath, counted to ten, found her place in the music, and waited.

"All right, then," said Dante. "Bar 45, once again."

38

"Thou shalt not make unto thee any graven image, or any likeness of anything that is in heaven above or the earth beneath."
EXODUS, BOOK 20

Erase me from the book.

What did it mean? Tom read the email again, more closely. Was he missing something? Was it a joke? Where was the connection between the Julie who had written "Keep doing your thing, dearest Tom. You are setting an example for those of us not as bold and courageous as you," and the Julie who was now writing:

> I'm sorry I didn't read your book when you gave me the opportunity to do so, because today I read the portrayal of my character. Her identity to me is unmistakable. I am stunned.

The violin's meaning played in tones beyond Tom's comprehension. Did she see her fictional representation as a twin? Dulcinea dancing hand in hand beside her on a paddleboard? Had she been bamboozled by her imagination?

Mirror images only reflect truth. Mirrors may dress reality up in images subject to the imagination's tailor, but an image remains a disconnected appeal to the imagination, a momentary break from reality. Childish game. Content of dreams. Fodder of fiction. Every day Tom had to accept reality in all its pallid aimlessness, investing images with passion and renewal in a fiction of his own design; every day he pulled a dream curtain aside to do so.

> In your attempt to stand up for what you believe is right and just, you have violated my trust and trampled upon the sacredness of generosity of the heart.

192

What was the "sacredness of generosity of the heart"? Charity for protestors? Had she been tithing while he'd been burning the boss at the stake?

> Either you have misunderstood our conversations, which I very much doubt, or else you are using me as a fictional pawn, thereby placing me in professional danger among my colleagues and, worse, misrepresentation among my students.

The classical musician had taken the romantic poet's bait. Eve had tasted false fruit in the temporary suspension of disbelief, engaged her insecurity gears before starting her professional engines: Moloch rising and speaking in tongues, Medusa spinning her wheels in the absurd. The common, coin-counting cold. Mumbo jumbo. Legal schmegal. Compromised logic where morality should be. Accustomed to unadulterated approval and applause, the prima donna had paddled out to the middle of the lake before she'd noticed no board under her feet. Tied to her day job, Julie was now begging Tom to save it.

> Because I don't believe it is your desire to cause me pain, I ask you to take on the responsibility of honoring my individual human rights. Erase me from the book. Edit all references to me. Delete my personal identity. Do this by Monday, or else take down all copies of the book and cease further distribution. Please, Tom, wipe me off of this, entirely.

Something in his head snapped like a broken spring and he slumped to the floor in a heap. He lay in a fetal position, aware only of his breathing and the sound of the wind in the pines.

But ... he was no Cyrano fawning at the feet of a Roxanne, no Don drawn to Dulcinea—he was a boss-firing poet with a pencil and eraser. He would wipe Julie from his mind.

He began with an armload of wood, some kindling, and a match. As the flames leaped in the heater, imagination caught fire. He watched another marathon bombing in Boston, another school shooting in Colorado, another drone strike in Afghanistan, another riot in Syria, and turned off the TV. Things fall apart. The center cannot hold, but Tom Freeman gardened among waves of autumn foliage and earth smells mingling with mature fruit and fading flowers. Late beans merged with early tomatoes. Cucumbers took aim at the broccoli to grow another week. Dead-heading magical marigolds, fawning over his giant comfrey, Tom sang a natural incantation to hollyhocks and dill; filled an album with parsley, radishes, beets, potatoes, carrots; and supernatural hope came home to his hollow, old heart.

I won't jump, Miss Julie.

One napping bumblebee in the marigolds. One sluggish toad crossing the path. One last squash hiding among fence-climbing cucumbers and shoulder-high pole beans. Picking up his pieces and putting them back together, Tom grabbed his fork, nudged the toad aside, and began closing the circle, turning manure into a medium of exchange.

This ripe tomato, fruit of his seed, a rough draft in June, a promise of bigger and better things to come, turned loose, shaken free from its dry hull to run the course of sun, rain, and soil. Flesh of his flesh pressed to his cheek. Inside, a chalice-palace: rows of sentries at attention, promises of fulfillment in the palm of his hand, the undeveloped ideas of tomato listening for "Go forth and multiply." Mere anarchy loosed upon the world. To compost or not to compost? To taste or to toss untasted? Blood of tomato oozing through his fingers, Tom raised two hands to the sky: "Take. Eat." Make art, not fear from birth to death, from surfer cottage to concert stage.

Dearest Julie, he wrote.

You are hurt. Melinda was hurt, and you supported her. I was hurt and you supported me. Mark died but his widow and children live, his work lives.

You know I would never hurt you. I care the world about your feelings, and will honor your request, take the book down, delete the online edition, ask everyone to discard it. All I ask in return is for you to read the book, objectively, in its entirety.

It addresses the hurts we inflict upon each other, and there is so much hurt. The book is about hurt, not you, or me.

39

"If it quacks like a slave, it is a slave."
OLD-SLAVE PROVERB

T om put the letter inside a copy of the book, and slid the book into a large envelope. Briefly he considered mailing it to the school, but if he did, Palma would have to write a parcel notice, place it in her mailbox, and Julie would have to pick it up. He was in a hurry. He addressed it to her lakefront rental and drove to the post office.

"How long to deliver this, Jim?"

"It'll be there tomorrow."

"Perfect," said Tom. "Good work, slave."

The postmaster mimed throwing the envelope at him.

At the bookstore on Front, Tom instructed the clerk: "I'm pulling the book down, Jeff; just for a while. I need to get a little thing clarified."

"They'll be right under the counter."

Tom removed the online edition and started calling people who had bought the book, including one special alumna.

"Are you kidding?" asked Elie. "Why?"

"Just do it."

"I will not. Last year we created a grassroots revolution that should be celebrated. *The Ping-Pong Club* is history, the document of our movement."

"Somehow I knew you'd argue with me."

"Is Julie behind this? Because it doesn't sound like you."

"I'd rather not say."

"Tom, listen. I may be nineteen but I can tell you something. Julie's ticket is her violin. After she's gone, and she will be soon, that book of yours will mean more to the school, a lot more, than to her."

"Right now, it means 'erase me from it' to her."

"Impossible. What she's asking can't be done."

"It would be difficult but not impossible."

"I'm telling you, it's impossible. Once an artist creates a work, he can't erase it. He can't take it down or discard it, because it's not his anymore, it's the world's. You can't take the book down any more than she can. Call me back when you've come to your senses."

His sister also refused to toss the book. "Poor little brother! So you've done what that crazy girl asked you to do? Is there anything you wouldn't do if she asked?"

"It's only a book."

"A book that cost you your job, your home, and now your sanity. I know how much work you put into it, Tom. You're acting strangely. Did you fall in love?"

"She could be my granddaughter."

"Oh, yes. You were dazzled all right, an old bumblebee waking up with spring fever, buzzing around an exotic lily."

Curses on that infernal engineer who'd laid the blurred centerline down the middle of an old slave's heart! Damn the wiles of women! A child had changed into shorts and tank top to tantalize with violin and paddleboard. Medusa had mimed a siren merged with a muse— and he'd jumped out of his truck like Cyrano after Roxanne, to career off the road in free-fall, and end up face-down, tongue-tied, and frozen at the feet of an Eastern sphinx rising from the ruins of Ozymandias.

"All right," Tom said, "I'm a bee. But a month ago, the woman was my strongest supporter. 'I'm sorry,' she said, 'I couldn't help you with armbands at the library today. You must tell me all about it.'"

"So, that's what you were doing. Telling her all about it."

Dull-witted, Tom took a breath. "She wrote, 'I continue to support you always going for what's right, really separating right from wrong.'"

"Word support."

"Not just words. How many times did you come to Armband Day?"

"Once."

"There! You see? Julie came out twice."

"I suppose you call 'erase me from the book' support?"

"The going got a little rough for her, that's all."

"I'm glad I never met her."

"If you had, you'd have seen a natural commander who knew what she was doing. Behind that cute little smile there was an executive ... the boss. Julie was my muse."

"I'm not amused."

"My inspiration! She'd say, 'I knew it!' and I'd have a page. She'd text 'You're a free man now,' and I'd have a chapter. *The Ping-Pong Club* came courtesy of the violin."

"So, you were using her."

"To get dismissed! Damn it, Sis, Julie wrote the book! She's my guru! My goddess!"

"Don't talk like that. You're too old."

"I feel old. Please, tell me again that there is life after death."

"Did I say that?"

"It's in the book. You said 'one sign of old age is memory loss.'"

"What was that I just asked?"

"Ha, ha."

"I do remember telling you one thing: Stop crying wolf."

"Me too," said Tom, "when the wolf was at the door."

"Times were tough then."

"They're tough now. Hey, do you remember Dad moving the family north in the old Ford?"

"How could I forget? I cried all the way."

"Not quite all the way. At a certain motel this side of Chicago you stopped."

○

Dustin phoned his congratulations.

"Fired the vice president? Woot! Woot! What a nice trophy for your wall, old slave."

"I was wondering, Dustin. You've read the book—care to add your comments to the back cover of the sequel?"

"Of course, I will. I must say, however, you give every indication of having gone off your rocker—caving to Miss Saigon. How could you agree to her request?"

"To give her some time. It's in the book."

"You're putting that in? A wacky woman stomping her foot?"

"She didn't stomp her foot."

"Explain why erasing her from it is in the book."

"Because I write like that, changing things. Because she's a sign of a large change coming—a change on a different scale from the change seventy-five years ago."

"I agree. The Great Depression was substantively different from the change we are about to experience."

"The Depression wiped out the entire economy."

"There's a quantitative and qualitative difference between that crisis and the one we are facing. The causes, for instance. The Depression was an accident, the result of over-reaching and under-valuing. This crisis will not be an error, and given all the warnings we've had, it will be no accident."

"Okay, Mr. History Teacher, are you saying the same brand of crooks will be at the top of the financial world?"

"Absolutely."

"This time, bringing the world to its knees on purpose—instead of incidentally grabbing the easy money?"

"They will be more circumspect this time."

"Not jumping from towers? Dustin, is there an overall pattern to this movie? A big picture?"

"Those at the top of the financial world define the big picture."

"How about the bigger picture? Beyond profit and loss? What pulled us out of it seventy-five years ago?"

"You're going to give Roosevelt the credit."

"Not. It was World War II, which he did his slavish best to keep us out of."

"I am surprised you didn't say strikes and sit-ins."

"John L. Lewis helped. Walter Reuther, too."

"Decent enough chaps, a cut or two above the thugs who followed them. Keep me posted, Tom, on terminating the terminator. I'll come back and spit in his face."

○

Tom arrived on the first anniversary of Occupy Front to find the small group of old protestors huddled under umbrellas.

> *To my Occupy friends:*
>
> *One of the ties that binds us together is our belief that history is on our side. As we've stood together in the snow and cold, the rain and wind, that one belief warmed our hearts. Those of you who have read it know that this belief informs* The Ping-Pong Club *from page one to the end.*
>
> *I'm sorry to tell you someone important to the book has challenged*

its distribution. I've decided to take a step back, remove it from the stores, and I'm asking those of you who have purchased it to discard it.

Sandra shook her head. "I can't believe you're taking it down, Tom. Why? Who is this 'someone important?'"

"Someone with a dimple in her chin and a Stradivarius under it. Someone with a smile like a soft summer cloud. A private someone who encouraged me to check out her Facebook page, who gave me a hug. Who gave me the book."

"Someone who now wants nothing to do with it." Sandra shook her head. "Is she schizoid?"

"She's brilliant. Very private, and very emotional."

"Well," said Sandra, hugging *The Ping Pong Club*, waving to a driver with his thumb up, "I'm not throwing mine away."

"Hello, folks," said a man in a blue business suit. "Name's Peter. I teach math over at the college. I just wanted to say thanks."

"Thanks for what?"

"For standing out in the rain. Speaking up for what you believe. Being true to yourselves. Rare qualities these days."

Sandra said, "It's just fear, you know, people have become mice. You shut your mouth and look the other way."

"We're showing art," said Tom, "not fear. The art of using your tongue, not holding it."

"Yes!" said Sandra. "Come to Occupy, then write about it."

"An old habit of mine."

Peter wanted to hear more but just then a yellow school bus cleared the crosswalk and rolled to a stop. Familiar faces in the windows. Interotten was going to the movies! Students began assembling in front of the theater.

Tom carried OUR NEIGHBORHOODS, OUR FUTURES, OUR VOICE over and said, "Hey, Dan. Great to see you again. Are you still playing ping-pong?"

Julie's violin student looked away.

Dropping his sign, Tom opened his arms. Moira was stepping from the bus. "Dear favorite ping-pong player! How are you? It's been a long time!"

Moira froze, glanced around. Her friends had turned their backs. She turned too, and pretended to resume a conversation, all the while looking at her shoes.

"Alex?" Tom offered the boy his hand.

An Alex cold shoulder too. *Ellie! Where'd our grass-roots revolution go?*

"We were watching," said Sandra. "They're all afraid."

"You say," wondered Peter, "you're writing about Occupy?"

Sandra held up the book.

"Let me see that." Peter thumbed through it. "How much?"

"It's not for sale."

"And why, may I ask, is that?"

Why, indeed, is that? *Why* curled into a question mark, dissolved, reappeared, turned into a sensuous violin F-hole and came into focus exactly where Julie coiled to smash a dot, a period into his head with such force he stood open-mouthed.

"I'm not sure."

"Well, I can't stay," said Peter. "Have to get back to work. Here's a twenty. Keep the change."

Across Front, the library board chairman stepped into the crosswalk, arm in arm with his famous author wife. Tom let out a low dog whistle. The chairman glared, snatched his wife by the arm, and continued to the theater.

"Interesting," said Sandra. "He doesn't seem to like you."

"And I didn't fire him, yet."

A car honked and Sandra waved. "By the way, Tom, your femme fatale is playing next month."

Tom stopped breathing. "Julie? She's performing?"

"Yes. At the Inverted Art Gallery."

Music hath charms.

"It's a funky little place," Sandra continued. "Cute though, and perfect for this sort of thing."

"What sort of thing?"

"A sort of women's liberation thing."

40

"I started at this crematory and it was immediately like, wah, wah, wah … a rotting corpse and I'm like grabbing, and its flesh slips off its hand as I'm trying to haul it onto a table."
CAITLIN DOUGHTY

WAH the red Jeep was parked outside the front door. It was early, no one around. Tom leaned against a wall and wondered what was WAH? Acronym? Anagram? Focusing on three black letters on the white decal on the rear of the Jeep, he suddenly had it. Wahini. The little surfer girl loved words and obscurity as much as she loved music and surfing. Voila! She'd dubbed her ticket to the beach with three letters resonating Hawaii.

"Why, hello, Tom! Are you going in?"

Offering Melinda his arm: "Where you go, madame, I follow."

They found seats near the front. Tom said, "Funky."

"Oh, Gina does it all. A genius! Organizing, designing, promoting. A one-of-a-kinder." Melinda indicated a display of jumbled plastic tubes. "Like the gallery itself. Have you been here before?"

"Just once. For a concert."

The pianist began with simple broken chords sounding like a lesson for an eight-year-old—primary notes in major relationships.

Two girls in camisoles walked on stage and Julie began playing a major scale, drawing out each tone, pianissimo, with minimum vibrato. The girls began stripping, slowly, button by button, looking each other in the eye. They then reversed their "dance," each putting her own camisole back on. In her bare feet, Julie played simple scales as the girls undressed each other, then dressed each other, maintaining somber eye contact, accompanied by a music lesson of scales played on piano and violin.

Tom leaned over. "I should have stayed outside."

"Wait," said Melinda.

A poetess came on stage. Although he had written many poems and was fond of erotica, Tom had never heard poetry like this.

Breathlessly, caressing each syllable, the poetess unclothed herself: You/ take me/ in the woods/ and I am a fox den/ a beaver ..."

"Poetic exhibitionism," snorted Tom. "Teenagers getting their rocks off." He stood and walked out.

A minute later, Melinda joined him. "Oh, come on. It's modern art. Might as well get used to it. Anyway, they're just warming up."

"Playing a bunch of scales."

"You didn't look at the program. Those scales are an instrumental poem composed by an Estonian dissident. Very political and influential. End-of-the-world stuff. Next is a Bach that Julie's been playing since she was nine. One of her favorite sonatas."

"Do you know Julie?"

"Gina and I are on the Community Arts Council; she introduced us. Come on, let's go back. Back to Bach." Melinda took his arm. Tom took a deep breath.

A partially dressed mezzo soprano came on and sang, "My poor soul, my heavy heart. I will never find you again."

"Never is right," said Tom. "This is Schubert, not Bach."

"Only for you did I go out," she sang. "Only for your smile, your eyes, the magic flow from your celestial instrument."

"I don't like Lieder," said Tom, "but celestial instruments are okay."

"Only for your kiss, your embrace, did I live. Only for you will I die."

Julie came on the empty stage in a floor-length, strapless, black dress, bare feet stepping cat-like to the front. Deep in her eyes was a mirror, her own personal Ground Zero—Bach.

Oh, my poor, darling! Please forgive this old fool! I deserve your every slap of scorn, your every spit of antipathy. Lash me with loathing, my muse, but do not look at me—oh, do not look me in the eye, or I will surely die.

O

It could only have been a dream. He rolled over, looked at the clock, and picked up the phone. "Who is this?"

"It's me! Doreen!" The girl garbled something to someone. Long past curfew. She was calling from her dorm room.

"I was asleep."

"This is important, Tom. Everyone's just getting back from orchestra. We had a meeting."

"A meeting?"

"A long meeting with the administration. The concert's been canceled!"

"Tomorrow night's concert?"

"Yes! The orchestra concert. Dante's been fired!"

○

Cruising to town, listening to Herbie Hancock's "Sophisticated Lady," Tom remembered Julie's Facebook post: a photo with the pianist. One sophisticated lady he knew played ping-pong.

At Hank's, the brunette pushing the kiddie shopping cart glanced up. "Omigod! I can't believe it's you."

Hugging his old top bagger, Tom asked, "These two bambinos yours, Sharon?"

"Yes! Barbie here's my doll baby."

"Beautiful, just like Mom." He handed Sharon *The Ping-Pong Club*. "This here's my baby."

"You're giving me your baby?"

"It's a clone. I've got another in the oven."

At the checkout, driving a full shopping cart, Darlene said, "Just the tape, Tom? You can go ahead. Hey, didn't Hank ban you from the store?"

"Guess he got tired of sending me to jail. These days I'm a regular, visiting old friends here."

"Sounds like the old Tom. Say, how about coming by for dinner?" Darlene winked. "I made spaghetti sauce, vegetarian, like you."

"I'll be at the library."

"Now you're hurting my feelings again." Humpty Dumpty's former secretary wrinkled her brow. "You know, Tom, I am actually embarassed, ashamed that he fired you."

"So you knew Z made the call, huh? How's retirement going?"

"I like not having to go to work, but in the evening I get lonesome."

"How long's Jethro been gone?"

"He died the week Hank's terminated you."

"Why aren't you shopping at Herb's like everybody else?"

"Would you believe my dad sold this building to Hank? Jeth was his first store director. We've always shopped here—why should I change horses in midstream?"

"Because the other horse is cuter?"

"Ha ha. Right now, this old gray mare is going home."

Tom slowly drove by the art school … someone was walking down the middle of the road—old felt hat, insulated red lumber-jacket, baggy pants, unlaced work boots. Staying right behind on the stranger's heels, Tom tapped the horn. Was he deaf? Tom tapped the horn. An Asian woman turned, made unsmiling eye contact, and stepped out of the way.

Armband Day could wait. Turning around, Tom drove back to the dead-end road and took it to the end.

No WAH. No red Jeep, but there was a sign in the front yard. For Sale. Tom pulled a leaflet from the box, read the price, and his jaw hit the ground. Three times the value of his own lakefront home! Humpty Z. Dumpster's annual salary! In the depths of the worst housing market recession in seventy-five years, the little surfer's rental was suddenly a summer vacation cottage for the one percent. The Realtor's photo from the lake showed no beach—just algae-covered water and a view pinched by overgrown forest—it was an old boathouse painted a dirty yellow. Something was fishy.

Tom went down the stairs, knocked on the front door, waited a decent interval, then went the rest of the way down to the lakeshore and walked out on the little dock. A loon paddled by. Tom skipped a stone, the bird took off, made a loop, and splashed down exactly where it had started.

Why, Looney, why?

From the end of the dock, the cottage was a small, unimposing bachelorette flat housing a question. Framing problem? Financing glitch? Owner a jerk boss? Tom climbed back up the stairs, knocked again, gave up, and taped an armband to Julie's door.

At the art supply store, he got in line to buy bulletin board paper—the raw material for armbands. Just ahead, an Asian woman was paying. Petite, dark-haired. Tom caught a fragrance of lakeside afternoons, heard the wash and splash of waves. Athletic build, orange top, black-silk slacks, high-heeled boots. The young woman set her purchases on the counter and brushed back hair black as Medusa's curse. Honey-colored, down-covered skin. A fallow field for his gaze. Oh, Beethoven! Eau de cologne! And a musical fragrance leaned him like a paddleboard against the little surfer's cottage. Jumping aboard, Tom closed his eyes and inhaled—paint thinner—exhaled, and opened them.

A dazzling smile. The Asian woman closed her purse and put a slip of paper on the counter. "Excuse me, sir, would you like this forty percent off coupon?"

○

Dear Tom:

I read your book. Guess I never realized how much political stuff was going on right here under my nose, maybe because Grounds is the last department to hear school news. It was a good read too, for this old conservative.

The dorm mom said they caught onto you because you left some notes behind in the practice room in the basement that alerted Dempsey to your students doing those protests. She also mentioned you could be losing your house. Is that true? Why would you risk losing your home? Why would you try to fire the boss? You never seemed like a vengeful person.

You know, Tom, I don't love my job. I like it. Except for those lazy kids Human Resources keeps hiring, screwing up the grounds I'm responsible for and getting away with it. Bing isn't the easiest person to get along with either.

You remember my son, Seth? Your ping-pong student at the school? Can I have an autographed copy for him?

Looking forward to the sequel.

Your friend,

Dave

41

> "He suffered from thinking his was an entirely unsentimental love,
> but in fact he suffered from thinking while Nature was busy
> with much livelier urges."
>
> SINCLAIR LEWIS, *CASS TIMBERLANE*

Armband day 121. Overcast. Prescient.

Tom handed a copy of the book to his favorite library user. "Thanks, old girl."

"You old rascal," said Nancy. She wrapped her arms around him. "How much did you pay this guy to write it?"

"He paid me."

Nancy donned an armband, took another to deposit on account, picked up *The Ping-Pong Club*, and disappeared inside.

"Armbands Are Free Speech. Mmm." The silver-haired lady in a tailored suit shook her head. "Hmm ... I'm not sure. I do, however, recognize a few names on the petition."

"How about wearing an armband today?"

"It can't hurt, I suppose."

"You recognize a few names?"

"Durwood. Carol, here, the Director of Admissions."

"Carol was dismissed."

"I knew her very well. And, I'll be darned. Here's Boyce."

"What?" Tom dropped the books.

"Boyce is my son," she went on. "I see Drake also signed."

"How do you know Drake?"

"He and I were original members of the faculty string quartet."

"You mean you worked at the school?"

"A century ago."

"A century? Was it before Dempsey?"

"Long before him. As a matter of fact, the president at the time just walked into the library."

"He did?"

"Irv Delaney, my father-in-law."

Tom's head swiveled.

"You won't see him, because he's waiting for me in the atrium. Give me your pen; I'll sign your petition."

"Ma'am." Tom picked up a book. "Can I give you something else?"

"Who is this author?"

"Tom!" The director of Interotten's motion picture department came up.

"Hello, Mason! And here's another book for you."

"Very interesting, Tom. Students have been fighting over the only copy in the MPA building. But it's slim, huh?"

"Part one is. You just made it into part two."

"Why Mr. Freeman!" Irv Delaney's daughter-in-law laughed. "It's a roman à clef! I'd be honored to find myself in its pages."

Around the corner, on his way to another volunteer shift, the former library director paused. "Are we having another armband party today?"

"Number 121, Gary. Welcome."

"You've got to be the most persistent person I've ever known."

"And you're the best boss I've ever worked for." Tom handed Gary a book. "Got something for you."

"*The Ping-Pong Club*! In print!" Gary gave Tom a fist bump before entering his personal legacy.

"Excuse me, young man." A ham actor who could have been playing Irv Delaney, pointed to the petition. "Does this, by any chance, belong to you?"

"Guilty as charged."

"Then I would suggest you get your facts straight. Melinda was not the senior reference librarian. She was one of several senior reference librarians."

Tom shrugged. "Details."

"Details, you say," said the cane pointer. "Details are important."

"I'll say they are. Ten librarians here, all senior reference, quit in protest."

"Details have changed the world. The first war was fought over one seemingly trivial detail."

"Well," said Tom, grinning, "shoot me and call me Kaiser."

"I'll give you another detail, sir. It was a Mercedes carrying the bomb that killed the Lebanese Chief of Security last week."

"I didn't know that. So what?"

"It establishes Germany as complicit. Russian and Iranian arms had been verified going into Syria and Lebanon until this."

"I'm still confused. So what?"

"The world no longer turns East versus West. A multinational crisis awaits us in the Middle East."

"And everywhere else. How about an armband?"

"An armband? Armbands are a detail that changed Europe. An armband with a swastika on it can be a lethal weapon."

"Looks like you're headed into the library."

"Into Reference, to be exact."

"Melinda's old department. Mel helped build the library."

"And I helped build the Berlin Wall."

"She actually did."

"You know, young man, as long as we have abandoned referential fact and are now speaking in parables, I also served as personal guard for Hermann Goering."

Something felt wrong. "Here." Tom held a copy of *The Ping-Pong Club*. "It's Armband Day and I feel generous. Have a book."

"Very impressive," said Goering's personal guard, pocketing the book. "What is your name, good sir?"

"It's there on the cover."

"Achtung! A cover!" Reaching into his briefcase, the gentleman pulled out a sheaf of papers. "What do you think this is?"

"A manuscript?"

"This, my authorial friend, is the thirteen hundredth footnote for my book, *The Rise and Fall of the Red Teutons*. It will be published in seven volumes next year."

"How about putting on an armband?"

"I will decline, sir, for personal reasons."

"Oh?"

"My wife is the director here."

○

Tom's neighbor waved a handful of leaflets. "Junk! It's ridiculous! Yes on this! No on that!"

"Yes on One," said Tom. "No on Two."

"Oh, you're such a liberal." She tossed it into the garbage.

"You're such a conservative." He loaded a pile of leaves into his wheelbarrow.

"I hate these political flyers and the ads on TV."

"Throw the flyers away."

"I just did."

"Don't watch TV."

"Okay, Mr. Liberal. Why no on Two?"

"Two is a ruse, Pam. Two is private enterprise's attempt to weaken unions and take money away from public education."

"But it's for grants to education."

"Courtesy of your tax money."

"Yes, but I can't vote against funding the education of American children."

"How about voting for someone who is in favor of tax money for public schools?"

"My son teaches in a private school. I'm voting for education."

"Well, that's better than voting for the hairdo."

"I have to remind you, Tom. I taught in the public schools for over thirty years. This is about choice."

"I taught in the public schools too. This is about money."

"I care about my son's family, their well-being."

"So, you're voting for your family's well-being?"

"Don't you care about your kids, your grandkids?"

"More than anything in the world. That's why I Occupy Front."

○

Tom held up his OUR NEIGHBORHOODS, OUR FUTURES, OUR VOICE sign, got a hug from Sandra, then ambled over to say hello to his favorite armbandit.

"Looking trim today, Rob."

"I'm eighty-four and I feel every minute of it."

"Want a few more armbands for the library?"

"Sure." Robert stuffed his pockets. "Now, where'd I put that damn thing? Oh, here it is. Have a look."

"I didn't realize the average American made forty-four thousand dollars a year," said Tom. "That's more than I ever made."

"More'n I ever made too. And look at the obscene annual salary of a defense worker."

"Eighty thousand. Union workers. Why am I not surprised?"

"That's nothing," said Robert. "Look at this chart. In 1982, the average

CEO pay was forty-two times the average worker pay. Today, it's three hundred and twenty-seven times as much—now that's obsce ..."

"Hey, guys," said the shabbily dressed man sporting a week-old beard. "I see you out here every Saturday. What's happening?"

"Occupy Front is happening," said Tom. "Join us."

"I gotta get to church." The guy moved in closer, and in a low voice said, "Did you see that homeless guy I was talking to? Claims he's Madonna's older brother. Swear to God."

"He is," said Tom. "I know Al."

"Madonna's big brother—homeless."

"So, what happened to you?"

"Me and the wife had it out. Couldn't take it anymore, didn't want to gob her face, so I walked out. No way I can go back now."

"Where are you staying?"

"At that church around the corner. Hey, I gotta run, they don't hold lunch for anybody, and I haven't eaten today."

"See you!" Tom waved good-bye just as a well-dressed woman stepped out of a double-parked Mercedes. "Hello, Bev!"

"Who's Bev?" asked Robert.

Tom was explaining to Robert, when a skidding Honda came to a stop, just nudging the double-parked car's fender. The driver's door opened.

Bev yelled, "Don't, Hamilton!"

Hamilton Z. Dempsey climbed slowly, deliberately, out of the Mercedes. The driver of the Honda, a girl of seventeen or so, had a look of terror on her face and a death grip on the wheel.

"What the hell do you think you're doing, you little bitch?!" The art school president pounded on the Honda's side window.

"Hamilton!" Bev tugged at his arm. "Please!"

"Don't you know where the brake is? Back this junk heap up! Open the door! Get the hell out of the car!" He banged on the top. "Do you have a fucking brain in your goddamn head, you ignorant little twit?"

Robert tapped him on the shoulder. "Excuse me, young man."

Z shrugged his hand off. "Out of my way, old codger!"

"You don't," said Robert, "have to shout. I may be old but I'm not deaf. You, sir, are out of order. Your language is execrable. My wife there, holding that PEACE sign, may be senile but her hearing is fine."

A staredown between Humpty and the octogenarian. The Occupyers held their signs and watched.

"It's all right, Hamilton." Bev pointed. "There's not even a scratch. Look."

"It's a company car," said Tom.

"It's insured," added Bev.

Z snarled, "A bunch of stupid girlies and sick, old coots." Scowling, he got back into the Mercedes and drove away.

Tom held his sign higher. "Hey, Bev, haven't seen you in a while. Did you manage yet to glance at *The Ping-Pong Club*?"

"Excuse me?"

"I'd like to know if you saw my book."

"What are you talking about?"

"I mailed a copy of *The Ping-Pong Club*. Did you see it?"

"I most certainly did not receive a book from you."

You didn't receive it because Hamilton opened the envelope, took one look, and mailed it back to me, with a note: "You are a sick old man, spreading trouble and dissent among the students to further your own sick purposes. Do not ever send me anything, anywhere, ever again, or you will be dealing with our lawyer."

42

"For in that sleep of death, when we have shuffled off
this mortal coil, what dreams may come?"
WILLIAM SHAKESPEARE, *HAMLET*

A spot of moonlight fell on his desk. The pen lay where he'd dropped it before collapsing into bed. Hand-printed text covered a white sheet of paper—the book arriving in the present—the now. He looked at the clock. Four a.m. He rubbed the sleep from his eyes. Through spasms of fatigue, he shook his head, remembered, got up, and paced the floor. Had it been a dream?

○

She is on a plane looking out the window, echoes of applause rolling away like distant thunder. The encores indicated it had been a good concert, well-attended and financed, sell-out crowds every day. Her performance had been as good as she'd expected, better than she'd rehearsed. "Fantastic fiddle pyrotechnics," wrote one critic.

Sheep-clouds sleep on a white quilt blanketing the earth. At the edges of the quilt, a sheet shimmers, the warm skin of life absorbing the sun's daily gift. A tiny lake, little more than a puddle, opens, like an eye upon the sky. Will she ever see her home on Grass again?

The phone call had come as she left the stage. It went through her like a lightning bolt and turned her into a well-tuned mechanical robot. She felt emptied and programmed for revenge.

Oh, if only she hadn't met the old man. How can he invade her privacy like this, parade her person around in public? She'd never misjudged character so completely. He dares use Mark's name! Tramples on his grave! If only she'd never gone to his armband days! Now the book was all over campus. She'll have to do something quickly before it's all over creation.

She should send an email to Dempsey: "Tom has reneged on his promise to take the book down. Out of common courtesy and consideration for my feelings, I am requesting that you make a formal campus-wide announcement. 'All students are hereby notified and required to bring any and all copies of *The Ping-Pong Club* to the Administration Office by noon tomorrow. After that time, students found in possession of the book will face disciplinary measures.'"

There. She leans back, studies the cloud quilt, and remembers. Her best violin student is, like Yu Liu had been, a favorite of the old man. Doreen will probably hide the book and take her chances on being expelled. If she does, others will.

What then? She could compose a campus-wide email: "Dear student artists, I need your help. Turn in one copy of *The Ping-Pong Club* to my studio by next Friday and receive a voucher worth $175, redeemable at the campus store. Two copies will give you $350."

That'll do the trick. Children love going to the store … and then it hits her. Doreen, like Yu Liu and so many other students, has a daddy who sends her hundreds of dollars every week for pocket change.

Aha! She will storm into Dempsey's office. "*The Ping-Pong Club* is a travesty of justice, an outrage, a violation of my privacy. You are giving the book a free pass, compromising my individual rights. I insist you use the full resources of the school to stop the book in its tracks. Sue the criminal who authored it. What are all your high-priced attorneys for anyway?"

Ha! His immoral book will land Tom behind bars. She rubs her hands together, then thinks, but if Hamilton Z. Dempsey had any intention of suing, he would have done so by now. He hasn't even banned the book; probably because he knows banning the book or suing Tom would turn *The Ping-Pong Club* into the worst imaginable thing: a hot commodity.

She racks her brain … what to do? She decides to ask her violin students to scour the campus from dorm to dorm and classroom to classroom. "Julie is calling a truce, burying the hatchet," they'll say. "She wishes to autograph each copy of *The Ping-Pong Club* personally. When she's finished, she'll return yours." How many kids will fall for the ruse? And how many copies are out there anyway? How many are in that secondhand store? Is there a single student who actually gives a crappy cadenza about her autograph?

Briefly, the idea of suing him herself dangles like bacon before a northern pike … then she realizes everything in the whole damned book actually happened! Suing is a black kite over a quilt of clouds blowing up a tornado. *The Ping-Pong Club* is true!

And on an otherwise inauspicious Sunday morning, at thirty years old and thirty thousand feet above the earth, Julie starts to cry. A minute later, she falls asleep. It will be dark when she pulls the red Jeep into the drive and gets her mail. *The Ping-Pong Club* will only be a bad dream.

○

A few years ago, Tom had helped form part of the zero in a giant human 350, the symbolic representation of the maximum parts per million of allowable carbon dioxide in the atmosphere of the only planet proven capable of supporting human life. Why didn't we get it? Governments get it, academics get it, the Pentagon gets it, energy CEOs get it—but the slave-hold is so busy getting and spending, they blame cows for farting? 9/11, the augury for a ball of hydrogen fire casting a shadow over all life, was a warning, a glitch, and Julie was a witness.

Diva-diverted, Tom follows an old-slave's inner GPS, turns off the highway, and drives down to the end of that narrow dead-end road. Every house is dark and curtained for the winter, awaiting the return of that inferno in the sky.

No WAH. Armband in hand, Tom steps from his truck into the wash and splash of waves on the lakeshore, the cry of a loon through the trees. The lake shimmers, no early-season fisherman is out trolling for bass, but a bass-drum rolls, humming from deep within the earth.

Has anyone checked her house? Tom jots a note: Heard a strange noise coming from under your house. He folds it into an armband and places it in Julie's mailbox.

He steps toward the lake, and smells it ... smoke. No doubt about it. Another step ... and the ground begins shaking like a leaf about to blow away. And he can see it! The house is on fire! A column of smoke and ash erupts, blotting out the sky. Flames burst through the roof, leaping toward the sun, going home. A roaring snarl of heat blasts him back, nearly blowing him away, and he turns and runs. Then turns back.

The next minute, the cottage is an inferno, a giant double orchestra is warming up, infernal timpani crashing and pounding a deafening din. Hell's atoms splitting, screaming, "DAMN!" In the conflagration are all of the little surfer girl's possessions, her violins, calendars, résumés, appointments, letters, acupuncture needles. Her music, books. Her mother's handmade wedding outfit.

Trembling, cursing, he scoops up snow, throws it at the flames, flings snowballs at the madness of fire climbing a satanic fuse in full discharge! A diabolical devil towers over him, laughing. Satan! Soul-seared, broken like kindling, an old slave stuffed with straw, Tom falls to the ground.

In what seems no time, the monster's appetite is slaked and the flames subside. Gasping for breath, trying to fill a hollow burnt inside his chest, Tom rises, wads an armband into a ball, tosses it at the flames. He starts his personal hell-on-wheels, spins the tires, and is dialing 911 before he arrives at the beginning of the dead end.

In the little gift shop, *The Ping Pong Club* lay as usual—six copies on the front counter—but today, a newspaper covered the books, and the article caught his eye.

Shawni frowned. "It's crazy, Tom. Since September my sales have been off ten percent. Is it possible President Dempsey warned the students about carrying your book?"

The headline read: **FIRE RAVAGES GRASS LAKE APARTMENT.**

> Departments from several districts in the area were called out to a house fire on Grass Lake yesterday. The small apartment on the shore of the lake appeared to be built over a boathouse or a sort of storage area. A fire department official commented, "By the time we got there, it was too late to save it. The location of the building was remote and some distance from the highway. We had trucks and personnel in place, but all we could do was contain. Fortunately, no one was home at the time." When asked if the home had been occupied, the spokesman declined to comment.

"The only Interotten customer I've had," said Shawni, "was a little Asian girl. Last week. Said she teaches violin."

"Thirty? Terrific smile? Personality to burn?"

"Yeah," said Shawni. "Pretty little thing."

Lowering his voice, Tom asked, "Was she driving a red Jeep?"

"I think it was a Jeep. Red anyway. Decal on the rear said WAH. She was shopping for a bride-to-be, a friend in California."

"She's there now," said Tom. "Probably surfing in the Pacific."

Shawni sighed. "Ah, I wish I was in California."

43

"Regular puzzle solving has a positive effect on the brain."

MAJID FOTUHI, *KEEPING YOUR BRAIN YOUNG*

A month later, the bass note was still murmuring when the phone rang.

"Tom? Lyle. Don't quite know how to tell you … can we get together?"

The bass note plummeted down his spine, rolled like thunder over the graves in Old Town Glades, and woke the depths of his being.

Silently cursing *The Ping Pong Club,* Tom said, "Let me guess. She fired you?"

"Joanne, I need help." After he sounded the call, Tom picked up his all-time favorite mail room helper, and drove to the stump in the park. Joanne ventured across the road; Tom settled down with a book of crossword puzzles. Six months and a dozen Armband Days had passed since the little surfer's house fire. Through Jeanette and Bernie, he learned the teachers had passed the hat, collecting enough to tide Julie over.

The old pine stump felt rugged as ever. After finishing a puzzle, he shifted his cushion—a bag of t-shirts—and glanced across the road to the main entrance. The school was preparing for another commencement, seven student revolutionaries and ten ping-pong players from last year would attend. Tom had alerted them all: he'd be right here, across from the main entrance with a founder shirt for any brave student who dared to violate Humpty Dumpty's prohibition.

"I found him!" Joanne crossed the road. "In the library. We chatted for an hour."

"Told you. Baxter's the nicest guy I know. Did you give him the book?"

"*The Ping-Pong Club*? Sure did; he said to thank you. But how did you know he was a crossword geek like you?"

"It's a long story."

Joanne settled on the stump, ready to listen.

"Once upon a time," Tom began, "Queen Off-With-His-Head was a perky princess with ambition and a crush on her piano teacher. He was a good teacher, too, but the queen saw a musical career befuddled by brilliance. You see, Joanne, Baxter possessed an all-consuming, encyclopedic memory. So one day, Alice suggested he apply for a job that just opened at the art school—accompanist. He got the job and they were married. They lived quite happily for a while, too, Alice bearing Baxter, to his delight, a son. Alice began moving through administrative ranks, making it up to the very pinnacle.

"Baxter was demoted slowly by Humpty, until he found himself planted alone in the basement, deep in the roots of school archives, where the old key plunker had job security. After twenty years, Humpty Dumpty didn't know how to get rid of him. No camper, student, or teacher knew as much about the school as Baxter.

"For a while after my termination, I visited Buddie's on Sunday morning. Sipping coffee there a few weeks ago, I spotted Baxter working over *The New York Times* crossword, and right away I recognized a lost brother. Over Baxter's shoulder, I solved one entry; he solved another, and the plan hatched itself. You see, Joanne, my kid brother, Landon, could also spend hours digging up crossword trivia from the graveyard of memory. He and I both loved searching for clues, scratching up facts and figures, and forgotten details. Especially, we loved the Sunday *New York Times* puzzle. Crosswords were the mortar cementing our relationship. I miss Landon.

"The next Sunday, I raced to the store, bought the paper, rushed home, and got to work, completing the crossword in record time. I drove to Baxter's and knocked on the door. 'Done!' I pronounced. 'Only took three hours!'

"'Oh, I've been done,' said Baxter, 'for a while.' We compared solutions and decided to call it a draw."

"Even though he won," said Joanne.

"Crossword combatants eschew competition."

"What are you talking about?" asked Joanne.

"He admitted the puzzle had been a tough one. I took that as a concession. Which is where we are now."

"It's a draw, huh? So, Tom, what's the plan?"

"He and I both like the Sunday puzzle. We solve until I can somehow get him to tell the truth about Alice, to put it out where everybody can see it. To be my witness."

"In court? So, the crossword book was a ruse to rouse Baxter's interest?"

"I do like doing puzzles, you know."

"What about 'Start no fear'?"

"That's why we're here today. Fifty alums said they'd come help protest. Occupyers, students, faculty, friends. I've even scheduled a special performer. Remember Louis Penfold?"

"That guy who sang at Occupy? Woo! Woo! Is he coming?"

"Said he would … hold on."

A big man in a security guard uniform was crossing the road.

"Uh-oh," said Tom. "Better hide those shirts."

Joanne covered the box. Tom called out, "Hello, Jack! Haven't seen you since Occupy Front. What are you doing in a school uniform?"

"I'm the new director. Got the job right after the election."

"Sorry about that."

"Of course," said Jack, smiling, "you mean you're sorry about the sheriff job."

"Ha, ha. Yes, of course. I voted for you, too, for all the good it did. Congratulations. You're a slave now."

"Never been anything but. Now, see here, Tom, you're not planning any trouble, are you? I warned Mr. Penfold, also warned the students, to stay out of the park, and not to get into any mischief."

"Mischief? I'm just spreading dissent among the students to further my own sick purposes."

"Ha!" Joanne laughed. "That's what Dempsey said about you!"

"Meet Jo, Jack."

"Hello, Miss Jo. Are you a student here?"

"Do I look like one?"

"Yes, you do. What's your last name?"

"I won't tell you my name. I don't have to. And I can be here if I want. It's a public park."

"Ohhh no, missy, you cannot. Not if you're a student."

"What are you gonna do about it?" Joanne stood.

Jack reached out for her shoulder. "Tell me honestly, now, Missy Jo, or whatever your name is …"

"Tess!" said Tom. "Her name is Tess Trueheart, Jack. She worked for me in the mail room. Graduated last year."

"True!" said Joanne, turning.

"Oh, no," said Jack, grabbing both of her shoulders. "If you're Tess, I'm Dick, the Sheriff of Nottingham."

Joanne twisted and slapped his hands away. "Try this, Dick!" She sprinted to the road, yelling over her shoulder, "Catch me, copper, if you can!"

"Okay, Tess," said Jack, "you win. Don't get into any mischief." Then, with a serious look, he said, "You know, Tom, you two troublemakers are asking for it. I'm not so sure I should leave you here."

"How about a shirt?" Tom held one up to Jack's broad chest.

"I know a few things about you, Tom. You're a decent chap who got the wrong end of a short stick. Believe it or not, I'm sorry about it, but it is what it is."

"True."

"And you'd like to get even."

"Untrue."

"Oh, come on, Tom, you can be frank. I'm your friend."

"I am frank and you aren't. I'm here to spread dissent and you're here to shut me up."

"You don't have a grudge against Dempsey?"

"There's not a vengeful bone in my body, Jack."

"'Start no fear?' What does that mean?"

"Show them art, not fear. It means we've got a big problem in this country, and I'm addressing it the best way I can." Tom faced the failed candidate for sheriff and looked him in the eye. "How'd you know about our 'Start no Fear' rally? Have you been peeking at my Facebook page?"

"Yes. It is public."

"You're a decent chap yourself. Join us, Jack. We won't bite. Stand up for art, not fear. Dempsey has you by the balls, and he knows how to twist. How much did he offer you?"

"Mmm …"

"It's okay, I won't tell anyone."

"Well, now. I like you, Tom. You're my kind of guy, and I'm not afraid of Dempsey. He said if I keep my mouth shut, which I'm not, I could be in six figures in a few years."

"Word raises."

"What? You were probably making close to six figures in the mail room."

Tom wrote a number on the old pine stump.

"Oh, my. You weren't even middle class."

"The earnings gap between boss and slave grows wider every day."

"Which is why I wanted to be sheriff. The boss."

"Even the sheriff must submit to authority."

"Right. The judge."

"Wrong. The other judge."

On cue, a sheriff's patrol car turned into campus. Tom stepped into the road. "As of now, Jack," he said over his shoulder, "I am submitting to your authority."

"Whoa there, mister mailman. Get your ass back here. You can't step on campus!"

The ex-candidate for sheriff hoisted extra-large trousers and started off in hobbling pursuit. Except for the blue security cap, he could have been a rhino on a run through the park.

44

"… and then we were running across the pasture toward the house without remembering when we got to our feet. We seemed to run forever with our heads back and our fists clenched before we reached the fence and fell over it and ran on into the house."

WILLIAM FAULKNER, *THE UNVANQUISHED*

"Action! Roll cameras!"

Tom starts to run, fast, then faster, past Admissions with a full head of steam, past Tom Jefferson dorm, ascending the seventh step to heaven, up the steps and across the stage of the outdoor auditorium, taking a bow before his imaginary audience, dashing past Humpty Z. Dumpster's office window.

At the ping-pong dorm, he stops. Reflection? Bottle cap spun to the ground? Outside Julie's studio window, a daffodil planted by one of her students blazes golden as sunlight, pure as a mountain stream. Farewell!

Farewell! Tom runs on, past the ping-pong dorm, past Visual Arts, scene of Medusa's transformation, past Mary Towney, where Queen Off-With-His-Head threatened to sue me. He splats through the mud where the director's purse fell. He tears past the chapel, scene of faculty and student recitals. He flies by Facilities and Human Resources and sprints down the stairs into the mail room, sweeps past a chipmunk on the conveyor belt into the past, and comes to rest. For right or wrong, for richer or for poorer, for love or for money, the old slave has arrived.

Joanne is running. "Wait! Tom, wait! You're not gonna believe this! There's security guys blocking every exit in the dorms. They even called the sheriff."

"I know."

"It's all over campus! And there's something else. My old English teacher just told me."

"Jeanette? She wouldn't snitch on me."

"I know! It's not that!" Joanne lowers her eyes, scuffs the ground with a shoe. "I'm sorry, Tom. Ms. Gordon confirmed it."

"Confirmed what?"

"Confirmed what *The Ping-Pong Club* hinted would happen."

It would never happen! Progress reversed! A broken Bach of promises and backroom deals! All his alarms off, caution flags waving, falling out of orbit. The chipmunk comes around the corner to see if the coast is clear; a sob breaks from the burnt-out hole in the old freeman's chest. "Shoo!"

"Julie quit!"

Tom falls. Joanne reaches to help, too late. "Oh, my god!" She cups her hand over her mouth in a silent scream, staring like Medusa at a dry seedpod on a withered stem in a heap of straw and stubble. Nothing is certain. Human endeavor a fabrication, the play of a limited imagination.

"Quiet on the set!"

"Action!"

Doors slamming. Dishes, pots, and pans crashing. Conveyor belts humming. Chairs skidding along the floor.

"Is he dead yet?"

"I don't think so."

"You're right."

"Stop blinking, Tom. You're dead."

A hand presses his chest, another his forehead.

Familiar smells—bacon, coffee, cakes, floor cleaner—reminders of routine, a job, remuneration. He moves a leg, lifts an arm, strokes a forehand loop. A paddle with his name on it is down there in the ping-pong dorm basement. Children at play—a little warm-up, the ball spun backward into his hand under the table—guess which hand and win first serve.

"Cut! Okay, Tom, nice job. That's it, everybody."

He opens his eyes. The cafeteria tables have been pulled into a makeshift cot beside the entrance. Through the window in the door, the lake shimmers green, unearthly, waiting. To and fro, faceless people carry trays and plates empty of food.

Matty is piling props on a cart. "We'll splice in the sound when we get back," he says to no one. He points, and a grip slides a tree of lights onto the cart. Mason walks in to consult with his student director, but Matty shakes his head. "Not now," he says. "Next we're shooting the life-after-death scene."

"You can go now, Tom," says Kylie, waiting to push the tables back. *"The shoot's done."*

The cafeteria door opens and Julie enters, chin high, head erect, eyes straight ahead. Never has she looked more beautiful.

Tom is shivering with cold and sweating as if in a sauna. A practice-room sauna. "Julie," he croaks.

"Yes?"

Words are tears. "Will ... you still ..."

"Will I still buy you that lunch? Of course, I will. Just as soon as you erase me from that book."

Jack waddles into the cafeteria and Tom musters all his strength. "Congrat— u—lations Julie."

"For what?"

"For keeping ... your integrity."

Jack levels a finger. "You there, Free Man! Gotcha covered. Stand down on the floor. Everybody! Over here! Cast, stand down on the floor! Hands behind your backs."

They form a circle, hands linked behind. On Tom's right, all in white and ready to take the stage, Yu Liu squeezes his hand. "It's not done? When will it be?"

Moira takes Yu's hand; Sven, Moira's. Someone comes and takes Tom's left hand ... Mark.

When will it be done? Thy will be done when the flag of the subconscious is burned and seared with warnings: Change course! Go no further! Instant death ahead!

Thy will be done on Mother Earth when Father Fire, this time, hovering over the carbon atoms of every home, school, church, and library, comes to take His bride.

Thy will be done in Heaven, as it was in the beginning, when the voice of God plays the *Sonata in A Minor* on a half-size violin as a nine-year-old, all the way through to the end.

PART THREE
INTEROTTEN

45

"The success of his novel will change his life, charge it with experiences at a more intense level; the people he encounters will have more sense of mission, be more exciting in both their good and in their evil."

NORMAN MAILER

Imagine the imagination never sleeps, she just takes to bed early, a little more tired than usual—nothing to shake a fist at, nothing to write home about. Good night, sweet dreams.

But in the middle of the night, you wake in a sweat. What's that? A plane? Through your ceiling of compromised security comes the bass drone! Fearful, trembling, you imagine the end is near, the word made flesh! In a spotlight aimed by the voice of God, your bed an ice floe in an ocean of flames leaping round on all sides, you enter a make-believe world on your belly. On stage, dressed all in black, is a cast of thousands. A beautiful cadaver plays the part of the violin. Opening your mouth to speak, you catch a muse of fire.

The plot is a Ponzi scheme around the voice of God. Everyone loses— you, your boss, your pipe-dreamed vision of support—even the owners of the theater lose. Under your bed, the red Jeep crashes, flips over, and you doze off, sleep shaking its fist at a fictional pawn. Silence, and then the blooming bud of perception takes the stage, a flower in her smile and a spark in her eyes.

Against this earthly background of workplace props, the silken shiver of her bow once again pierces your heart. *Arco!* A mirage of song and word dances forward. The fleeting sacred invades the profane, trumpets announce an original composition for violin, and presto! A new arrival: the virgin conceives.

Exiting the stage, she takes the nonessential parts: horoscopes, acupuncture needles through the brow, repositories of hope and trust. Vetoing the president of mind, she carves the white meat from a wasp and leaves the bait for a black widow borne on her arrow to pick your skeleton clean. Tossing the last crumb—love—into her bag, she bows, waves, blows a kiss, and the curtain comes down.

The earth forever moves from shadow to light, night to day, as memory, the messenger, moves from past to present to enter your orbit and crash into your future. For too long you stay in bed. A patriarch falls in the forest. Sweat and blood and random coincidence strike the pine stump. A fallen fawn waits for danger to pass before springing to its feet to rejoin the cast.

You open your eyes. A partially completed *New York Times* crossword puzzle—charred, covered in dirt—is at your feet. The dragonfly on your knee unfolds its wings in the sun, turns into a maple seed. A chipmunk scampers over the puzzle and darts into a fallen log.

Art lifts the ban. Awareness rises. Baxter raises his baton, and one by one theater majors step into roles written for them hundreds of years ago. One school year ends, another begins. Alone among pines you stand, find your center of gravity, get in your truck, and drive to the store.

○

"I heard about Julie's fire." Darlene stepped aside with her cart, inviting Tom to take her place in line.

"Thanks, dear." A regular customer, delighted to be back in his old store, Tom paid for his armband tape. "Don't take any wooden nickels, Mary," he said to the cashier, then waited in the bagging area to watch the former executive secretary load the belt.

"I also heard," said Darlene, placing a can on top of a loaf of bread, "the faculty took up a collection. She lost everything."

"She move in with Drake and Jorna?"

"Yes, unfortunately. At least she wasn't hurt."

Freeing the bread, Tom said, "She was hurt."

"Horrible. Enough to make a grown woman cry. Everyone was talking about it." Darlene swiped her card. "What's wrong with this?"

Doing double duty ringing up purchases while eavesdropping on a conversation, Mary pointed at the card. "Stick it in the chip reader."

Darlene tried again. "I heard they held a meeting to help her out. Julie was so popular … oh, dear. It's still not working."

Mary rotated her hand.

Darlene tried again. "What do you suppose caused the fire?"

"Who knows?" said Tom. He finished bagging Darlene's groceries and put them in a shopping cart. "But I do know why Julie quit. Because of the book."

"Your book? *The Ping-Pong Club*? Come off it, Tom. It was because of the fire."

Mary handed Darlene her receipt with a patented thank you, a packaged smile, and a sigh of relief.

Tom sighed too. "Julie was afraid her job was toast; she'd be just another fire in a book of Hamilton Z. Dempsey firings."

"Why'd you say Hamilton made the call? Alice was your boss."

"Alice told me, Daryl, and Keith when she handed me my pink slip. *The Ping-Pong Club* was too hot for her to handle."

"It's okay, Tom." Darlene put a hand on his arm. "I don't care."

Tom pushed the cart to the door. "See you later, Mary."

"Oh, wow," said Darlene in the parking lot. "I just thought of something. Humpty Z. Dumpster meant to fire Julie, missed, and fired her house!"

"Humpty Dumpty doesn't miss. Julie fired herself. Like me."

"Well, it's over now, thank God."

"It's not over, it's a break. A calm before the storm. Another boss will come in, clear the ground, hang his nameplate, call a meeting: 'Time to move on, folks …'"

"I don't get it."

"He may even fire someone. It's what middle managers do—ignore the coming storm. No more business as usual, Darlene. The underground plates have shifted."

"What on earth are you talking about?"

"I'm talking about a quiver on the cosmic seismograph."

"The cosmic *what*?"

"Seismograph. The new boss will have to think twice before he fires someone." Tom finished setting Darlene's groceries in the trunk of her car and closed the lid. "It's time."

"Time for what?"

"For slaves to speak out. Slaves like me. Like Julie."

"She wasn't a slave. You can call her a slave until you're blue in the face but she was different."

"She was a virtuoso … a paddleboard rainbow."

Darlene nodded. "She was beautiful."

"She wanted to be bolder and more courageous."

"Well, of course." Fluttering her eyelashes, Darlene said, "We could all be bolder and more courageous. But I'll say one thing about you, Tom; you're persistent."

A beer truck, diesel droning dully, backed slowly to the freight door of the store. "Thanks, Darlene." Tom leaned against the trunk of the car, remembering.

"I like Hank's," said Darlene, her voice coming as if from far away. "They've got good meat here." She pointed across the road. "But over there, at Herb's, cashiers start at nine dollars an hour."

The voice on the phone: "Uncle Landon's dead!" The shockwave was a typhoon coming ashore; your world tipped, ripped open. Your instincts grew limbs, climbed your inner walls, leaped from your chest like spiders hunting flies. The bass drone became a river in flood, burst its banks, blindsiding your boatman with an unruly rudder, and you capsized, fell to the floor. Suddenly you were running into the forest, fighting for air, yelling, Landon! You ran for miles. Landon! Tossing your brother's name to the wind, planting a decimal point on the bottom line of the brick wall you built between truth and fiction. Landon! Another needle under tall pines on a branch of fathers and sons broken off, falling from an everlasting sky. Landon! You ran and ran until at the old pine stump you fell to your knees and heaved words, columns, pages, books onto the ground, sobbing until your breath fled on firefly wings and left you gasping for air, and there was only silence inside.

Darlene grasped his hand. "So, Tom, will you keep handing out those old paper armbands at the library?"

"I don't know. The old slave is feeling his age."

Like someone reading in bad light, she looked Tom straight in the eye. "I hate that word."

"Age?"

"Slave! I wish you'd call a job by its proper name: director, associate, vice president …"

"Dog-shitter. Asshole-she-ate. Vice-producer."

"Oh, piddle. Why don't you call yourself the old serf? Call me the little serf-er girl?"

You remembered the next day. The campus was a-buzz with students arriving from all over the world, meeting old friends and greeting new— moving their lives to Interotten. A new school year about to begin! A fresh season of change! You remembered the packages arriving, box after box, addressed to a certain Julie. You stacked them in a corner of the mail room.

After sorting the incoming, delivering to Humpty Z. Dumpster's office, and making the first campus run, you were metering outgoing when a dazzling smile appeared at the window.

"Hi, there! Any packages for me?"

"Let's see ... for Julie?"

"Yes!"

You placed the packages on the conveyor belt. "That your red Jeep outside there?"

"Yes!"

She went out to load the Jeep. Through the open hatch door you asked, "Are you a teacher?"

"I'm a musician."

"What do you play?"

"Violin."

"I calls them as I sees them. Right now, I sees a beer truck."

"One of the last," said Doreen.

"What do you mean?"

"You haven't heard? Hank's is closing in a month ... going out of business."

46

"I don't miss my thoughts. Whatever they are thinking in there hidden from my awareness doesn't harm me or anyone else."
ANDREI CODRESCU

On the phone: "Dustin! Good to hear your voice."

"I called, Tom, because Dean Warren emailed me to say Miss Saigon is pissed off. I mean thoroughly."

"Miss Saigon?"

"Do you remember posting a status on Facebook that wasn't exactly complimentary to Humpty Dumpty?"

"I post a lot of over-ripe fruit."

"I don't know how you get away with it. Anyway, you wrote a few words about our violin friend, and the dean shared your post with her. You know, Tom, after you came that day looking for her, I started paying more attention to your book. That 'ping-pong club.' That 'Queen Off-With-His-Head,' 'voice of God' claptrap. You could be in some serious shit. Harassing is a crime."

"Grist for the gossip mill."

"She also made allegations pertaining to a fire at her cabin—you know, that lakeside cottage? She was renting it. It belonged to a mutual friend Hamilton Z fired years ago."

"I read about the fire in the paper."

"Miss Saigon accuses you of burning it down. I'm aghast, Tom, and surprised you aren't. Don't you feel a bit under a cloud?"

"Like I said—news of the fire was in the paper. Julie demanded I throw *The Ping-Pong Club* away, and I almost did, but instead I put it in the compost where it belongs. Compost: proof of life after death. It's in the library."

"Listen, Tom. Before you go off, it doesn't make any difference to me what happened to your book or what sordid things people claim about you. I'm no witness, and no longer an employee of the school—I'd just like to know as much as I can about the tyrant screwing my friends. Jim admitted there are no legal incriminations involving his cabin. Thank God. I am concerned, however, about Julie's claim of harassment."

○

"Fictionalized!" Tom turned into the familiar alley and parked. "A drama of ancient tribal customs. Orchestrated by the students! Ever been here?"

"No." His sister looked around. "You say there's music?"

"Music, dance, drama—an historical performance! Welcome to the Inverted Art."

In the vestibule of the little gallery, a small string ensemble was warming up. The violin looked, smiled, and put her bow down.

"Tom!"

"Doreen! Are you guys playing tonight?"

"Yes! Our first concert of the year ... my senior year!"

"Four years of practice! Practice rooms rock."

"I wish we were still down there playing ping-pong."

"Me too, if you'd learned how."

Doreen stuck out her tongue.

"Meet my sister, Betty, a ping-pong clubber before there was a club."

"Glad to meet you. Enjoy the show, Tom!"

They found seats in the front row. The program said: "Every element of this opera, the entire production and direction of this performance except the plot was created by students; they wrote the script, built the sets, composed the music, and improvised on it."

Betty murmured, "What an intimate little venue."

The lights dimmed and the band began to play. The Boss entered: "All will take their places and their turns."

A spotlight fell on a beat-up cardboard box front and center, so close Tom could touch it.

"You will draw your number," said The Boss. "One number for each, one at a time. All right! Begin!"

A hush fell. Names were called. One by one the actors stepped forward.

Betty whispered, "Why are they all acting so frightened?"

"The Boss," said Tom, "is brutal. The box is scary—it's the status quo."

"What's scary about the status quo?"

"No one wants to break with tradition."

The final actor to draw a number, an Asian girl named Estelle, reached into the box. The chorus moaned, "Oooooh noooooo." Doreen's violin screeched cacophony.

Estelle held the slip of paper. Full vibrato she sang: "Almighty God, what have we become? When will we be free?" Her hands trembled violently; her soprano voice could have been the wailing lament of a child lost in the wilderness.

Betty elbowed Tom. "Shh, little boy. Grow up."

Tom's lips wouldn't stop quivering.

"She won," said Betty. "Be happy for her."

"Too late. Money has declared war on people. Anno Domini. Redistribution of wealth in the form of population control. Estelle will be stoned."

"For what purpose," sang Estelle, "do we live?"

A bass began the chant: "Lottery in June ..." A soprano picked it up; another bass came in, a tenor, an alto, and then the entire troupe of singer-actors circled the stage, each holding a fictional ear of corn like a knife and intoning with increasingly restless sadness: "Lottery in June, corn be heavy soon."

Other members of the audience were dabbing their eyes with tissues.

"Come on, little boy," Betty whispered. "Let's go."

"After you, sis. Anyway, it's almost over."

○

On the shoulder of the road the deer lay on her side, one leg over a partially delivered fawn ... earth to earth ... Tom brought an oak branch down hard twice. He dragged the carcasses farther off the road, and laid them in a hollow slowly filling with leaves. The doe's eyes continued to gaze upon her killer.

A firetruck roared by, its siren screaming MAMA MAMA, and then everything grew still. He caught a glimpse of something moving in the trees ... another fawn? An older, wiser sibling?

The red Jeep! He peered closer. The Jeep was pulling into the little surfer's cottage. Except it was blue! And then it was gone; in its place, a pile of rocks and broken slabs of concrete. Chunks of brick, glints of glass, splinters of charred wood. And a sign: For Sale.

A question too hot for his sleeping brain to handle veered, swerved, wobbled, and crashed into the ditch, flipped over on its back, and lay there, wheels spinning.

47

"The steady onslaught of information about a problem over
which people feel little sense of personal agency gives
rise to a feeling of futility—informed futility."

SANDRA STEINGRABER

Morning commuters sped past. Behind Tom, the Firestone Inn
loomed dark and shuttered. Once a venue for B.B. King, Bo Didley, and
other blues artists, the Inn also drew Interotten students vying for the
privilege of performing on its stage; its unique setting in a northern pine
forest attracted folk-music fans from all over the Midwest. Hundreds of
student dreams were born at the Firestone. The inn was a treasure house
of extraordinary memories but also abounded with rumors—of a casino
in the kitchen, of an upstairs brothel, of Jimmy Hoffa buried out back.

A small car stopped and Tom climbed in.

"Well?" asked the driver, the Democrat candidate for the U.S. Senate.
"Did you bring it?"

Tom handed George *The Ping-Pong Club*.

From the backseat, a voice: "Where's mine?"

"Here you go," said Tom. "Free of charge, but not of innuendo."

"Sign it, please," said Fiona.

Tom autographed the book, George stepped on the gas, and off they
went to Little Big Rapids College and a conference on Women and the
Environment.

"Who's the speaker?" wondered Tom.

"Sandra Steingraber," replied Fiona. "A biologist."

"She's an environmentalist," said George. "And a poet."

"And a mom," added Fiona, "who just got out of jail."

Fiona and George filled Tom in during the three-hour drive; by the time they arrived at the college, a block-long line had formed outside the auditorium.

"Nice crowd," said George. "Practically all women."

"I expected there to be a few more informed followers of the masculine persuasion."

"Men are pigs," said Fiona. "Boars in suits."

"Present company excluded," said George. "I'm so glad you came, Tom, and so excited to see your book. I can't wait to read it."

"Watch out, George. He'll put you in it."

"That would be interesting." The Senate candidate went off to glad-hand the girls; while Fiona, sporting a red-white-and-blue button, busily handed out brochures.

Tom pointed to Fiona's collar. "What's that mean?"

"What's what mean? Oh, my GMO button? It means Get the fucking Men Out of fucking politics."

"Ha ha." Tom chuckled. "Or Go Mad Online."

"George Mendez of the people."

"Grand Motherfucking Old party."

"Get Me Out of this place. General Motors Owns you. We've got hundreds more … oh, look. It's starting."

A hostess gave a short history of the group and the purpose of the meeting. The treasurer's update followed, then a panel report; finally, the featured speaker stepped up to the podium.

"It might be easy to wish you'd skipped this show altogether," began Ms. Steingraber, "once you get my message."

Like a teenager, Fiona nodded her head.

"Our environment," the speaker went on, "is centered in the most serious crisis in history; we've built our house on un-decayed dead plants and animals."

Stunned, Tom got Sandra's message.

After touching on the oxygen cycle, photosynthesis, parenting, and high school education, rhyming them all with her experience as a biologist and mother, Sandra threw nonrenewable resources over the heads of her audience and out the window. "Those dead plants were squashed into petroleum, gas, and coal. We know where they came from, how they got there, and why we're willing to risk our children's futures burning them, but we don't know their whole story. We don't even know how nature manages to split the water molecule."

Tom felt like they were all drowning in scientific analysis and he was a bystander at a firestorm in an oil field—an irrefutable crisis of our own making. Hit broadside by the fact—no future with fossil fuels—he vowed to get rid of his truck and never drive again.

Ms. Steingraber delineated the problems associated with global climate change and zeroed in on fracking. No doubt about it. The extraction process known as horizontal hydraulic fracturing defined a world with no future. "We worked," she said, "against corporations poisoning the environment for years ... protesting, making phone calls, writing letters and media stories, calling press conferences, circulating petitions. We went to jail. And we finally won! If we can ban fracking in New York, you can do it here in Michigan!"

Tom jumped to his feet, applauding wildly. "Yes," he yelled, "we can!"

Fiona joined him, then George, and then the entire audience of feminists stood, giving the speaker a standing ovation.

George said, "I want her autograph." He and Tom got in line with other autograph seekers. "Good speech, eh, Tom?"

"I'd say. What's with the book?"

"Sandra's novel: *Raising Elijah*. Here, have a look."

"Hmm." *Index, bibliography, table of contents.* "It's not a novel."

George had Ms. Steingraber's ear. "... what about money for wind or solar?"

"Solid investing," said the environmentalist, "in the future. In people. In food."

Tom interrupted, "Ms. Steingraber?"

"Call me Sandra."

"Call me Tom. I grow my own food."

"That is great ... if you are organic."

"I am. Listen, Sandra, I looked at your book. You said that when your son found out about fracking he burst into tears."

"That was ... difficult. Elijah was five; we were at breakfast. We had a No Yuck rule at the table—no outbursts, scenes, tears—but he wouldn't stop crying. I said I was going to stop fracking. Just like that, he stopped crying."

"It really happened? Weren't you afraid? I mean, of going to jail?"

"Luckily, I had the support of our faculty committee."

"Sandra, I've gone to jail too, for protesting."

"Protesting what?"

"Vietnam."

Sandra nodded. "People should speak up against war. I chose to protest pollution and the poisons in our food."

"You're an informer informing the unread," said Tom, "in the age of information. You call it 'informed futility.' The more people learn, the more paralyzed they become ... silenced, incapable of taking action."

"For sure. Yet action is precisely what is needed. Don't stop. If one person speaks up, steps up, others will follow, it's like David slinging pebbles at Goliath. We must speak up literally, figuratively, and often against abusive corporate authority. This war will take our wallets, our voices, and our votes—every pebble we can muster, in fact."

"I'm mustering. Here's my pebble." Tom handed Sandra a copy of *The Ping-Pong Club*. "Can one jailbird give another a book?"

"Hold on." Sandra ducked behind the podium, dug into a bag, brought up a copy of *Raising Elijah* …fledgling authors figuratively on the same page. "Fair trade?"

"Calling it fair trade doesn't make it fair."

"Call it free trade then."

"I call *The Ping-Pong Club* a novel."

Sandra laughed. "My book's the furthest thing from a novel."

"Will you autograph it, please?"

"Of course, if you sign yours. But is yours really a novel, Tom?"

○

After the long drive home, they were approaching the Firestone Inn. In the backseat, Fiona had found her very own chapter and verse in the book. "Yow!" she giggled. "I didn't say that!"

"I said it," said Tom. "Turn left, George… and, please, turn the radio up. The news is on."

"Okay, Tom. You think Bernie should have been on the ticket?"

Tom put a finger to his lips.

The news was devastating.

"Trumplestiltskin?" Fiona shouted. "Are you fucking kidding me?"

"A tidal wave has hit both coasts," said George, pulling into Tom's driveway.

"And hit," said Fiona, "the Democratic National Committee between the eyes."

"Looks like trouble," said George, "on homefield."

"With a capital T," said Tom.

"We'll be looking for some extra canvassing help on my race."

"Count me in."

48

"The very existence of libraries affords the best evidence that
we may yet have hope for the future of man."

T. S. ELIOT

Bursting like a dolphin through the surface, the boy waded to shore, climbed onto the beach, and put a finger in the air. "One." Hopping back and forth on bare feet, "But at the Albatross Club," he said, "we do three."

"C'mon Sven," said Tom, throwing a towel in his direction. The boy threw it right back, dove in, came out, turned around, dove back into the lake, and came out shivering. Tom threw him the towel again; this time the boy kept it. "It's a ritual," Sven said, quickly drying himself off. "Third time's a charm."

Tom handed him a dry shirt. "Albatross Club, huh?"

Ah, yes, you've been there where your eldest was born just across the bay. Erica was born without defects, a beautiful perfect baby in every way, unlike you ...

"Sorry. This boy will never walk. The Achilles tendons are too short." *The doctor shook his head.*

"Please, Doctor," *pleaded your mother.* "Can't you help?"

"It could cost you an arm and a leg."

"We're new here," *said Father.* "I'm a shoe clerk at Penney's."

"Tell you what. There's a surgeon in Canada who's having success splicing primate tendons. He just lengthened an ape's Achilles. It's a correction, though, not a cure."

"I believe in you, Doctor," *said Mother.*

"I believe," *said Father,* "in the New Deal."

"These are tough times," said the doctor. "FDR is helping us get through it but we must all pitch in. Well, let's have a go at Tom's feet."

"How much?" asked Father.

"No charge."

And so, the tendons on your corkscrew feet were spliced and plaster casts applied. Every Sunday for the next year Father drove you to the hospital to have the old casts removed and new plaster applied. One day, as your brother and sister were playing hide-and-seek, you stood for the first time on wooden crutches and took a step, a step that set the tinder in tendons aflame and you grew wings. You were a great white heron parting low ebbs of fear on high winds of hope, gaining altitude and momentum: "Look, Ma! No hands!"

Al looked like he'd been sleeping in his clothes for a week. The homeless man levered a bicycle up the stairs from the river, eyed the cash in Sven's guitar case. "All right!" he said, nodding his head and drumming handlebars with his fingers. The bag of returnable bottles draped over the bars rattled with the beat.

Sven was finding his groove. Pedestrians paused to toss coins and the occasional bill into the case. A girl of four or five watched Tom put a dollar in, asked her mother, got the dollar, and followed the leader. Across the river, another busker pounded on a tambourine. All up and down Front, amateur musicians framed chord changes, sang, and fiddled away in the time-honored tradition of busking.

"Ooh! Wahh!" sang the bike man, bobbing his head, snapping his fingers—a live, impromptu rhythm section.

"Hello, Al," said Tom, clapping the man on the shoulder. "Haven't seen you in a while."

Eyes closed. "Don't hit me, man." Squinting, "What's that on your front?" Tracing the letters on Tom's shirt, Al tried spelling, "I A-m T-h-e … what the fuck? I can't read the rest."

"Take your time."

"F-o- …" Al scratched his chin. "You are the fonder?"

"I am the founder. In six languages."

"You foundered sumthin'? No shit."

"Found means start."

"Whatzat at the bottom … hey! Izzat that place down the road? With all those rich chinks and big-ass buildings? My sis wanted to go there."

"Madonna would have fit right in at Interotten. The kids aren't all rich. Many have to borrow to pay the tuition. They're all talented though."

"Whadja do there?"

"I was the mailman." *Sealed and delivered. Water under the terminatin bridge. A knife etching a scar on the heart.*

"Dooby-dooby-doo." Al danced a flamenco step.

Sven put down his guitar and clapped: "Ole! Ole, Al!"

"Al's a friend," said Tom, "from Armband Days."

"Got the feet," said Al, stomping. "Ain't got no band. No dough, neither."

Sven shook the money from his guitar case into Al's hands.

The homeless man stuffed his pockets and hurried away.

"Looks like Al's on a mission to the liquor store," said Tom, "and forgot his bike. It's okay. Put it in my truck. We'll see him at the library."

O

Kate came hurrying up. "They're watching you."

"Good."

"Whenever you come into the library." She pointed with her head. "The new surveillance cameras."

"Then they know I just put seventy-seven armbands into your nonfiction department."

"Oh, dear."

"Sven's planting more in fiction."

The reference librarian almost dropped her books.

"Cat's out of the bag, Kate," said Tom, "and it's got the library's tongue. What're they gonna do? Ban me?"

"If she sees you putting those black things in a book."

"Like that black thing?" A bookmark protruded from a book in Kate's hand.

"Oh, dear."

"The library's in mourning. Lyle's premonitions were correct. He was fired for being in a book. Melinda was fired for not being in the union."

"Oh, Tom, it was awful! A policeman came upstairs with the chairman of the board. Karen hid in bound periodicals. I went into the ladies'. The director is a witch!"

"Man, do I miss Lyle. My best boss ever."

Kate wrung her hands. "Lyle's career is over; Melinda sued the library just to get her retirement. Oh, Tom, the armbands are so right, so true. I'd help … except I need my health insuran—" She put a finger to her lips.

Pushing a cartful of books, the former director came around the corner. "Look who's here. How're things going, old slave?"

"Hi, Gary. Hey, whatcha got there on top?"

The Ping-Pong Club! Catalogued, stamped, and wrapped. Tom opened his book. "Someone actually checked this out?"

"How would I know? I'm just another slave now."

"A slave with his name on the wall outside."

"Pah. The people of this city built the library with their taxes. They own it. Besides, you know darn well Melinda had more to do with building it than I did. Well, it was nice seeing you again, old slave. Gotta get back to work."

Kate watched Gary disappear into the stacks. "Lyle's last evaluation," she said, "was a catalog of lies ... twisted facts and contrived complaints."

"Was that snitch hanging around ... overweight, frumpy?"

"Big Ears. She'd camp over there by the computers pretending to read. We had to be careful. My goodness, Tom, your book is true! Nonfiction! How the plot thickens!"

In the empty atrium, Tom joined Sven on the bench overlooking the flower garden. Warm sunshine cascaded down through floor-to-ceiling windows. Opening his case, Sven tuned his guitar while Tom bent over the unfinished jigsaw puzzle on the table.

"How'd it go in fiction?" said one arm bandit to the other.

"Great." Sven turned a fret. "No one said a word."

Tom put a puzzle piece in place. "How long can you stay?"

"I'm flying back to Stanford Sunday," replied Sven. "So, a couple days. Final exams are in two weeks."

"Congratulations. After all you went through. What a story you could tell. The actor tried to kill himself, became a musician."

"Hey," said Sven, "it's all good. I'm still here." He finished tuning, played a Spanish cadenza.

An elderly woman walked into the atrium, took a chair beside the piano. "Oh, good. Music in the library."

Segovia interluding with Rodrigo, music soared up the stairs into the reference section, turning fact into fiction and reason into rhyme. A few more patrons walked in and sat down. Listening to Sven's guitar reach for the sky, with sublime authority and sun-charmed chords, Tom closed his eyes. A flicker of a lash and memory took off like a swallow ...

49

"Hope sees the invisible, feels the intangible, achieves the impossible."

SUNDAY CROSSWORD PUZZLE, *NEW YORK TIMES*

When he opened his eyes, Sven was gone and Al was sitting there, talking to himself and counting on his fingers. "One and one are words. One and two are words."

"One and two," said Tom, "are three."

"Words are numbers," said Al. "Numbers are words."

"Where is everybody? Where's Sven?"

"The word's out. The weirdo mailman's out."

"I'm not a weirdo. You're the weirdo."

"You're a weirdo out of postal codes."

"Postal codes? They're my codes, Al."

"Good code slaves doin' their jobs. Code one to two codes. Two codes to a crowd. Three crows crowed a crowd. It's a murder! Fire them all!'"

"Al, you're nuts."

"Fire the crows. Fire! Fire! Fire!"

"Shh. Listen to me. I worked my tail off twelve years in a row and didn't speak up."

"Twelve years in a row—plenty of time to crow. Caw, caw!"

"You're a nutcase!"

"The mailman's a nutcase, a nuttin' again case and no tellin' how but the Chinaman knows, he knows you come in pairs. You and know-nuttin' you."

"Damn it, Al. You're starting to piss me off."

Sven returned and picked up his guitar.

"Twelve months," said Al, hands fluttering in the air like bat wings, "in a year. Twelve hours in a day. Your lucky-ducky day lasted twelve years."

"Be quiet." Tom glared at the homeless man.

"Okay, ducky," said Al. "Now, here's where it gets inneresting ... twelve doubled is two-faced. Twenty-four is twelve doubled! Three two-doubled years makes twelve months. A year."

"Shut up, Al, you tinpot Madonna. You've been smoking too much wee ... wait."

"Wazzat?"

"Shh!"

Sven put down his guitar. A siren was coming closer.

"Comin' to a library near you," said Al, raising a finger, pointing. "Lights, camera, action!"

"Shh! Something's up."

The siren stopped and an EMT ran up the stairs. Sven was right behind.

"Sumbody musta called for special delivery."

Tom stood. "Shut up, Al."

Sven leaned over the railing. "The director's had a stroke! They're taking her out now. She's done, Tom! It's over!"

It doesn't interest me if you believe in one God or an infinite number, I only want to know if you're awake and wise enough to know when imagination is alive.

Tom staggered upstairs. "Sven, help. Al, help. Pull all the armbands from the books. Every one. Every last armband."

○

Over the next few months, Tom worked on it. He pulled armbands from books, going through them page by page by page, sometimes driving to town just to pull armbands. He'd stop at the library on his way to chorale rehearsal and pull them; he'd stop on his way to Occupy Front.

One day, after terminating two hundred armbands, Tom stood at the crosswalk with fifteen oldsters and their signs.

Sandra pointed to the theater marquee, *Twelve Years a Slave*—BEST MOVIE OF THE YEAR: MICHAEL MOORE.

Hmm. Why not? Tom got in line for a ticket.

He hadn't watched a movie in years. In the window of the bookstore was a new display: the cover of a book had a cartoon drawing of a boy with a slingshot and, towering over him, a fearsome giant. Tom pressed his nose to the glass. The boy was leaning on a crutch. The book's title was *Dismissed*.

50

"I don't always free the slaves because when I do somebody shoots me."
STEPHEN COLBERT

Nineteenth-century Washington, D.C. was the pinnacle of American slavery, the hub of human trafficking. The owners fed lavishly on the racist link through the Industrial Revolution that defined African Americans as investments; slavery became the golden calf that kept on giving. By day, the founders enacted bills of indemnity, signed deeds of transfer; after dark, their lackeys bought and sold human beings.

Just "business as usual." By day, revolutionaries composed *requiems magnificent* and Articles of Confederation; after dark, these profit-oriented butt-kissing dealers did their shady business in back alleys and warehouses. Just buying and selling—slave masters on salary, the first middle managers in an industry of forced labor, mutilation, whipping, shackling, branding, imprisonment. Never mind the rampant poverty and sickness, never mind the broken families and forced migration, never mind the fact that white men too poor to own slaves died in grotesque numbers protecting the rights of a handful of greedy plutocrats—slavery was boss.

But Solomon is no Uncle Tom. He is a free man. Handsome; imposing in suit, vest-coat, tie, he is a black man of resources, an alpha male. Adam in the garden of forbidden fruit. He speaks engagingly in public, sends his kids to good schools, plays violin at recitals and in salons with other chamber musicians. He gives to the poor; on Sundays, he plays in church. At the drop of a hat or a dollar he'll fiddle for a hoedown.

Off-camera, Solomon is targeted by snake oil salesmen who know how much he loves to play his violin, and sucker him with promises of fame and fortune. Like Adam, Solomon swallows the apple hook, line, and sinker.

Suddenly, he's in a boxcar loaded with human cargo headed south; in no time, he's swimming in sweat and blood, picking cotton, and dragging logs overland. He gets an idea: tie the logs together and raft them downriver.

Tom Freeman: "Good idea, slave! Save time and money. Atta boy, Solomon!"

"Quiet down front!"

Tom stuffs popcorn into his mouth. Master puts Solomon's idea to work and puts Solomon back in the cotton fields.

Scene: A candle burning in a darkened corner of slave quarters. Solomon is mashing hardwood bark, pressing and drying it, adding crushed burnt seedpods to oil, dipping a feather in. He writes late into the night.

Footsteps. Solomon puts out the candle.

Sniff. "A candle? You can write?" Slugfest. Solomon scores.

Scene: In the moonlight, Master ties Solomon to a tree, whips him until he's a broken straw, a broken bow.

Scene: The wee hours of the morning. Master enters the slave-hold and pulls a black girl to the floor. She doesn't resist. Rape is part of the job.

Scene: Solomon hightails it for the river through fields and woods, stumbles over a body. Another body hangs from a tree. Laughter. Solomon is surrounded by white men who beat him and carry him back to the slave-hold.

Scene: Stage left, enter the Canadian.

Scene: Solomon escapes to Upper New York, meets his granddaughter, a good slave raising her kids. SHH! She must keep her family together. Her great-great granddaughter Michelle must also keep her family together. Solomon's memoir confirms conditions in Louisiana, *Uncle Tom's Cabin* blows the whistle on a legal system preventing owners, even kind owners, from treating their slaves well. George Washington emancipates hundreds of his own slaves but does not apologize or give them references or severance pay and never appoints one of them to his cabinet.

PS. After the Civil War, freed slaves became the fastest growing segment of the population, a fact that stoked fear in their white countrymen.

PPS. Solomon's book *Twelve Years A Slave* became a best-seller in the black market before disappearing for over a century. It was rediscovered at a flea market.

After the movie, Tom was steering his truck through light evening traffic. Bully bosses with privilege were direct descendants of slavery. The fruit on the tree of knowledge was a gargoyle perched on an evangelical post outside a church guarded by sentries in white sheets. He was thinking of chaining himself to the White House fence when his phone rang.

The voice on the other end shook but was familiar. "I heard you put me in the book."

"Ari?"

"My name is Cassio. Am I in the book or not?"

"There's a character who resembles you. Just a minute." Tom pulled over to the side of the road.

"I didn't give you permission."

"Have you been drinking?"

"Nary a drop! Long time, no sip. Have YOU been drinking?"

"It must be three a.m. in Israel, for God's sake, and you're phoning me about *The Ping-Pong Club*?"

"Why didn't you ask permission?"

"I don't need permission. The book is a novel; its characters are private property. As a writer, you should know that."

"You should have asked. As a common courtesy."

"Sorry."

"They're watching you, you know."

"Probably. Hamilton Z pays his snitches fairly well."

"Tom, why declare war?"

"Students declared this war, and you helped with those Ides of March stickers."

"I wish I'd never seen them."

"Are you in Jerusalem?"

"I am in Haifa. The only thing I'm fighting for is Cyprus."

"Ari, always the actor."

"I am not an actor. I'm a poet."

"And Cyprus is a red wheelbarrow on which so much depends; a ping-pong game between Israel and the West."

"What are you talking about?"

"Oh, nothing. Power versus ping-pong."

"I will tell you about power, Tom. Last year, students elected me President of Student Council ... that is power. But Humpty Dumpty has much more power. Students have none! Our education is a *rara avis*. The real Interotten will never be again."

"Nobody knows the future. Humpty will be gone soon. Help me fire him, send him packing with his tail between his legs."

"Wouldn't you rather spend what time you have left tending your garden, mulching your tomatoes? You are fighting thin air, Tom, writing on the walls with no ink. Your novel is over. The school is an insignificant chapter in our lives. Our goal is not to change the school; it is to change ourselves."

"You're changing as we speak."

"End the book. Start a new chapter."

"I just started a new chapter. You're in it."

"I'm done, Tom. You are one foolish old man. Students know you're on our side; I've made sure of that. But that book you're writing can hurt us."

"You're a rock, Ari."

"I am a rock ... a rock that stays where it belongs, that won't let anybody kick it out."

"Stubborn as a mule."

"I must have got that from my grandmother. Listen, old man, don't do anything crazy. You know the students love you, for the shit you're disturbing, standing up for, speaking truth. But Humpty Dumpty eats two of us over easy for breakfast. We need to keep our asses safe."

"You're too good for his grill."

"And you're too good to be trying to change another corporate asshole president's diaper. Kylie's the new President of Student Council. It needs to stay that way."

"You just said you were President."

"I was. I quit. It's private. Also, please don't tell anyone about this conversation."

"Of course."

"You must not think I am afraid. Drunk, maybe. On wine and wild women, but not afraid."

"Come back, Ari. Meet me at Buddie's."

"I will come back. But you will never see me at Buddie's. I'm washing my hands of this."

51

"True democracy is neither convenient nor politically correct,
does not tolerate laziness or comfort or conformity for conformity's
sake and has a hard time with majority rule … in fact, the greater
the majority, the greater the threat to true democracy."

MICHAEL NUNN

Stopping at Buddie's for coffee, Tom took a table near a group of teens chattering away as if they were the only patrons.

"I got it! You guys, we can have fish and chips in the mall!"

"I'd like to go to a movie," said a boy in a blue shirt.

"I need to shop," said a girl in a red sweater.

"Walmart's good!"

"But will we be back in time for dinner?"

"The bus is never on time."

"Who cares? I have to shop. I need new shoes. Look at these crocs!"

"You're like so beautiful. Like, they're clogs."

Tom stood. "Excuse me. When's the bus?"

"We can only ride the bus on Saturdays."

"It's every day," corrected Blue Shirt.

"But we're talking Saturdays—going to the mall!"

"Excuse ME!"

"Sure thing, batshit."

"Excuse me, sir," said Red Sweater. "Didn't you used to work at the art school?"

"I remember!" said Blue Shirt. "In the mail room! But weren't you … let go?"

"I was fired," replied Tom. "How many of you are four-year?" Three students raised their hands. "Do you remember the ping-pong club?"

"I do!" said Blue Shirt. "The student protest thing?"

"Wait!" said Red Sweater. "Kylie and Kris were in my dorm! Kris said there was a book?"

"Omigod! I got a copy! *The Ping-Pong Club!*"

A blonde girl asked, "Did you write it?"

"I'm still writing it."

"Kylie told me she was in that book."

"Matty told ME he was."

"Matty! Matty was so cool!"

"I've seen your movie," said Blondie. "It was Kylie's junior film thesis."

"OMIGOD, I loved Kylie's movies."

"Ready position!" On the balls of his feet, Tom stroked a high forehand loop with an imaginary paddle. "Kylie and Matty were members of the club," he said. "Great ping-pong players."

BANG! The door to the kitchen closed and the manager of Buddie's came striding over. Silent as blind mice over bread crumbs in the pantry, the students waited for the all-clear signal.

"Can I have a word with you?" Steel Rims motioned to a table in the corner, and the old table-tennis teacher waved good-bye to the teens.

Steel Rims placed a booklet on the table. "These are all over the restaurant."

The founder's booklet! "Compliments of the ping-pong club." Hmm. Elie was gonna change it to "courtesy of."

"Boss," Tom asked, "can I buy you a cup of coffee?"

"What is this booklet all about?"

"A collection of the founder's ideas."

"Founder? Of what?"

"Interotten. Some of his thoughts on education."

"How did it get here?"

"Beats me."

Steel Rims squinted. "What's on the back of your shirt? Chinese? German?"

"In six languages—'we are the founder.' Art and education are absolutely necessary in today's world."

"Hmm."

"Especially where Washington and Wall Street are in cahoots."

"What? What does that even mean?"

"It means money is doing the talking."

"That does not matter one whit. Trouble talk. It doesn't belong in here. Buddie's is not a platform for you or your politics. You're pushing my buttons, Tom."

"Trouble talk? The value of Art?"

Steel Rims exhaled loudly, a deer coughing. "I'll ask the questions. What were you talking about over there, with those students?"

"Old times. The good old days."

"That is a lie. You were talking about that book you wrote. I know all about the trouble it caused. You think that there's some kind of conspiracy against you."

"It's a novel, not a conspiracy."

"Huh! You have quite the imagination, I'll say."

"Thank you."

"I did not mean it what way! You don't get it! You don't respect authority! You don't seem to understand that this is a restaurant, not a meeting hall."

"I love Buddie's. It's my kind of restaurant."

Steel Rims' eyes flared. "It is MY kind of restaurant."

"I'll say this, you are the boss here."

"I am," said the boss. "And you were once my customer. That's it. I'm closing the door. You are no longer welcome here."

"Did Humpty call you?"

Steel Rims stood. "You are off limits now. If I see you in here again, I'm calling the police." She strode into the kitchen.

Tom handed copies of *The Ping-Pong Club* to six kids staring wide-eyed. "Gotta go, guys."

Red Sweater wanted Tom to autograph it.

"Sir," asked Blondie, "that movie you were in? My brother played on the soundtrack."

"Your brother?"

"Sven."

O

The Ping-Pong Club is the WORST book ever written!

Palma's Facebook message hit Tom like a cudgel to the knees.

And you're still not satisfied! Now you're writing a SEQUEL to inflict as much suffering as possible. Do you enjoy hurting people? Or just like driving them away?

251

Tom replied: Every slave who drives away causes pain.

What a ridiculous caricature! You make it sound like I helped you with those stupid armbands at the library! You know I never did. You even accuse my son of being a drug dealer. THANKS, YOU TWAT.

Couldn't have fired the boss without you.

Are you shitting me? That is a lie … a bald-faced lie!

A novelist's characters speak for themselves.

You're not a novelist! You're an attention-whore! Your book is a monument to self-gratification! You think you're some kind of hero who wants nothing more than to be a martyr!

I'd rather be a martyr than a slave. Tell me, Palma, how goes it in the mail room?

Eat me! I'm unfriending you. Liar! You're nothing but a self-aggrandizing old fart!

○

During the final days of the campaign, polls had George with a slim lead. Tom and other Mendez-For-Senate canvassers traipsed from door to door, house to house, neighborhood to neighborhood, gathering signatures and hanging leaflets on doorknobs.

Then an out-of-state brochure appeared in mailboxes throughout the district, with a photo of George's opponent shaking hands with supporters and a message distorting George's positions on everything from guns to gay marriage. The pamphlet even hinted that George was homosexual. Fiona couldn't stop crying.

"Tom," said George, "we are on a yellow-brick road to hell in a handbasket."

"Money is in the driver's seat."

"Absolutely correct. Elections today mean little more than appointments to the status quo."

Tossing a box of Mendez-for-Senate leaflets into the back of his truck, Tom sat slumped behind the steering wheel. It had been a long day. He started the engine, waited as traffic zipped by, found an opening, and steered into the right lane. This four-lane through the south end of town could have been a commercial looking for a new TV show, with all the new retail outlets popping up on both sides.

The left-turn lanes were dangerous though. Tom slowed to forty as the traffic light ahead changed to red. An oncoming car put on its brights … *WHOA. Asleep at the wheel?* Tom flashed his own bright lights and the other driver dimmed.

The light changed from red to green.

He'd make it easily, cruising along just under the speed limit, free as a bird, glad corporate-style management, bossy bosses, and wrongful termination were things of the past. Forget them.

The light ahead beamed the all clear—an open green door. Simple. Obey the rules, stay in your lane, keep up with traffic, and you will arrive home safely.

52

"The deer in that beautiful place lay down their
bones: I must wear mine."

ROBINSON JEFFERS

He can see the light, green as a pasture, and then he can't. A
mountainous wall rising out of the gas station on the right keeps rising
and rolling and stretching across the road from one side to the other,
filling his windshield. NO! NO! Slamming on the brakes, Tom hears
skidding—and NO! enters his eyes like a shadow. An immovable
midnight force strikes him from behind, a giant bull buttting him in the
back, throwing him forward, to collide with the seat belt across his chest.
Screaming, "NO!" his earthbound transit is an irresistible bullet hitting
the eye of the bull—the belt. Every ounce of fear leaps from his body, his
mouth falls open, his heart stops, and all the air in his lungs escapes in a
whooshing rush.

He opens his eyes. Where's the traffic light? A plume of steam rises
from the engine of his truck. He's inside a mountain, looking down at
his hands on the wheel. Somebody is standing in the road, in the middle
of the northbound lanes, directing traffic around him. Somebody walks
over, peers through the windshield, opens the door.

"Are you all right?"

"I don …" He tries to answer. Something is wrong. He doesn't know
if he's all right. His body is separated by a wall from his self. "I think I'm
…" He closes his eyes. *I think I'm a visitor here, a visitor who took a wrong
turn—a tourist without a map, a temporary hired to fill a gap. Tom, the temp.*

"Hit him square in the gas tank. Right there."

"Did you see it happen?"

"Yes. Here comes the cops."

"Oh yay. Lookee at that."

"Fuel tank. Diesel in there. Good thing."

"He hit the brakes ... hard ... lookee the skid marks."

"If he'd hit the big tank ..."

"I know. I got a full load in there! We'd have blown this whole side of town to kingdom come."

Siren murmuring a moan an octave below the bass drone, the ambulance weaves through the cars stopped along the side of the road.

A cop asks the driver of the truck a load of questions, comes over to help Tom get out of his truck. "You gonna be all right?"

And up Tom's spine, his very own emergency vehicle transports him to another time, another space, where sirens drone.

O

Doors closed, lights off. Tables set and ready for play. A Make Art Not Fear poster on the wall with a face he seems to recognize. Julie? Steps coming down the stairs. An alto voice: "What are you doing here?"

"I'm looking for Julie. I think."

"She is not here."

"This is the ping-pong club?"

"It's after taps. Go back to where you belong."

"Wait ... Your voice ... push your hood back. Let me see your face."

"Don't come any closer. There are others behind me."

"Do you work here? Were you fired like me? Please, I need to look at your face. It's a blackhole."

"I am a rover. And you are a stray. You do not belong here."

"I'm scared."

"Don't be afraid. I am never frightened."

"Are you the founder's daughter? Karma? Here, let me touch your hoodie. Silk! It's not uniform."

"You are the one out of uniform! You're off limits. And, truth, you smell to high heaven."

"Do you live here, Karma?"

"Art lives here."

"Does Art play ping-pong?"

"NO." Karma punches numbers on her phone. "Jack? Six here. I've got an intruder in P Dorm—a dead male. Says he's looking for Julie. What? You sure? No one ever died here before? Roger. Go ahead, I'll wait."

Tom stands. "I have to go to the bathroom."

"Wait! Hold on! Jack, he's getting away!"

The lights dim. A whirling dervish sweeps the floor, flips Tom upside down like a windblown leaf. Powerful hands take him by the shoulders, lift him to his feet, lock on the shackles. "Step along now."

"I'm old. I can barely see."

"You're fine. Keep moving. Time is money."

"I'm not fine and you're not Karma."

"I am a keeper. This is the furnace room. Let's go."

The giant toad sitting on his chest waddles off. Tom tries to sit up, manages to get all the way up on one elbow before falling back in a heap. The bass drone returns.

The nurse smiled, put down her book. "Well, look who's here."

"Barbie? Am I dead?"

She rolled up his sleeve. "Nope, not yet anyway. Hmm. Pulse is okay. Your memory seems to be all right too."

"You're a doctor now?"

"Physician's assistant." Barbie stuck a thermometer in his mouth. "You had an accident, tried to blow up the whole south end of the town. How do you feel?"

"Fine. I guess."

"Something for the pain?" She pressed a rubber pad, glanced at a gauge. "Blood pressure normal, heart sounds good." She turned some dials, checked a chart. "For Pete's sake, Tom, you're not a young buck anymore! It's a miracle you're still alive. You got a little case of costochondritis … inflammation of the soft tissue in the chest cavity. You'll have to rest for a little while—maybe for quite a little while."

"That tanker didn't stop."

"And your airbag didn't go off."

"Wasn't my fault."

"You're right about that. I asked one of the cops who was called to the scene. The driver of the truck didn't yield. There were witnesses all over. That's one of the busiest intersections in town. Nope, the accident sure wasn't your fault, Tom. No sirree. But you're alive. You must have saved up some good Karma."

O

For a few weeks, his heart rebelled, refused to be a team player. Tom had to coach and coax his ticker along, calling on Landon for support, for help climbing the stairs one at a time, taking their time, stopping often to rest. Up and down, up and down, then take a little break on the bed. A few breaths, then up and down again.

One special morning, Tom walked to the mailbox and back. Cold air awakened his limbs, gave him a lift. Next morning, he marched all the way around the block, stopping only once when the drumroll inside his chest threatened to escape confinement.

He was alive. He was alive and it was like life before the automobile— before freeways, coal mines, and climate change. Getting out the old bike, he took his life into his own handlebars, stood on one leg, hoisted the other over the seat, found the pedal, and took off down the two-lane highway toward campus.

Danger flew by. A Lincoln Navigator honked, crossed the centerline to pass, and a semi-tractor and trailer going the opposite way touched its airhorn, scaring the bejesus out of him.

Pedaling hard, he flew down the road and his imagination caught fire. He was on the way home, passing the pine stump, when the plot thickened ... roadkill. Smooth suede skin torn, ears and tail missing. Flies flitting over eye sockets, crawling into nose and mouth. One thigh is a grocery aisle for a family of mice, the other an avenue into the anus for an invading army of ants. One celebrating centipede reaping rewards amid yellow jackets paying their last respects. A mob of orgasmic sow bugs browsing the ears, unaware they're on the menu for roving ravens. The ribcage a picket fence around a balloon of bliss for silent slugs. Grave-robbing robins staging entrances, whistling while they work. Beautiful pungency.

"Shh." Fingers shaking, Tom strokes the brow, traces the stillborn ends of an acupuncture needle. "Not a word." He holds the head in his hands, nose pointing the way, one hoof brushing the ground.

With a grunt, he hoists the doe to his shoulders and down the trail of tear droppings they go. At Admissions paying their trespass dues, by the chapel bowing down, outside the ping-pong dorm serving a warning: "Make art, not fear."

In the foremost lot, Tom kneels and lays the voice of God to rest in his old parking space. He puts an ear to the lips and hears the fear of the hunt. He wipes his nose with a leaf from the earth and inhales the smell of the chase. He licks the slick she-shell and tastes the sky catching fire. Taking charge of death, he shrugs one shoulder inside, slips the other in, and pulls the pelt over his head. He slides in a loving hand, glides like a surgeon down the spine counting the ribs, caressing each as he goes, blessing the bones. He lowers the curtain behind the long neck, eases in a hip, twists and squirms down to the prim haunches, slithers down to the desperate subdivision, thrusts in one leg, then the other, and scrambles to his feet, hooves clicking, pawing the ground. It was time to return the voice of God to sender.

At the Firestone Inn, he hears:

I'm feeling so low and blue. My heart's full of sorrow.
Don't know what I'm gonna do. Where will we be tomorrow?

King Pleasure! Kansas City here we come.

53

"She'd seen the coral reefs bleaching out
and dying fast all over the world."
BARBARA KINGSOLVER

As the weather grew colder, Tom began sleeping through the night. His headache eased, the improvising drum inside his chest resumed its normal beat, his appetite for life returned. One clear December day, he rode all the way to Hank's and back, the bruised bags Barbie called lungs greedily gulping fresh air. His internal drum slowly but surely got in sync with the rest of his biological orchestra and flooded his brain with oxygen.

The oil company's check—a thousand dollars for the loss of his truck—arrived. An early Christmas gift, a winter carol. The next day, it started to snow. Tom decided to bike to Occupy, and pedaled by the Firestone singing, "Where will I be tomorrow?" The snow kept falling, all the way to the bus stop, where, unaware, he was being watched, he put his bike on the front rack and got on.

Sandra almost dropped her sign. "Tom! You're panting like a slave."

"Snowing pretty good the last few miles."

"Where's your truck?"

"At the wreckers."

"So that's why you haven't been here the last few weeks. Wait a goldarned minute! Good heavens! Did you ride your bike the whole way?"

"Biked to the bus and rode the bus to town."

"What happened?" asked Peter. John, Sandra, Robert, and the rest of the Occupyers gathered round.

"What's costochondritis?"

"I'll bet it costo a lot."

Robert, the octogenarian, clucked his tongue. "An old man like you."

"It cost," said Tom. "I'm supposed to take it easy. Might be a couple years on the mend ... or forever."

"Are you seeing a physiotherapist?"

"I'm stretching, walking, running," Tom said. "And biking."

"Well," said Sandra, "I think you're crazy biking in the snow."

○

His faithful sister donated a neon-green tam, a fluorescent-yellow hoodie, and Tom kept both hands on the handlebars—except when he was passing the president's for Humpty's middle-finger salute.

One morning, a school maintenance truck was parked on the shoulder in front of the mansion. Leaning on a shovel was an old friend. "How come, Tom, you put me in your book?"

"I didn't put you in it."

"You sure did ... my words, anyway."

"Not your words."

"Well, that letter on page 212 ..."

"Dave. I hear you. Please, understand. Those are my words."

"You trying to get me fired like you? I been here twenty years, the wife too."

"I remember we had some great conversations in the cafeteria."

"Me and the wife worked our whole lives. I was hoping to retire next year. Now, I don't know if I'll have a job tomorrow."

"I'm sorry," said Tom, and meant it.

"It got worse after you left ... everybody in a sweat about Bing or one of his stoolies, looking over their shoulders. They'd eavesdrop on us, too, poking their noses in ... remember Jakob?"

Tom nodded.

"Last week he walks up to Bing, throws his cap on the floor—his uniform cap—tells him to stuff it and walks out."

"Jakob was a good mechanic."

"Security's all over the place, with sticks up their asses asking if we seen you on campus. 'What'd he say?' 'Which way'd he go?' Shit! Now I'll have to tell Bing about this conversation ... you do know you're on campus, right?"

"You don't have to tell the boss a thing because I'm not on campus. I'm on the shoulder of a public road."

"It's bad for employees, but what about the kids, Tom? Students all worried sick they'll get kicked out! It ain't fair."

"It isn't fair. It's life."

"There ain't no place left where you can get a job like this. My kid's in college. You know how much that costs?"

"How is Seth? He still playing ping-pong?"

"Ping-pong? History. It's all too risky, Tom. I can't take no chances. We don't want no more trouble." Shaking his head, frowning, Dave shoveled sand. "You hear? No more."

A side-swiping, sand-spewing snowplow came barreling down the road throwing snow to the tops of the trees. Tom gave Dave a shove and the two old friends jumped into a bank of snow up to their crotches. The plow disappeared around a curve. Laughing, they stomped around the shoulder, slapping snow off.

For a minute, Tom stood at the gate and peered down the winding drive that led to the president's lakeside residence. *Locked? Sensors? Yard lights? Chain-link fence around the property? Humpty, you're secluded and insulated inside the founder's dream of community and inclusion.*

"Oops." Tom got on his bike. "Gotta catch a bus. See you, Dave; tell Seth I'll spot him five points."

"No more ping-pong, Tom. No more trouble."

"Kansas City, here I come," Tom sang, getting in line with the students waiting for the next bus.

"What's in the bag, Caruso?"

"Kylie! Didn't see you! How's my old movie director?"

"How'd you get your pants all wet?"

"Playing! Jumping in and out of snowbanks, dodging snowplows." Tom reached into his backpack. "Here."

"The *Ping-Pong Club*! Am I in it?"

"Is Humpty a bully?"

Kylie laughed. "Is Trump" she asked, "the Pope?" She turned a page. "Whoa … 'to be continued?' What'll you call it when it's finished?"

"Think of a title."

"Thanks! I'll read it tonight."

The bus pulled in and Tom and Kylie got on. Students were still boarding when the golf cart with the school logo drove up. "Hold it there, driver!" The Director of Security climbed aboard. "Tom! What in hell do you think you're doing?"

"Hi, Jack."

"Doggone it, Tom, you got me in a quandary. Been watching you riding that bike by campus. How long you been catching the bus here?"

"Oh, two weeks, I guess, more or less."

"That was your bike on the bus yesterday?"

"Hoisted it up there on the rack myself."

"And then you got on?"

"You're sleuthing me out, Jack. You should run for sheriff again; I'd vote for you."

Laughing, "Me too," said Kylie.

"You aren't old enough to vote."

"I will be in a month."

"Okay," said Jack, "that's enough." He looked Tom in the eye. "You can't be here. Do you understand?"

"I am here ... on the bus."

"YOU can't be on campus. You're not welcome."

"I'm on public transportation."

"YOU. CAN'T. BE. HERE!"

"Sir," said the driver, "are you getting on?"

"NO!"

"Looks like you're getting on ... you're blocking the door."

"What's your name, driver?"

"My name is Marlene. Please, get on the bus, or off."

"What's your last name, Marlene?"

"I don't have to tell you."

"You're not answering my question."

"On purpose," said the bus driver. "That'll be three dollars, please."

"All right, Marlene, you win this round. You'll change your tune on the witness stand after we subpoena you and charge you with aiding and abetting. I'm serious."

"You're seriously riding to town if you don't get off the bus."

The Director of Security stared at Marlene. Bug-eyed students in the back stared at the security director. Marlene tapped the horn, started the engine. "Now."

"Jesus H. Christ," said Jack, shaking his head. "I'm sick of this. All right. I'll have nothing more to do with you and your bus today. But you keep off campus, Tom. If I see you here again, I'm calling the police."

54

"Schools that give students meaningful opportunities to exercise their First Amendment freedoms are safer and more successful learning environments than schools that treat students like prison inmates."

CHARLES HAYNES

"Marlene, no more high jinks."

"Ha. No more 'hi, Jacks' either."

Kylie wondered, "What was Security all frizzed about? Can't you catch the bus on campus? Why would he make you get off? You'd just get back on again, down the road."

"Jack's just doing his job," said Tom. "How's school?"

"Oh, I must be dreaming. My film *Dusk Matters* won first prize in the student category at Cannes! And next week, I'm going to Washington! To meet President Obama!"

Gazing out the window, Tom said, "What a feather in your cap." *What a small world ... one president greets another. Kylie, meet Barack. Humpty, meet Trumpty.* They flew by Buddie's and the new greenhouse.

Two minutes behind schedule, the bus passed the new compost outfit—appropriately named Interotten—and Hank's and Herb's. Halfway to town, Marlene was back on schedule and the snow had completely disappeared.

Kylie continued. "This semester, I'm working harder than ever! I just wrote a new film! *Dusk Matters* was on racism; this one's on sexual assault."

"Humpty Dumpty treating you guys okay?"

Kylie grew thoughtful. "It's not about him."

The forest gave way to abandoned farms and subdivisions and bait shops as Kylie connected the dots for her old leading man ... a strong girl's story of hurt and pain—of rules enforced, of art mismanaged, of hormones controverted, of expulsion and termination.

"The deans act like students are criminals. Check in! Check out! Every move monitored, supervised, measured. Everything done by the book. No exceptions, no humanity. Dorm mothers playing wardens, counselors sniffing around in our past and present for stuff we may not know ourselves, watching us like hawks for the tiniest telltale sign, snooping in our closets looking for rubbers, butts, roaches, anything they can pin on us. They're prison guards violating us all day every day, peeking and poking and prying."

"I remember Josiah," said Tom. Amid accusations, warnings, and threats, under the atmosphere of fear over the school, Josiah had been dismissed. Sighs of relief. Then, in the ensuing campus-wide hush-hush, three male students had been expelled without cause or reasonable justification.

"Josiah," said Kylie, looking at Tom, "got what he deserved."

"And Sven? What was the skinny on Sven?"

The film-maker became a cougar growling through gritted teeth. "The skinny on Sven? There was nothing! They had nothing on Sven! He didn't do a damn thing!"

"No alcohol? No joint?"

Kylie took a deep breath, sat back, and the bus pulled into the mall. A dozen students walked by, heading for the exit. In a low voice, "After Sven tried to kill himself," she said, "there was a rumor going around."

"Rumors can kill."

Choosing her words, Kylie went on: "Josiah said he thought he could smell dope in the mail room. We all knew that Sven worked in the mail room."

"He did. So did a lot of other students."

"And then Josiah notified Dean Warren!"

"Coincidentally, I mailed Dean Warren a copy of *The Ping-Pong Club*. She returned it with a letter that she copied to Humpty: 'Do not send me anything again. Do not use my name, even cleverly disguised, in your letters, Facebook posts, or other writings—or you will regret it.' She's as afraid for her job as everyone else and is just enforcing Humpty's rules, doing his bidding, and trying not to upset too many parents and donors."

"Dean Warren expelled Sven, my leading man. She should be fired!"

"Sven's father was institutional tech; he knew what was going on. Dean Warren won't outlast Humpty." Tom noticed Kylie's arm. "Oh, my God. How did that happen?"

It can't happen here; the guards won't allow it. You're eighteen, going to class. Josiah follows. You run into the park; he's right behind, making comments, asking questions, telling you things you shouldn't know. You're President of Student Council; he's a square peg in a round bubble. He doesn't know his part in your movie. He's a turd among goldfish in a shark movie; a sick, wilted dollar sign in a revolutionary, sublime, oil painting.

You are a middle-aged woman working in a children's museum. Your studio wall is covered with prints, photos, poetry. The sign on your door, Men at Work, isn't graduate school; Men at Work means your imagination never gets to sleep.

One night you're setting up the death scene, cutting in the next-to-last soundtrack. If you get the Spanish guitar right, the movie will play itself. Kicking off your shoes, you pull the script and play the scene.

There's a draft of air, the door opens. The lights go out and a hand covers your mouth. Another pushes you down. You hit the floor screaming, "No! Josiah! No!"

"I can't tell you," said Kylie, "yet."

"Let me see that arm." Tom rolled up her sleeve, held the girl's hand, saw the tears.

"I can't," she said. "They'd start watching every move, opening our mail, eavesdropping on our phones." The bus began to move. "Oh, shit. I was gonna get off."

"Marlene!" yelled Tom.

"No, it's okay," said Kylie. "I can get off at the station." Marlene shrugged and kept driving.

Tom patted Kylie's hand. "Good. You can tell me about your new movie." The scratch in her arm was deep, a stark, accusatory line. "Does it hurt? The arm, I mean."

"Yes, but expulsion can kill you."

"Larry recovered from it, and graduated. He visited me a month ago at my home. Now, tell me about your new movie."

"It doesn't matter."

"I'd get that arm looked at in the clinic if I were you."

"And answer questions on how I got it? No thanks. I want to graduate. Fuck the deans, they're tools. I'm sorry, Tom, about the ping-pong club."

"Don't be. You guys were fantastic, Student Council rocked, and I got the best present of all. By the way, Kris told me why she quit the club."

Kylie looked her old actor in the eye. "I know why. She cried for a week. Kris is a woman with heart, and she's smart."

"Is she ever. She's an adult."

"Boys and girls are people, Tom. Gays are people too."

"Hey, George Mendez, a politician I know, is gay."

"And people are lovers, old slave. Ah, love! Love! I want to throw love everywhere."

"Interotten is all about love."

"And there's so much love! Every variety of love!" Eyes ablaze, Kylie's hands on love's piano played fortissimos of fantasy in the air. "Lakes, pines, music—love! Contagious, collective love, Tom! It's the theme of my new movie, set in the dorm where we played ping-pong."

55

"An aroused German Shepherd mounted another dog; Kevin was right on it with his camera. Both dogs were male though, and someone yelled, 'Stop filming!' Apparently it's taboo to even imply that the dogs of Nazis are queer."

MICHAEL MOORE, *HERE COMES TROUBLE*

On his way to Occupy, Tom was biking past the old pine stump when he heard the bass drone. On sudden impulse, he turned and coasted down memory lane to the dead end.

Gone like smoke into the heavens, the little surfer's cottage had slipped away like a figure of speech, meshed like melody with music. But Santa had come down the chimney to cover the costs of constructing a new lakeshore rental—real estate. For Sale. *Wonder how much they're asking.* Tom jotted down the phone number. Something was lying in the grass … WAH! Decal of muse! Shining in the sunlight, bright as the flame on top of a candelabra.

Head aching, hands shaking, he looked around. He placed WAH over his heart, then slipped the decal inside Julie's mailbox.

Halfway to the bus stop, a car stopped across the street. "Hey!" the driver yelled. Fisherman's hat, sunglasses. "Come over here!"

Tom pushed his bike closer.

"I got a problem," said the man, taking off the sunglasses.

"Hello, Jim. What's up?"

They locked eyes in a staredown. Jim's books on big-game hunting filled a shelf in the library, remembered knocking on Jim's door and getting his signature on the armband petition and his vote for George Mendez.

A gust of wind from the lake bustled through, broke up the staredown. "What's up, my ass. I want to know what you're doing here."

267

"Bicycling. Touring the neighborhood."

"Bullshit." The big-game hunter's storied temper was off like a prairie grass fire. "You don't live here."

"I live on Forest Lake. Don't you and Lynn live there too?"

"You know where we live. Don't get smart."

"Wait. You live on Forest. Do you own property on Grass? Was Julie's cottage ... yours?"

"That house is my property. What were you doing there just now?"

"I was just pedaling by. It's a public road."

"You were not *just* pedaling by!" Jim shook his head. "You stopped, looked around like you didn't want to be seen—like that time you put in your kayak and paddled around like you owned the joint—and then you picked something up and put it in my mailbox."

You read the book.

"Don't deny it. What's up with you, anyway? How many times have you done that? Were you thinking of putting something else in there? You do know it's private property. That mailbox is mine, opening it's a federal offense. As far as I'm concerned, right now, you're on thin trespassing ice."

"I'm standing in the road."

"What is up with you? Playing games? Talking about free speech? Don't try to silence me. You write about workers' rights. Well, I've got property rights."

Tom nodded. *So, you were Julie's landlord. The voice of God found shelter in your domain.*

"Well? Do you respect property rights?"

"I was thinking about Julie." *My fictional pawn in the game.*

"She's gone and she'll never come back, thanks to you—quit the best job she ever had because you fell overboard like a drunk trying to swim. You turn everything you touch to shit!"

"Guess you read the book."

Jim clamped a jaw like a lion over prey too big to swallow. "You call it a book?" Clenching his fist: "*The Ping-Pong Club* is the biggest pile of horse shit between two covers ... unadulterated garbage. Calling yourself a writer by copying down what people say and hiring an editor ... that doesn't make you a writer. Printing a book doesn't make you a writer. Writing is a job. It takes talent to build structure and character and plot! Writing is damn hard work, not playing God in a schoolyard."

"The old slave would agree."

Jim jabbed a finger into Tom's chest. "A writer has to build it and then tear it all down and start over again. That's the kind of work that makes you a writer! But you built your book on thin air, with no foundation at all … you're not a writer, you're a phony! An imposter! A mailman who's been terminated! You're a failed musician, a senile dumb cluck with one foot in the grave and the other on my property!"

"How'd the fire start?"

"You know, smart-ass, I've had it up to here with you. You're a blemish on the art of writing and an embarrassment to the school. Get the fuck out of here! Go home! Why in the name of Satan, sweet Jesus, and the Pope are you pissing around in front my house?"

"I think I just found out."

○

Through Irv Delaney, Tom learned that Alice had stage IV cancer. Devilish and intransigent, the disease had hidden for years undiagnosed while the Queen lopped off the heads of her fellow slaves. Her axe-wielding became too much for her fifty-nine-year-old body, and she became a breeding ground for festering malignant cells.

It was a twenty-mile ride to knock on the door of the former president. Irv had put on a few pounds but still had that youthful twinkle in his eye. "Good job, Tom, biking all the way here … Hey, I read *The Ping-Pong Club*."

"How'd I do with your character?"

"Too straight-laced. No sense of humor. My eyebrows are not exactly bushy. Other than that, I'd say you painted a forgivable portrait."

"Have you talked with Baxter?"

"About Alice?" Irv shuffled his feet. "Yes. It wasn't easy. The doctors have given up hope."

The thing about old age is you cry a lot. Driving a bulldozer or a laptop, riding a bike or doing the dishes, listening to an old song or singing a new, the tears come on without warning and there's nothing you can do about it.

Irv made a cupola with his fingers. "It's too bad. Her family has notified the school she'll forego any and all treatments. She's ready to face the music."

"Alice is a fighter."

"She's also pragmatic. Confrontations take a lot of the fight out of you. What a shock, eh? I'd say she's taking the news remarkably well. Who knew?"

"She knew."

"You're probably right."

"She knew when she started going along with Humpty, when she began playing his terminate-to-intimidate game, when she fired Bernie, when she fired me. But she was handcuffed to a fire-at-will-and-don't-tell-Bill game that went into overtime, and she lost. Nobody wins at fire-at-will."

"Baxter must have known."

"Oh, he knew. Alice told him to keep it confidential—for the sake of the school." Tom crossed his heart, turned a pretend key in his mouth. "Baxter's brilliance has a blind spot ... Interotten."

"Baxter," said Irv, "would never say a negative word about the school."

"Interotten is cool. Things there are beginning to heat up."

"Why do you say that?"

"Because it's true. You can't shove the crying babies under the bed forever. I hope that when the time comes for Baxter to tell the truth, Alice is still here, still cheering him on."

Tom felt for the kickstand. *I'm a flake of snow in a midnight universe fallen in the path of a plow.*

Chin on cupola, Irv looked affectionately at his old mailman. "Me too."

Tom swung a leg over the seat and got on his bike. "Good-bye, Mr. President," he said. "Give Alice my best."

"I will," said Irv. "Godspeed!"

56

"We are but dust in the wind, fallen angels, imprisoned if we forget to pay our bills, but he can shoot an innocent citizen on the busiest street in America and he gets to walk away and continue to lead our country as if nothing happened."

ISIAH SMITH, JR.

Entering the church, Tom could hear the voice of God. *What are you doing here, Tom?* He looked around, listening. No Julie.

"Singing," he replied to the roof and climbed the risers, joining Baxter in the tenors.

"Begin," said the composer, lifting his baton, "with the angels."

"Green fields of summer," sang the angels.

Dan Forrest put a finger to his lips. "Half that volume. Eyebrows up, now. Head voice." They started over but down came the baton. "Shh. Again." One bar in, Dan put a finger to his lips; you could hear a pin drop. "Once more." The sopranos gave it their best head voice and two bars later, "Great. Now, half that volume."

So it went, note by note and bar by bar, tightening and tuning, honing entrances and exits, sharpening sharps and filing flats for two hours.

"Great," said Dan. "See everybody Sunday, in the auditorium. Two o'clock sharp."

On the way out, "I'll probably be flat," said Tom.

"Get those eyebrows up." Baxter raised his. "Use that head voice. I have a good feeling about this concert ... 'Green ...'"

A door opened and their conductor joined them in the hallway. "Tenors, unite! You have nothing to lose but your cadenzas." Dan laughed. "You guys sounded good."

"Thank you," said Baxter.

"I'm a baritone," said Tom.

"A baritone singing tenor?"

"We needed tenors."

"That's really decent of you. If I'd known you were singing higher than your range, I could have written your part down a third."

"That's okay, Mr. Forrest."

"I was just kidding. Call me Dan."

"Thanks, Dan. Can I give you a copy of my book?"

"Only if you autograph it."

Tom signed his name, added his email.

A baritone also on his way out asked, "Haven't I seen you on campus?"

"Who, me?"

"Yes, Tom, you," said the baritone. "I'm on the board."

"Of trustees? Wait …" Vision blurring, Tom was back in the ping-pong dorm. "Oh, my God! Is your daughter a student?"

"She was. I'm so glad to finally meet you, Tom. And glad we're in the same choir. My name's Hornblat. Do you have an extra copy of your book for me?"

"Yes, of course!"

Tom walked out of the church, spiritually on air. Two birds with one score! Two readers with one rehearsal! The book was marketing itself. Singing "Green fields of summer," he got on his bicycle.

Someone cleared his throat. "Allah be praised!"

"Ashqar!" Tom shook hands with the physics teacher. "How are you?"

"I'm good. And it was good to hear you sing. In forty years of teaching, I have never witnessed more tangible proof of the existence of God." He gestured toward the girl beside him. "My daughter, Ara, is singing in the sopranos."

"Stellar! There must have been an eclipse today."

"Ha! No! No eclipse at this longitude! I just loved listening to you. What was that song? That extraordinary piece of music?"

"An original composition by our conductor."

"The world is becoming one in song! Thank you, Tom, for singing, and for your dedication to overcoming fear."

"Just singing my part."

"A musical mammal singing his part! Before I forget, I must thank you, once again, for the camera obscuras."

"Forget it. The postal service will."

"We all miss you at the school."

"God Almighty, do I ever miss Interotten."

"You will recover. You are strong. All the world's a stage."

"Isn't that *Hamlet*?"

"Act Two. A hard act to follow." The physics teacher laughed and put an arm around his daughter. "We are so blessed, Tom, and so proud. Ara will attend Interotten next year. She's a singer! She'll be in my class!"

"Congrats. Would Ara like a copy of *The Ping-Pong Club*?" The girl glanced at her father, shook her head.

"No, thank you, Tom" said Ashqar. "We'd like to read it but your book is—shall we say—making waves. Now, I make waves myself—magnetic waves—and I must continue making waves, doing my best for my students and my children, continuing to labor under this atmosphere of fear in a strange land. So be it. There are worse fates."

"What are you saying? Who'd Hamilton dismiss now?"

"Caroline was notified yesterday."

"Caroline?"

"The new violin instructor."

Julie's replacement! She'd barely rosined her bow! Z was firing on all cylinders.

Ashqar sighed. "So it goes. We'll be off now." Hand in hand, two followers of Mohammed wove their submissive way through the parking lot to their car.

Back on his bike, Tom had a pilgrimage to make. Up the road, parallel with the ridge overlooking the town, he rode an old deer trail to lay his bike in a clump of bushes. Snapping his fingers, singing "The Virgin Mary Had a Baby Boy," he reached the summit, and suddenly there it was: his gateway to the promised land—an unobtrusive ranch-style, three-bedroom, with a two-car garage. No WAH.

On Facebook, Julie had cried:

How I miss you dearest Mark, how I need you. You were the conductor who changed our hopes and dreams, our very spirit. I swear I will fill the gaping hole you've left here in this nation, in Colombia and Panama, and everywhere, so that someday the world will know your spirit as a rising shining star. You will come forth to bravely lead us, and we will link arms, hearts and souls in music.

Shades drawn, garage door closed. Tom took a deep breath, corralled himself, and ... footsteps. Light, unhurried, feminine steps going from room to room. Humming "the virgin Mary," sweating like a knight in armor who'd just been caught chasing a scarecrow, Tom knocked softly.

The footsteps stopped. In deathly silence, he knocked again.

The door opened a crack.

Dark, beautiful eyes squinting, glaring. "Yes?"

"Sorry to bother you ..." The door started to close.

"Wait." Tom put a hand on the jamb. "Can we talk?"

"You, you …" said the widow, "are not welcome here."

"Please. Can you tell me what happened? Where's Julie?"

The eyes grew until they were twin moons, two rising and shining stars, filling with tears in a dark abandoned sky of yesterday's eclipses.

"She was Yu Liu's and Doreen's teacher," said Tom. "Her students want to know what happened—how they can help."

"Let her students find her if they want to help her so badly."

"Connie …"

"Don't Connie me! How dare you?! How dare you come to my door? What in God's name are you thinking?"

"Is Julie … around?"

"Do you have an ounce of decency? Have you no respect?" Her jaw clamping like a grindstone on steel, the widow of woe spit sparks, her eyes flashing like lightning. She hissed, "You have no business being here. You are invading my privacy! You are trespassing!"

"Mark was my hero."

"My husband was not your hero! He was a good man! He would never say those things."

You read it!

"In the library, you told me he said those things. At the Inverted Art Gallery, you told Julie and me that one of his orchestra kids did it—snitched on him. Connie, two of Mark's orchestra kids worked in the mail room. I know the snitch; she played flute."

"Don't! Just don't! I'm warning you."

"Mark hated Hamilton's terminations, hated the Thanksgiving Massacre—fifty-three fellow teachers were fired with one bullet, and eight full-time faculty quit. Those things were true. I read Hamilton's warning letter to him."

"You are lying. For shame. How can you write such libel? How can you put it in a book? You defile our family's name! You have placed me in professional danger."

"It's the truth."

"You call it the truth. You think that you're the victim, but you have brought all this on yourself. My husband was the victim. You have made my children and I the victims."

"Mark died because Hamilton fired him."

"You do not know that!" The widow's eyes narrowed, and she spat out, "You do not know anything! I have children in school! I need my job!"

"We all need our jobs."

"What did you say?"

"I'm sorry."

"You should be!" Pounding her skull with her fists, Connie moaned. "Oh, I may as well be dead too. Why, oh, why did you write *The Ping-Pong Club*? Throw that *chupacabra* away!" She hurled an imaginary book to the ground and stomped on it. "Go away, please, before you burn my house to the ground like you burned Julie's!"

Staggering backward, Tom tripped, almost fell.

"Leave now, or I'm calling the police!"

Singing, "Julie! Juuulie!" Listening for her voice, Tom felt the tears rising.

"Go away, firebug!" Connie's rage followed him down the trail. "Do not come here ever again. Do not contact my family in any way. Do not write about us. If you breach my family's privacy again, I will sue you down to your last penny! You will regret ever having written a word about my husband! Go now! Go!"

57

"Fiction's logic dances, singing out of us; escaping us to pull
nonfiction out by the aching, broken world we face each morning."
TERRI GLENFIDDICH

On Friday, before the election, George Mendez held a flyer. "Have
a look. 'Health costs? What does Mendez think this is … Russia?'"

"Huh?"

"A flyer that came in yesterday's mail. One of them," said the Senate
candidate. "Here's another: 'Isn't Mendez's support for gay rights queer?'"

"Omigod."

"And this: 'Where's your immigration papers, George?'"

"Bastards."

"And this: 'Mendez can't read. The Second Amendment says Hands
Off My Guns!'"

"It doesn't say that at all!"

"Of course, it doesn't," said George. "It doesn't say anything about
abortion either … 'Gorgeous George supports partial-birth abortion.' Or
how about 'Don't worry, Mendez. Obama's got your back.'?"

"Lotsa cash," said Tom. "Boom. Dark money on the drumhead."

"Cry babies," said Fiona. "Losers. We're so far ahead of little lord
Fauntleroy now, it doesn't matter."

"Only four percentage points ahead," said George. "It matters."

"Yesterday," said Tom, "it was closer to a seven-percent advantage, if
you can believe the poll responses."

"People want change."

"They want," said George, "to get the money out of politics."

"They want meaningful change," said Tom. "This is for-profit
mudslinging. Negative campaigning."

"Well, there's still four days until the election. We'll see what tomorrow brings."

○

Tomorrow brought another bombardment of hate mail hitting every mailbox in the district with incendiary charges, discriminatory statements, and racist insinuations. Out-of-state money, super PACs, and oil-industry marketers were pulling every string to win this seat. On Tuesday, by the slimmest margin of victory in the electoral district's history, two hundred and twelve votes, Jamie was declared the winner in his first campaign for political office.

At campaign headquarters George said, "Money wins again."

"Whoopee," said Fiona. "The sell-out jerkoff swapped his Bermuda shorts for slacks. Now he's promising to make us great again." She sneered. "Where've I heard that before?"

"Not from me," said a voice.

Everyone turned. Bart Stupak walked in, having stopped by to offer his commiserations. Tom took advantage of the surprise visit to hand a copy of *The Ping-Pong Club* to his former Congressman.

○

Call time three hours away. The *falsetto* second tenor put on black shirt and pants, grabbed *The Ping-Pong Club*, and, singing *libera me Domine*, rode his bicycle all the way to Interotten. Wavelets lapped rhythmically along the lakeshore; low sunrays flirting with clouds made coloratura rainbows over the water.

A clear ride with minimal traffic and a soft breeze for tailwind. Past the **No Trespassing-Construction Zone** sign, he pedaled, then turned down a road through faculty housing. He got off the bike at the vacant volleyball courts, and, walking down a trail he once used to deliver the mail, arrived at the intersection of earth and water, and there he laid his two-wheeler down in a swath of tall grass.

Not a soul in sight. A loon lifted her yodel to mark his return.

Music in hand, Tom navigated the pines around the ping-pong dorm and walked to the back of the auditorium. No one here either. He closed a hand around the final rays of the sun, shadowed himself to the front, and surveyed the courtyard … dozens of concert-goers waiting for the doors to open, chatting on the benches. No sign of security. Tom got a grip on the here and now, approached the portal to ponderous performances, and, with a hand on the door, hesitated.

A soprano chirruped. "Why, hello, Tom."

He held the door. "Head voice, Giselle." She laughed.

Right behind, at the doorway to happiness, two old friends came up, arm in arm, munching ice-cream cones.

"Jared! Ginger! How're things?"

"You lost, Tom?"

Jared licked a swab of ice cream, took a bite out of the cone. Tom held out his hand. "Long time, Jared, no see."

Ginger raised her eyebrows. "It has been a while," she said.

"Oops," said Tom. "Almost forgot. I'll bet the wedding was a great experience. Musically, that is! Congratulations."

Jared asked, "What wedding?"

"A little birdie told me you got married."

"Our wedding was seven months ago."

"I knew it!"

"But," Ginger put in, "Daryl and Tammy's was last week."

"Brigadoony honeymoony!"

Jared had another lick. "What's that supposed to mean?"

"Oh, nothing. A happy wish. Where'd you get the ice cream?"

"You know where."

Tom eyed Ginger's expanding midriff. "Whoa? Are you two expecting?"

"Yes, we are, as a matter of fact."

"A musical miracle! I'm so happy for you guys. Is it a boy?"

"It is a she."

"A new soprano for the choir! I hope Dempsey doesn't fire you."

"Dempsey is not gonna fire me."

"I hope not. He's prejudiced though; not the most musical middle manager, and a mite mental about money."

Ginger opened her mouth and bit her lip.

"I hope, future soprano mother, he doesn't fire you either. Say, Jared, do you remember conducting our choir?"

"No."

"It was a few years ago; we were doing the Verdi." Conducting an interview, Tom waved *The Ping-Pong Club* like a baton. "Didn't you conduct Mendelsohn's *Elijah*?"

"I've never conducted either Verdi or Mendelsohn."

"How about the Fauré *Requiem*?"

"You're frigging off your effing rocker."

Ginger had turned to watch the setting sun's heavenly remains—a slice of orange floating above the surface of the lake—then made up her mind: "I remember the Fauré *Requiem*."

"A requiem for the dead," said Tom, handing Ginger the book, "and a revolution for the living."

The former dorm counselor said, "Yu Liu told me about this."

"Yu was a prize," said Tom. The orchestra was warming up. "My best mail room worker."

"She didn't understand," said Ginger, "why students were walking out of class. If she had, she would have joined them. Yu did not like President Dempsey."

"Yu played ping-pong with me … so'd Julie. Asians are ping-pong freaks."

"Racist remark," said Jared.

Ginger shook her head. "Hamilton's the racist, Jared. Not Tom. Yu should know."

Tom laughed. "Humpty Dumpty sat on a *basso continuo*!"

"Hey," said Jared. "Weren't you banned from campus?"

"You'd better leave now, Tom," said Ginger. Taking Jared by the arm, she put a hand to the side of her mouth. "One thing I know for sure," she said, "Julie agreed with me. And Yu."

58

"Art is always at the door looking for a way in."
OLD-SLAVE PROVERB

A few members of the chorale stood waiting for their call. Like a doorman on the alert, Tom watched and listened. An alto went inside the auditorium, followed by two sopranos. Shadowing head voices, Tom stepped inside.

"We're downstairs." The warm-up conductor pointed.

"Why, Tom!" Orchestra President Crystal Wyng, a former Interotten vice president, handed him a program. "It's been a long time. Good to see you."

"You too, Ms. Wyng."

"Howdy stranger!" said Irv Delaney. "Don't tell me you rode your bike all this way."

"Oops." Tom dropped his music. "Hi … sorry." He got down on his knees, sorting through it. "Good to see you, Irv. Going to the concert?"

"That's right."

Trembling, fumbling with sheets of music, Tom said, "Enjoy the show."

"Break a leg."

Tom's heart lodged in his throat. Mini earthquakes scampered up and down his spine. A wave of nausea arrived and he ducked into the men's room. In the mirror, brow awash in glistening beads of sweat, lips the pale-blue of a stillborn, a reflection stared at him. He moved his lips, the reflection didn't.

Still the truth, still the breathing pulse of life, is a song of hope, a picture of light that only breathes freely when oppression writes the score. Changing constantly, suspended in the watery space between water and air, between the material and the immaterial, the seal swims forward and backward. Desperately, the sea urchin finds life-changing footholds in meaningful engagement. The killer whale sings to its prey. The sponge's song of love in the stillness of hate is a flame gasping and grasping for air.

Truth, that imperfect blending of opposites, is only one reason for being but it can bring the world to its knees. Truth is the marriage of fire and water. It is here. It is now.

Hitching up his pants, Tom winked, gave his reflection a thumbs up. Ready, Eddy? He walked back into the foyer.

Three basses led the way: "Let's go." And a barbershop quartet of inharmonious trouble headed for the basement. Tom, Joe, Ed, and Anderson immediately started talking about the hockey game.

"I thought the Wings had it."

"They did."

"Until overtime. How about that save by Dom from behind the net?"

Suddenly it grew quiet. "What? You again?"

"Hi, Jack," said Tom. "Did Jared call you?"

"Shut up." Grim as the grin of a gargoyle, Jack commanded, "Come along, Tom."

They climbed the stairs. Tom turned and started walking toward the lake and his bike.

"No, you don't." The gargoyle pointed. "This way."

Crowd killing time … friends, faculty, family, and students milling around over ice cream and soft drinks.

"This way?" Tom spotted Cordell, Cam, Ashqar. He turned. "Are you sure?" On a bench, Drake and Jorna laughed. Boyce chatted with Jake. Over near the ping-pong dorm, a group of students in dramatic dialogue. A small string ensemble gigging love songs in the gazebo: Palma and Rolph leaning together, holding hands.

"I'm not parked," said Tom, "that way."

"C'mon, get going. Back to your car."

"My truck, you mean. It isn't that way—or the way you're pointing."

"Where is it?"

"At the wreckers."

"Oh, for Christ's sake." On his cell phone, Jack's ghouly grin turned into a scowl. "Hold it right there! The office says we need a photograph."

Tom posed. Jack shot.

"Okay, old man. Let's go. Move it!"

"This way?"

"Yes! Now, move it!"

Tom walked on air into the crowd of smiling faces. He waved to Jeanette on the bench between Kylie and Matty and blew the Student Council President a kiss.

"He's coming eastbound toward the mall and main entrance."

"Congratulations, you two." Tom formed Vs for Tammy and Daryl and put one V over his heart. "I shot an arrow in the air; it feathered down I know not where ... but it was close to Interotten." Tammy smiled.

WHAM! Jack slammed a fist into his back. Tom staggered.

"Move it!" said Jack.

On the ground lay Tom's program! *Green fields of summer.* With his name! Suddenly realizing eviction, banishment, termination, and dismissal were all just part of the program, he gave the soiled, torn program to Daryl.

A percussion instructor twirled his sticks, hit the bass drum. "Howdy stranger! Long time no see!"

"Hi, Gil!"

Another punch in the back. "I said move it!"

Tom stopped, looked the Director of Security in the eye. "Don't. Touch. Me. Jack."

Eyeball-to-eyeball, a silent power struggle ... then Jack blinked, Gil hit the bass drumhead, and Tom wended his way through the crowd.

He fist-bumped Jon, and a girl in the crosswalk waved. "Wahoo!" she warbled. "If it isn't the old crusader!"

"Cheryl! Are you building a guard house?"

"I'm on duty. Hey, guess what I found in the bookstore? *The Ping-Pong Club*! I didn't know you were an author. I read it in one sitting. Is Hank's that store down the road?"

"Actually, I made Hank's up."

"Hah! You got that girl in it too, who was fired ... Sharon? She had the job I was after. Do you remember interviewing me for the job at Hank's? You said I was too young."

"And look where you landed."

"I was one lucky little bitch. What a dickhead that store director was! I was so glad you fired him. Your book almost made me cry with the shit that's happening here. Hear about Ron?"

"Ron who was thinking of quitting?"

"Yeah. Humpty Dumpty fired him."

"Hold on," said Jack to the phone. "He's talking to staff."

Cheryl stepped into the crosswalk, moved a barricade for a cement truck.

"Tom," said Jack, "hit the road!"

Tom waved to Cheryl, and started walking slowly down the road.

"That does it." Jack punched numbers into his phone. "Hello, Sheriff's office? Yes. Interotten. We got an order on a guy under surveillance—name's Freeman, Tom Freeman, an older ex-employee. Yes, it's a legal order … What? Like I said, a no-trespassing order that has been in place for over a year. Yes, in the auditorium … he resisted arrest, refused to leave … Wait, there he goes."

Cheryl waved. "See you later, Tom!"

59

"Unless you believe sitting at a segregated lunch counter or standing in front of a line of tanks in Tiananmen Square is a waste of time, resistance is anything but futile."
SANDRA STEINGRABER

Switching on his flashlight, Tom walked under the last street light, left the road in the dark, and followed the airstrip that ran along parallel to the road. The moon brushed the tops of the pines, raising shadows of doubt and prickly premonitions. A car drove slowly by ... *Cop?*

The taillights disappeared, silence returned, and Tom stepped onto the runway. A lonely hoot owl lamented. *Follow me.* Hoofing it, he picked up his pace and hit the end of the runway trotting. Hastening down the footpath, he hustled by the Firestone Inn, crossed the road with pounding heart and dead battery and only the moon for light, and, singing *Dies irae*, covered the last mile home as though he'd biked it.

O

He woke sitting in a chair at three a.m. The imagination does not write, it only dreams. The world revolves, doesn't revolt, and the sun rises. Resistance grows, carbon in the atmosphere grows, and one petition fires the boss, one novel tips the scales of justice. Imagination, one way around reality, lifts the subliminal caution sign around peace and prosperity. Putting pen to paper puts the period on the impertinent predator precariously perched on his pretend wall but Tom knew the imagination does not write.

A few stars were still out. Tom switched on the light, crawled from bed, and by six o'clock, he was pounding the pavement, thumbing a ride. A car came up behind and blew by; a pickup without a muffler roared past. A mail truck flashed its lights and almost ran him off the road, then veered into the opposite lane, swerving to avoid a head-on collision with a delivery van going the other way. Thumps up, Tom kept hitching. A logging truck with its brights on laid on its horn, a van slammed on the brakes but kept going. Finally, his neighbor Sue pulled over and dropped him at the door of Admissions.

The sun awoke yawning, wondering what Tom was doing on campus at such an ungodly hour. He scurried past Security to the lake ... his bike was still there! He raced around the main gate and pedaled home as fast as he could.

As he rolled into his drive, the cruiser was right behind.

"Tom!" said the cop. "Trooper Truman ... man, you were moving there! Glad I caught up with you. This your place?"

"Yes."

"What were you doing on campus, testing the water?"

"Joining my chorale. Singing."

The trooper glanced at his phone. "Okay, that jibes with Security. You have a little run-in with the Director?"

"He wouldn't let me get my bike. He clobbered me."

"And you left on your own? You didn't resist?"

"I said, 'stop hitting me.'"

"That doesn't qualify as resistance. But I have to tell you, Tom, if I'd been there, I'd have arrested you and taken you to jail."

"Are you arresting me now?"

"You just admitted that you committed a criminal misdemeanor. A warrant for your arrest will be issued."

"Are you arresting me now?"

"I can arrest you now—or later, after the warrant is issued."

"When's that?"

"Well, the prosecutor's been busy—you know, the holiday and all. In a week or so, he'll order you to appear and set bond."

"What's bond?"

"Temporary release while they schedule a trial. That is, if you want one."

"You didn't say what bond was. Money?"

"Yes. Money. Bond guarantees your appearance in court. How much is up to the judge."

"It's up to me if I get a trial?"

"Yes. It's a free country."

"No. It's a sold country."

"Now see here, Tom. Jack's been patient, looking the other way. And, I can be patient too. Let's say bond is, oh I don't know … have you got a hundred dollars in your bank account?"

"No."

"There's a bank next to that old grocery there … Hank's? Scratch together a hundred and I won't take you to jail tomorrow."

Tom shook his empty wallet. "This is my bank account … wait." He pointed toward the garden. "Trooper Truman, do you like peas?"

"That there's a good-looking bank account," said Trooper Truman. He tried an edible peapod. "Good eating too. What's with the pile of wood?"

"Winter heat. Brought in on my shoulder, cut with a bow saw."

"A hand saw? Must be two cords of wood there. Okay, I'm out of here. Have a hundred ready in the morning."

"Tomorrow's Saturday. The bank's closed."

"That's right. See you Monday morning then."

○

Tom passed the hat at Occupy Front.

"Hey, bro, whatcha doin' with the collectin' plate?" Al said. "You be trespassin' on my turf? Why you stealin' from me?"

"Bond, Al. It's for my bond."

"Oh, ya." Al put his hands up, gave Tom some space.

Sandra asked, "What did you do now?"

"Just trying to sing on campus."

"Trying to sing at an art school? How dare you?"

"Got kicked out and assaulted by the Security Director as he escorted me off campus."

Tom collected eighty-seven dollars from his fellow Occupyers.

"Crackpot charge," said John. "Bonkers. The school's trying to break you. You should have hit that asshole Security Director right in the nose. In this jurisdiction, you have a better chance with an assault charge, like that guy riding by here on his bike, clubbing Rob and me, and getting off scot-free."

○

Long ago, the county courthouse had been a Methodist church. An architectural marvel of elaborate stone masonry and stained-glass windows, the building was now a civic fixture dedicated to a former governor, Will Mannekin.

The trespasser entered the old courthouse with more than a little trepidation and was greeted by a guard in uniform.

"Cell phone off? Belt, watch, coins, keys in the basket."

Tom obeyed instructions and stepped through the Trojan-horse metal detector.

"Spread your legs." The guard waved a wand over Tom's feet, checked his ankles and crotch. He shook his head. "Lift your arms."

"John?"

On his knees, "That's my name," said the metal detective. "You used to work at Hank's?"

"You were my bagger!"

John stood. "Turn around, please." He finished scanning and handed Tom his basket of beeper metallica. "My mom used to work there too. You remember Marion?"

"How could I forget? My night cashier, helped me close the store."

"Yep. Well, Mom was fired."

"Ugh. Let me guess. Stealing beer from the back of the store?"

John nodded. "Unfortunately. And that was the least of it. She was charged and found guilty of fraud. Stealing night deposits. She's been here a number of times. Hey, are you still a vegan?"

"Forty-three years now."

"No shit! Hard to believe!"

"I find it hard to believe that Hank's is closed."

"I know! Hank's was there before I was born! Hey, Tom! Are you still working in the Interotten mail room?"

O

Outside the courtroom in the old chapel, his lawyer nephew tried to explain what an arraignment was. "Let's say you're running a steeplechase. Lots of jumps. An arraignment, Uncle Tom, is the first jump through an assortment of legal hoops."

"Legal schmegal hoops, you mean. How many?"

"Hoops? Depends. I'd take your case, but I'm busier than hell right now. In any case, you need an attorney. Your extremely low income means the judge will ask if you want him to appoint one. Remember, Uncle, you have a right to legal assistance."

"Appoint a lawyer for a trespasser? How much will it cost?"

"A few hundred dollars, maybe. The judge will also ask how you want to plead—innocent or guilty."

"I want to plead pissed off."

"If you plead guilty your case can be decided immediately."

"Guilty of what? Of getting angry? Of looking the boss in the eye? I didn't give him a shiner like he deserved! His lackey Jack hit me. Humpty just wants to shut me up … what do you mean, 'decided immediately'?"

"The verdict. You might consider standing mute."

"Mute? What's that? Why?"

"To exercise your full legal options. There's no huge advantage or purpose in it but it sends a message. Standing mute produces the same result as pleading not guilty, brings the appropriate search-and-seizure motions, and serves for any defense, factual and legal. Your case is so uncommon, there could be benefits. And don't forget, you have the right to a jury trial."

"A jury trial? Why?"

"Because in the first place, you have a constitutional right to one. You're innocent until proven guilty. Anyone accused of any crime, including trespassing, has the right to be represented at a trial before a jury of his peers."

"My lips are sealed. Mute I stand."

"The judge will set a date for the jury selection—shouldn't take too long—then he'll set a trial date. And I'm sure you know, Tom, but I gotta remind you—a criminal trial could get a little media attention. It's up to you. A criminal trial would also be your opportunity to call the president to the witness stand."

My legal shmegal nephew's a smart dude. "Whoop de doodle dee! And ask him why."

"Yes. Why did he do it? Why'd the president of Interotten slap a fired old geezer who delivered his mail, with a no trespassing order?"

"To shut me up. I guarantee it."

"It is what it is. Something else occurred to me today on the way here. His intimidation tactics—warning students not to speak with you, threatening to take legal action against you distributing your book on campus—could be interpreted in some courts of law as violations of your right to express yourself."

"Humpty's pissing on my Constitutional rights."

"Well, no. Not exactly."

"He's pissing on *The Ping-Pong Club*."

60

"Spirituality wasn't just a belief; it colored everything the
Anishinabek did each day of their lives."

BOB DOWNES

Shaking the ground, dump trucks and earth-movers rumbled and
rolled; a battalion of slaves in hard hats moved in, on, and around piles of
lumber and cement blocks. Humpty Z. Dumpster's construction project
was full-steam ahead, blanketing the ground around the old pine stump
in a cloud of dust.

Tom looked at his watch. With a sigh, he got back on his bike; a man
came hurrying up. "Hey, sorry I'm late."

"Never mind," said Tom. "You came!"

"What's with the guard house across the road?"

"It's to keep me out, not you."

"Ah! So, where do you want me to infiltrate?"

Tom pointed. "Through the barricades."

"Sure, as long as they don't stop me."

"They won't. They're busy. Here."

"What'll I do with it? Who gets it?"

"Nobody in Interotten knows you; so you can walk straight to
Administration. Go upstairs, turn right, then all the way to the end. Last
office."

"Got it."

"Don't talk to anyone until you're inside the building and into the
outer office. If the president's there, put the subpoena into his hands and
get his signature."

"What'd you call it?

"A subpoena. Get his signature on it. On the copy … and bring it back
so we can notarize it."

Being a radical at heart, Mr. Jones observed convention with a wink. "Who're you?"

"My name is Henrietta Hefner, Mr. ...?"

"Jones. Boss in?"

"Hmm." Humpty Dumpty's new secretary wanted to know what was in the envelope.

"A subpeanut."

"Did you wink at me, Mr. Jones? If that was intentional, I'm sorry. I can't accept a ... what did you call it?"

"Subpeanut. For Mr. President."

"This is very unusual, certainly. I mean, I can't receive it, whatever it is, if it's intended for somebody else, now can I?"

"You better. It's some legal schmegal for your boss. Where's he at anyway?"

Henrietta nodded toward a closed door. "He can't see you—not now anyway. He's in a meeting."

"That's okay." Mr. Jones pulled up a chair. "I can wait."

"Oh, but ..." Henrietta shook her head, pulled a strand of hair, looked around, appeared to make up her mind. "I'll be right back," she said, and walked out of the office.

Mr. Jones leaned back and lit a joint. Five minutes later, Henrietta was back, accompanied by the president's personal envoy. Beverly had been Irv Delaney's chief diplomat, executive assistant, number one trouble-shooter, and now she guarded Z's inner sanctum and privacy with diplomatic zeal. Her job had proven challenging during the turmoil of Bernie's dismissal and the ensuing student unrest, but Bev was a professional and handled it with aplomb. Putting her phone on speaker, she set it on Henrietta's desk and dialed. It rang and rang. She let it ring.

Finally, "Yes?" The voice was that of someone awakened from a nap.

"Pat, there's someone in the office, says he has a subpoena."

"What's it about?" asked Interotten's lawyer. "The new guard house, by any chance?"

Beverly and Henrietta exchanged puzzled looks. "We don't know," said Beverly with a shrug. "He says it's for the president."

"Well, give it to him, then."

"He's in a meeting."

"Go ahead, deliver it ... wait. Who's in there with him?"

"Excuse me, sir?" Beverly looked at Mr. Jones. "There's no smoking in here."

"Who?" asked the attorney. "I don't know what you're talking about."

"Pat," said Beverly, "there's a man in the office here, who delivered the subpoena. Hamilton is with the contractor for the security building."

"At the main entrance? I need to talk with him. Put Roger on."

"He's in the meeting, but I'll tell him."

"Have him," said Pat, "call me immediately. And as for the subpoena, look at it. Is it dated correctly? On court letterhead? Stamped? Is there a trial date at the bottom?"

"Look," said Mr. Jones. "Somebody here's gotta sign this damn subpeanut and I gotta get it notarized."

"I heard that, delivery boy," said the attorney over the speaker. "Bev, it doesn't matter who signs it, you or Henrietta. You're just acknowledging you received it."

Mr. Jones stood, dropped his still-smoking roach to the floor—mission accomplished. "Thanks, cluckadoodledoos."

"Cluckadoo …? What in the world?"

"He's leaving, Pat," said Henrietta.

"Thank God," said Bev.

The inner-office door opened. "What's all the fucking ruckus?"

"Sorry, sir." Henrietta hastily handed the subpoena to her boss. "This is for you."

"Where'd you get it?

"There was a delivery guy …"

"What? A delivery guy? What'd he look like?"

"He looked," said Henrietta, "maybeee … like Tom Freeman?"

"Tom Freeman can shove this up his arse."

"He wasn't as old as I thought he was."

Bev cleared her throat. "Um, Hamilton?" Shaking her head, she put a hand over her eyes. "He wasn't Tom." Responsible, dutiful Bev had known the old slave for years, also knew a thing or two about the law. "Subpoenas are ordered by a judge. If we've signed for it, as we have, then we have to deliver it to whomever. If you've seen it and refused to sign it—or if you sign it and don't appear where and when it says to appear—the judge will hold you in contempt of court, and then issue a warrant." She paused for dramatic effect. "For your arrest."

Henrietta moved over to stand on the roach.

The door to the inner sanctum opened once more and the guard-house contractor emerged. "See you tomorrow?"

Humpty Dumpster nodded. "Ugh, Beverly, what's that smell?"

61

"Until parents, donors, and trustees all get involved in direct
opposition to the kinds of things that have occurred, I
don't hold out hope for change anytime soon."

DURWOOD

His lawyer and the prosecutor had been huddled for an hour and a
half in the judge's chambers working a plea bargain—whatever that was.
As long as they called Hamilton Z. Dempsey to the stand, Tom didn't
care what was going on in there. If Humpty had to tell the truth, it would
open a Pandora's box of wrongful terminations. "Because I could," was
a cop-out.

Tom was now glad that he hadn't subpoenaed Baxter. The cancer
raging through Alice's body wouldn't quit and now the old key plunker
was in the hospital himself. He'd caught his wedding ring on a chain-link
fence and fallen, pulling his finger out of the joint. A freak accident, but
the finger had to be amputated. His old crossword friend would never
play piano again, but it didn't stop him from sending Tom this Facebook
message:

Tom: Where the bus stops could be pertinent to your case. The
school does not own that property. It's on the former public road
right of way and is owned by the state park system. An agreement
was put in place twenty years ago to let the school use the
parking lot area but that land where the bus stops still belongs
to the state. It's in the Campus Master Plan; I helped work out
the details when I was on the faculty committee who prepared
the Plan.

The plea bargaining ended and the jury entered. The prosecutor and
Tom's lawyer, also named Tom, walked in.

Lawyer Tom: "All set."

Freeman Tom: "Not all set! Where's Humpty Dumpty? Where's Dan and Kerwin? Keith and Daryl? I gave you a dozen names … Naomi, Bernie, Jeanette …"

Lawyer Tom: "I got your letter. I had to pare down the list."

Freeman Tom: "You what? Pared down my witnesses?"

Lawyer Tom (whispering): "Not so loud. Some on the list I called. Some I didn't. Don't worry, I got this."

Freeman Tom: "But Kerwin? Dan? My conductors! They've got the training, the ear, the experience! They can answer our important musical questions!"

Lawyer Tom: "It's all good. We know your attendance was okay, you paid your tuition. You know how to sing."

Freeman Tom: "I'm talking art! Fearless work! Besides, I gave you that list a month ago!"

Lawyer Tom: "A few subpoenas weren't delivered in time. I had to waste an hour or two with the sheriff. They should have been delivered yesterday … don't worry about it, Tom."

Freeman Tom: "Yesterday? Are you kidding? Kerwin and Dan travel the world! Conducting, giving seminars. Did the sheriff hand deliver them or just put them in the mail?"

Lawyer Tom: "Shh."

Of course. Shh. What if we dragged everybody in Hamilton Z. Dempsey's administration and the entire Board of Trustees into court? Shh. What if we caught him in a bald-faced lie, administered Z's coup de grace, fired him back right here in court? Shh. What if the middle managers have already taken over? Shhhh.

Anderson arrived. Tom gave him a thumbs up.

Freeman Tom (sighing with relief): "All right! Call Anderson first. He knows I've been singing baritone for twenty years, and knows that I moved to tenor to help the musical balance."

Lawyer Tom: "Shh. Check this out—their last offer."

Freeman Tom: "No deals!"

Lawyer Tom: "The prosecutor's all over it. Judge Sikpak approves."

Freeman Tom: "The prosecutor's hands are bloody! He's a criminal! I want Humpty Dumpty on the witness stand."

Lawyer Tom: "Yes, I know. You've made that pretty clear. Now, keep it down. And listen up. They'll dismiss the breaking-and-entering charge if you plead guilty to trespassing."

Freeman Tom: "What's the penalty?"

Lawyer Tom: "Ninety days for the B & E, thirty for the trespass. Of course, there are fines and fees for both. Take your time. You don't have to accept their offer right now."

Marlene and Jack, witnesses for the prosecution, entered and took their seats. Humpty Dumpty arrived with Henrietta, Beverly, and an entourage of security personnel, deans, administrators, lawyers, and … *Hornblat! I'm so glad to see you.* They all took their seats. Humpty loosened his belt, belched, and leaned back, scowling.

Freeman Tom: "How long have I got?"

Lawyer Tom: "Don't worry. Take your time."

Freeman Tom: "How much are we talking about?"

Lawyer Tom: "For the fines?"

Freeman Tom: "For the legal schmegal! For going to trial!"

Court-appointed, Lawyer Tom would get his two hundred fifty dollars, the minimum fee, no matter what Freeman Tom pled. If, however, the deal was off and a trial was on, Lawyer Tom would have to work for every penny, calling witnesses, researching backgrounds and facts, investigating each and every detail in the case and arguing them.

The courtroom grew silent.

"All rise."

Judge Sikpak entered.

Freeman Tom (sotto voce): "Ask him now. Why the ban?"

Lawyer Tom (standing): "Your honor, may we approach?"

Two mouthpieces huddled with the judge.

Lawyer Tom (returning to the table): "Nope. He says it's not part of your case."

Freeman Tom: "It IS my case! The reason I'm here!"

Lawyer Tom: "Hush. You don't need a contempt charge added on."

Freeman Tom (pointing at Z): "I'm charging the Terminator with contempt."

Lawyer Tom: "Are you crazy? Have you ever been examined by a psychiatrist? They've made their offer. Take it and Judge Sikpak may reduce your sentence."

Freeman Tom: "Reduce it from thirty days? And a penalty? They're drawing blood from a turnip! Ask why!"

Lawyer Tom: "It's been decided."

Freeman Tom: "Why is why I'm here! Why is why Z's there! Why did you take this case—for the money? Or because it was the right thing to do? There's a reason! A reason for everything. What in the world is wrong with asking why?"

Lawyer Tom: "The judge has decided. It's out of our hands."

Freeman Tom: "I want to know why!"

His Honor brought his gavel down. "Quiet in the court."

Lawyer Tom: "Shh. Time's up. Well, what do you say?"

Freeman Tom: "No deal without why."

Judge: "Is counsel ready?"

Lawyer Tom (standing): "Yes, your honor. After careful consideration the defense has—reluctantly—decided to reject the prosecution's offer of the plea bargain."

Freeman Tom: "Not reluctantly."

Judge: "Then, we'll proceed."

Lawyer Tom: "Ladies and gentlemen of the jury, it seems the times, in the words of the bard, they are a changing. And so, it seems, are the characters. The heroes are now villains, the villains heroes, and the lawyers—in the words of another bard—should be tortured and hung by their heels until they scream for mercy. Shakespeare wrote 'Kill all the lawyers!' for a trial where, as simplistic a villain as you'll ever find, pled guilty and got off. Seems absurd, right?

"But Shakespeare saw the larger issues of truth and justice, law and equity, as anything but absurd. The absurdity lies in assuming that the words he put in his characters' mouths are his own personal views. Like the bard, my client believes that the law favors the rich. He uses words to make a point—words like 'Employees haven't a shred of free speech left' just as Shakespeare was also making a point, using words like 'kill all the lawyers' in order to draw attention to a contradiction. He didn't have a problem with laws favoring the rich because there were no laws at the time favoring the poor—illiteracy is easier to govern.

"Shakespeare was simply illustrating the absurdity of such laws. We have the same absurdities and contradictions today. Lawyers and laws for the disadvantaged, the poor, the ignorant are hard to find. Ignorance of the law is still no excuse, and the duel between right and wrong is waged in the shadow of justice. Ladies and gentlemen of the jury, trusting that you don't vote to kill me, I have a question for you: who knows upon whom—the defense or the prosecution—lays the burden of proof?"

"No idea," said a male jurist in the back row.

A woman in the front piped up, "You?"

Lawyer Tom bowed, his hand sweeping the floor, and, shaking his head, he sat down.

Freeman Tom could hear the guilty verdict coming.

Marlene testified Tom had been on the bus, Jack confirmed it, and it was Humpty Dumpty's turn to take the stand.

Lawyer Tom: "Did you terminate Mr. Freeman?"

Humpty Dumpty: "Yes."

Lawyer Tom: "And did you ban him from campus?"

Humpty Dumpty: "Yes."

Lawyer Tom: "Mr. Dempsey, is there an ultimate authority to decide who gets to step on campus and who doesn't?"

Humpty Dumpty: "That would be me."

Lawyer Tom: "You and you alone?"

Humpty Dumpty: "That is correct. Why do you ask?"

Lawyer Tom: "Why do I ask? I ask because of 'Why do you ask?' Your Honor, the witness is leading the question."

Prosecutor: "Objection!"

Judge: "Sustained."

Lawyer Tom: "Your honor, the witness asked 'Why do you ask?' I was answering his question."

Prosecutor: "OBJECTION!"

Judge: "Sustained."

Lawyer Tom: "Mr. Dempsey, you don't like Mr. Freeman, do you?"

Prosecutor: "OBJECTION, YOUR HONOR!"

Judge: "Objection sustained. Strike from the record."

Lawyer Tom: "No further questions."

Judge: "Mr. Dempsey, you can step down."

Anderson took the witness stand and testified to Freeman Tom's membership in and value to the chorale. Lawyer Tom asked if the orchestra had rented the auditorium and, therefore, had tenants' rights to its use.

Anderson: "Yes, the orchestra was tenant; they invited the chorale to sing along."

Judge: "Any further questions?"

Prosecutor: "No, your honor. We rest our case."

Judge: "Mr. Freeman, would you please stand? How long did you work at Interotten?"

Freeman Tom: "Twelve years."

Judge: "That's a long time, long enough for you to get to know a lot of good people there ... teachers, students, staff, alumni?"

Freeman Tom: "Some of my best friends."

Judge: "And you admit to trespassing—knowing it was illegal? Are you sure you understand the nature of your actions? More to the point, do you respect authority?"

Freeman Tom: "Depends on the authority, your honor. There were three reasons for my actions. The first was: the bus and my bike were my primary means of transportation. They still are. I can't afford a car."

Judge: "So you just sat there, and rode the bus onto campus?"

Freeman Tom: "I got off the bus many times before it stopped at Interotten."

Judge: "I'm talking about the time you were sitting on the bus and Mr. Armbend told you to get off."

Freeman Tom: "Jack gave me no such order. He didn't have the right to order me off. There were witnesses ... a dozen students, the Student Council President, the bus driver ..."

Judge: "We've been through all this in plea bargain. Never mind. I'm curious, though ... you said there were three reasons for you to go on campus ... to trespass."

Freeman Tom: "My second reason was conscience. I felt obliged to make public the crimes President Dumpster committed."

Judge: "Crimes, Mr. Freeman? What sort of crimes?"

Freeman Tom: "Firing hundreds of my friends for no good reason."

Judge: "He can do that. It's perfectly legal."

Freeman Tom: "It's wrong, your honor. It creates, as one of the teachers there put it, an 'atmosphere of fear.' Wouldn't you know it, my fearful friend has now been fired. The third reason is this: I'm writing a book about this."

Judge: "A book? What kind of book?"

Freeman Tom: "An autobiographical novel. A roman à clef. The first part, *The Ping-Pong Club*, is already published."

Judge: "You published it? Is it copyrighted? Filed with the Library of Congress?"

Freeman Tom: "Yes."

Judge: "And you're still writing this 'novel'? Can I buy a copy? Is it for sale here, in town?"

Freeman Tom: "It's at the bookstore on Front, where Occupy takes place every Saturday. It's in the library."

Scratching his chin, Judge Sikpak looked sharply at the jury forewoman who'd just pronounced a guilty verdict. "Hmm. Autobiographical … means it's true. I'll have to buy a copy."

Freeman Tom: "I can give you one."

Judge: "Why would you give your hard work away?"

Freeman Tom: "I didn't write it to make money. In fact, I'm giving all profits from sales of the book to needy and deserving Interotten students."

Judge: "Well, I can't accept your free copy."

Freeman Tom: "I understand."

Judge: "Anything else you want to say before I pass sentence?"

Freeman Tom: "Yes, your honor, there is something I want to say. It's one of the reasons for my actions. I just put it in my book. A reliable source has told me the school does not own the property where the bus stops."

The prosecutor jerked as if he'd been shot in the back.

Judge: "Go ahead, Mr. Freeman."

Freeman Tom: "The bus stop is owned by the state park system, not the school. It's a campus drive, all right, but the drive is a former public road right of way and was deeded to the state park. The land is owned by the state."

Silence in the court.

Judge: "Um … Mr. Freeman, that's astounding news. Would you care to identify your reliable source?"

The jury fidgeted. Their job done, it was time to go home. Tom made eye contact with the forewoman, a dead-ringer for the library director.

Freeman Tom: "I can't do that, your honor." *Baxter isn't ready yet to join the Queen.*

Judge: "You don't have to. All right then, sentence is thirty days, with two weeks held in abeyance, plus six hundred dollars in fines and costs, and two years' probation. While on probation, you are not to talk with students or staff. You cannot be within half a mile of school property. When driving by campus you cannot stop."

Tom inched backward until he stood next to Humpty Dumpty. "Like I said, your honor, I don't have a car. What happens when I'm riding by campus on my bicycle?"

Judge: "Don't stop. And please, Mr. Freeman, give authority some respect.""

Tom nodded, reached to shake Hamilton Z. Dempsey's hand. *No hard feelings, Mr. President?* Humpty snorted, turned his back. The courtroom deputy attached handcuffs and shackles, and shuffled Tom off to jail.

62

"Oh, he'll give me names. He owes me. He was horrified about
protesting at the wrong address. You should have seen them,
they just picked up their signs, apologized, and headed out.
They even picked up their trash."

BARBARA KINGSOLVER, *FLIGHT BEHAVIOR*

Tom was no neophyte jailbird. He knew terrible things could
happen here; he kept his head down. His five cellmates called him Old
School, never asked what his name was.

Dogeared paperbacks lay around; he read another *roman à clef*—*On
The Road*—for the first time. He received a letter from his sister, "never
understanding why he wanted to go to jail." He started writing Betty
back but tore up the letter. He attended church a couple times in a large
cell down the hallway and enjoyed the change of scenery.

One day: "Freeman! You have a visitor."

In the visiting room, Tom saw nobody, just a wall of glass, then looked
again. On the other side of the wall, his reliable source was putting on
headphones—fiction was becoming incarcerated reality.

"Did you get my message?"

"Yes! Oh, Bax, I'm so glad to see you! Thank you for coming! This is
worse than the emergency room. Did you bring the new crossword?"

"Did you get my message?"

"I got it. It saved my butt—would have been ninety days for sure. Hey,
what's up? Are you sure you're okay?"

Baxter's hands fluttered like moth wings.

Tom placed his palm on the glass. "Omigod! Is it … Alice?"

"Cancer. She passed ten days ago."

"I am truly sorry."

Baxter matched Tom's hand finger for finger with one exception. "She's in a better place."

For a minute they held hands through glass. "Much better than here," said Tom. "Alice dedicated her life to her job—she fought Z on termination after termination. She was the queen, and did not deserve what he did to her."

"The memorial service was today."

"Wish I could have gone."

"A humbling ceremony. Very difficult for me. Had to leave part way through."

"Did Z go?"

"No."

"He'd have faced a chorus of boos."

"Very likely, but he didn't attend. I was on my way home, passing the courthouse, when I remembered you."

"I'm so glad you remembered, and so sad about Alice. She made the school what it is, and everyone knew it. Bet it was standing room only in the church."

"Four hundred in attendance, a thousand cards. Live music. Commiserations all around. Memories multiplied by memories."

"She will forever be the queen."

Baxter ended the high nine on glass. "Some nicknames, however," he said carefully, looking Tom straight in the eyes, "are like the buck that stops here. Last Tuesday, Dempsey enforced 'early retirement' and fired me."

Saddened by the news, Tom was not surprised. Z's favorite targets were older staff—'excess baggage' he called them. Old bags didn't protest, they took their lumps like good slaves and quietly carried them away. Baxter was no exception.

His friend's visit lifted Tom, gave him wings to fly above the fray, and for a figment of a moment, he was free—Baxter's confidante and crossword competitor singing in his cell. He could almost hear the little surfer girl accompanying him on violin: Green fields of summer! High at the head of a flock of boss-firing birds of a feather he flew.

Humanity had arrived at the crossroads of rich and poor, freedom and slavery. For a fictional moment, Tom felt like a freeway engineer defining how to approach that crossroad, life's major intersection, and how to move in, not move on. Moving in instead of moving on can make all the difference, the difference between an encyclopedia and a crossword puzzle—and you can fire the boss.

On the night before his release, Tom asked a cellmate what his plans were after he got out. An African American arrested in a nearly all-white northern community for failing to properly signal his intentions—Ivan was now dead broke and homeless but not, he declared, without hope.

"My plans," he said, "are to stay out of jail. And to get my online business running again. I'll be out of here in six months."

"Good luck," said Tom. "If you like, you can stay with me until you're back in business."

They exchanged email addresses. Tom lay back, dreaming of tending tomatoes and beans and writing the last chapters of his book—perhaps even riding his bike to campus … *Palma still there? All his friends been fired? How many fled?* He was dying to visit the mail room; he'd kill for a veggie wrap at Buddie's.

"See you in the morning, Ivan."

"Thanks, Tom. You're a godsend."

If only he were a godsend. If only the world spun fair and free. If only more worker bees realized how simple it was to decapitate the queen.

If only yes, if only … if only he were a fly on the wall at the trustees' meeting in a nearby state, where his trials and tribulations were at the top of the agenda.

63

"In 1977, we first proposed the existence of a professional managerial class distinct from the old working class and the small business owners to explain the tensions that culminated in the political backlash that led to the election of Reagan."

BARBARA EHRENREICH

"So, there it is." The big man opened his palms, turned them so the entire board could see he was hiding nothing. "It's a game—a real game with a loser and a winner—and right now Freeman is winning—by messing around with the rules."

Truth to tell, the CEO of Tanker Model Industries and Chairman of the Interotten Board of Trustees didn't like games. Ferlin Butterworth did, however, like winning; and he could prove it with eight active equities and twelve prime investment holdings. He operated a wealth of emerging markets and strategic investments, owned three townhouses, and oversaw an office with a breathtaking, panoramic view of downtown, harbor, and lake. He liked views, though, about as much as he liked losing; he'd forever fought the fear of falling. Losers fell.

From here, his view plunged a quarter mile down to those poor two-legged ants bustling about the business district. He turned from the window, lowered his corpulent flesh into a chair, and groused under his breath: "A bunch of boardroom buffoons waffling in apoplectic indecision. About as useful as a Greek chorus. Curses on them. Curses on this damn acrophobia. Curses on Hamilton Zippo Dumpster. And curses on this epic hangover banging nails into my eyes!"

Ferlin cleared his throat. "Well, is he crazy, or is he smarter than we think? George?"

"Who knows?" replied the chief executive and executioner of Boxmore

Cosmo. "I don't. And I don't care. Put him away and throw away the key. Whatever works."

Sonder, the attorney for Interotten, said, "He just served thirty days in county."

Tom the fly circled the table.

"It's a public relations stunt, pure and simple," said Coffer, the tea magnate.

"A first-time-lucky stunt," said Boxmore with a shrug.

"Balls." The Fulsome Scholar Head of Renaissance Oil was always researched and referenced but could be blunt. "First time, yes. Lucky, no."

"Of course, it's a stunt!" said Beasley, University of Wetlands dean. "Freeman's a clown standing on his head in a comic-book courtroom!"

Ferlin gritted his teeth, shifted in his chair. Incomprehensible. Every board he'd been on engaged in a direct discussion of the issues and based their decisions on that discussion. But he was waltzing with warranted womanizers, worrisome wimps and wackos who wasted working hours while they fried this bored chair's bacon. Planting his feet, Ferlin looked around, made eye contact with each of the wackos: "Can anyone here explain to me why any sane person would choose to be terminated?"

"He's one wily coyote!"

"What do you mean? 'Choose to be terminated'?"

"Some things," said Craftly, president of Power Engineering and Solar Exploration," are inexplicable. Why, for that matter, would any sane person choose to go to jail?"

"I overheard two guys down in the bar," said Seldom, maître d' at Budweiser, baron of Wall Street, and Super Bowl ad-boy genius, "talking about Freeman. He's off their charts; they're giving odds he wins."

"Winning," interjected Coffer, "isn't part of the game if losing isn't an option."

"Well," said Sonder, the only woman on the Board, "I learn more from losing than I do from winning."

Coffer exploded: "Winning, at least, means staying out of jail!"

"We live between two opposites," replied the attorney. "Right and wrong—balanced by justice. Winning and losing are relative. Going to jail is no more losing than is staying out of jail."

"Freeman, the ex-con," said Fulsome, "would agree."

"As would Nelson Mandela," added Sonder.

"I've been reading our writer friend's posts on Facebook," said Seldom. "It's weird. He's broke, been on the dole since Hamilton fired him, yet he self-published that book."

"And," added Sonder, "he's making Hamilton do the work of calling the cops on him."

"As he tests the water," said Fulsome, "again and again."

"He's in over his head," Boxmore said, "not testing the damn water. Hamilton's got him now. Game over."

"He's out of jail," said Seldom, "and still writing that book." Tom flew to the ceiling. "There seems to be a lot of copies. Any idea who's behind him?"

"He must have enlisted the help of a poltergeist."

"Ahhhh! I wouldn't mess with the satanic asshole."

"The devil's in the details."

"Ask the fly."

"We are talking," said Ferlin, frowning fiercely, "about Freeman and his book."

Hornblat stood. "Listen to this." He pulled a paper from a stack on the table. "It's his HR file: 'Tom maintains perfect attendance. He's dependable and takes initiatives, he never gets frazzled, even handling large volumes of incoming and outgoing mail.' And this: 'Tom saved the school $33,000 last year alone.'"

"Where'd he save that?"

"In postage," replied Hornblat. "I know Daryl. His employee evaluations are typically extraordinarily modest. He wouldn't say those things if they weren't true."

"Didn't you just say," asked Sonder, "that Freeman had been invited to star in some student movies?"

Hornblat flipped through the papers. "That's right ... here: Daryl says 'his acting roles are important illustrations of how Tom supports the Interotten mission.'"

On cue, Craftly coughed. "He's an actor all right."

Beasley bellowed, "The satanic asshole was making porn flicks when he should have been working."

"Not at all." Hornblat shook his head. "Daryl says 'Tom takes the initiative to get his work done even if it means staying late and coming in early. He never asks for overtime, instead using his personal time to perform roles in Motion Picture Arts Department student theses.'"

"Fake!" Boxmore sputtered. "Filth! Work of the devil."

"It's all water under the bridge," said Coffer.

"Motion Picture Arts," said Ferlin, "is going strong—part of the curriculum. Hamilton created the department."

"Freeman's movies," said Fulsome, "are stereotypical student film."

"A few years ago, I saw one," piped up the former governor of the state, Will Mannekin, "at a film festival on campus. He's as good an actor as we deserve."

"I heard he paid you a visit, Will."

"He did. He gave me a copy of his book and asked me if I'd write a letter to Hamilton requesting lifting the ban so that he could sing."

"And did you write it?"

"No. I did offer to pay him for the book. He wouldn't take it … got on his bicycle and rode away."

"Is that when you called the cops?"

"I didn't call them; my housekeeper did. I wouldn't call the police for that."

"Every run-in he has with the law is free publicity!"

"His movies," said Craftly, swiping at the fly, "are free publicity."

"His book is free publicity! A local paper, the *Northern Progressive Press,* reviewed it, said it was well-written."

"The reviewer called it a game of guess who," said Ferlin, "and suggested it could lead to a libel suit."

Coffer declared, "We can't let him get away with it! He must be stopped."

"Before that book becomes a best-seller."

Sonder the lawyer said, "For what it's worth, Freeman has promised to donate all proceeds from sales of his book to deserving Interotten students."

64

"In 2008, we were a society that watched as those who
obeyed the rules got played by Wall Street and Washington."
THOMAS FRANK

"Ridiculous," said Seldom. "There's no way in hell we lose; no dime
novelist is gonna clog our gears."

"Remember," added Craftly, "he's still banned."

"Freeman," said Fulsome, "isn't going anywhere."

"He's scheduled to sing in a concert on campus," said Sonder. "His
Facebook friends are writing letters of support asking us to let him sing.
Staff have been replying to those letters all week."

"Four hundred letters," said Ferlin, "asking Hamilton to let him sing."

Coffer said, "He has four hundred liberal friends! Big deal! Wasting
administration time! Reds have monkey-wrenched our elections, the
economy's crumbling, and Freeman's friends think he should break the
law!"

"Our staff," said Fulsome, "is handling the letters. The election is over.
The economy's not crumbling."

"Profits are up. Unemployment's down."

"What about the asset price bubble?"

"It's a story of less than ample returns, yes, but think globally not just
the U.S. In the bigger picture, the economy is expanding."

"Equities and holdings," said Boxmore, "are below targets."

"Short term," responded Craftly. "Liquidations of pay benefit
positions. Funding for private equity calls."

"Boom and bust all over again."

"Too simplistic." Sonder shook her head, shooing the fly. "I think,"
she said, "every trustee—in fact, every employee if not every student—
should read the book."

"I second that," said Hornblat.

"Hamilton banned it," said Ferlin.

"And played right into Freeman's hands," said Fulsome.

"Look here." With a forefinger Hornblat speared a blurb on the back cover. "'Determined underdogs battle a stifling bureaucracy.'"

"Who wrote that shit?"

"Here's another: 'An educational haven taken over by cynics trading on the brand name.'" Hornblat raised the book like a flag. His voice trembled. "It's become a game of Guess Who; the only thing missing is my daughter's name."

Boxmore came to peer over Hornblat's shoulder. "Quixotic whistle-blower? What's that? Who's Dante?"

"Former orchestra director," said Ferlin. "Hamilton fired him."

"A week after Dante was dismissed," said Fulsome, "he won that high school orchestra award from *Downbeat Magazine*."

"It's still shit."

"My daughter was in the orchestra," said Hornblat. "And in the ping-pong club."

"That's too bad." Coffer frowned. "Does anyone else wonder how a poor, scruffy old man alters the way we do business?"

"They say a small group of dedicated kids can change the world," said Sonder.

Boxmore sputtered, spilling his coffee.

"Those dedicated kids," said Beasley, "apparently have nothing better to do than hack Ham's emails! And send him a photo of a pile of shit!"

"The hack," Ferlin growled, "is irrelevant. Does Freeman sing or not?"

"What's in it for Interotten?"

"Is the budget on our agenda?"

"No," said Ferlin.

"Will it be majority rule or not?"

"What difference does it make if he sings or not?"

The Chairman of the Board hit the table with his fist—a gunshot into the air. "Hamilton Dumpster is what difference it makes! Glowering, growling, "This game's for keeps."

"I move," said Sonder, "we tell Hamilton Dumpster to let Freeman sing."

Boxmore mopped his lap with his shirttail. "This Freeman—is he a nigger? Take him out back with a rope."

"I can't believe," said Craftly, "you said that."

"Shall I repeat myself?"

"He's white," said Ferlin. "A white Canadian."

"I say we ignore him."

"I second the motion to let him sing."

Boardroom abuzz, Governor Mannekin stood. "I read the book … an amazing story of heartbreak and loss for so many. These are difficult times. Art needs a home. Music eases the pain … I say let him sing."

Beasley pounded a fist in his palm. "The changes Hamilton has put in place in procedure, policy, and personnel are positive and absolutely necessary, the leadership we need to guide the school forward. We must change with the times. It is neither easy nor optional; it is hard work making Interotten work!"

"Hamilton has had an impact all right."

"Hear, hear. We're lucky to have him."

In the uproar, Hornblat stood, hands in the air, holding the book. "The ping-pong club was a gift Hamilton didn't accept, but the students did … and it changed everything. Doreen wouldn't talk about it much. The group was tight-lipped. A boy was expelled, a girl suspended. Another student attempted suicide." Hornblat wiped his brow. "Doreen did, however, tell her mother and me a little story about our tone-deaf president."

"Go on."

"Hamilton had called the leaders of the ping-pong club—the President and Vice President of Student Council—into his office. He warned them that if they didn't cease with the protests he'd sue their parents."

"Oh, my god! What else?"

"Ham-handed."

"He wouldn't dare sue," said Sonder. "Bad PR. Expensive."

"He isn't stupid enough," said Seldom, "to risk his job with a lawsuit."

"Yes, he was bluffing, of course," said Hornblat, "but it worked: no more student protests, no more talk of walking out, no more student bill of rights. Freeman was suddenly alone and Hamilton took advantage of his sudden loss of student support and fired him. The break-up of the club broke something off inside Doreen. She stopped practicing and began failing classes. Her mother and I became afraid she'd try something like her friend Sven."

The boardroom suddenly turned frosty. Tom needed coffee; he flew to the table and crawled inside a cup. Eyes glazed, Hornblat tugged at his shirt cuffs. "I'm not sure how to say this—it seems unreal, fictionalized—her violin teacher noticed that something about Doreen was wrong. Virtuoso violinist, international celebrity, Julie was also an educator. After lessons, the two girls, teacher and student, would talk, sometimes for hours. Julie told my daughter how to spread her wings and fly."

Tom flew to the ceiling.

Hornblat continued. "Doreen heard how Hamilton invited Julie to be a guest on his radio show: an hour-long weekly program of conversation, conflict, and concertos. For most of those shows, Thad worked the control room.

"For the record," Sonder interrupted, "Ham fired Thad too."

"They were off-air," said Hornblat, "on a break … Thad put on Mozart's violin concerto."

On the ceiling, Tom cleaned his ears, listening.

"Hamilton looked his newest faculty member in the eye, asked where she was born. Julie replied, 'In America.'

"'I mean, which state … California?'

"'I was born in Washington.'

"'Not D.C.? The state of Washington?'

"'Yes.'

"'And your parents?' Ham probed."

"'What about my parents?'

"'Were they also born in the state of Washington?'

"'No, they weren't.'

"'Where, then? China?'

"'My father and mother were born in Korea.'

"'North Korea?'

"'Yes.'

"'Were they Korean War refugees? Did they have their yellow cards? Did they get their American citizenship?'

"'What does that have to do with anything at all?' replied Julie, who knew this conversation was getting out of line.

"Ham pushed on: 'What does your birth certificate say?'

"'Are you implying that I'm lying?'

"'I'm implying that you could be recruiting there, in North Korea. Or California.'

"'I said I was born in Washington, not California.'

"'San Francisco has lots of you people.'

"'*You people?*'

"'I know you were in Colombia with that leftist orchestra leader, Mark. And here you are, intermingling with that mailman and those student troublemakers.'

"'You call what I do *intermingling?*'

"'I call it what I want,' continued Ham. 'You're intermingling when you should be teaching. You're intermingling when you should be working. Recruiting is part of your job description. It's in your contract.'

"In the control room, Thad held a finger to his lips and mimed, 'One minute.'

"'I recruited in Colombia,' said Julie. 'I helped Mark with his National Youth Orchestra. There are student musicians in that orchestra who would love to come here, who could attend Interotten—if you provided a financial aid—except you've made it clear they're not welcome!'

"'Those kids are fake. They're not musicians.'

"'You are so wrong!' said Julie. 'They loved learning classical music! They were devoted to Mark!'

"'Bunch of wall-climbing beginners. Part-time parasites.'

"'You don't know them! I'm beginning to think you fired Mark for helping Colombian kids, for telling the truth. He loved Interotten! He died of a broken heart.'

"'Huh. The bleeding heart liberal had a coronary.'

"'You are heartless! A bully! Termination killed my friend!'

"'Look, Miss Shanghai or whatever you call yourself. I've had it with you and your liberal bullshit. This conversation is over.'"

Hornblat shook his head and sat down. In tomb-like silence, Tom circled the table, zeroed in, and thrust one of his flexible sensory antennae into a pitcher of cream. He flew to the window. *Where, oh where, have you gone, my musical muse? Colombia? New York? California?*

Ferlin cleared his throat.

Hornblat said: "Julie didn't hold back, or keep it to herself. In a week, Hamilton's effrontery was all over campus. A hundred students already riled up about Bernie getting fired, started meeting and organizing; the ping-pong club came along, and here we are."

"Whew. That was … unfortunate," said Coffer.

"Hamilton certainly should have asked the Board about banning Freeman. Too late now."

"The book," said Hornblat, "is in its final stages before publication."

"I move we adjourn," said Boxmore. "Nobody here knows this mailman or his motives, or what this vote will mean to Interotten."

"Some of us do," said Ferlin. "Yes, Will?"

The former governor struggled to his feet, holding onto the back of a chair for balance. "Last week," he said, "I talked with Keith."

Tom flew down to Will's head and planted a drop of cream on his earlobe.

"Go on," said Ferlin.

"Keith is filling Alice's position—and now, with Hamilton history, he's number one in the chain of command."

"Yes, he was right under Ham. Keith is now boss."

Governor Mannekin straightened his back, clamped his jaw. "Keith would like the Board of Trustees to know that he's in favor of lifting the ban; the orchestra rented the auditorium and invited the choir. Freeman's in the choir, has been in it for twenty years. Lifting is perfectly legal, logical, and I believe it is just. Keith knows Freeman. He was his boss. He supervised him the entire twelve years that Freeman worked in the mail room; he played ping-pong with him, golfed with him, bowled with him. Keith sees no reason why Freeman shouldn't be allowed to sing on campus."

"Thank you, Will," said Ferlin. "Keith's a good man."

"He is. Furthermore," added the former governor, "it's only for this one concert, not carved in stone or anything. Lifting the ban would go a long way toward healing some pretty deep wounds in our community."

"Anyway," said Coffer, "Ham's as good as gone; he's all packed up and moving back to Kansas."

"We are first and foremost a music school," said Craftly.

"Oh, for God's sake, let him sing," said Seldom. "What's the harm?"

"Lift the ban," said Hornblat.

"I'm for it if Keith is," said Fulsome.

"Makes all the sense in the world to me," said Sonder. "A progressive win-win situation. Legally, at least."

Coffer made a sour face. "I guess," he said, "I'm in."

"So," said Ferlin, "I'd say we're ready to vote. Without further ado, do I hear a motion?"

65

"Never doubt that one determined truth-speaker
can change Interotten."
DEAN ROBB, ATTORNEY AND FAMED CIVIL RIGHTS ADVOCATE

T he email arrived just in time for breakfast.

Good morning, Tom. I'd like to speak with you regarding the
possibility of your participation with the choir on campus next
week. Please let me know the best time to meet.

Sincerely, Jack Armbend

A glitch! Roll over, Beethoven!

Tom poured another cup of tea, slathered a slice of toast with peanut
butter, and typed:

Immediately, if not sooner.

Too good to be true! What was up? Could Humpty feel a twinge of
guilt, or was he gone? Did the shadow board suddenly find a heart? Tom
knew there were donors tightening their purse strings: he'd talked with
them, watched angry alums argue with administrators. Had Humpty
seen the founder's phantom prowling campus perimeters?

Tom finished his tea, rinsed his cup... What if it was a trap, a bogus
invitation? What if the police were waiting for him at the auditorium
with his ticket back to the slammer? What if he'd done it all for naught?
Wasn't the most illusory dream worth a try? He'd been down so long,
everything looked like up now ... and he heard the call.

No time left to twiddle dee dee.

Slipping a copy of *The Ping-Pong Club* into a hip pocket, he hit the road, pounding the pedals as hard as he could, ignoring his pounding heart, and in twenty-five minutes he was at the Security Director's office in the guard house at the main entrance.

"Come in, Tom." Jack pulled out a chair, handed him a four-by-eight sheet of lined notepaper: his ticket to freedom. Through tears of joy, Tom read the short but sweet means to an end of sorts. Hurriedly written in a humdrum bossy manner, the agreement laid out the rules: No verbal contact with students. No distributing material of any kind. Arrive on time and go directly to the auditorium. As soon as the show is over, leave, and go straight home—no ambling around, no unguided tours, no peeking through the construction fence around the new music building soon to be dedicated to Baxter. No strolling down memory lane to the mail room. No ping, no pong.

Tom wiped his eyes.

Jack smiled. "Here's a pen."

Hands flapping like the wings of a fly, lifted by imagination's tailwind to find its way home, Tom wiped another tear and signed on the dotted line. Laughing like a lost loon, he dropped the pen. Jack quickly bent to pick it up, offered Tom his hand.

"I see you're still riding your bike. Does that mean you'll be riding it here next week when you come to sing?"

"For sure. My happy means of transportation."

"Be sure you stop at Security on your way in to get your happy clearance papers. They'll be ready and waiting."

"Yessiree." Singing hallelujahs under his breath, Tom felt for the book in his hip pocket. "How about it, Jack? Would you like a copy?"

"You gotta be kidding … you brought one in here? Look here, Tom, we don't need any more of your wrongful-dismissal conspiracy crap. We got a hundred fifty of the damn things." Jack took the book, opened a closet door, and threw *The Ping Pong Club* inside. "Been confiscating them from students and teachers, parents and alumni, for months. And, until we hear otherwise, we'll just keep doing our job."

"You just stole my book, boss. Thank you."

"You're welcome."

"I guess Humpty Dumpty is still on his wall."

"Humpty Dumpty, as you call him, is as good as gone. He told me to tell you good-bye."

"Tell him it's been a barrel of fun."

"I will. The new president arrives tomorrow. What a breath of fresh air for Interotten."

○

On the day of the concert, The Ides of March were in the air, but nary a cloud was in the sky and nary a care burdened Tom pedaling down the shoulder of the road in concert garb. Four words—as good as gone! He'd fired the boss!

He coasted up to the old stump marking the trail into the state park. Leaving his bike on the shoulder, he stepped over a fallen log and took the road less traveled. Gentle rustle of wind through oaks. Nesting songs of finches. Croaking frogs in a nearby pond. A scuffle of squirrels in scrub shade. A warm, spring wind came up whispering, "Be not afraid."

Climbing the embankment to the footpath singing, winging it, swinging his arms, Tom entered the unknown future. In the little clearing the doe lay still as death, white as a cloud, a pile of bones picked clean, and left to bleach in the sun.

Kneeling, he solemnly lifted a sliver of bone, an arc fit for the elfin bow of a youthful violin. Feather-light, stone-tight, it was an instrument strummed by the gods, humming with stories and deeds, vibrating with musical gravity. If only his muse of fire hadn't abandoned ship, she'd be playing for him today.

Tom set the fragment of breast between his thumb and middle finger, felt the edges, snapped his finger. The bone spun lazily in the afternoon sun, went into orbit to cross the road, returned, and came to earth, snuggling into the leaves beside the old stump. For the first time, he saw the plaque on its anchored steel stem:

Who is King of the Forest? This ancient Eastern White Pine is a remnant of the old growth stand that provided the lumber to rebuild Chicago after the great fire.

Ducking a low-hanging branch, Tom walked to the edge of the road. Angels of light, shining arias, lyrical rainbow prisms of welcome danced on the gray granite walls of the auditorium.

Almost home, he pinched himself, then looked both ways—and the red Jeep roared by, missing him by the slimmest figure of speech.

Made in the USA
Lexington, KY
17 November 2019

57186387R00179